To Brittany
From Papa

Oct 5 2001

# The Nez Perce Trail

# The Nez Perce Trail

by

**Vernon L Harris**

with

**Lee Nelson**

ISBN: 1-55517-464-7
v.1

Published by Bonneville Books

Distributed by:
925 North Main, Springville, UT 84663 • 801/489-4084

Typeset by Virginia Reeder
Cover design by Adam Ford
Cover design © 2000 by Lyle Mortimer

Printed in the United States of America

**DEDICATION**

To Shirlee,who fulfilled my life

To my Mother, one of the Camas Prairie Martins,
who first took me there when it
was at its loveliest.

And to my Father, who led me along the trails,
beside the streams and lakes,
and over the mountains which were
once home to the people of this story.

# IN APPRECIATION

The writing of this book would have been impossible without the help of the following people, whom I thank personally.

Sue Cox, word-processor extraordinaire, and her engineer husband David, a computer expert. Neither they nor I envisioned the extent of this project when Sue offered to do the typing.

Dr. Julene Butler, Professor of Library Science at Brigham Young University, who tracked down books for me through inter-library loans, critiqued parts of the manuscript.

Dr. Donald Freedman and Joe Palmer, who steered me away from some ridiculously obvious pitfalls.

My two sons, Brent and Robin Harris, who made objective suggestions on the manuscript in spite of warnings about the halo effect of family criticism.

Bill and Millie Shelley, hwo read it all when it was long and awkward.

The staff at the Nez Perce National Historical Park at Spalding, Idaho, warned me that the Nez Perce language is extremely complex, which I soon learned to be true. It can only be written correctly by using Universal Linguistic symbols. These are hard for me, in spite of struggling with them in the Navajo language, and I suspect the average reader would stumble over them as I do. So I took the lazy way and used common phonetic spelling, deliberately avoiding complex words and phrases. So thank you and forgive me, Diana and Judy.

The historical basis for this book came from a wide variety of sources and authors. Some were important for a single brief account of an event or a person which sparked a wider search. Because of their concentration on the Nez Perces or on some related subject, the following authors were most helpful: Robert G. Bailey, Merrill J. Beal, Fred Bond, Mark Brown, Angie Debo, Bill Gulick, Francis Haines, Alvin M. Josephy, David Lavender, L.V. McWhorter, and Herbert J. Spinden.

## How It Came To Be
## **A Prologue**

As prairies are measured, it wasn't much; only a few thousand square miles perched on a plateau between Idaho's lower Salmon River to the west and the Clearwater River to the east. A low mountain formed its southern boundary, and on the north it broke off into canyons leading to the lower Clearwater Valley. It was called Camas Prairie, after the June blush of blue Camas flowers in its marshy meadows. In 1877, when this story begins, it had only the beginnings of a few small villages, but it was a crossing for miners seeking gold in the mountains to the south and east; and it was home to a few hardy ranchers, and to the packers and draymen who carried supplies to them and to the mines.

Other people, long established, lived along the streams and canyons below the prairie, and crossed back and forth between the Salmon and Clearwater countries, camping in season to harvest the bulbs of the Camas flowers. Their ancestors were among the primitives who, over many thousands of years, left Siberia and crossed Beringia, to trickle down ice-free corridors through Canada; perhaps as long as ten thousand years ago some of them reached the valleys of the Salmon, Snake, and Clearwater Rivers.

Long before the memory of any we will meet in this story they had called themselves Nimipu, "The Real People." Lewis and Clark in 1805 called them the Chopunnish, after the Clearwater's North Fork. A few years later some Frenchman saw Native American people in the Snake River Country wearing shells in their noses and called them Nez Perces: "Pierced Noses." Actually it wasn't the Nimipu who had their noses pierced, but they got stuck with the name, just as most of the native peoples of the Americas are called Indians because that's what Columbus called a few of them in 1492.

The Nimipu probably never numbered more than six thousand, but their ancestral home was huge. They wandered freely from Oregon's Blue Mountains on the west to the Bitter Roots, where Idaho meets Montana on the east, were loosely bordered on the south by the Salmon River flowing westerly across Idaho, and on the north mingled compatibly with related tribes beyond the Snake River. Hostile tribes to the south and east limited their movements and challenged their lives on the fringes of this far-flung domain of more than 26,000 square miles. After horses reached them in the early 1700s they became wonderfully mobile, and more aggressive, and traveled often to the buffalo country to the east.

The great treaty-making frenzy, encouraged and softened in the public mind by "manifest destiny," swept westward, and the first of these farces was foisted on the Nez Perces and their neighbor tribes to the north and west in 1855. The resulting Nez Perce Reservation included the majority of their homeland and was no apparent threat. But in the early 1860s, easily gathered placer gold was found at several places on the reservation, and thousands of miners swarmed over Indian lands with impunity. They demanded access without interference, and the 1855 treaty was revised. Then in 1863 a new treaty was made, and this time it served the white man's needs very well and left the Nez Perces with less than 1,200 square miles, including very little of the mountain country The People loved.

The 1863 treaty was signed without protest by the chiefs of bands living in the lower valleys of the Clearwater and Snake Rivers, for their homes were within the reduced reservation where they had long been settled around missions and schools. But several bands from the rugged mountains of the Salmon and Snake Rivers along the adjoining fringes of Idaho and Oregon would now be robbed of their ancestral lands, and their chiefs did not sign the treaty. Among these "non-treaty" chiefs was Tuekakis, whose band, the Walwama, ranged the valleys and upland meadows of the Grand Ronde, Wallowa, and Imnaha Rivers of eastern Oregon.

When Henry Harmon Spalding, first missionary to the Nez Perces, baptized Tuekakis and his wife, he changed his name to Joseph, and called her Aseneth, harking back to the biblical Joseph and the wife given to him by Pharaoh. Their first son, as in that biblical account, was named Ephraim. The name of Old Joseph was abandoned by Tuekakis when he forsook Christianity, and the young Ephraim soon became known as Joseph. He in his own way would also become a legend.

The Treaty of 1863 was ignored by the non-treaty Nez Perce bands for years while the other bands were being civilized on the small reservation. The U.S. Army was very busy with the Civil War when the treaty was signed, and then after the war was busy subduing other Indian tribes farther east. By the mid-1870s the pressures for land and the careless attitude of the few small "free" bands were too strong. The wandering Nez Perces were ordered, by force of law and the U.S. Army, to report to the Agent on the reservation at Lapwai. And in June 1877 they gathered at a traditional campground for a last few days together. They were only a day's ride from the reservation boundary.

---

My earliest memories are crowded with street scenes, fairs, horse parades, and rodeos at Lewiston, Idaho. There in the 1920s and 1930s the Nez Perces were part of the daily crowd on Main Street, which parallels the Clearwater River. At fairtime they trailed from the reservation to the fair-grounds with hundreds of horses, and rode in every parade on these high-colored mounts—pintos, roans, appaloosas, piebalds—their trappings decorated with beadwork, porcupine quills, elk teeth, ermine tails, and feathers. They formed their own parades, camped inside the racetrack oval at the fairgrounds, and were fierce competitors in rodeo events. Then, as now, there was feminine royalty for all such celebrations, and I remember the Nez Perce festival "queens" and "princesses" as among the loveliest of women. They were vibrant, charming, always smiling, and superb riders.

But through those years I never met or personally spoke to even one Nez Perce, though my father had friends among them. They had their own schools and churches at Lapwai and Kamiah, and sent flashy basketball teams to tournaments.

The culture of the times effectively separated us through attitudes, reminders of the horrors of the war they were said to have started, and by calling the women "squaws," the men "bucks," and the babies "papooses." I never imagined speaking to one of them on the street, or when mingling with them in Al Newell's Pawnshop, where their lovely beaded buckskin handiwork was bought and sold. Al had a magnificent collection of Nez Perce and other Indian artifacts, and the pungent odor of willow-smoked buckskin always comes to mind when I think of that intriguing store.

But the "Indians" were different, like the nuns from St. Joseph's hospital, and my young Protestant mind placed them all in the same logic-tight compartment. Then at age 16 on a bitterly cold November night after an elk hunt, I met Harry Wheeler. He was solid, thoughtful, deliberate of speech, mellow and warm. He had graduated from the Carlisle Indian School in Pennsylvania and had played on Pop Warner's Fabulous Redmen Football Team. He repeated the oft-told stories of the hidden ball play and other tricks of that impressive team. And on that starry sub-zero night I saw the Nez Perces as Real People.

---

A few years later on a bright summer morning my U.S. Forest Service work crew filed past a Nez Perce camp. A small boy stood by a footbridge over the nearby stream while we crossed. I exhausted my entire Nez Perce vocabulary—except for counting from one to five—and said, "Tac Meywi." He flashed a big smile, and that evening as we returned from work he was crouched in the brush scanning the face of each man ahead of me; and when he saw me his face beamed in a full, toothy grin and he said, "Tac Kulewit."

My working Nez Perce vocabulary had just doubled; I could now say "Good Morning" and "Good Evening." Over sixty years have passed, but I still see that boy's smile and remember how I felt as I walked away. How precious are the bridges built of the languages we speak, if only a few words.

Many of the people in this story are real, and I hope their roles, whether historical or fictional, closely portray the lives they led and the parts they played in their time. Several of the Camas Prairie people are historic, including my grandfather, Mortimer S. (Morty) Martin; my great-uncle, Seth Jones, several civilian volunteers, and the controversial mercenary guide Ad Chapman.

There were Martins, Joneses, Cones, and Henleys living on or near Camas Prairie in the 1870s. Their roles in the story are fictional, as are those of the Phelps family.

All principal military leaders are historic, and we have tried to portray them accurately in the human, if not always humane, roles they played in the pursuit of the non-treaty Nez Perce bands. Glances into their backgrounds, ambitions, and frailties are based on historical accounts of their lives. Agents and others mentioned at the real village of Lapwai are also historic.

Daytime Smoke and his genealogy are historic as is Fred Bond, the river boatman. They are portrayed in historic settings with fictional details. All the Nez Perce warriors are historic, as are their leaders. They fought, suffered, and died in the manner and at the places described. Detailed episodes are at times fictional, but based on historical events. Chiefs Sitting Bull and Moses were real people.

The other Nez Perces are historic, but their stories are sometimes fictional. The setting, and the people involved in the valley called Hey-ets Pah, are entirely fictional.

There was a reportedly beautiful Chinese girl in Warrens in the 1860s. Several varied historical accounts and at least one screenplay have been written about her life. The story of her tender romance with Lucas Phelps is fictional, as is he.

Some say every writer's first book is an autobiography. That is not true in my case, but my ancestors and friends are in the story, along with my love for the land where they lived, and for horses. To quote T.K.Whipple: "We live in the civilization they created, but within us the wilderness still lives. What they dreamed, we live, and what they lived, we dream."

# CHAPTER 1

The gathering hadn't started off well, and General Oliver Otis Howard was irritable and threatening as he faced the men before him. His sideburns and stiff square-cut beard bristled with anger as he said, "If you people hesitate to come to the reservation, soldiers will be used to bring you here; and if you keep insulting me, I will arrest you and send you to the Indian Territory."

Several Nez Perce men drew back, showing fear. They had heard this threat before—to be sent to "Eikish Pah," The Hot Place. Howard smiled to himself, sensing their alarm. He adjusted the pinned-up shirtsleeve which hid the remaining stump of his right arm. The forearm and hand were buried somewhere in Tennessee

"We'll recess the council until tomorrow," Howard told them. He had found a soft spot, and waiting overnight would give them time to think it over.

Chief Joseph's Wallowa band sat cross-legged on the ground in an army tent with General Howard and his aides, Indian Agent Monteith, and the interpreters. During an opening prayer, a Catholic priest had beseeched the Holy Father to open the hearts and minds of these misguided Indians. He prayed they would join their enlightened brothers already on the reservation, listen to the wisdom dispensed today, be done with their wanderings and horse racing, take only one wife, become faithful Catholics, and live by farming.

As the priest spoke, a happy group of the "enlightened" and their plural wives were gathered at a meadow a few miles up Sweetwater Creek beyond the watchful eyes of the missionaries, where they had laid out a rough track and were joyously racing their multi-colored ponies. Joseph's implacable bronze face belied his impatience with all this and with the increasing pressures on the non-treaty Nez Perce bands, but his powerful athletic brother, Ollokott, was not so restrained; his anger and frustration were evident. And listening outside the tent was Yellow Wolf, Joseph's nephew, too young to sit in council and almost obsessed by hatred of the white man.

White Bird, now past seventy-four winters, arrived with his band the next morning. The old chief, still vigorous and erect, realized the white man could no longer be resisted; but he also had within his band some resentful young men whose relatives had been beaten and murdered by white men along the Salmon River. What might they do?

And from the Clearwater's middle fork came Looking Glass, athletic and stubborn, but realistic about the whites, and not really wanting war. With him were some Hasotino relatives from the lower Snake River near Lewiston.

From the mountains between the lower Salmon River and the Snake

River came the irascible and fearless old Toohoolhoolzote, fiery, defiant, and prepared to fight to the death for his freedom. The harsh-voiced old Dreamer Orator was a follower of Smohalla, the Dreamer Prophet, who taught that all dead Indians from all tribes would arise, unite, and drive the white man out of America.

Toohoolhoolzote was perceived as a threat by Howard, for Joseph earlier had stated that he would speak for all the non-treaty bands. He now upheld his reputation: "There is really nothing to talk about," the chief said. "We are fighting for our homeland, our free way of life. Your own people value freedom above life and should understand this."

Joseph, still seeking to delay any final decision, asked for a recess which Howard quickly granted with a feeling of relief, having sensed the growing resentment among the chieftains. Besides, it would be good to have on hand the troops who were already on the march toward Lapwai.

During the three-day recess, ill feelings increased among the non-treaty bands, and Howard's apprehensions grew. Non-treaty strength had grown with the arrival of many newcomers, especially two Paloose leaders from north of the Snake River. They were Husishusis Kute— "Little Bald Head"— a Dreamer-Prophet and strong orator; and Hahtalekin, head of the largest free Paloos band. Both leaders had stayed in their ancestral homeland, ignoring demands to move to the Yakima reservation.

After the recess, the council started quickly and Toohoolhoolzote attacked at once, destroying Howard's hope of an easy solution: "The earth is my mother, and must not be cut with shovels or plows. You would not so treat your mother. Your soldiers will cut us off from the lands which have always been ours. As Indians, we are chieftains over the earth. We cannot sell or give away our mother."

The old man's fire and passion stirred up the non-treaty Indians, and Howard became increasingly impatient as his attempts at reconciliation failed. "I stand here for the U.S. President," Howard said. "My orders are plain and will be executed. Will you obey the orders of the government?"

"So long as the earth keeps me, I want to be left alone," Toohoolhoolzote said. "You are trifling with the law of the earth. The others may choose their own way, but I will not live on a reservation."

Howard completely lost his temper at hearing this, and assisted by Captain Perry he took Toohoolhoolzote to the guardhouse while his friends watched in disbelief. The assembled Indians were shocked and silent. They had seen the ultimate insult in Howard's attitude and words, his loss of patience and his temper, and most of all in his jailing of one of their council participants. The chiefs left quickly with all of their confidence in justice and fair treatment destroyed. A sullen and bitter Toohoolhoolzote remained in the guardhouse for seven days.

The resolve of all the non-treaty chiefs was now broken and they agreed to select reservation land. Some said, "Howard has shown us the rifle," but all knew the futility of war; and the humiliation being forced on them would rankle forever. All stayed at Lapwai for a week or more as land was selected for Joseph, White Bird, Toohoolhoolzote, and their bands. An area was chosen on the upper Clearwater above Kooskia close to Looking Glass, who already had land on that river. Husishusis Kute agreed to bring his Paloos band to the lower Clearwater near Lapwai; but Hahtalekin, bitter and resentful to the end, went back down the Snake River to join his band at the mouth of the Paloos.

On the day Howard released Toohoolhoolzote from the guardhouse, he issued his final decree to the non-treaty bands. "You will have thirty days, and no more, in which to come on to the reservation."

In spite of protests that the time was far too short and the Snake and Salmon Rivers were rising rapidly each day, Howard was still immovable and he picked up a letter from the table in front of him: "You are risking fights with impatient settlers," he said. "Just today I received this letter from some of the people on the Salmon River, complaining about troublesome members of White Bird's band."

So the leaders returned to their own lands. Joseph, Ollokot, and their men went to the mouth of Joseph Creek to join the rest of the band, where they found troops camped nearby. Their young warriors were ready to fight, saying; "If Howard wants a war, we'll give him one."

The fierce, raging Toohoolhoolzote came down from the hills, encouraging the incensed younger men. "I will join you. We must fight like men, and not be driven like dogs from the land of our birth."

But Joseph and the elders of his band again convinced the hostile ones to be still. "They are many and we are few. Soldiers are camped very close to us and we might defeat them, but others are at Lapwai and more coming there from Walla Walla. Would you rush us into a bloody battle and risk the lives of our people?"

Their words were effective. Even Toohoolhoolzote became solemn and constrained, realizing that the Indian way of individual decision and action without censure by others was not wise at this time.

While Joseph and most of the men were at the council at Lapwai the rest of the band had almost completed the annual springtime move to Oregon's Wallowa Valley. There was a sense of serenity and peace as the tipis went up on the meadows along the river. Flowers bloomed everywhere as the children played happily and the young people swam in the deep pools.

But the happy years of complete freedom were long gone, and the more recent years of ignoring the ever-threatening encroachment of the white man were now past. Howard's final edict had reached the people in Wallowa Valley, and they had hurried down to the mouth of Joseph Creek to meet the leaders returning from the council.

Joseph pondered what lay ahead. "We have always known where we were going, how life would be, and that we would come back to our home here," he thought. "This time we do not know what our lives will be like. Will we find the things we need on the Clearwater? Big country for our horses to run in? Hunting in the back country? Enough salmon? The bands now living around Lapwai hunt very little and aren't allowed to travel to the buffalo country. they must live on what the agent gives them."

Joseph rationalized, though not convincingly, that perhaps life would not be too bad on the Clearwater. Still, within his mind was a persistent threat—the angry hearts within his own band, and some of the others as well. Could that anger be controlled until they had all moved across to the Clearwater and were settled away from Howard's troops? Could his high-spirited men accept the loss of the many horses which were now in the hands of white settlers? Could they adjust to the confinement to be imposed upon them in just a few days?

But the decision had been made, and he gave the direction, "Get ready to move to our new home. Round up horses and cattle, as many as can be found."

The excitement and anticipation of a voluntary move would have made the 30-day limit a challenge, but now the band's bitterness and the fear of Howard's troops made the joyless task even worse. Thousands of their horses and cattle needed to be rounded up, but the animals were now spread across hundreds of square miles of high country. Ollokot and Yellow Wolf immeidately summoned their best young riders in hopes of finding all they could.

"Search the prairies and meadows first, then the wide canyon bottoms and the broad ridges," Ollokot directed. "We will find more stock there than anywhere else. It will take too much time to drive them out of the deeper canyons and narrow draws." So the arduous task was begun.

Toward late afternoon of the second day Ollokot and Yellow Wolf were riding back toward camp trailing a large herd of horses when Yellow Wolf glanced toward the top of the ridge. He saw two white men on horses hiding among the trees.

"They are watching us," he said. "They know we can't find all of our horses and cattle, and probably saw the bunch that escaped behind us into that little draw."

He knew that without weapons any pursuit of the suspects was futile, and as the sun sank and the dust began to settle, the two white riders angled down the ridge seeking the strays which had disappeared up the draw. That night they forced 23 beautiful Nez Perce ponies westward to their own ranches.

That night Joseph called a council, where Yellow Wolf stormed, "They are stealing our horses and cattle! We must go after them! Ollokot and I saw two of them today. The rest of you have seen others. We must fight them!"

But Joseph, as usual, was the conciliator. "There is too much to do. Besides, troops are camped nearby and will support the settlers if we attack them. We have found a lot of stock, and we'll find more." Joseph's words did nothing to ease the pent-up anger of the young men, but his wisdom was again recognized.

The urgent pace of gathering livestock continued. The young men scoured the hills each day, riding for punishing miles, returning after sundown; and each day their hatred grew deeper as they realized how many horses and cattle were being left behind.

Joseph, his role of peace chieftain now most evident, had gone quietly about organizing the move. Heyoom Yokikt, his first wife, needed no real direction but felt her spirits rise a little at Joseph's quiet comment, "It would be good if you could help the women get started, unhappy as they may be."

Springtime, his younger wife, her belly swollen and heavy with child, knew her own role and quickly started accumulating the family's belongings. Meanwhile, Ollokot's wife Wetatonmi and his other wife Fair Land were assembling their family items and preparing packs to be loaded on the horses. The preserved beef and wild game that couldn't be carried were stored in anything that could be found and then buried in the ground. Joseph and others still hoped they might return to this summering place.

Heyoom Yokikt reflected sadly as she packed cherished items. "Here are the ceremonial robes and headdresses which we have used for so many years. And here are those two beautiful horn bows which Ollokot and Joseph made when they were young. How we laughed at them when they decided they would make the strongest bows any of us had ever seen, but they were right!"

And so it went with Heyoom Yokikt and the other women as they packed blankets, clothing, tools, braided grass bags and the many buffalo robes, so prized and so valuable for so many purposes.

Joseph still could not accept this might be a final farewell to the Wallowa country, so he summoned his brother Ollokot and together they rode through the meadows. Here they had grown up, found their wives, raised their children, and struggled to provide wise leadership to the little band. After an hour's ride in silence, they came to a spot where strong poles were still lashed together to form a tripod. There was a slight mound of earth, and the rocks placed to protect the grave were scattered about.

"Here is where we buried our father so many winters ago," Joseph remembered. "It is sad that we have all become too busy to keep a horse-hide hanging over his grave. I promised him just before he died that I would not sell this land, and I have kept that promise, but now we must leave our home."

There were some memories of happier times, but they couldn't fight off their depression. They soon turned their horses back toward camp, where they would toss restlessly all night awaiting the dreaded departure.

The next morning the solemn band began the trip, heading toward the lower valley of the Imnaha River. Then from that narrow, lava-walled canyon they drove their vast herd eastward over a great ridge and down to the Snake River. The sight of the raging water filling the canyon bottom again caused their anger to rise as they remembered the stubborn white man Howard and his refusal to allow a few weeks until more of the stock could be gathered and the crossing was safe.

Their anger soon fused with fear. All of them had crossed this ford many times, but only the strongest attempted it with the water at this height. All were amazed at the churning, rumbling river. They watched as the great torrent washed sand and gravel from beneath the large boulders on the river bottom, which then rolled and tumbled downstream, their roar adding to that of the thundering water. Thus the sand bars, the depth of the water, even the shorelines, were changed from year to year, and this familiar crossing was now terrifying and formidable.

But the crossing must be made. As the bravest riders on the strongest mounts drove cattle and horses into the boiling eddies and powerful current of the river, everyone else began making bullboats, bent willow frames covered with buffalo hides. And upon these boats they piled all of their belongings, with the young, weak, and old ones riding on top. Skillful riders and strong swimmers towed the tossing bullboats over the treacherous river, trying to follow the course set by those who had first ridden across. But this was seldom possible. The bullboats—with their riders desperately clinging on—were swept far down the river until they were finally dragged over the rough boulders onto the shore.

Yellow Wolf segregated some of his favorite horses and drove them into the river, but their intended course was impeded by bullboats and thrashing cattle. His noble horses were swept downstream to where the river was funneled between large rocks and the force of the surging water was impossible to overcome. Yellow Wolf managed to stay afloat by holding onto the tail of his horse, he saw some of his favorite ponies perish in the roaring current, their bodies finally still and floating passively down the river far below him. Tears of rage and frustration filled his eyes and he stood on the shore, exhausted and shaken. He threw his head back and gave an anguished cry to the sky.

The agony and torture of the crossing continued into the next day. The river banks for several miles were strewn with the dead bodies of once-beautiful horses and cattle, and many of the band's possessions were damaged beyond use. Though bruised and battered, all of the band members somehow crossed the river safely.

The weary people scoured the riverbank, searching among boulders and thorny bushes for possessions that could still be used, while others gathered the children together and prepared food. The men assembled the livestock, destroying those injured beyond help and noticing with sullen resentment how few young colts and calves remained, for most of them had perished in the torrential river.

Joseph decided it would be best for everyone to rest through the night, and the next morning they climbed out of the steep, narrow canyon of Divide

Creek, crossed the plateau that would become known as Joseph Plains, and descended to the Salmon River. That river also was high and treacherous, but the crossing was made with the loss of only a few horses. Then the caravan of dejected, tired people struggled up another rough trail, riding weary horses and leading others carrying heavy packs.

Behind the pack animals came hundreds of other horses following the narrow trail beneath the sheer lava walls of Rocky Canyon known as "Split Rocks" as they climbed toward Tepahlewam. Here by the Camas Meadows the Nez Perce bands had gathered for countless generations.

In the past this had been a happy trip and all had eagerly anticipated reaching the lake, shimmering blue under the prairie sun. But today there was no anticipation, no playful banter, no talk of horse racing or feasting. Joseph and his brother Ollokot rode in silence, apparently calm; while others seethed with an inner rage that showed on their bronze faces

Following closely behind the leaders were their wives and families. Heyoom Yokikt rode her pinto pony with quiet grace. Fair Land, whose soft eyes, gentle disposition, and deliberate approach to life's problems complemented Ollokot's ebullience. Then came Wetatonmi, her two-year-old son, Jumping Rabbit, dozing behind her saddle. Behind Wetatonmi rode Springtime, Joseph's younger wife. Her dun-colored mare walked the rugged trail with deliberate care as if she knew the meaning of the swollen belly which her rider attempted to ease by placing a rolled blanket over the mare's withers. On this pad Springtime could rest her abdomen by placing her forearms on the blanket and leaning forward. She had borne two other children, and childbearing was no special concern to her or to the other women of the band. Yet today, in the aftermath of the arduous trip through the canyons and rivers, she wondered if this trip would ever end.

Behind Springtime rode a slim, graceful girl-woman named Payopayo Kute, or "Little Bird." She rode a proud Appaloosa gelding that she and her foster uncle Ollokot had broken. She'd named him "Hawk Who Rides The Wind," and the girl, like the horse, appeared to have withstood the rigors of the trip better than most. She was eager, though, to reach the top of the canyon where she could dismount, stretch her legs, and bathe in the lake. Now she rode up beside Springtime, asked how she felt, gave her a drink from the gourd hanging on a thong around her neck, and then took a small sip herself. Her eyes shone with the joy of her life, in spite of the bleak future facing the band.

Just behind Little Bird, sometimes riding beside her with admiration in her eyes, was Kapkap Ponmi, Joseph's twelve-year-old daughter, who was usually called Running Feet.

Following the leaders were the rest of the band, including other families, their children drowsy or sleeping behind their mothers, young boys and girls too tired for their usual flirting and chattering. Then came the loose horses, an unbroken string walking the narrow, twisting trail in single file.

The mares, their udders engorged and teats dripping rich milk, were followed by their hungry foals. The day's march had allowed very few stops, and the smell of the oozing milk tantalized the almost frantic colts.

All of the horses were restless and irritable in the heat of the June day and because of their need for water and grass, which they could sense nearby but couldn't reach. Several seasoned young riders kept the main herd closed up and moving; behind them came the stallions, separated from the herd before the march had started at the Salmon River early that morning. High-spirited and fractious, the stallions were dangerous when mixed among the herd, for if aroused by the scent of a mare in heat they often caused great confusion, injuring other horses and sometimes riders.

So this was no ordinary camp movement for the band. Increasing numbers of white settlers, pressures from the government and the edict by General "Cut Arm" Howard had forced this march. Now on this early June day in 1877 this little band of Nez Perce Indians, carrying all its earthly belongings, was moving up the trail toward Tepahlewam and the end of freedom.

It was late afternoon when the leaders prepared to make camp by the lake. Joseph and his two wives, along with Little Bird and Running Feet, waited patiently in the shade of small trees as the long string of horses emerged from the head of the canyon. They picked their own packhorses from among the earliest arrivals, and the women began to set up the camp. Lodge poles recovered from a cache under nearby trees were placed to form the conical tipi skeletons, which were then covered with buffalo hides.

Soon smoke drifted upward in the still air as cooking fires were built. Other women of the band found their packhorses and rapidly erected their tipis. Children scurried everywhere. Dogs ran in delighted circles, barking and yapping. Foals, deprived of food for several hours, nursed happily, and their mothers sighed with relief. For more than an hour the horse herd streamed from the canyon, joined those of other bands camped nearby and spread out to drink noisily from the lake and feed on the lush prairie grass. Many rolled in dusty spots, while others ran with tails and manes flying. The stallions, no longer segregated, sought the willing mares.

Little Bird, after helping set up the camp and prepare the evening meal, walked slowly around the lake and soon saw the horses dotting the prairie, their sleek hides glistening in the level sunlight. She found Hawk and he responded to her low call. He nuzzled her affectionately, and nickered as she stroked his soft muzzle and arched neck. Her eyes roamed over the large herd of horses. "How beautiful they are," she thought.

As Little Bird mounted Hawk and rode along, the beauty of the horses and the prairie had turned her thoughts away from the tensions within the band and the dark feelings of recent weeks. Now her spirits rose with the westerly breeze blowing from the head of the canyon, rustling the sweet prairie grasses and mingling the fragrance of a myriad of flowers. But she couldn't shake one troublesome question: What changes must her people face, living in a strange land?

Little Bird had ridden farther than planned and suddenly, as she crested a low ridge, several brilliant flashes of light caused her to blink. Though bewildered at first, she soon realized that these were reflections from the windows of a ranch house nestled at the foot of the mountain a few miles eastward. Then she recalled last year's camp at Tepahlewam, when the band had come to gather camas roots. During that time she had ridden Hawk across the prairie and upon emerging from a small grove of trees, she had come face-to-face with a young white man mounted on a large black horse.

She was startled only briefly, for she knew that a white family lived in that direction. Yet the fears and resentment voiced by Yellow Wolf, Ollokot, and other men, even the women, had left Little Bird suspicious and wary of contacts with the settlers, including this one now facing her. His look of insolence and a touch of arrogance were irritating. Little Bird had been to the mission school at Lapwai many times and had heard Joseph, Ollokot, and others speak English, so she knew a few words. Refusing to back away, she told the boy, "My people are camped by the lake. What are you doing here?"

The boy's response was quick, and Little Bird saw the glint of hostility in his eyes as he spoke. "I live here! You must have seen our house. My father, Lucas Phelps, built it years ago."

Little Bird held her temper and cautiously appraised the lithe young man, somewhat older than herself. He had solemn blue-gray eyes, a strong mouth, red-blonde hair curling around his ears and hanging below his collar; and the muscles of his shoulders and upper arms stretching his shirt. His hands were rough from hard work; and he was confident in the seat on the black horse, probably from riding a lot.

As they watched each other, Little Bird heard herself ask, "And do you have a name?" Irritated by her curt, almost haughty, tone, he answered in spite of his feelings, "Kirby." Then, with curiosity in spite of his inherent dislike, he looked more closely at the slim girl on the obviously well-bred Appaloosa. Her hair was a bit untidy, done in waist-length braids. Her eyes were large, wide-set, dark, almost smoky; with features finely chiseled, high cheekbones, skin dusky, now a bit smudged; clothing part Indian, part white man's, hand-made buckskin tunic over store-bought pants. And around the tunic was a brilliant blue-beaded belt.

Slowly, Kirby realized he was staring. Little Bird realized that too, and again felt rising anger. Hawk shifted a little and pawed the ground, and the black horse became restless. Feeling no need for further talk, both Kirby and Little Bird turned their horses about and rode away.

As Kirby headed home, he felt relieved of the intensity of the dark eyes, the sardonic half-smile, the almost-defiant tilt of the head, the ripeness of the trim body. Shutting out these impressions, he muttered aloud, "Insolent little bitch! 'What are you doing here?' and 'Do you have a name?' Dad would call her a heathen!" So Kirby had ridden home, turned the black loose in the pasture, was quiet through supper and went to bed early. Sleep was elusive, disturbed by flashes of blue beads encircling a slim waist.

Little Bird had turned leisurely back to Joseph's tipi, the softness of the prairie twilight calming her mind, but annoyed that she could not simply dismiss this boy—he called himself Kirby—as just another arrogant white man. "I live here," he had said, as if that gave him some kind of right to the prairie. "Well, he's no part of my life," she thought to herself.

And during that summer Little Bird had not seen Kirby Phelps again, for his work with the family cattle took him in other directions, and she had gone back across the rivers with Joseph's band.

## CHAPTER 2

Lucas Phelps had lived on the ranch near the lake with his family for several years. He was a burly, powerful Scot, only five feet nine inches tall but weighing 240 pounds. He had massive arms, red hair, and a full red beard, and the sandy hair on his barrel chest curled out over the top of his shirt and grew close to his Adam's apple. His piercing blue eyes, with wrinkles at the corners, and his ready smile belied a basically stubborn nature, but also showed an optimistic view of the world about him and a refusal to be riled at much of anything.

As a boy, Lucas had quarreled repeatedly with a stern Presbyterian father on a rock-laden farm in Vermont. He finally rebelled at the strict discipline and unrelenting religious routine, and at age 15 left home for the gold fields of California. He had no money and only a few personal items, which he guarded closely and carried in a small bundle over his shoulder.

He made it to Sutter's Mill in California, but found very little gold. After a year or so he drifted eastward, working odd jobs and learning a smattering of farming and blacksmithing, to which his rapidly maturing body and heavy muscles were well-suited. By 1856 he was beginning to feel at home in the Walla Walla country of Washington Territory, but in the early 1860s he became restless.

Lucas heard a man named Pierce had discovered gold far up the Clearwater River in Idaho on a creek called Oro Fino, so he collected his wages and the small share he had in the blacksmithing business and moved on. But the Nez Perces had protested the arrival of the miners and the crafty Pierce had pulled back, deliberately waiting for public pressure and political expediency to allow return to the Oro Fino. Soon the existing treaty with the Nez Perces was amended to allow travel to Oro Fino Creek, and Lucas went there. Here he was more successful, built up a reasonable stake in gold dust, and soon was so infected by gold fever that when news came of a rich strike south of the Clearwater he took off with other men, deliberately traveling through Indian lands and ending up at Elk City. He did well there and soon moved west to Florence to join the biggest gold rush since Sutter's Mill. His stake grew rapidly, but the wild, lawless life and the lure of gold, girls, and whiskey insidiously wore him down. He struggled to remember his strict Presbyterian background, but the loneliness and the lack of anyone who cared led him deeper into gambling, to which he was soon addicted. He started drinking heavily and could no longer resist the girls.

One night, while winning significantly, Lucas detected a slight-of-hand trick by an opponent which threatened to wipe out his winnings. Lucas challenged him, knives flashed, and within seconds the man lay on the floor in a pool of blood. Within the hour he was dead.

The next morning Lucas awakened in a puddle of his own vomit, with a throbbing headache, a livid red slash running diagonally from his right shoulder across his breastbone, and the sudden realization that he had nearly been killed. Later he learned that the other miners had been aware of the dead man's cheating and none of them held any grudge against Lucas. But a crushing sense of futility and guilt almost overcame him, and he realized that his life was a shambles and it was time to move on.

The next morning he packed his few belongings, including several little bags of gold dust, and walked out of the camp. Perhaps somewhere to the north he could find people who lived in houses, or at least orderly cabins, had children, tended their gardens, and tried to make some sense out of their everyday lives. He remembered a little place called Mount Idaho and another, slightly to the west named Grange Hall. There were a few people in each, as well as other settlers scattered around the nearby prairie. At this point, one place seemed as good as the other.

A few miles out of Florence he remembered that he had eaten no breakfast and stopped at a spring by the trail for a sparse lunch. As he rummaged through the pack his hands touched the little buckskin bags. He felt the familiar tingling in his spine that always occurred when he saw gold. The old fever was returning, and he asked himself, "Why am I going north? Why not try Crooked Creek, or the Oro Grande? How about that man just last week who talked about the big strike on the south side of the Salmon River? I've never been across the Salmon River. But no! That's only going back to the same pointless, clawing life that I've known for the last several months. I'm beginning to have the feeling that I'll never have enough gold. If I don't walk away from it now, I probably never will."

While occupied by these thoughts, Lucas had been replacing the contents of his pack and hefting the heavy bags of gold dust. Then he heard a click just behind his head and felt the hair stand up on the back of his neck.

"Stand up, stranger! Turn around real quiet and slow with your hands raised, and step away from that pack."

Lucas turned slowly, raising his hands slightly at the same time, and looked directly into the barrel of a revolver. Behind the barrel he saw a bearded, grizzled face, tight lips that were smiling very slightly, and a long thin nose—from the bridge of which a livid scar extended across the cheek. Above the nose were the hardest eyes Lucas had ever seen.

"Nice little buckskin bags you've got in your pack there," the man said. "Ounce for ounce it's the most valuable thing a man can have, except for diamonds, which aren't much good around here. Now if you'll just move back a couple more steps, I'll relieve you of that gold."

Those flint-like eyes reminded Lucas of a rattler he had seen recently, lying on a ledge at eye level, coiled and tail buzzing. Lucas had backed slowly away from the snake, but there was no backing away this time. Lucas began sorting out possible ways to fight back: "If he just diverts his eyes for one split second, or perhaps when he reaches down to pick up the gold bags..."

Help came suddenly. A badger blundering through the brush disturbed a hornet's nest and one angry hornet struck the stranger's face. He raised his hand to slap it away, and turned his head, and in that instant Lucas leaped to the left and swung his right arm up under the wrist holding the gun. One shot went into the air and before the man could get off a second, Lucas had driven a knee into the man's groin and then they were on the ground, flailing and cursing. Lucas managed to grab the gun hand with both of his, avoiding a second shot, and as he wrenched the gun loose it fell in the dust.

Suddenly Lucas' eyes were aflame with blinding lights as a great, crashing noise exploded in his head. He found himself groveling in the dust, attempting to regain his feet. As he slowly recovered, he felt the blood oozing down the side of his head, saw the rock with which he had been struck and the contents of his pack littered about on the ground. But the heavy little buckskin bags were gone.

The impact of losing the fruits of months of work slowly penetrated Lucas' dazed mind and he felt the need to wash his hands and face and refresh himself in the water of the spring. As the cold water stanched the flow of blood from the head wound, he began to feel better and walked back to accumulate his belongings.

"Well, Phelps, where do we go now?" he idly asked himself. "In the last two days you've managed to kill one man, barely miss being killed yourself, and lose your entire stake of gold. What's next? Is it back to something that looks a little more like civilization? Or is it to some other lousy mining camp?"

As he stooped to pick up the scattered items, something glinting in the grass caught his eye. Looking more closely, he found one little buckskin bag, empty, but in the grass around it was that soft glow that comes only from gold. His mind again went back to his experiences along the way, especially at Sutter's Mill in California, where he had seen his first gold, felt the tingling thrill of it, and watched the frenzied pursuit by others, which he soon joined. He remembered vividly the first time he had watched a man take a board, hold back the water in a flume box, and show him the gold accumulated behind the upstream side of the slats. The miner had an almost fanatical look in his eyes as he said to Lucas, "I came all the way from Brazil, saw some gold there, but nothing like this! Of course, only a few people strike it so soon or so rich."

Now Lucas stood holding in his hand one little empty bag, and looking at the gold scattered through the dust and grass at his feet. Then he carefully scooped up every grain he could find, filled the little bag, and put the rest of the mixture of gold, grass, and dirt into a large bandanna, tying a knot with the corners. "There's a lot of dirt in there," he thought to himself, "but it sure is heavy. Probably enough to get me started somewhere else."

Having searched through the remains of his pack, he found some food, had a good drink of water from the spring and by nightfall was well on his way to the other side of the Salmon River and the little town of Warrens.

The Salmon River canyon south of Florence was an impassable gorge with perpendicular cliffs, rockslides, giant boulders and pinnacled ridges leading down to the river, a blue thread in the darkening shadows of the evening. Lucas was exhausted and by sunset he was forced to seek shelter under an overhanging rock. He gathered some leaves and pine needles and made the best bed he could, but he slept little until first light.

By late afternoon he had descended to the river, where a crude ferry was available for crossing. The lonely-looking little man who ran it seemed delighted to have company and talked continuously as he prepared to make the trip across.

"Mighty glad you came along. We been waiting for you. We got a spyglass up there in the house and we watch the trail. Saw you start down over an hour ago. Awful lonely down here through the winter when hardly anybody travels this way to Warrens."

The man talked on and on, but when they reached the shore the fare had still not been discussed. "What do I owe you?" Lucas asked.

"One dollar, cash or gold dust," the ferryman said. "If you want supper tonight, a place to sleep, and breakfast in the morning, that'll be another fifty cents."

A home-cooked meal, and hopefully a soft bed, was almost more than Lucas could imagine, and he readily agreed, pulling out the handkerchief containing the gold dust mixed with dirt. The little man scratched his head and said, "Well, I ain't seen it mixed with dirt like this before, but I guess we can figure out something."

He had a little balance with tiny weights and they finally agreed on enough of the mixture to equal one dollar and fifty cents. The little man, still talking, now led the way across the beach and up a trail. Well above high water mark they entered a small, crudely built cabin where a thin but sprightly little woman came toward them.

"Got company tonight, Ma. Hope you're fixing a little extra."

"Yes, I figured we would have," she answered, glancing at the spyglass lying on the table. "Gus, you haven't introduced us. Been talking a blue streak again, I suppose." Gus, apparently having been chided before, merely grinned and said, "I'm Gus McGreggor, and this is my wife, Bess."

"I'm Lucas Phelps, and much obliged for your hospitality."

Lucas was ravenously hungry after most of three days without much food, and the meal of boiled potatoes, biscuits, small delicious chops and lots of hot coffee was surprisingly good. Not having seen any livestock except two rather thin donkeys, he asked about the meat.

"Mountain sheep," Gus replied. "They come down to the river all the time. Nobody bothers them much and they're easy to get. But the weather's warming up now and we'll have a garden growing pretty soon."

With supper over, they sat on the little front porch while Gus continued to talk. Bess interrupted him to ask Lucas about the lump and raw-looking bruise on the side of his head. He made some excuse which seemed to satisfy her and she quietly left the room, returning soon with a pleasant-smelling ointment. She first cleaned the wound then rubbed the ointment on it. "That should help," she said.

The sun had set and soft shadows were deepening among the cliffs on the south slope across the river. Bess saw that Lucas needed sleep and led him to a small shack behind the house. Inside was a soft pile of hay, cut from a narrow meadow beside the river. A big, slow-moving dog of uncertain lineage had trailed along from the house and now flopped down on the hay, obviously planning to spend the night. Lucas was soon comfortable between clean blankets and with a pillow which Bess had provided for him. The roar of the rapids in the river below was softened by distance and intervening willow thickets. A catbird called from near the small stream which ran past the cabin and a nighthawk, pursuing insects high in the air, ended its dive with a sighing moan. Up on the hillside a coyote began a characteristic series of staccato yelps and was answered by another farther away. The old dog sighed in his sleep, Lucas spoke to him softly, and the big, bushy tail flopped against his leg as Lucas drifted off.

---

Slits of sunlight beamed through cracks in the shack wall as he slowly awoke, and Lucas savored the smell of frying bacon and brewing coffee drifting from the cabin. Soon breakfast was over and as Lucas prepared to leave, Gus pumped his hand while Bess softly touched the wound on his head. She wished him well, and then Lucas resumed his journey.

He soon looked back down the trail and saw the smoke from the little cabin rose straight into the air, the sign of a clear, calm day. Then his thoughts turned back to the pathetic, lonely couple he had just left. There was longing in the woman's eyes as she touched his cheek. The night before as she dressed his wound she had talked about the loss of their five-year-old son, gone now for ten years. Ten whole years! And they still referred to it as a checkpoint in time, after which things around here had been "a little lonely." What a struggle their life must be there on the bank of the river, scratching out a bare existence on the tiny income from the ferry. How old are they? Fifty? In the soft glow of the canyon twilight, do they still feel tenderness and affection? How many couples like them are scattered along these lonely canyons with their dreams of riches long dead?

---

As Lucas entered Warrens he found tents, shanties, and even dugouts everywhere. An enterprising man had set up a small sawmill and a few shacks had been built of the rough, whip-sawed lumber. The short main street, still rutted and muddy from the winter snows and spring rains, hosted only a few shabby buildings. A general store accommodated the post office as well as an assayer's office for the gold. Beyond that, there were only a couple of cheap hotels and several makeshift saloons.

Considering the hotel rates, Lucas figured he might last a week or two on the gold dust he already had, but it was critical he find more soon. His search was discouraging; though. No one wanted a partner without money and there were no claims available which looked promising. The miners, generally, were loners and the only sense of welcome that Lucas felt was when he went to buy a drink, especially if he was the least bit encouraging to the girl who sidled up to him at the bar. Soon it became apparent that gold mining there would not be very successful. But every saloon had active games and there were several tents set up entirely for gambling. "Well, Phelps," he thought, "you were pretty good at this for awhile. Maybe you'll have to go back to it now."

In the following weeks Lucas began to win enough small to moderate-sized pots to at least sustain him from day to day. There were as many Chinese in Warrens—"Chinks," everybody called them—as there had been in Florence. Most were miners, often working the poorest claims. With few exceptions they were detested and ridiculed by the white men. Among the Chinese residents a small, self-assured man stood out, for he did nothing but gamble, obviously had plenty of money, and usually was at the high-stakes table. His name was Ah Fong, and he commanded a rare respect among the local miners and gamblers. Lucas saw him almost nightly in one of the gambling joints, soon recognizing him as a determined man with a keen mind. His eyes met others with a calm, unflinching gaze, his face unreadable.

Then one morning Lucas met Ah Fong on the street, but he was not alone. Following him at a designated and respectful distance was a slim Chinese girl in a coolie shirt and trousers and wearing a conical straw hat, not an uncommon sight in Warrens. But this girl was different. She walked briskly rather than shuffling, and her uplifted chin and general bearing showed a person who met life on its own terms and was subservient to no one. That night Lucas asked another gambler about the girl.

"Oh, that's Mei Ling. She's Ah Fong's girl, and nobody messes with her."

"Is she his wife?"

"No, slave girl. Came here with Ah Fong last summer. The story among the other Chinks here is that she came to San Francisco from Shanghai. Her beauty made her valuable property and she was kicked around among the various tongs in San Francisco. Probably isn't much she hasn't been through. I suppose Ah Fong won her in a Mah-Jong game or something. Cute little trick, isn't she?"

Lucas felt that description fell far short of describing Mei Ling, and agreed with himself that he certainly would not mess with her, as he remembered Ah Fong's hard eyes.

As the days passed, Lucas' skill in gambling grew and his winnings increased. At first he was concerned about the safety of his growing stash of gold dust, but then was assured by acquaintances there was no problem—immediate hanging was the penalty for theft of gold dust with no questions were asked. Among Lucas' winnings was a magnificent blood bay mare, half Morgan and half American Saddler, and with the mare, he had won a fine Spanish saddle and bridle, both intricately decorated with silver. His recreation now was riding the mare along the streams and through the meadows in the surrounding mountains.

Lucas began to sense that his standing as a gambler was high and his skill virtually unchallenged, but the old urge to move on had come again. Then one night as he watched the play at the various tables his eyes rested on Ah Fong. He suddenly realized that here was his ultimate challenge. Ah Fong, in turn, was quite aware that Lucas was the only man in Warrens who could challenge him, and he knew Lucas had been accumulating quite a pile of winnings. So setting up the game was easy.

The play started the next evening shortly after supper, and by 11 p.m. all the other players had dropped out. The stakes of gold dust, coins, and other valuable items lying on the table were large and growing with each game. At the end of one hand won by Ah Fong, Lucas had lost his gold watch. On the next hand, Ah Fong bet and lost a huge diamond ring. Finally, the showdown had arrived. Lucas had left at one point and returned with all of the gold from his stash. Ah Fong, likewise, had everything on the table. Lucas raised the ante one final time. Ah Fong glanced at his cards, excused himself and left the room briefly. When he returned, the beautiful Mei Ling was walking behind him. Then he sat down and said, "Mei Ling is now part of the pot," before calling Lucas' hand.

In the stunned silence within the gaming tent, no one moved, hardly breathed, or cleared a throat. The sound of a horsefly circling the lantern was like a buzz saw in the smoky air. Then the two hands were laid on the table. Lucas had won!

The imperturbable Ah Fong arose, smiled thinly, nodded formally to Lucas, turned from the table and left the hall. The release of tensions was loud and boisterous, and brought calls for drinks on the house. Mei Ling looked at Lucas, walked slowly around the table, bowed solemnly, and said in a soft voice, "I am your servant."

Lucas' mind was in turmoil. The game had ended so suddenly that the final action by Ah Fong was not yet a reality. Gold, watches, diamonds, horses, saddles—these things he could understand. But a woman? Then suddenly he heard his father's voice which seemed to be saying, "Heathen woman," or at best, "Pagan." Though Lucas was never quite sure what the difference was, he had come to understand at a very young age that neither of these compared in any way to a Presbyterian. And wouldn't this woman be even worse if she were considered as property? How has all this mess happened? And how can

I get myself out of it? Father was right, and I want nothing to do with this woman, cute as she may be!

Lucas had recently acquired a small cabin with a lean-to in back for the mare. Since the game for the evening was obviously over, he started home—and soon discovered that Mei Ling was following at a discreet distance behind him. "Doesn't she have any place of her own?" he thought. "Does she think she's really my servant? Does she think she's going to live in my house?"

But that was exactly what Mei Ling intended. She spoke little English, but when they arrived at the little cabin, Mei Ling followed Lucas in and immediately began looking for ways to make him more comfortable. He pushed her aside, ordered her to sleep in the hay, and dropped off to sleep. But the next morning she was back, preparing breakfast when he awoke.

In the sunlight that streamed through a small window, he got his first good look at her and drew a sharp breath of surprise and amazement. The straw hat was gone. She wore a turquoise blouse, and her slight but shapely figure moved gracefully about the cabin as she tended the food on the stove. Her eyes met his directly, with no sense of servitude or subjection, and that bothered him. His former safe and comfortable impression of her as a slave girl was being replaced by the uncomfortable realization that here was a mature, self-sufficient woman, with softly curving lips and almond eyes and tawny cream skin. Her jet black hair caught little glints of sunlight coming through the window, contrasting delightfully with the turquoise of her blouse.

Lucas began to feel a glow of warmth and excitement at her beauty. Then he realized, "I'm still in bed! How do I get out with this female wandering around my cabin?" After a few minutes, Mei Ling went out to the spring for a bucket of water, and Lucas leaped out of bed, jumped into his trousers, and was buttoning his shirt when she returned. The trip to the spring had taken Mei Ling several minutes, and she returned invigorated by the walk. Her eyes sparkled, her skin glowed, and the tiniest beads of sweat stood out on her forehead. As she moved past Lucas to set the water on the table he was sharply aware of her nearness and the scent of her body. He wanted to reach out to her, to touch her, and perhaps even to embrace her—or should he simply thank her for preparing his meals?

She turned to him with a faint smile, and those large almond-brown eyes looked directly into his with honesty and openness, and perhaps even an invitation. But suddenly he was back in Vermont, sitting between his mother and father in church, and the preacher was talking about the "strange woman," and his tight-lipped father was nodding his smug agreement. That night Mei Ling again slept on the hay under the lean-to.

Lucas had given up prospecting for gold but his gambling luck continued to run high and his stake increased. He sensed, and tried to push aside, his growing need for Mei Ling. Meanwhile, she was there each morning, discreetly entering the cabin when she knew he would be up and dressed, fixing his meals, keeping the cabin clean, washing and mending his clothes and then returning to sleep in the lean-to each night amid the smell of hay and horse manure.

## CHAPTER 3

Lucas became increasingly fond of riding and was out on the bay mare almost daily. He came to appreciate the mare's great strength, stamina, and speed, and he grew to love the animal more each day.

Late one afternoon Lucas returned from a ride to find Mei Ling in the cabin preparing to place dinner on the table. She seemed strangely moody, and though she did not usually eat with him, tonight she deliberately fixed her own plate and sat down at the table across from him. He said nothing, but here was that warm feeling again and that exciting, vague scent of her body. "Where is it written that I'm supposed to understand women, much less this strange one, who is willing to sleep in the hay?" he asked himself. After supper, he went for a short ride and then to the gambling hall. Again his luck was good and he returned home feeling very secure. As he unsaddled and tied the mare he glanced cautiously under the lean-to, but Mei Ling was not there. He cautiously entered the cabin and there on the floot she sat. He noticed she'd brought in her blankets and pillow. With sparks in her eyes and no smile, she defiantly said, "No like smell of horse turd. No like noise of horse chomping on hay all night. No like dogs sniffing around my bed. I sleep in cabin."

One day in early spring, Lucas traveled to the Salmon River to visit with Gus and Bess. The trip was easy on the mare, but he sensed that things were not well as he approached the ferry. He could see signs of general disrepair and no evidence that Bess had started a garden. As he neared the cabin, the old dog greeted him listlessly.

Bess answered the door and welcomed him warmly, but without her usual enthusiasm. Gus sat in a chair and shook Lucas' hand without rising. Bess prepared a meal, even simpler than the one on Lucas' first visit. As they ate in silence, Lucas realized that one thing missing was Gus's continual talking. Not really knowing these people very well, Lucas decided it was best not to invade their privacy.

As he prepared to leave Bess followed him out on the porch to say good-bye, and Gus having wished him well inside the cabin, again without rising. As they stood on the porch, Lucas turned to Bess and said, "I'm concerned about Gus. He's not the man I met last summer."

"He's this way most of the time," Bess sighed. "He's been losing steam for several months. I have to help him with the ferry now when we have a passenger, but I think he'll perk up now that the weather is warmer. Lucas, we sure do appreciate you coming down, and I hope you'll return. We seldom see passengers a second time. Will you come again?"

"I'll try," Lucas replied. "Thanks again for the meal."

---

Soon after Mei Ling moved into the cabin a comfortable pattern developed. She continued to arise before Lucas and managed to be gone while he awakened and dressed, seeming to sense his shyness and respect his privacy. There was little conversation between them, for Mei Ling's English was poor and Lucas felt no responsibility to help her improve it. But how could he complain at having the cabin clean and orderly, washed clothes available and hot meals prepared each morning and evening? It was wonderful! After all, wasn't that what a woman was supposed to do? Especially a slave woman?

Then Lucas began to realize there was much more to it than the clean cabin, the washed clothes, and the meals. Just having someone else there, even if she was a heathen woman who slept on the floor, was beginning to get to him. He had not yet realized that he was falling into a trap, even though he found himself thinking about her during the day as he gambled or rode the mare across the meadows. Then one night as they sat after dinner, he watched as she painted little bowls and vases. She had built a small oven out in front of the cabin where she fired various items made of clay from the creek bank. Apparently she had brought paints with her from China. He was fascinated as her quick strokes produced foliage, flowers, birds, fish, and other patterns on each little item. She always finished with a single Chinese character, like a signature. Her face was serene and calm, and her hair glinted again in the lamp light. She sensed his eyes watching her and turned toward him with that shy, faint smile that brought the warmth to her eyes and a strange glow within him. Lucas couldn't help thinking, "She may be a heathen woman, but how precious she is! I no longer want her to go away."

Late in the afternoon, Lucas had seen massive thunderheads gathering in the west. Now Mei Ling had put away her paints, cleaned up the dishes, and lain on the floor to sleep. Lucas was dozing off in his bed when he heard the mare scream in terror as the first jagged dagger of lightning slashed the sky. Thunder crashed and rumbled overhead as the clouds were torn apart and air masses collided. Repeated flashes of lightning and peals of thunder continued for several minutes and the cabin was brilliantly aglow as if spotlights flickered through the small windows.

Then came the wind, tearing and clawing at the cabin. Lucas could hear shakes being ripped from the roof. Rain came in roaring torrents and the hastily built cabin, anything but tight, leaked in several places. Lucas feared for the mare, but was afraid to go out in the storm to calm her.

In the midst of the surrounding confusion, Lucas suddenly felt a thump on the bed, a cold draft around his shoulders, and a warm, trembling little body pressed against him. "No like storm," she said as she rested her damp head on his shoulder and put her arm across his chest. Lucas felt the smooth, firm softness of her, and again caught the subtle, exciting scent of her body.

As the storm moved eastward, the lightning flashes became less frequent and the rumbling of the thunder more subdued. Mei Ling quit trembling, but made no move to go back to her blankets on the floor. The bed was warm, her hair had dried, and Lucas realized he did not want her to leave—indeed would not allow her to. Then, as if by the brilliance of the passing storm, Lucas realized that never in his life had he given or received love and warmth from another person. On the farm in Vermont, there had been much talk of love, and much praying, but he had no memory of tenderness or affection, or even real sympathy. Now his deprivation swept over him, and he felt that he would never be lonely again. Mei Ling was in his arms and her mouth was sweet and warm against his. "No matter how she got here, this is my woman," he thought to himself, and neither the word "slave" nor the word "heathen" came to his mind.

As spring blended into summer and the days warmed, Mei Ling and Lucas would walk the hills or ride double on the mare, reveling in the beauty of their world and the unspoken realization of their love. The inexpressible loveliness of the land about them and the clear, endless sky overhead became as a world apart from the bawdy life in Warrens, and the couple spent as little time as possible at the cabin.

The weeks that followed were almost idyllic. Lucas' luck was good at the tables, and Mei Ling started working in a restaurant. Lucas had always been a loner, but now he began to open up and became friendly with several people around the town. He grew to like one young man, Early Jorgenson, a roustabout for one of the companies which handled the loads of freight brought into Warrens by pack trains.

Like Lucas, Early had not been very successful at mining, but he was no gambler. He had a beautiful young Swedish wife named Anna who worked at the restaurant with Mei Ling, and the two women had also become friends.

Early and Anna had recently arrived in Warrens and had not heard the story of Lucas winning Mei Ling in a poker game. One day Early asked Lucas, "How long have you and Mei Ling been married?" The shock of the question was too much for Lucas, and he mumbled, "Oh, not very long." But that night in bed the full import of the question struck him. He could feel the soft warmth of Mei Ling close to him and listened to her contented breathing. However, he seemed to hear his father's voice thundering the Seventh Commandment and quoting other scriptures about marriage and husbands loving wives—-and of course, avoiding heathen women. It was a restless, tormented night, and by morning Lucas had decided he and Mei Ling must be married. There was no preacher in Warrens, but he would find one in the closest place possible.

But before he could do anything about finding a preacher, he was hailed on the street the next morning by a miner who had recently come across the Salmon River. "Hey, Phelps," he called, "have you been down to the ferry to see old Gus yet?"

Lucas remembered that the miner had told him several days before that Gus and Bess were not feeling well and would like to see him. In the almost mystic happiness of being in love he had forgotten. Now he must go and see them.

Quickly he saddled the mare, rode past the restaurant to tell Mei Ling he would be gone possibly overnight, and soon he was hurrying down the steep mountain trail. As he descended, an ominous foreboding came over him. Drawing closer, he searched the area around the cabin, looking for any sign of life, but seeing only the two donkeys sleeping in the shade. Then his eyes moved to the river, scanning the shoreline for the ferry, but it was not there!

Now Lucas' mind seemed to work in slow motion. He saw the breadth of the river as one scene, expecting to find the ferry on the far shore, but then he saw it swaying slowly in the middle of the river, its cables at a slight angle to the current. His worst fears became evident as he noticed the ugly, ominous presence of magpies and ravens sitting on the ferry railing while others circled overhead.

The chilling sight of the birds had immobilized Lucas, and he sat for a long moment before regaining control. Now his mind raced to find ways to get onto the ferry, knowing that he must but dreading what he would find there. He was a poor swimmer and knew that the water was very cold. Could he make it out to the ferry? The current not far downstream was very strong, and if he miscalculated the angle when entering the river he would miss the ferry and be swept away.

Then as he glanced at his strong mare, he noticed the heavy saddle strap across her chest. She could pull the ferry to shore with the saddle! He found a strong rope and some baling wire near the cabin and soon had one end of the rope connected to the ferry's bowline and the other end attached to the saddle horn.

Fortunately, the beach was wide and solid, allowing enough space for the mare to slowly tow the ferry to shore. The staunch mare strained and heaved, her bulging thigh muscles taut and knotted, her breath coming in deep gasps. When she paused briefly to rest Lucas feared the ferry would drag her into the river, but she groaned and tugged, kicking up spumes of sand behind her. Lucas led her, and when he saw that the bow of the ferry had touched the shore he tied the reins to a bush. He rushed across the beach and secured the ferry, then ran back to unsaddle the trembling, exhausted horse.

The ravens and magpies had flown away as the ferry approached the shore, but as Lucas turned from the mare he saw that they were again settling on the deck. He fought a sickening revulsion as he hurried to the bow and climbed aboard to chase them away.

Gus lay on the deck in full sunlight. Before Lucas could grasp what had happened, his mind was imprinted with the startling, grim details. The flaming red bald spot on Gus' head was like raw meat, and what was left of his face was even worse. His gray hair was tousled and bloody and matted. Only one ear remained, and his eyes were now just empty black holes.

The river's current made the ferry's wooden structure creak and a lonely wind played a mournful dirge on the cables. Lucas was almost overcome, and with a shudder he covered Gus' wasted body with a piece of canvas. Then he crossed the ferry to find Bess. The frail woman lay in the shade of a tattered blanket hung over a cable and Lucas first thought she also was dead. He was relieved to detect a slight breath, though. Holding the rail with one hand, he reached down with the other to dip water from the river and sponge Bess' arms and face. In a little while her eyes fluttered open, but she was not able to speak. He soon carried her up the shore to the cabin with the faint hope she'd pull through.

He did all he could for Bess, tended the mare, and ate what food he could find before dropping into a shallow, disturbed sleep. He soon returned to Bess' bedside, and she asked for water. Then, holding Lucas' huge hand between her worn, emaciated palms, she haltingly told him what happened.

"On Monday we took a man across the river. Coming back, Gus began feeling faint. He kept trying, but suddenly he collapsed. I could do nothing by myself, and the boat slid back to the middle of the river. I tried to do what I could for Gus, but I wasn't strong enough to move him. That evening he died. And then those horrible birds began circling, cawing and chattering! I kept them away for awhile, but by the time it got hot the next day, I had no strength left. I couldn't stand to watch what they did to Gus, and their squawks almost drove me crazy. I prayed and I cried. There was no water on the ferry, and I couldn't reach into the river. Finally, I passed out. And then you came."

Bess drifted away then; and Lucas thought she still might make it. But when he awakened the next morning she was dead, and he began the heavy-hearted task of taking Gus and Bess to where he knew they would want to be. Methodically, he forced his mind and body to take each step. Finding some old blankets, he tenderly wrapped the bodies and loaded them on the ferry. Then he caught the two donkeys, led them aboard, and tied them up. Fearing that he might not have the strength to pull the ferry to the opposite shore from the middle of the river with the weight of the bodies, the donkeys, himself, and the mare, he tied her securely to the stern and she swam strongly on the downstream side. He somehow managed to reach the other shore, where he lay on the deck for an hour, regaining his strength. Then he carefully loaded one body on each donkey, mounted the mare, and started the long trip up the mountain toward the head of Slate Creek.

By mid-afternoon clouds obscured the sun and a chilly wind sighed through the tops of the pines. As the funeral caravan rounded a sharp curve, he glanced back at the pathetic bundles draped across the two donkeys and was suddenly and desolately alone. But by nightfall his work was finished. Two fresh mounds were made in that quiet mountain place, covered with big stones to discourage digging by wild animals. Between the new mounds was a tiny one, now overgrown by grass and a lonely clump of late summer Indian

Paintbrush.

He slept between the mare's saddle blankets and early the next morning left the donkeys to themselves before riding back to the Salmon River. He was too tired to manage the ferry, but he urged the mare across and rested awhile at the little cabin. The lonely old dog did not offer to follow when Lucas started back to Warrens. He arrived at a hot spring by the trail where he bathed as his mind struggled with the last two days' events. He hoped in vain to just wash them away.

Mei Ling was not there when he reached his cabin. The cabin was strangely silent. There was no sign a meal had been prepared, or any freshly painted vases drying. With growing alarm he hurried to the restaurant. As he entered all activity stopped. Two Chinese men sitting over their teacups arose and disappeared into the back room. Mei Ling's friend Anna came forward, her eyes unsmiling as she took his hand.

"Ah Fong came back," she said. "He has taken her to San Francisco, and some say they may return to China."

Lucas' first frenzied impulse was to flee, as he had run from his father as a boy, to burn away his fury in blind action. Even the gentle bay mare became a victim of his rage as he saddled her to escape into the mountains. But the sight of Mei Ling's firing kiln outside the cabin brought a flood of memories of the first real love he had ever known. He must bring her back!

He frantically returned to the restaurant. "Come with me, Early," he asked, but Early declined, for Anna was pregnant. "Then I'll go alone!" Lucas said. "There's no horse in Warrens that can outrun this mare."

Anna urged him to take food, warm clothing, and blankets, and at his cabin, he saw the heavy little box Anna had given him when she told him Mei Ling was gone. It was filled with gold dust, left for him by Ah Fong. He had hurled it in anger and shattered the mirror behind the bar, but now he realized it was worth hundreds of dollars. He put it in his saddle bag along with his Colt revolver and cartridges. Mei Ling's little painted vases tore at his heart, and he carefully wrapped two of them to take with him.

# CHAPTER 4

Lucas punished the mare mindlessly as he rode westward, but gradually the powerful surge of her easy lope soothed him. "Early said an old miner named Hank Meacham is traveling with them, and he'll need his rest," Lucas thought. "Their horses can't be very good. I'll catch them within two days."

It was dusk of the second day when the wind in Lucas' face carried a faint smell of wood smoke. He had traveled hard for 36 hours without rest, forcing the mare relentlessly, devouring the miles but sensing now she was tiring. A few miles back the tracks of two horses had joined the three he was following—travelers from some nearby ranch. So he proceeded cautiously, peering around trees at each bend in the trail, and he smiled grimly when he saw a barely discernable film of smoke among the trees away from the trail. Leaving the mare well-hidden, he crawled ahead from tree to tree. Soon there was a little more smoke and, dimly, he saw three horses hidden among brush and thick lodge-pole pines. Their camp had to be there in some tiny opening in the dense thicket.

He returned to the mare, picketed her in a meadow to feed and rest, huddled in his blanket, and waited. At midnight he crept past the three worn-out horses and into the black, thorny thicket, and in two hours he crawled only 50 feet. Nervous sweat filled his eyes, trickled down his neck as thorns tore his face and clawed at his clothing. In the next hour he moved only 20 more feet, inching and waiting, straining his eyes to see through the tangled foliage. Suddenly his shoulders pushed through the last branches. He had blundered into the tiny camp circle, and in the misty dimness of gray dawn he saw three blanketed figures, barely discernable on the ground. He dared not move, fearing the sound of his own breathing and the alarming boom of his heartbeat. Three people not ten feet away! But the light was still too dull. Which one was Ah Fong?

So he waited, ready to pounce, while the light grew brighter and no one moved. He feared a trap, but now he knew from the size of the three huddled forms that Hank was the big one to the right, Mei Ling the tiny one in the middle, and Ah Fong lay to the left. A low moan triggered Lucas' swift leap, and with the Colt cocked he snatched the blanket from Ah Fong—only to find a mound of rocks, grass, and pine needles. Another groan from the right and Lucas whirled with his trigger finger constricting. He almost shot Hank Meacham, whose half-glazed, rheumy eyes stared pleadingly above a dirty gag which encircled his gaping jaws. The gag was attached behind his neck to his wrists and ankles, all drawn together and lashed tightly below his shoulders. Now he shook with sobs and tried vainly to move.

What Lucas had thought was Mei Ling was just more blanketed debris, and he knew he had been totally outmaneuvered. But before he untied Hank he circled the camp, still finding nothing but the three depleted horses—and only one saddle!

"We traveled without rest," Hank told Lucas. "Before daylight the second morning Ah Fong stole two fresh horses from a ranch near the trail. I've been here since early yesterday. They didn't sleep here, must have hurried right on after he slugged me and trussed me up."

Angry and humiliated, Lucas untied Hank, left him to shift for himself, and drove the mare mercilessly on around Payette Lake. She's had food and a night's rest, he thought defensively, but she can't keep this up much longer. So, fifty miles south of the lake he left the mare and took a gelding from a herd pastured by the trail—really just a trade, he rationalized. He steeled his mind against the pangs of deserting the mare and spurred the fresh mount down the winding, rocky canyon of the Payette River. By the time he reached Boise he was riding his fourth stolen horse which—along with some gold dust—a horse trader took in exchange for two strong geldings.

At Boise no one remembered seeing a Chinese man and a girl. After all, there were hundreds of them going to and from the mines at Idaho City. And the railroad he was hoping to find somewhere in northern Nevada was stalled in the Sierras near Donner Pass.

"You'll have to ride these horses to Truckee, maybe farther," the horse trader said, almost gleefully. Lucas felt resentful, but just groaned and rode out of the Boise River Valley, across the broad Snake River plain, and up the long, tiresome, sage-covered hills to the rim of the Great Basin. Gold Fever had controlled his mind and driven him blindly forward when he crossed this formidable basin as a boy in 1850. Now, consumed by his longing for Mei Ling, he was depressed by the immensity and desolation of the seemingly endless, thirsty land. It was pure luck he found two usable springs, which eased their sufferings as Lucas and the horses struggled southwesterly over crumbled lava and salt-encrusted mud.

Days passed with no sign of another human. Lucas sagged in the saddle, unaware of time, changing horses frequently, sharing their fatigue. Then one evening he saw lines of stakes with little flags, and two men on horseback. Surveyors, far ahead of the railroad construction crews! They shared water and food and hay with him, but hadn't seen anyone recently. "Follow these stakes and you'll find the railroad," they told Lucas. "They're somewhere this side of Donner Lake."

Three days later Lucas saw swarms of blue-clad Chinese coolies, shoveling into carts the rock blasted from the canyon wall. Others graded the roadbed or set in place the heavy ties on which were laid the long steel rails. Then came the resonant, rhythmic thunk of sledges on spikes, securing rails to ties. These scurrying little men were building a railroad a mile or more every day.

Locomotives pulling flat cars supplied the workmen, then moved back up the finished track. Lucas rode the trail upstream to Donner Lake, where he stared past mountains of rails, spikes, ties, tools; extra locomotives; and dining tents. But there were no rails leading up the canyon above. Why would a railroad start in a wilderness and come from nowhere?

Lucas questioned the foreman, who said, "Charley Crocker couldn't wait."

"Who's Charley Crocker?" Lucas asked.

"One of the Big Four, the guys building this railroad. Charley never had a day's experience building anything, but he's moving this Central Pacific like you wouldn't believe! It's finished from Sacramento to Cisco, but all those tunnels and bridges and snow sheds this side of Cisco killed a lot of time. Now it's the big tunnel that's the holdup, 1650 feet long through the top of a solid granite mountain. Charlie wouldn't wait, so we moved everything it takes to build forty miles of railroad over that mountain, most of it through the snow! Now we're laying tracks while other crews finish the long tunnel."

Lucas was still dazed: "All this stuff came over the mountain through the snow?"

"We built sledges of long split logs with hewn ends like runners, long enough to haul locomotives and steel rails," the foreman said. "Sometimes they slid over the horses and oxen. Talk about Hannibal crossing the Alps!"

Lucas listened politely, but was restless to be moving on. He was pleased when the foreman said, "I'm going to Cisco for supplies. You can ride with me in the wagon. Can't take your horses, but they're exhausted anyway. You can trade them for the wagon ride. Same deal I made with a couple of chinks a few days back."

Lucas was shocked: a couple of chinks! A few days back! But he said nothing, agreeing to the trade. The foreman also agreed to store Lucas' silver-mounted saddle, and made out a receipt, saying; "You'll have to find me wherever the tracks end when you come back. Maybe Reno or Winnemucca. Who knows?"

As the stiff-sprung wagon jolted up the mountain road, the foreman talked on. "All the steel for this railroad traveled over 18,000 miles by sea, from east coast ports, south around the cape, north to San Francisco, and across the bay to Sacramento. At one time, there were thirty ships bringing us locomotives, rails, spikes, everything we need."

Lucas grew impatient, desperate to know more about the "two chinks" already mentioned. He tried to casually back into the subject, but they were close to Cisco now, and he had to trust somebody, so he told the foreman his story, claiming Mei Ling as his wife. The man said nothing, but as they entered Cisco he wrote a name and address on a scrap of paper and handed it to Lucas. The brief note said, "Ras, have plenty of coolies for now. Do what you can for this man Lucas. O'Malley."

Lucas was on the first train west out of Cisco, and the next day he stood before a weather-beaten building on Levee Road in Sacramento. A sign above the door read: WALSH ENTERPRISES: ERASTUS WALSH, PROP.

Ras Walsh was a lean man whose thick glasses seemed to augment the startling ice-blue of his eyes. His parchment-like skin was stretched over high cheekbones and he was entirely bald. Lucas thought of a billiard ball. Ras did not speak, and his face was impassive as he read the note from O'Malley and listened to Lucas' story. Was there the faintest flicker from the cold eyes when Lucas mentioned Ah Fong?

Ras swiveled his chair to a credenza behind him, poured brandy into two snifters and handed one to Lucas. It was only then that Lucas noticed the luxury of the office: deep carpets; rich draperies; classic oak furniture, ornately carved desk, and fine paintings. The coolie business must pay very well, thought Lucas.

Finally Ras spoke—in a deep voice far too strong for his thin face and narrow chest: "I, of course, see no one. But I have sources, expensive sources, who may be of help. It will take time. Find a rooming house and wait."

"That's all?" Lucas said loudly. He stood to leave, but the penetrating eyes held him. Lucas finally opened his saddlebag and asked, "How much?"

"Two hundred, to start."

Two hundred dollars! Almost half of Lucas' dwindling gold dust! But Ras weighed the fine dust, offered no receipt, only gave a curt "Thank you." He still had not smiled.

Lucas in his anxiety had scarcely noticed the Chinese girl at the reception desk when he arrived. Now as he looked at her his loneliness swept over him. She returned his gaze, her face unemotional and serene but touched with a faint sadness. As he turned to leave she said softly, "You must be patient."

As Lucas walked through Sacramento he realized that the saddlebag was a poor place to carry his gold; so he converted the dust into greenbacks and spaced them evenly around the money belt he bought. Then he picked one of the many rooming houses, poor as they all looked, paid a week's rent of $3 in advance, and settled down to wait.

The first week started with expectation and ended in despair. "The girl said I must be patient; how did she know that?" he asked himself.

Lucas walked the rutted streets of the town each day, scanning hundreds of Chinese faces until they all seemed to look alike.

In spite of three devastating floods and a fire which destroyed half the town, all within the fifteen years since the gold rush, Sacramento was now quivering with the prosperity of the Central Pacific Railroad. Everyone and everything seemed to flow through and enrich Sacramento. Lucas sensed the excitement through his depression as he wound his way through the crowds and shops.

But more days and nights of inaction fed his despondency, and he seldom left his cluttered little room with its tiny window and sagging bed. He had not eaten for three days, and a moldy sandwich lay on the dresser next to an empty beer bottle. A flickering candle sputtered and smoked. Why did he light it at all?

He finally started out to find food and noticed a neatly sealed envelope on the floor just inside the doorway—no name or address, only the return: City of Sacramento, Office of the Mayor. Just part of the railroad publicity he thought, and threw it on the dresser. He was back in an hour, less hungry but more frustrated, and he started in a burst of energy to clean up the place. On the dresser he saw again the envelope, its neatness an irritation, and he listlessly opened it and read:

The Mayor and City Council
Request The Honor of your Presence
At A Reception
Honoring the Founders and Celebrating the Great Progress of the Central Pacific Railroad.
The Mayor's Residence; Half after Six
Dinner to Follow
12 November, 1867
RSVP only if not attending

"None of my affair," he grumbled as he idly turned over the card. Suddenly he stared and his hand shook, for precisely centered above the printer's embossed mark was a single Chinese character—Mei Ling's signature.

If was a 6:15 on November 12, when Lucas, in rented evening dress and driving a rented carriage, arrived at the Mayor's Residence on a hill overlooking the junction of the two rivers. By habit, he was fifteen minutes early for an event which might start, casually, by seven. He saw no one on the broad front porch or near the doorway, so he circled the spacious grounds, located all the drives and entrances, tied the team to a hitching post and waited for the reception line to form.

Polite, questioning glances slid along the line ahead of him as Lucas, a total stranger but as handsome as any man there, was murmured from hand to hand, a rather strange process to him. He was beginning to be amused when the line ended with four big, self-assured men and their impeccably groomed ladies; and he was quickly ushered to a table partially hidden by potted palms.

Soon the four apparent honorees were seated at the head table and Lucas was impressed by how much they looked alike: deep-set, penetrating eyes under high, bold foreheads, with firm chins made more so by heavy beards. They had the look of quiet confidence and the smell of money. These Big Four were the owners of the Central Pacific Railroad.

The were Leland Stanford, former Governor of California, President of Central Pacific; Collis P. Huntington, Vice-President; Mark Hopkins,

Treasurer; and Charles Crocker, self-made Chief of Construction. All had profited from the lure of gold, making their considerable fortunes in groceries, hardware, mining supplies, and trading. All had helped form and were leaders in the Republican party. They'd helped elect Lincoln and kept California in the Union.

Some would say they were greedy, manipulative, swindling opportunists; but others would call them geniuses. All those terms applied to one or all of them at some time. But they were building the far western link of the first transcontinental railroad; and that, plus their calculated exploitation of California's rail and water transportation over decades would make them obscenely wealthy.

They would leave legacies and monuments which Americans would come to treasure: the Leland Stanford Junior University; the Huntington Library and Art Gallery in San Moreno; the Crocker-Huffman Companies Merced Irrigation District; the Top of the Mark in San Francisco. And on Nob Hill would rise four palatial mansions, each costing in its day a king's ransom and each achieved through the gentle, or not-so-gentle, persistence of a Big Four lady.

Dinner was an awkward affair for Lucas, whose tablemates tried to ignore his use of the place fork for the shrimp cocktail and the dessert spoon for the soup. From beyond the potted palms came the sounds of chamber music. There was a pause, a change in quality, as exotic strains in a minor key and limited range, no more than five notes, rippled from strange-sounding strings, almost wiry, but sweet. Lucas leaned to see around the palms. The woman playing the entrancing music faced half-away from Lucas and wore lustrous gray pearls set like a cape on her shoulders. Her hair was swept high above her graceful neck and held with a tiara of larger pearls, crowned with diamonds. The long, sensitive fingers caressed the strings, and she seemed half asleep when the song ended.

When she turned, Lucas almost lost control, for Mei Ling looked directly into his eyes. Her face showed no emotion, but her almond eyes, full of love, said she had watched him since the moment he parked the carriage. Now the eyes retreated, became obscure, and said, "Wait!"

Dessert was served. Lucas absently used the soup spoon to eat the marzipan, but tasted nothing, waiting while the tables were cleared. The music stopped and Mei Ling placed her instrument in a simple case. She looked once at Lucas then walked quickly toward the kitchen. He left the house by the front door, fighting to walk slowly, casually; then he blended into the shadows near the servants' entrance from where he could see the hitching post. She had outrun him, and now he saw a flash of white as she disappeared into the carriage. In seconds he was on the driver's seat, seized the reins and started the horses toward the front gate.

"Drive slowly," he told himself. Soon the mansion was behind them and a trembling Mei Ling nestled across Lucas' lap, still wearing the lovely and expensive white sheath and jeweled tiara.

———

The day Ras Walsh took Lucas' money and said "Wait" was one of the very few times he had seen a client face to face. Coolies were bought and paid for through one of his close-mouthed agents, and few people even knew Ras existed. The Mayor's reception was also a rare occasion for Ras, but to stay in business long after the demand for coolies ended he must know the railroad crowd. Ras considered himself a connoisseur of music, and now judged the chamber group as almost acceptable, at least for Sacramento. He was enjoying the shrimp cocktail when he saw Mei Ling; and through the rest of dinner her fragile beauty and quick, delicate fingers so charmed him that he knew he must have her. "Why have I not known about her before?" he pondered. The answer came quickly when Ras saw Lucas emerge from behind the palms and follow Mei Ling.

———

Lucas held only a steadying rein, letting the horses find their way down the twisting road toward the Sacramento River. As a precaution he stuck his Colt behind the wide cummerbund, which also covered his money belt. The horses moved placidly under the dim starlight and soon were near the livery stable. Lucas looped the reins around the whip socket, then held Mei Ling close. The desperate, lonely times and thirsty miles all fell away as she turned her face to be kissed, but suddenly she shuddered.

"Don't go to stable!" she pleaded. "Danger there!" Lucas drove on slowly, looking for a side road, but soon strange hoof beats clattered on the cobblestones and Lucas whipped the team into a full gallop.

"Go to the wharf!" shouted Mei Ling; and she pointed the way as the carriage swayed around bends and lurched around corners. The horsemen were closer now and Lucas feared the sound of pistol shots, but none came. They wanted Mei Ling alive!

Warehouses fronted Levee Road, and behind them the wharves sat high above the river. Lucas whirled the carriage through an alley and parked in the dark shadows of a warehouse, then lifted Mei Ling from the seat. They started to run; but her dress allowed her only short steps and she tripped, falling against Lucas. He quickly slung her over his shoulder like a sack of wheat and ran on, but there was nowhere to hide! No open door, crawlspace, or even an empty barrel! They were trapped! Dusky figures emerged from three sides, and the fourth side was the river!

Carefully Lucas lowered Mei Ling to her feet and held her close with his left arm. His right hand drew the Colt, but he knew he had no chance to outshoot these men. He was glad that his black evening suit blended into the night. Then a moonbeam flashed through breaking clouds and Mei Ling's white gown glowed softly. In that instant she twisted from Lucas' encircling arm, lifted her skirt above her knees, and ran across the main wharf onto a projecting dock. As the clouds again parted, the moon lighted Mei Ling's silken white sheath like a headless wraith.

In the faint moonlight reflecting from the water Lucas detected dim figures moving toward Mei Ling. The Colt was leveled and aimed, but the risk of hitting her was too great. He squinted, blinked, searching the darkness, and then he was shooting frantically at vague forms in the dark, firing again and again until he heard the clicking of the hammer on empty cartridges. Searing his mind was the last thing he had seen before firing—a glowing streak of light descending from the dock into the murky water below.

The slap of running feet echoed from warehouse walls and then there was silence. Lucas ran out on the dock, removing his coat, ready to dive into the river. But he heard only the water swirling around the pilings, and could see nothing, not even his own patent leather shoes. Could she swim in the long, restricting dress? How far had the water carried her by now?

His parents had feared water and had kept him away from it, so he was a poor swimmer. He sank down against a piling and sobbed as he had often done as a child when there was no one to comfort him. After a while he returned to the carriage, climbed onto the seat, and drove aimlessly. His mind was so dulled that he scarcely heard the rustling sound behind him just before a flash of pain exploded in his head. Then darkness.

---

Wind through the slats of the cattle car swirled dusty manure over the little blue-clad men huddled around a brazier where they cooked rice and kept boiling water always ready for the staff of life they called tea. The coolies were barely awake after a bone-chilling night in the lurching car—the Central Pacific's answer to delivering workers to keep the track moving eastward. But these were tough, resilient people. Their basic needs were met and the $35 they received each month, less the cost of rice and tea, were sent to relatives in China or hoarded to purchase steerage tickets to get themselves back home. But they were as close to happiness as they would ever be in this life. Only the designated overseer of this group had gone near the strange, big white man lying at the far end of the car.

His sandy-red hair was matted with blood from the raw lump on his head, and he wore only one shiny patent leather shoe. He had lain there in the same condition, making no sounds, since the coolies were herded into the car in Sacramento. Well, someone else would have to deal with him when they reached the end of the rails.

The cattle car was empty now and Lucas was bumped and jerked as it was switched onto a siding. His head throbbed and flamed, and his mind and eyes failed to focus. The flat plank floor tormented him as he turned gingerly, feeling for the position of least pain. As the morning warmed, and flies swarmed over his bloody scalp, he could tolerate no more and painfully pulled himself up, gripping the slats, finally leaning against the wall. There he waited until he felt less dizzy and could focus his eyes; then he shuffled along the wall, sat down in the open doorway, and looked at his dangling feet, one bare, one in patent leather.

After awhile he recalled the events in Sacramento and understood why Mei Ling had jumped into the river—she could not again face life as a plaything. Ah Fong had likely sold her, probably through Ras Walsh, to Sacramento's Mayor. Once Ras saw her he wanted her for himself. But most of all, she had seen that her glowing white sheath was an easy target, with Lucas as the backstop.

An hour passed before a yardman came along the track.He stared and grinned, then helped Lucas to walk. Within another hour Lucas had found the foreman O'Malley, who was apologetic, and effusive in offering help. Yes, he still had the silver-mounted saddle, and led Lucas to where he could buy new clothes. Lucas unbuckled the tattered cummerbund—and stared at his naked waist; his money belt was gone! O'Malley was, of course, sympathetic, but could not give away company merchandise such as shoes, pants, shirts or gloves, but he did offer Lucas a job. O'Malley turned Lucas over to an assistant who said jobs were scarce for white men.

"The chinks do most of it," he frowned, "and they're good. Can't work chinks and whites on the same crew anyway." But there was one job done largely by white men, though Lucas groaned inwardly as he watched the stocky Irishmen work. But what else could he do? He had clothes and food to pay for, and horses to buy! So he became part of a ten-man rail-laying gang. Five worked each side of the roadbed and their only job was to lift 600-pound iron rails from a small car, carry them forward, and set each down on ties already in place. Back and forth, 600 pounds each trip, hundreds of tons each day carried, then set down on the ties.

Within three months Lucas' once-flabby body was as hard as the iron he carried. The rails now stretched across the Nevada desert to Winnemucca, and Lucas was ready to start back to Idaho. On payday he paid for the two horses and had a few dollars left.

Lucas found O'Malley and said, "Just wanted to thank you. You've helped me through some bad times. I'll always be grateful."

"You've been a good worker." O'Malley hesitated. "No hard feelings over Ras Walsh or anything?"

"It's all in the past," Lucas replied.

A voice interrupted: "Boss, there's a problem." It was Ryan, who brought to O'Malley only the hard problems. "Be right there" answered O'Malley.

The impatient Ryan led O'Malley to the tracks where rails lay loosely on the ties and no one was working. "What's wrong?" demanded O'Malley curtly, glowering at the sturdy Irish spikers standing idle.

"That clumsy Flannigan hit Murphy on the foot; he'll be off for days!"

"Replace him!"

"No spikers available, except this little fart who claims he can do the job," snarled Ryan, pointing to an undersized coolie who stared back defiantly. "Look at the little runt! He's a chink! We've always used Irish spikers."

"We'll lose days waiting for a replacement," O'Malley said firmly, unwilling to lose even another hour. "give the little guy a chance!"

Lucas paused on a rise to look back at the familiar scene—the leading edge of a railroad being built, where he had at first almost perished in the heat and punishing work; now he saw only O'Malley and Ryan confronting a very short coolie holding a mall with a sawed-off handle. Lucas stared, not knowing why, then rode away.

There were grumblings and hard looks as the Little guy gripped the short-handled spiking mall and took his place opposite Flannagan. The spikers loved the sound of their slender malls sinking spikes into solid wood, but now they heard a new kind of music, more rhythmic, more precise and perfectly timed, as the Little Guy swung the short-handled mall, alternating with the blows of his partner. It was the same metallic, resonant beat, this symphony of sound and motion which had first drawn the Little Guy to the end of the track during a blizzard in the High Sierras where the falling snow muffled the music to piano. And since that day spiking was the only thing: thunk-thunk, thunk-thunk, thunk-thunk; two malls, six blows, two spikes nestled in the wood, tight against the flanges of the rail.

No one knew much about the Little Guy and no one cared; just one of the 15,000 coolies in the hum-drum routine of building a railroad: tea, rice, work, tea, work, tea, rice, sleep, tea, rice, work; relish the rare change in diet once in awhile; cherish the accumulating gold coins—the same unbroken cycle day to day, week to month; try to forget the hundreds who were too close to the exploding dynamite or were swept into the canyons by snow slides where they would lie forever, humiliated by unmarked burial in a foreign place.

There was one person who noticed things about the Little Guy: August, the locomotive fireman who smiled a lot, talked little, and loved his great throbbing engine. About two months back he had seen the Little Guy steal wads of the clean cotton waste normally used to wipe the engine parts; the next month that had happened again. And each morning he had watched the coolies facing away from the tracks as the sun glistened on their golden streams, but Little Guy was never there with them. Now, for the third time in three months, August again saw Little Guy stealing waste. It was cheap, but the stealing could end in real trouble. When stopped by August, Little guy looked up at him unperturbed and with no apology, and he saw in the weathered, piquant face, the unflinching eyes, the half-smile, a serenity which he envied. Both understood their little charade as August handed the waste back and climbed the ladder to his locomotive. He would never see the Little Guy again, but their secret was safe.

---

The railroad moved on without Lucas, and on May 10, 1869, Leland Stanford emerged from his luxurious private car at Promontory, Utah, to drive the golden spike symbolizing the joining of the Central Pacific and the Union Pacific Railroads. The Mayor of Sacramento was also there that day, along with others of note; but he did not see the coolies in the crowd, just as he had never seen the thousands like them who thronged the streets of his city. And he was in a hurry to get back home; for just as he was leaving The Residence he had learned that Ras Walsh had found for him a beautiful Chinese sculptress who would be waiting when he returned.

After the ceremony at Promontory many Chinese, no longer needed, simply walked away. Many would join the thousands then living in Idaho Territory. Among them was the Little Guy, who hoped she might be re-united with Lucas in Warrens. Sometimes she thought of the coolies who had pulled her, half-dead, from the Sacramento River.

---

Lucas Phelps' journey out of the Great Basin took two weeks, for his horses were rejects, tired out from pulling loads of rails; and Lucas had no incentive to do much except just keep going. And always there was the crushing loneliness. Though the months of carrying iron rails had toughened his body and melted away some thirty five pounds, the total lack of companionship had deepened his depression as he rode northward.

A savage early-winter storm struck as he rode over the rim south of the Snake River, and driven snow forced him to find shelter among stunted pinion pines and dry sagebrush. For four dark nights and three bitter days the howling wind robbed him of sleep and threatened his life. The already-lean horses gnawed on juniper limbs and cried in the cold, and one of them died. Lucas walked for three days down the long slope to the Snake River, leading the second horse loaded with his saddle and belongings. At Bruneau he made another horse trade. He also took the rancher's advice to avoid the high Payette Lake country and go instead over the Weiser River Divide and down the Salmon.

A week later Lucas sat on the divide north of Whitebird Creek. He was worn out, cold, and broke. Below lay Camas Prairie and to the east the tiny settlement of Mt. Idaho. He somehow made it there, and L. P. Brown, proprietor of the new hotel in Mt. Idaho, took one look at Lucas and put him to bed. It took several days of sleeping in comfort and eating good food before he could talk rationally. Then Mr. Brown talked to him quietly, and liked him, learned he had worked as a farrier and quickly found him a job.

Mt. Idaho was a way-station for pack trains carrying supplies to the miners at Florence. The rocky trails wore out a lot of horseshoes and Lucas was always busy. He was courteous in a distant kind of way, but talked little and seldom smiled. He became a familiar, silent fixture around Mt. Idaho and at Brown's Hotel where he continued to live. And there, some two years after his arrival, he first noticed Jenny Wilton, the manager of the hotel's restaurant.

Jenny was quiet, efficient, attractive in a dignified way, and had brown hair and blue eyes. Lucas found out she was two years older than he, and sensed within her an underlying sadness. They saw each other often as time went by, and gradually became friends, though neither seemed willing to divulge any confidences. Lucas could not think of talking about Mei Ling and he wondered in turn why Jenny never mentioned the father of her handsome two-year-old son, Kirby. But over the next year they became quite close and a few months later Jenny accepted his proposal of marriage. There had been no deep passion, no physical intimacy and no profuse expressions of love, yet each knew the other's heart and sensed the unspoken pain of the past. No searching questions were asked and both were willing to start anew, realizing the strength they could share.

Lucas had saved most of his earnings as a farrier and Jenny's salary from her job in the restaurant had accumulated. Both understood the need for permanency in their lives and had ridden together westward across the prairie where, a few miles from a small lake, they found the spot they were seeking. On a slight rise above the prairie was a meadow of several acres nestled against the hill, dotted with large Ponderosa Pines and close to a fresh-running stream. At the edge of the meadow beneath the pines they built the cabin where their daughter Phoebe was born a year later.

The years passed and their small herd of cattle increased on this homestead. From time to time small bands of Nez Perce Indians camped over by the lake, often rode by the cabin, and Joseph, their tall, impressive leader, sometimes stopped. He had spent much time with whites and spoke some English, though he was more comfortable with the jargon common among neighboring tribes to the north and west. Once a vigorous younger man, Yellow Wolf, accompanied Joseph and spoke curtly, though not unkindly, to their son Kirby, who was quite taken by him. Kirby had grown to be broad and muscular like Lucas, whom he now thought of as his father, and had his mother's blue eyes and steady disposition.

Now it was late spring of 1877, and for some time tensions had built as stories circulated about the Nez Perces arming for battle. Lucas and Jenny had seen various Indians riding back and forth; and though Joseph had not stopped by recently, no one had bothered them. While Lucas disliked all Indians, both felt some security in their long-established relationships with the roving bands. They had no forewarning that their peaceful world would soon explode around them.

## CHAPTER 5

A year had passed since Little Bird and Kirby had first met. She now sat on Hawk, looking at the bright reflections from the ranch house windows and remembering the bold, somewhat arrogant boy on the black horse. It wasn't a pleasant memory. Perhaps tomorrow after the morning work was done she'd ride this way again. "I still need a bath," she thought idly.

From the ranch Kirby had heard the sounds of the arriving Indians, seen the horses on the prairie and the evening campfires. "I better ride over there in the morning—don't want those dirty Indians too close. I'll just keep track of them."

Upon returning to camp, Little Bird hurried to a tipi set up away from the main camp—the women's lodge. Here the women went each moon when, as a missionary woman had said, "the custom of women is upon them." No man ever thought of entering that lodge, or even coming close to it. Women in labor also used the lodge, and there Little Bird found Springtime, her time now very near. She had gone there as soon as the tipi was erected after the arrival of the band.

Sighing with relief, Springtime had lowered herself laboriously to the comfortable buffalo robes, easing her aching back and swollen legs which had become worse during the demanding trip. Little Bird drew back the leather flap covering the tipi opening and spoke softly: "Are you well, my sister? Do you need a little extra food or perhaps a drink of water?"

Springtime's reply was low and throaty and Little Bird wondered if she might be feverish, but she said, "Thank you little one, I am all right. I am happy to be here in this place so familiar to us all. Soon I will no longer have to endure this pounding and kicking on my belly. You are a woman now, and I would like you to help me be relieved of this baby. I will be glad if you will see that my cradle board and other things I need are ready."

Feeling secure about Springtime, Little Bird murmured a soft "Tac Kulewit" and went to Joseph's tipi, thinking of the harsh life of the band's women. "They do all the hard work of packing, moving camp, preparing food, drying salmon, tanning hides, making clothing, and now I am part of it," she thought.

Before going to bed Joseph had talked to the leaders of the other bands, but still he was restless and worried, for the grudging agreement of the chiefs and the near-rebellion among some of the younger warriors threatened the decision to settle on the reservation. Awake on his robes, he thought back to the Clearwater River land selection. While not acceptable to any of them, it was at least better than hot, treeless 20-acre farm plots on the lower reservation along Lapwai Creek or at Kamiah. They would have good spots along the river for fishing, and hunting toward the river's headwaters was still good despite the encroachment of thousands of white men.

After sleeping poorly for a few hours, Joseph arose at first light. The quiet serenity of the June dawn did little to improve his spirits as he caught and saddled Ebenezer for a ride. As he skirted the camp he encountered Yellow Wolf returning from a nearby grove where he had relieved himself after the night. Joseph's "Tac Meywi" was acknowledged with a perfunctory grunt.

Joseph admired this nephew of his, although the youth hated the white man perhaps more than anyone else in the band. His other name was Heinmot Hih Hih, White Thunder or White Lightning, and Joseph reflected that these names fit him well. But his real name, Hemene Moxmox, spoke of great strength and fighting ability, which were certainly part of Yellow Wolf's personality. He reveled in hunting grizzly bears and was renowned for his horsemanship. He had a slight droop in one shoulder, the result of a fall from an unruly horse, and sometimes seemed to display it like a badge. Joseph had watched him become a strong leader among the warriors of the band and now felt concern that Yellow Wolf might lead some of them into war.

Having cleared the camp, Joseph began the ascent of the mountain, longing for one last look across the Salmon and Snake River country. Although a final conference with the other leaders was necessary, he was not prepared for it yet. He must free his mind of lingering hostility and resentment.

Ebenezer took the slope with his usual vigor. Joseph needed a big, powerful horse that could carry his 210-pound body all day without fatigue and felt secure in the surging strength and willing movement of the great gray-brown gelding with the silver mane and tail. Finally they reached the broad saddle overlooking the canyon of Whitebird Creek, where they paused for Ebenezer to blow and for Joseph to reflect.

Only a sliver of sunlight had cleared the mountains to the east and in the morning stillness the canyon lay in deep shadow. In the depths below him Joseph could pick out the mouth of Whitebird Creek where it joined the Salmon River, and far beyond he saw the towering peaks and spires of the snowcapped Seven Devils range piercing the sky. The sun cleared the eastern mountains, and a new day had come to the Salmon River country, but Joseph knew that beyond the Seven Devils lay a sparkling blue lake and the Valley Of The Winding Waters. How could his people ever live in happiness anywhere else?

As Joseph mused, everything about him seemed to shimmer and disappear. Then a warm, glowing light enveloped him, and he perceived that his Guardian Spirit, his Wyakin, was beckoning to him. He moved with it, disembodied but acutely, totally aware of all around and below him, infused by visionary power which transcended all time and all distance. His Wyakin soared beside him, and he spoke to it as they traveled together:

"My heart is glad that my Wyakin has joined me this day. I have been confused, and much in need of guidance."

"Yes, I have been aware of your troubled mind and have waited for you to summon me. Together we will seek the best way for you and your people to go."

"Below me, my heart sees Whitebird's people, all busy catching and drying the big salmon," Joseph said. "They have all been feasting. I see their great herds of horses roaming the hills, and the men are enjoying races. Then to the south of us I see the Esmine, the Snake Creek band; and there to the north, are the Tamanmu. To the west and north are other bands. Each band has always lived separately, but now the white man is forcing us together for defense."

Joseph's vision continued. "Near the Grande Ronde river is the place of my birth and childhood, and now I see my father and mother, Tuekakas and Asenath, hurrying along the trail. Her belly is big with child, and it appears she will not reach home in time. But there is a cave just around the bend of the trail, and the horses enter. Asenath slips from the saddle, and a few moments later my birth takes place.

"My father was the spiritual leader of our band for many years and was baptized by Spalding, the first of the missionaries, before I was born. Spalding also gave my mother the name Asenath out of his Bible. Did you know my parents?"

"No, I do not know them. They had a different Wyakin, but because you came through them, and they are part of you, I know their hearts."

"Very soon after I was born, my father took me to the mission at Lapwai, where I was baptized. Our people first learned something of the white man's God from those first two white men who came over the mountains long ago, and stayed for awhile with old Twisted Hair on the Clearwater. They told of a far place called St. Louis, and they talked about teachers coming to us. After several years, they did come.

"Spalding—a Protestant, they called him—built that first mission, down at Lapwai, and helped our people in many ways. My father, Tuekakas, renamed himself Joseph soon after he was baptized. At first, the missionaries called me Ephraim, but later I too became known as Joseph."

"And do you still pray to the white man's god?" the Guardian Spirit asked. "Do you have a good feeling for the missionaries?"

"Father remained a Christian for more than twenty winters, and during that time I saw much of the missionaries and learned much of their story; but through the years, the white man has forced most of our people and almost all the other tribes onto reservations. The papers which some of our people signed were honored only until the white man wanted more of our land."

"Do you believe that the missionaries, or the white man's god, are really responsible for all of these troubles?" the Gaurdian Spirit asked. "Do you not understand that it is men, and not the Great Spirit, that cause all of these things to happen?"

"Yes, I understand that, and my father believed that at first," Joseph said. "But when the missionaries and the army men and the government agents, who were all hand in hand, joined together to take our land, my father's confidence in all of them was shattered."

"That is understandable, Joseph, but I believe that many of the white men have good hearts. I believe many of the missionaries truly wanted, and still want, to help your people. Some people in the government have good hearts, but many strive for land, wealth and power. They are great in number and are surrounding you from all directions. I believe the decision which you have already made, to go to the reservation, is right."

The Guardian Spirit said no more, and gradually Joseph realized that he was by himself, and that the aura of light and the feeling of peace were gone. Ebenezer still stood in the shade of a tree. Joseph approached him quietly, swung into the saddle and headed down the mountain. Ebenezer knew the way and Joseph was free to reflect upon his Guardian Spirit search as a boy. After several days high on the mountain without food and water, he hadn't seen any special images. There weren't encounters with ferocious animals—there had been only peaceful things, and a sense of serenity. Some doves fearlessly landed on his shoulder and ate seeds from his hand. And at the Guardian Spirit dance, it wasn't able to demonstrate anything like the other young people did. How could a muscular, strong-looking boy do a dance showing how the doves performed? So all of his life Joseph had chosen the peaceful way—speaking with moderation, often with wisdom, sometimes visiting the homes of settlers, talking quietly with them.

Now he thought of the several treaties, all aimed at the white men gaining control of the Nez Perce lands and the inescapable conclusion—submission.

## CHAPTER 6

A good night's sleep following the stressful trip raised the people's spirits. The women were up early cooking the breakfast meal, and soon were headed for the camas fields with their digging sticks. Others were gathering the heating rocks and digging the holes in which a fire would be built and the huge mounds of camas bulbs would be cooked. By evening, all would be feasting.

Little Bird helped with the digging of camas and, when a large pile had been accumulated near the fireholes, she walked to the women's lodge to call on Springtime, who was miserable but smiling. Then Little Bird walked toward the lake to have the bath for which she had been longing.

---

Kirby had been tired after the previous day's work and slept later than usual the next morning. Awakened by sunlight streaming through his window and remembering the sounds of arriving Indians, he dressed quickly and after a hasty breakfast mounted the black and headed toward the lake. He slowed the black as he approached the lake's east end and stopped in a grove on the slope. He could see a group of women and children bathing in the lake; and, though Little Bird was not with them, he felt his temper rise as he remembered their meeting the previous summer. He tied the horse in a thicket and walked toward the lakeshore with plans to follow it to the camp.

As he approached the lake his view was obscured by trees, but suddenly he heard the ripple of water and a gasp. He turned quickly to see Little Bird standing at the edge of the lake, no more than thirty feet away and facing him. Kirby stared, stunned and immobile, for Little Bird had loosened her braids and her glistening black hair hung down over her shoulders, only partially covering her firm, pointed breasts and flat belly. She wore a pure white dentalium necklace with a carved shell pendant—and nothing more. Kirby had recently seen his developing 13-year-old sister almost naked. She had grabbed frantically for anything to cover her body, her hands fluttering wildly in several directions. But this naked, bronze girl facing him showed no such concern, and stood silently.

"Should I turn away?" his mind screamed. "Should I run? I seem unable to move!" Little Bird made the first move. Sensing his confusion and relishing her own control, she said slyly, "Hello, Kirby."

She turned slowly, the sunlight glistening on her graceful shoulders, delicately flaring hips, and smooth rounded buttocks. Then she casually lifted her loose buckskin dress from a nearby limb, slipped it over her head and stepped out of the water onto a convenient rock. Kirby's mind was in total turmoil. "What kind of girl is this? How am I supposed to act, and what do I say now?"

Little Bird, still enjoying Kirby's embarrassment, suppressed a smile. Close living in the winter lodges and tipis with Joseph's family, often including Yellow Wolf, left very little concern for privacy. Unclothed bodies were commonplace and generally ignored. Now she looked again at Kirby, realizing that he had grown taller and showed a maturity that was lacking the previous year. Still, the glint of disdain in his eyes irritated her, and she turned quickly toward camp. Aware of her taunting, Kirby went to his horse and angrily rode back toward the ranch. He'd seen enough of this wild Indian girl. He smiled and thought, "Actually, I've seen nearly everything!"

---

Lucas was always surly when Indians were nearby. At supper he growled, "Damn savages are making more noise than usual this year! I sure hope Joseph can control them." Kirby said nothing and went upstairs to bed, but sleep was elusive. Somehow he resented Lucas' attitude and argued with himself that the girl by the lake hadn't looked like a savage, although she didn't act very civilized either. Then he dismissed her. "She'll be gone soon, along with the rest of that scruffy bunch."

"Kirby," Lucas said at breakfast, "your black needs new shoes and I'll take care of that today. Will you take another horse and ride up to the mountain pastures above the lake? See if the grass there will support a few more cows and calves. But watch out for that old maverick cow with the twisted horn! If she's calved she'll be meaner than dogwater."

The trip to the high pasture was usually a welcome change—but not today, for the young mare Kirby had saddled was jumpy, fought the bit and shied at everything, even an occasional butterfly. He had to ride her intently, never relaxing. At the upper meadows he rode among mother cows resting on the grass, placidly chewing their cuds while their frisky, white-faced calves bounded across the meadow with tails high or engaged in head-butting contests. The mare was almost calm after the demanding climb, and Kirby began to relax, relishing the mid-morning sun. He watered the mare in the creek and let her rest while he walked upstream for his own drink.

"The grass is plentiful and the cattle look good," he thought, "but there should be more of them. Better check the lower meadows on the way home."

Well below him and to the west was the Indian camp, a disorderly cluster of tipis. Kirby could hear dogs barking, and a few smoldering morning fires sent slender columns of smoke into the clear air. The lake sparkled beyond the camp and the prairie stretched away to embrace a few light clouds far to the north. More well-fed cattle dotted the little meadow where Kirby sat on the mare. She moved down the hill and he eased her around a knoll into a secluded cove, thinking of the lunch in his saddlebag and a rest on the grass.

The calm was shattered by an angry snort from the right. The startled mare leaped to the left, and for one terrifying second Kirby, in mid-air, stared into the wild eyes of the gaunt one-horned maverick, her wobbly-kneed calf half-hidden behind her. As Kirby tumbled to the ground, the brawny cow bellowed, lowered her head and charged!

Kirby rolled downhill, frantically dodging the scythe-like sweeps of the horn and the stomping hooves. The frenzied animal lunged at him repeatedly, never allowing him to regain his feet as he scrambled through brush and brambles and was slammed against the rocks. He did avoid direct thrusts of the fearsome horn, but he was gasping for air and his legs burned. Then in a roaring, blinding flash it was over as a broad, flint-hard hoof crashed against his skull!

The sweating, riderless mare, after a run of three miles, collapsed at the ranch corral in late afternoon; and, within minutes, Jenny was circling the lower trail while Lucas rode up and around the mountain. Somewhere within that circle they must find Kirby.

---

The hands were strong but gentle, moving lightly over the battered, swollen head, searching with more pressure the joints and bones of the limbs. Kirby's first feeling was of throbbing pain as the hands sought serious injuries. Then there was a pungent aroma and warmth that soothed his flesh and eased his lungs before he returned to darkness.

Jenny found the mangled body and was sure Kirby was dead. She steeled herself to kneel beside him, choking back her tears, not wanting to look closely at his almost unrecognizable face. Then he groaned deep inside, and as she was about to speak his name she heard someone calling. She yelled a reply, and soon Lucas joined them.

An hour passed before Kirby could stand with Lucas and Jenny holding him up. After several tries, Lucas got him onto a horse's back and Jenny rode behind, her arms holding Kirby in the saddle while Lucas led the way back to the ranch house. With Kirby in bed and Jenny applying home remedies, Lucas rode to Mt. Idaho and brought the doctor; he found no serious injuries but told Jenny to keep Kirby quiet for at least a week.

The next morning, Lucas rode out to "shoot that damn cow as I should have years ago!" He returned with a tiny calf in front of his saddle. "Found him nuzzling his dead mother, trying to nurse," Lucas reported. "She'd been shot and her hind quarters cut off and dragged away. Thieving Indians, I suppose." Then he seemed to forget the whole matter and went about his work. As Jenny kneaded the daily bread dough, she recalled finding Kirby on the hillside. He had lain on a narrow, flat spot, the only such place around from which he would not roll down the hill. His head, though a mass of contusions, was clean; and there had been that strange, rather pleasant, smell about him.

Kirby's head cleared a little by the second day and he tried to put events in the right order, but by the third day there were still only questions. Whose hands had touched him and brought that wonderful, soothing feeling? And why didn't the cow finish me off after I passed out?

Kirby was nearly back to normal on the sixth day, and he saddled the black and rode away. His fast recovery ended the matter for the others, but he needed answers.

The hillside was an unreadable jumble of horse, cow, and boot tracks so, riding in circles, Kirby found other trails: the mare he had ridden walking into the cove, the cow stomping, and sliding down the hill into the maze of other tracks. The second circle crossed the trails of Jenny's horse coming from the north, Lucas' from the south. But from the west, one horse had entered the cove and left again; two other trails led to and away from the hillside where Kirby had been found; all three of those horses were unshod.

The sun was low and Kirby was tired when he reached home. Jenny seemed anxious, Lucas preoccupied, and Phoebe was still repulsed by Kirby's scabby head and grisly, unshaven face. No one talked, and Kirby mulled a remaining question—what were the Indians doing there?

In a few days Kirby was back at work, walking carefully and wincing at times as he helped put up the first crop of meadow hay. Lucas became more surly, listening each night to the boisterous Indians, but Kirby was more concerned about what had happened the day the cow attacked him. He finally decided on a direct approach—he would find the girl. Though he didn't know her name, he certainly would recognize her.

The camp went quiet as Kirby rode in. A few children eyed him suspiciously and ran to their tipis. Then a broad, robust man with upswept hair emerged from a tipi and unemotionally asked, "What do you want?"

"I am looking for a girl," Kirby answered, groping for the words to describe her. Immediately the tipi flap was opened and Little Bird emerged. "It's all right, Joseph," she said quietly. "I know him." Joseph nodded, and returned to the tipi.

"Much too easy," thought Kirby. "But there she is, and what do I do now?"

She broke the awkward silence. "What is it you want?"

Kirby dismounted and said, "I must talk to you." She hesitated and frowned, but followed him as he led the black to the edge of camp. He dug for a way to start, conscious of his ugly scars and scabs, which she seemed to ignore. So he started in the obvious way. "I was attacked by a mad cow," he said hesitantly.

"I know."

"But how?" he asked. Then he answered himself. "You were there!"

She made no reply, but took the black's reins, mounted easily, rode to the nearby horse herd and returned, leading Hawk. No one showed any special interest as Kirby and Little Bird entered the camp to saddle Hawk. Then they rode across the low ridges bordering the prairie. Kirby finally asked her name, and she answered contritely, "Payopayo Kute, means Little Bird."

"Now, about the cow?" Kirby asked, unwilling to wait longer.

"Yellow Wolf drove her away from you and shot her," Little Bird said casually. "He told Heyoom and we came to find you." Then she added, "Heyoom makes good medicine."

Kirby, baffled and speechless, looked at her curiously. These people had saved his life, yet she acted as if that was routine on the prairie. They rode for awhile in silence, still sensing the distrust between them and wondering why they were there together. Kirby was still very young by the white man's standards and life on the isolated ranch meant very few young women had been part of his life. Not that he hadn't daydreamed a little as he watched the Martin girl from a nearby ranch, and once he had even danced with her after a potluck dinner at the schoolhouse. But this one—this Little Bird! She's so self-assured, so calm about everything.

After awhile, their tensions relaxed and their minds more at ease, they paused on a low hill overlooking the prairie. Glancing down at the Tepahlewam camp, Kirby remembered the recent rumors of war. "Will your people fight?" he asked.

"Some older men would like to fight, but know we cannot win. Many angry young men want to fight, but are held down. Joseph wants peace."

Shaking off the ominous feelings, Little Bird suddenly said, "Let's race!" She loosened the rein, urged Hawk with her knees, and was off across the ridges. Kirby was caught off guard, but the big gelding leaped into action as he felt Kirby's heels in his flanks. Little Bird rode with total abandon, leaping rocks, logs, and small creeks. She was as one with her lovely horse, and Kirby marveled at her grace and skill while he reveled in the flowing speed of the powerful black beneath him.

Little Bird was not to be caught, and finally Hawk slid to a halt by a little stream beside an aspen grove. There Little Bird flung herself from the saddle and waited for Kirby, who was only a few seconds behind. The horses, sweating and blowing, drank greedily from the stream and then wandered off to graze in the nearby meadow. Kirby and Little Bird walked a short distance up the spring stream, where they drank deeply of the refreshing water.

Little Bird had been here before, and soon found a grassy spot in the shade of a pine tree. Here they stretched out side by side, listening to the whispering sound of the low wind through the long needles and a bluejay chattering at some unwelcome intruder. The stresses of war, the conflicts within the band, and the reservation all seemed far away. After awhile, as the sun dropped and the shadow of the pine tree moved away from them, Kirby arose and helped Little Bird to her feet. Slightly drowsy, she stumbled a little and swayed against him. For an instant he felt the warmth and fullness of her—and a stirring that was quite different from dancing with the Martin girl. After riding back to the edge of the camp they paused. Little Bird finally said, "Tomorrow, by the creek."

In the days that followed, fears grew among the settlers as rumors of possible Indian attacks spread across the prairie. Lucas and Jenny were increasingly concerned as the sounds of drums and revelry from the camp drifted on the wind during the evenings. Kirby was gone for awhile each afternoon with a regularity which was puzzling and he seemed strangely detached, talking very little during the evening meal and often drifting off to bed without saying good night.

Now, as mid-June approached, Kirby and Little Bird roamed the countryside on their horses, growing closer each day. Once day she seemed troubled. Kirby questioned her and she answered, "The anger among the young men is growing. Joseph and Ollokot are worried, but I believe they will control things. A short time remains, and within three suns we will be moving to our new home on the Clearwater."

Little Bird suggested that they meet earlier the next day, and when Kirby arrived, she said, "Let's ride down Rocky Canyon to the Salmon River. With these horses, it's a short trip." So down the winding trail they went, the sound of the horse's hard hooves on the rocks echoing among the canyon walls.

When they reached the river, the sun was high above them. Little Bird had brought a lunch of cooked camas bulbs, which were new to Kirby, but he found he liked them. She also had pemmican of deer meat and fat and huckleberries, and they drank from a clear stream that tumbled into the river.

They had eaten lunch in the shade of willows near a broad gleaming beach and now lay on the soft sand, half-asleep. As usual, there was little talk between them, and little needed. Kirby began to doze, reflecting quietly: "This lovely girl has finally gotten to me. My folks suspect that something is going on, but don't know what."

When he awakened he listened for her soft breathing, but heard nothing. He reached out to touch her, but she was gone. Then he sat up quickly and looked about, but saw only her tracks leading over a slight rise on the beach. Leaping to his feet, he followed the tracks, coming suddenly in view of the river—-and there she lay, floating lazily in the circle of a revolving eddy, her long hair waving in the current behind her.

When she saw him she turned over, started swimming, and her brown body flashed through the water like a graceful otter. As she approached the shore, she called and beckoned to him to swim with her. "But how can I?" his mind demanded. "I can't take off my clothes and run across this beach in front of her. Maybe I could swim with my trousers on, but that would look foolish and she might laugh. So I'll just tell her I can't swim."

So he told her that, and went back to the willows; then he saw her clothes lying in a heap on the sand. He was astonished as she walked up the beach naked and casually stood before him in the ripe beauty of young womanhood. She soon came near him and stretched out in the shade of the willows, carelessly covering part of her body with the buckskin dress retrieved from the little stack on the sand.

They lay apart for awhile, with Kirby's body tense and rigid, aching with his need and his shyness. Then she turned toward him and their hands touched. He felt her trembling, the buckskin dress was gone, and they were in each other's arms, all their tenderness and passion closing over them.

They rode back up the canyon in inexpressible wonderment, lost in the newness of feelings that come only with first love, and only to the very young. The sun was sinking behind them as they followed the lengthening purple shadows into the gorge, while the last glow of orange-gold faded from the ridges above.

They stopped often to kiss and hold each other, and by the time they approached the head of the canyon their leisurely movement up the trail brought them into flickering patterns of moonlight shining through the trees. At the edge of the camp they paused and urged the horses close together, where they held each other for a long moment. Then they moved apart; agreeing to meet again tomorrow at the spring by the aspen grove.

Little Bird slipped quietly beneath the leather flap into the tipi and among the sleeping figures, listening to the familiar pattern of breathing. But the pattern was not complete, and she knew that Running Feet, her little shadow, her constant admirer, was awake, waiting for her. Little Bird whispered, "Hello, Little Sister," and heard a murmur followed by a soft, contented sigh.

Meanwhile, Kirby closed the door of the ranch house as quietly as possible and moved up the stairs, attempting to avoid the one tread that always squeaked. But it didn't matter, for Jenny had been awake, and spoke to him softly as he went by her room: "We will talk in the morning."

The time spent with Kirby and her concerns about the unrest within the camp had occupied Little Bird's mind for several days, and she had thought little about Springtime; now she hurried to the temporary women's lodge. Before lifting the tipi flap, she heard low moans and deep guttural breathing. Glancing inside, she saw Springtime writhing in pain and ran to find Heyoom.

"The baby is coming!" Little Bird cried. Heyoom assembled her birthing kit, and together they ran to Springtime's side. Running Feet was close behind.

Springtime lay on the buffalo robes, her eyes closed, her back arched, breathing in great gasps through clenched teeth. Heyoom waited patiently, and soon helped deliver Springtime's baby.

Now for Hewoom one task remained. The umbilical cord, left hanging on a tipi pole, was taken down and suspended over the warming fire, where it would remain until dry and shrunken to a fraction of it's present size. Then springtime would place it carefully in a small buckskin pouch to be attacked to her baby's cradly board, thus assuring the fertility of the future bride. And because of the glorious spring, with flowers appearing sooner than usual, Springtime named the little girl Early Flower

## CHAPTER 7

The idle time in camp at Tepahlewam had been enjoyed by all for a few days. Looking Glass, who had brought his people from the Clearwater to be with the other bands, had returned home believing that the rest would soon join him on the farthest reaches of the reservation, where they could be happy. But the diversions of horse-racing, feasting, and games could not for long drive away the shadows, and the sound of drums and dancing mingled with war chants each night.

Some said, "It's all right for Joseph to be peaceful. That is his way. But we are being forced to give up the country and the ways we have always known!" And they pretended that the nightly revelry was real preparation for war, and that they were real warriors.

Then, with only a day or two of freedom remaining, they staged a celebration with a warrior parade and all of its symbolism, during which Wahlitits and Sarpsis Ilppilp rode double on a bareback horse at the rear of the warrior column. As the excited horse was ridden through the camp, he pranced through a pile of kouse roots spread out to dry. Upon his wife's complaint, Yellow Grizzly Bear rushed from his tipi, and shouted at Wahlitits: "Why do you destroy my wife's food? If you are so brave, why don't you kill the man who murdered your father?"

Several other families and some of the warriors heard this challenge, and, in the Indian way, said nothing. But the insult was there. And now Wahlitits lay on his bed, brooding and thinking of the day's events. "Yellow Grizzly Bear did not need to stir up old feelings by challenging me to kill Larry Ott, the white man who killed my father, Chief Eagle Robe. Killing him would only arouse the whites and bring trouble on my people. But he has questioned my honor, and all will say I am no man if I do nothing."

So Wahlitits found his cousin Sarpsis and, after recruiting his nephew Wetyetmas as a horse holder, they rode over the divide above Tepahlewam and thundered down the long, bare Whitebird Canyon slopes, determined to find and kill Larry Ott. They splashed across Whitebird Creek and passed their band's usual camp, now vacant and lonely in the early morning light, then hurried on south, up the Salmon River, around the great loop called Horseshoe Bend, past Slate Creek to the place where Eagle Robe had lived on land given him by Larry Ott. But Ott had fenced off Eagle Robe's garden for himself, and then shot him.

"Now we will kill him," Wahlitits thought as they came near Ott's little shack. But on this day Ott, perhaps seeing the Indian riders coming, had fled and couldn't be found. Discouraged and frustrated, they picked up Wahlitits' wife at her place on the Salmon River and headed for the home of Richard Devine a few miles upriver.

"Devine will pay for his cruelty to our people," Wahlitits stormed. "He chased my mother and sister with his vicious dog when they were picking blackberries, and he set the dogs on others of our band too. But especially will he pay for killing poor old crippled Dakoopin. Maybe he would like to try killing me!"

Night was falling, so they slept with their pent-up anger near Devine's shack. In the morning, they left Wetyetmas holding the horses, pushed open the door of Devine's house, and shot him dead. With their blood lust inflamed and their need for further revenge tormenting their minds, they braided red cloth in their hair, painted their bodies and their horses in brilliant colors, and rode toward the farm of another old enemy, Henry Elfers. They staked their horses in his oatfield to get his attention, then they crouched and waited. It was a short wait, as Elfers stormed into the field, brandishing his bullwhip. Sarpsis leaped on him, riding him to the ground, and Wahlitits killed him with one shot. Then they caught his favorite horse, a roan stallion, which they let Wetyetmas ride, and they started back down the river.

On the way back to Tepahlewam, intent on reporting their success to the assembled band, the four avengers terrorized other whites; and at Whitebird Creek they chased Samuel Benedict from his store, firing at him as he disappeared into the brush. He had once shot and wounded Sarpsis, who had regularly sold whiskey to the Nez Perces, and was well-known for short-changing Indian customers.

As they rode back up the steep south-facing slope toward the divide, Wahlitits stopped by Round Willow, a thicket a mile or so from the top. "We did these killings on our own," he said. We must not make it look like others were involved. While our revenge is for everyone, not just my father, it was never my plan to start a war. Wetyetmas, you ride on to the camp and tell them what we have done, and also tell them we plan to punish others tomorrow. These who want to go along must make their own decisions to do so."

Wetyetmas, well-mounted and enjoying his role, rode the beautiful roan stallion into the camp. The camp was aroused as Wahlitits rode about, telling of the killings, and of his plans to return to the Salmon River. But he asked no one to join him, saying they could decide on their own. It would be said, later, that Two Moons of Joseph's band urged all warriors to join in other forays and share in the revenge.

---

Joseph's band had been without fresh meat for several days, so a visit to the cattle herd west of the Salmon River was necessary. He summoned Ollokot and several other men. Wetatonmi, and Running Feet; the women, as usual, would be the best help at butchering. All were glad to be back on their horses and away from the tensions of the camp.

Riding with the group was Welweyas, wearing an attractive beaded buckskin dress made by the neighboring Shoshones. Welweyas' precise black braids, hanging well below the shoulders, complemented the soft creamy-white bucksin. "Hardly the dress for butchering cattle," thought Running Feet.

The little group filed down Rocky Canyon under a cloudless June sky, a string of packhorses following. The trip was exhilarating, and upon reaching the river there was much shouting back and forth with the young men guarding the cattle on the far side, for the river was calm here and the strong voices carried clearly across the water and echoed from the cliffs.

All waited on the east bank for the chosen cattle to be driven over, except for Ollokot and Running Feet, who loved to swim their horses across the river. As they rode their dripping ponies up the west bank, they were greeted warmly by the young herdsmen, who had been here alone since the band crossed the river two weeks before. They had gambled, raced their horses, played all the games they knew, grown bored and restless. All the girls were miles away at Tepahlewam, so they eyed Running Feet with renewed interest. She had been ignored while among the older girls but now stood alone, suddenly much more mature, her wet dress clinging tightly to her slim body.

Ollokot diverted the young men's attention, led them out to the cattle herd, and selected several fat steers which were driven across the river to a grassy meadow just above the high water line. There the butchering was started, all working quickly, preparing the big steers to be loaded on the pack-horses.

The men stripped to the waist, their bronze muscles dripping sweat as they wrestled the heavy carcasses into position for gutting, skinning, and quartering. The women, who avoided baring their bodies except when bathing, rolled up their sleeves and patiently suffered as the sun rose higher. But no one noticed as the lovely bucksin dress came off over Welweyas' head. All had seen this transformation before as Welweyas used his strong arms to slice open the belly of a big steer. Running Feet had often wondered about Welweyas— this person, this woman? this man?—and tried to sort out the pieces of the puzzle. But all they could do was observe his bizarre behavior, the mood swings, and the change from man to woman within hours or even minutes. Of course, they knew nothing of the confused hormones, the uncertainties, the tormented mind and body!

As the first steer was dressed, Wetatonmi had deftly cut out the big succulent tenderloins from their fatty beds beside the spine and below the last ribs. Then she seasoned them with herbs and a little precious salt; and now, the butchering done, all were gorging themselves on their first fresh meat in over two weeks.

While mist still masked the river, the men were loading the big quarters of beef, two shoulders on each of the larger horses, two hams on the smaller, all loads slung and balanced to rock with the horses' motion, the hides tied securely on top, one to each larger horse. Both meat and hides were made more precious now by the uncertainty of the future. Would they see this cattle herd again?

Joseph led the way back up the canyon; Wetatonmi and Running Feet, more than comfortably tired by their always-heavy share of the butchering, were soon nodding to the sleepy rocking of the horses' gait and rhythmic hoof beats.

As the pack train neared Tepahlewam, Joseph saw a lone rider racing to meet him. His first thought was of his wife, Springtime. Had the baby been born? But no, that would have excited no one. Soon the rider was seen to be Two Moons, who drew his horse to a stop and hurriedly blurted out the story of the Salmon River killings.

"It wasn't our band, Joseph! It was Wahlitits and others of Whitebird's band! And they want to take others back to the Salmon River to kill more white men!"

Joseph, sick at heart, hurried to the camp and found many tipis down and people loading packhorses, though confused, frightened, and unsure of where to go.

"We must wait!" Joseph exclaimed. "We must talk to Howard. These killings were for revenge by only one young man! Howard will not hold the rest of us responsible. He knows we are here with all of our bands, and are ready to go to the reservation."

But the others would not listen. One fierce young man shouted at Joseph, "You and Ollokot are like old women! You are not the fighting leaders! You do not support us, and want to give in to Howard! You are traitors!"

But Joseph held his peace and returned to camp, knowing his people would need his guidance in the days ahead.

---

The day Wetyetmas rode the proud roan stallion into camp, Yellow Wolf had watched eagerly, trying unsuccessfully to control his envy and his passion to join Whitebird's young warriors. "I must be loyal to Joseph," he thought. "He will return tomorrow and will need my support."

But when Wahlitits and Sarpsis returned, repeating the story of their deeds, its daring was increased as others joined in the chance to prove their manhood and to seek retaliation; and Yellow Wolf, caught up in the emotion and frenzy of it all, seized his weapons, and was soon mounted and pushing his horse toward the river. These avengers, 18 or 20 of them, were about to close the door on any possible peace and seal the fate of the last free-roaming bands of Nez Perces.

On Whitebird Creek there was a second, vicious attack on Samuel Benedict's store, and Benedict was shot as he ran across a log footbridge and fell into the creek, his body rolling and turning as it was swept away by the swollen, churning water. A store employee made it across the bridge but was killed on the far side. Mrs. Benedict and her two children escaped into the brush beside the creek and were not pursued; since they hadn't caused the Nez Perces trouble.

Down Whitebird Creek, closer to the Salmon River, was a second store. Some of the avengers knew that its proprietor had once surprised and overcome a Nez Perce man, tying him up in his tipi and repeatedly raping his wife as he watched. Now, as the raging warriors rode away from the burning store, one exulted, "He will never bother our women again!"

Yellow Wolf watched these violent acts of death, this swift and final retribution justified by the moral code of his people, but he could not take part. At times he would start, lift his gun, then hesitate, his frenzied companions seeming not to notice. The same code supporting the murders now controlled his actions—the revenge was not for acts against his band, and his loyalty to Joseph must be honored.

Whitebird's people paid no attention as Yellow Wolf rode back up the canyon, driving his pinto mercilessly, ignoring his basic regard for horses. From the summit he could see a cloud of dust on the prairie beyond Tepahlewam. There was the band, moving away from the deserted camp; but their progress was moderate and he soon overtook them, riding quietly to his usual place in the procession. The unspoken signal of relief in Joseph's eyes was full reward for Yellow Wolf, and nothing was said.

---

On the day that Little Bird first heard about the Salmon River killings, Kirby had gone to meet her at the aspen grove, but did not find her. No word of the killings had yet reached his family and thinking that he should not invade the privacy of the camp, he returned home. The next day he went back to the grove, but again Little Bird was not there. His anxiety and desire to see her compelled him to ride toward the camp. As he skirted the shore of the lake, he saw a dust cloud ahead and a column of horses approaching, and he quickly rode into the shelter of nearby trees. Soon he recognized Joseph and Ollokot leading the band and, looking farther to the west, saw that no tipis were standing. Then he saw Little Bird and the other women riding behind Ollokot and Yellow Wolf. And there was Springtime, her cradle board lashed securely to her back. The light-footed mare carried her carefully, and the day-old baby slept peacefully.

"They are moving their entire camp, and all look so grim," he thought desperately. "I must talk to Little Bird!" Quickly he rode out of the grove toward the moving band until Yellow Wolf saw him and raised a warning hand as Little Bird rushed past and joined Kirby at the edge of the trees.

"You must come no closer," she said. "Whitebird's young men have gone to the Salmon River and killed several white men. Many other angry men are down there now, searching for the whites who have hated us in the past. There will be more killing."

"But where are you going?"

"To Sepachesap, that cave on Cottonwood Creek, to join the other bands. I must go now." She wheeled Hawk and returned to her place in the column.

From the protection of the grove Kirby watched the band file by. Then behind them he saw another dust cloud, and soon the band's horse herd rumbled past. In disbelief, Kirby rode back to the abandoned camp. A few little wisps of smoke rose from the trodden earth beneath which the final fires had been buried. A coyote skulked nearby, looking for morsels of food. Kirby slowly turned toward home, his mind numb. After awhile, the black stopped and Kirby looked up to see the ranch house. As Kirby walked in the faces of Lucas, Jenny, and Phoebe told him without words that news of the Salmon River killings had reached them. By this time tomorrow, they would learn of many other killings along the river, but would not foresee the firestorm of hate and rage that would race across the prairie and reach into their own family.

At dawn the next day horses thundered up to the house and loud, urgent knocking rattled the door. Motioning his family back, Lucas opened the door to face two of his neighbors, now shaken and fearful. "The Indian attacks are spreading! More people have been killed between here and Slate Creek. Some from the Salmon River have already arrived at the Mt. Idaho Fort, and the rest of us are heading that way. You'd better get your folks and your livestock together and follow us."

Lucas thanked his neighbors, who turned their horses and headed off to the east. Quickly, he sent Kirby to round up the cattle and told Jenny and Phoebe to begin packing while he gathered weapons. In less than an hour their most needed belongings were in the back of the wagon and their fastest team was pulling them rapidly toward Mt. Idaho. Behind them a mile or two came Kirby, driving the livestock.

## CHAPTER 8

Following the killing of Samuel Benedict, August Bacon, and others, the Salmon River Avengers, led by Yellow Buffalo Bull, raged upstream toward Slate Creek, killing additional white people along their way. They were possessed by unlimited passion, and to them their actions were justified, since there had been 30 or more known murders of Indians by white men in recent years, all within or near the Nez Perce country. Yet during the same period, one white man was convicted by a jury at Boise, Idaho, of murdering an Indian and was sentenced to die—but there is no record that the condemned man was ever executed.

Whites saw the revenge killings as attacks by mindless savages, a company of fiends who enjoyed killing for its own sake. Reports of the depredations over this three-day period would be conflicting and include stories of both actual and unconfirmed atrocities. One story alleged the murder of a woman by Chief Joseph, who in fact was far down the Salmon River butchering cattle on the day she was killed.

Unaware that the bands camped at Tepahlewam had departed for Cottonwood Creek, Yellow Buffalo Bull and the avengers rode out of Whitebird Canyon to the divide to look down on the deserted camp. "They're gone!" said Sarpsis.

"Yes," answered Yellow Buffalo Bull. "And there below us is the dust of a wagon and livestock, heading east. There is only one man with the cattle. We must catch the wagon before it gets close to the village." So they angled down the mountainside, aiming at a spot where they could intercept Lucas as he drove toward Mt. Idaho. But they underestimated the one man with the cattle.

Kirby, riding the big black gelding and driving the family herd, was more than a mile behind Lucas and the wagon. Yellow Bull and the warriors attempted to stay hidden behind trees, but as they crossed a gap between two groves, a pinto horse was visible for a second or two. This caught Kirby's eye as he glanced up the mountain. Quickly discerning the trail of warriors, he abandoned the cattle, lashed the black into a full gallop, and was at the wagon while the warriors were still several hundred yards away.

"We must protect ourselves!" cried Lucas; and swiftly they pulled the wagon close to a bank beneath dense trees and tied the team and saddle horses deep within the grove. Then, with Jenny and Phoebe helping, they turned the wagon on its side, crouched behind it, and prepared their weapons. They had several rifles, two pistols, and a good supply of ammunition for all of them. Lucas, Kirby, and Jenny immediately had rifles in their hands, while Phoebe stood ready to supply reloaded rifles as necessary.

The avengers, surprised by Kirby's sudden arrival and expecting a short fight with easy success, now saw a well-fortified position and pulled behind a nearby thicket to reconsider. The warriors figured the odds at seventeen to two, because they did not consider women as fighters.The Nez Perces also were well armed, so the attack came swiftly. Their strategy was simple—ride rapidly around the perimeter, firing in from the flanks at the ends of the wagon when possible. And Yellow Bull exulted: "Now we are many and they are few, and they will not survive long!"

They were wrong, for Lucas, Kirby, and Jenny fired deliberately, and Phoebe always had a loaded gun ready. The results were deadly: within minutes the 17 warriors were reduced to 12. But there was one weakness in the Phelps family position, for to their rear were only trees and they lost track of the numbers. Though they knew that five warriors had fallen from their horses, they did not notice now only ten were riding in the circle. The other two, unmounted, were creeping into the grove from behind the wagon.

The black gelding gave a startled nicker as an unfamiliar body brushed his flank and he smelled a strange odor. Lucas, Kirby, and Jenny whirled simultaneously, and the two warriors who had planned a silent attack on two men suddenly faced three rifles. They fired immediately, but were dead before they could reload.

Kirby and Lucas quickly turned their attention to the ends of the wagon, their vulnerable flanks. Again their aim was deadly, and two more riders were taken from the circle. But when Lucas turned to grasp a reloaded gun from Phoebe; there was no gun. Phoebe lay slumped over the rock where she'd been sitting. With a horrified moan, Lucas turned to Jenny, but her lifeless body, cradled like a little child, was swinging slowly in the arc of the lower wagon wheel.

The surviving riders, including Wahlitits and Yellow Buffalo Bull, surprised by the deadly fire from behind the Phelps wagon, disappeared across the prairie toward Cottonwood Creek.

---

People stop to stare, and fear smothers their hearts as they watch the wagon slowly move from the edge of Mt. Idaho toward Brown's Hotel. Some of them recognize Lucas and Kirby on the wagon seat, their eyes downcast, their faces streaked with tears, and even their horses showing grief. All along the street the somber, silent people sense the tragedy moving before them, and their hearts weep for the two pitiful little figures carefully covered with blankets in the back of the wagon. Mr. Brown, Jenny's old boss at the hotel, meets Lucas and Kirby at the door, embraces them, and escorts them without words to a quiet, private place.

The little graveyard, on a slight rise above the village, contains only a few graves, for Mt. Idaho is a young town and has seen only a few accidental deaths and even less from natural causes. A minister from the family church has finished speaking, and now, as preparations are made to lower the rude caskets into the graves, Seth Jones, who had befriended Jenny in her early days at Mt. Idaho and is related to the Martin family on the prairie near Lucas' ranch, speaks the final words that will mean comfort to both Lucas and Kirby.

"Surely these were the two people of all on this earth most dear to you," he said. "You will mourn now for awhile, and cherish the happy memories; but you need not grieve, for grief is born of remorse, and remorse comes only when we do not give all of our love and all of ourselves to dear ones while they live. And now we commit their bodies back to the earth, and their souls back to their maker."

With fear all about them, and within their own hearts, Lucas and Kirby did not return to the ranch. They had their horses with them, but their cattle were scattered and perhaps might not be found again; and for a time life in the empty ranch house would not be bearable, so they accepted Mr. Brown's invitation to stay at the hotel in Mt. Idaho, sensing, but not saying, a return home might be a long time coming. Both knew, somehow, that they would be drawn into continuing tragic events on the prairie.

Depredations by the enraged Indians continued across the prairie as they attacked wagons, burned homes, and killed indiscriminately. The nation was incensed, and territorial governors of Idaho, Washington, and Oregon took steps to provide militia. The Military Department of the Columbia swung into action, with communications reaching all the way to Gen. William T. Sherman in Washington D.C., the same Sherman who ten years earlier had said of Indians in general, "They all have to be killed, or be maintained as a species of pauper."

Ironically, someone in Sherman's background must have respected one of the greatest Indian leaders of all time, for the "T" in his name stood for Tecumseh.

Now with military forces being marshaled from all directions, the non-treaty Nez Perce bands, realizing the hazards of their present spot on Cottonwood Creek, streamed back to camp on the lower reaches of Whitebird Canyon. These small bands, with a combined fighting force of not more than 200 men, hardly supported the exaggerated terror which thrilled the public mind. Some reports claimed that a confederacy of tribes, with as many as 1,500 armed warriors, was about to ravage the entire west.

The same day that Lucas and Kirby, bearing their sad load, reached Mt. Idaho, an urgent letter was dispatched by Mr. L.P. Brown to General Howard at Ft. Lapwai. In addition to those of Jenny and Phoebe Phelps, it reported the deaths of other people on the prairie and along the Salmon River. Within an hour Howard received a second letter describing more deaths and urgently requesting help in arms and ammunition, and that all travel across the prairie be stopped.

Within hours, two companies of cavalry were en route to Mt. Idaho under Captains Perry and Trimble. With them were First Lt. Edward R. Theller, two other officers, and 99 enlisted men who had been employed as clerks, carpenters, and blacksmiths. They were not properly drilled and were not encouraged to have regular target practice. They were mostly raw soldiers who were poorly supplied, provided with old guns and inadequate ammunition. Hardly an impressive force.

At times General Howard referred to Captain perry as "Colonel" and as the troops departed, theirs was a comfortable farewell:

"Good-by, colonel."

"Good-by, General."

"You must not get whipped."

"There is no danger of that, sir."

In camp, on Whitebird Creek, Joseph agonized, and tried to convince the other chiefs that in some way a truce could still be made with General Howard before he sent his troops against them. But of course it was too late; it probably had been too late since the hour when Richard Devine was killed. But even then peace might have been achieved had there not been a second foray to the Salmon River, for the bands might have been willing to give up Sarpsis and Wahlitits as murderers and proceed to the reservation. But after those additional killings, that possibility was gone. The devastation along the river and across the prairie had finally branded the non-treaty bands as red devils who simply must be eliminated. The country's honor was at stake, especially that of the army, from General Sherman in Washington to Captain Perry in Idaho, slogging his troops through a rainstorm toward Grangeville. Certainly not forgotten by the people in general, and the military in particular, was the fact that just short of a year ago, George Armstrong Custer and two hundred and fifty men were slaughtered near a stream in Montana called the Little Big Horn. The public was not yet aware that Custer had ignored warnings that he was overwhelmingly outnumbered and had led his troops in a direct frontal asault against several thousand Sioux and Chyennes.

Now in this June night Little Bird, Heyoom, Springtime nursing her new baby, and Running Feet dozing on a buffalo robe, listened to the increasing noises of revelry all about them. The salmon River Avengers had returned from Benedict's store with whiskey, and the looters on Camas Prairie had found more, so the sounds of the camp were those produced by that whiskey as the men got drunk, some of them beyond the point of being of any value as warriors.

Whiskey! The most potent of the white man's weapons in subjugating and manipulating the Indians.

# CHAPTER 9

Only two days had passed since Lucas and Kirby had left their loved ones in the Mt. Idaho cemetery. The passing time had not lessened their pain, and the terror gripping the town only added to their misery. Perhaps there was one benefit— they didn't have much quiet time to reflect. They still felt bitterness and anger against the killers, though, and when the call came for volunteers to join with the military, both signed up quickly. Now they watched Captain Perry and his bedraggled troops struggle into Grangeville.

The 104 men and officers comprising F Company and H Company had left Lapwai at sundown the previous day; and, as the sun sank again, the pitifully exhausted horses and bone-weary men dragged into the little town.

Lucas stared in disbelief at the horses. "How can men treat their animals in this way?" he asked Kirby. "And is this an army?"

"I'm not sure I believe it," Kirby replied. "Let's talk to some of the troopers." They soon learned that the dejected young men had ridden for most of the past 24 hours, having stopped at Cottonwood for only two hours for breakfast and to let the horses graze. Then one young trooper added, "At least we will get to sleep overnight here."

But the trooper was wrong. Captain Perry had talked with anxious settlers in Grangeville who had seen the Nez Perces crossing the prairie heading for the Salmon River, and they insisted that Perry must overtake the Indians before they escaped back across the rivers.

Perry decided a move was necessary that night. The need for rest and food was everywhere apparent, so a meal was started and hay provided for the horses, some of which were so depleted that they lay down and refused to eat. With preparations barely started, the men hurriedly ate half-cooked army beans, then struggled into their saddles.

As the long column rode toward Whitebird Creek more of the problems of this military unit became apparent. Though the men's nonchalance might be attributed to their youth and exhausted condition, that did not explain it all. There was no sense of military discipline, no apparent feeling that they were headed somewhere to do something important; and what troubled Lucas the most was that no one had any accurate knowledge of their destination. The one person in the group who claimed to know the lower Whitebird Creek area was the self-appointed guide, Ad Chapman.

Lucas did not like this tall, flamboyant man in the white hat, and wondered how much he really knew of the details of the terrain where the Nez Perces were camped. Lucas had ridden through it a time or two, but couldn't recall many details. So why should he have confidence Captain Perry would be able to deploy his troops in a fight?

---

No one in the Nez Perce camp slept that night, for scouts had seen the troopers crossing the prairie toward Grangeville and followed their progress. Now sentries were located far up on the ridge. More warriors continued to get drunk through the night, and by first light only sixty-five or seventy were able to fight, and even some of them were far from alert. But preparations were made, though there was no overall direction of the effort, for this was not the way of these people. Each band, and each warrior within the band, made individual preparations, gathering their best was horses and tethering them close by. Strategy was not entirely lacking, as the best rifles were handed out to proven warriors, for much would depend on them; others who knew how to use them received muskets or pistols, and some had bows and arrows, or even war clubs and knives. Yellow Wolf, only twenty-one years old, was not recognized as an experienced fighter, and carried his own bow. Welweyas, leaving the buckskin dress in its grass bag, stripped to his loin cloth and eagerly awaited a weapon; but he was given only a stout club, which he grasped firmly as he mounted the little brown mare. Little Bird, Wetatonmi, and other women were directed to deliver extra horses to the fighting men in the event they were unhorsed or their mounts became tired on the steep, rocky mountainside.

On one issue there was agreement: there would be one final attempt to achieve peace. They were not yet on the warpath. They were Nez Perce people prepared to defend themselves if necessary; and, knowing the landscape intimately, they planned their deployment. It was simple and basic and involved a most important principle of combat: enfilade—fire at the flanks; so they placed major groups of warriors on each side of the route they expected the soldiers to take. Others would be concealed behind rock outcroppings and in ravines directly in front of the approaching soldiers. And having made these simple preparations, they took one last step to support their effort for peace; they appointed a negotiating party, and the white flag was to be carried by Wettiwetti Howlis, whose name, ironically, meant 'malicious weasel'.

---

Captain Perry has his troops marching in a column of fours, thus making their formation shorter, more compact—and more vulnerable. He hears sounds which are not common to the early morning, and knows that the waiting Nez Perces have been warned. Then he sees in the distance a group of unarmed Indians carrying a white flag, and beyond them are warriors on horses. His apprehension has crystallized, and all his senses seem terrifyingly acute. He hears a single shot ring out, and sees Ad Chapman reload his rifle and fire again. Lucas realizes that the distance to the peace party is long, and is not surprised that no one there falls. Then he hears the plop of a bullet, followed instantly by the sound of a shot fired from behind the peace party and he watches, his perceptions in slow motion, as Captain Perry's bugler tumbles from his saddle.

Now the jumbled, rocky ravines and lava mounds become a frenzied scene of horror as rifle fire rolls and reverberates. Officers desperately shout commands, horses plunge and scream in agonized confusion! Cold terror grips the inexperienced men, while the more seasoned make valiant attempts to hold the units together. The second bugler is also dead, and Perry is never able to signal his platoon leaders. Panic soon takes over and only one thought remains. Escape!

Lucas' mind, like a detached and calm observer, records a series of impressions:

A large man with upswept hair gallops past on an iron-gray horse, firing his rifle and rapidly reloading. Chief Joseph!

Lucas turns to see several troopers fighting desperately with their backs against a sheer, rocky bluff. Mounted warriors stream past, hanging from the protected side of their horses, then dismount to pour deadly fire into the troopers while their horses wait patiently. By now not many troopers are firing; and most are retreating in disorganized, terrified panic.

Across a nearby hillside rides a slim woman on an Appaloosa horse leading two other mounts and Lucas watches as she proceeds up the canyon.Then he remembers seeing that horse and that young woman beside Kirby on the black gelding in a meadow near their ranch and he understands Kirby's absences.

Suddenly Ad Chapman is back among the volunteers as they sit on a small knoll, not one having fired a shot. Then Chapman is leading them in retreat up the canyon, leaving behind the shouting soldiers and the exhausted horses which made it down the mountain but cannot make it back up. Lt. Theller and eight men lie crumpled in a blind pocket at the base of a cliff, and scattered over the devastated area are 25 other lifeless bodies.

Captain Perry's mind is numb, frozen by paralyzing and uncomprehending fear, groping for the why and how of such a disaster, trying somehow to find a way to regroup his shattered troops. Then he too is in frenzied retreat, his gasping breaths mingling with those of his struggling horse.

The battle lasted only a few minutes. By 9 a.m. all of the volunteers were back in Mt. Idaho, having started with better horses than the soldiers. The warriors dogged the weary troopers to within four miles of town, further harassing and terrorizing them. Other troopers whose horses were shot or too depleted to travel, straggled back on foot over many hours, including First Sgt. McCarthy, whose 16 mile trip took three days.

Thus, in a matter of minutes a small force of about 65 Nez Perces, some of them drunk, some with only primitive weapons, killed 34 of a supposedly potent troop of 104, driving the survivors back over the mountain in total disarray. No Nez Perces died, and only three or four were wounded. How many more of Captain Perry's troops might have died had not the white man's whiskey diminished the Nez Perces' fighting abilities?

Little Bird, riding Hawk and leading two spare horses, had paused on a hillside to watch the furious battle, which had ended so quickly that neither Ollokot nor Yellow Wolf, whom she was supporting, needed a spare mount. In the midst of this melee she glanced toward the knoll and saw, among a group of men not in uniform, a burly man on a strong iron-gray horse. Both horse and rider were familiar, somehow; but in the excitement of the battle Little Bird forgot them and turned toward camp, expecting to be needed if there were injured warriors. Wetatonmi rode up as Little Bird approached the tipi, and together they tethered the unneeded horses, both solemn and relieved at finding that none of their people had been killed or seriously injured.

Now Little Bird sat in the shade of a tree near the tipi watching as the warriors moved among the fallen soldiers and their horses, gathering weapons, ammunition, saddles, and other items of value. Many of the men had chased the retreating soldiers and volunteers up the canyon, and Little Bird could hear occasional gunfire. But then her thoughts turned back to the big man on the gray gelding, and suddenly she knew. She had seen the same horse and rider while with Kirby not far from his home.

"Where is Kirby now?" she asked herself. "It appears his father is fighting our people. Will Kirby also be drawn into this war?" As she glanced up the canyon, the crest of the mountain seemed formidably higher and the pine-studded slopes and Camas meadows around Tepahlewam seemed very far away.

## CHAPTER 10

Joseph, Toohoolhoolzote, White Bird and the others were too emotionally exhausted to meet after the battle, but agreed that tomorrow a council was necessary, for they faced a major decision—where do they go now? Joseph scanned the country in all directions around him, and it seemed that the rugged but familiar hills had become forbidding and impenetrable mountains. White men were just beyond those mountains wherever he looked. And he was right, for the forces against his people were being marshaled everywhere, and could indeed be brought from any direction.

The camp settled into a restless sleep, only to be broken by Yellow Wolf, who had been posted as a sentry on the mountain. He galloped into camp and said, "There are riders coming over the mountain, too far for me to tell who they are. But I thought you should have warning."

"The extra warning is good, Yellow Wolf," said Whitebird. "We must always be alert now." So he sent scouts up the mountain to relay information back to the bands, and soon one of them returned, saying, "They are some of our own people, returning from the buffalo country!"

Soon they were close enough to be recognized, and Joseph exclaimed, "It is Rainbow and Five Wounds; back from their long hunting trip!" Quickly the leaders of the column reached the camp and dismounted. The lean Five Wounds, tall and athletic, embraced Joseph, and close behind came Rainbow, a shorter, compact man, alert and vigorous.

Now the somber feelings of the camp imposed by recent conflicts and the battle of the day before were replaced by excitement and joy, for these were old friends, returning after two winters far beyond the big mountains. There was much hugging and laughter, and more than a few tears. The young men among the hunters eyed Little Bird and Running Feet, for some had marriage on their minds and may have seen desirable brides in Montana, but had lacked enough horses or other items with which to buy them. Heyoom, Wetatonmi, and Springtime found relatives among the women who had just returned, and there was much visiting and showing off of babies, some now almost two years old. And the men, in the way of all hunters, proudly displayed the pack loads of dried meat and the many buffalo robes. The meat would be gladly shared, but the robes and hides would be exchanged for rifles, better clothing and, as always, horses. Who ever has enough horses?

Soon Five Wounds and Rainbow had selected a camp spot, the packs were unloaded, the women were erecting the tipis, and the tantalizing aroma of boiling buffalo meat drifted through the camp as the women prepared a meal for everyone; and all relaxed as the high excitement of the day softened to the comfortable ambiance of pleasure that comes when friends reunite.

Joseph walked to the bustling new camp, and found Five Wounds and Rainbow watching leisurely as their women erected the tipis. A round-faced, smiling woman approached Rainbow and spoke to him briefly, then turned to her work, her noticeably fat bottom swaying as she walked. A little boy, perhaps a year old, toddled happily along behind her.

"The buffalo country was good to you this time, Rainbow," Joseph said. "And do you have a new wife?"

"Yes. She is a Crow. Her father demanded two of my best spotted horses. Her mother thought she was a little awkward, and named her Waddling Duck." Then he said, with a slight smile, "But she has been good for me in every way."

"And you also have a new son, a strong boy."

"He walked early, and already speaks some of our language, which his mother is learning too. We call him Small Duck."

The day had ended happily, and the people of the camp in their light-hearted way tried to push aside reality—but it remained. Now the chiefs of the bands, joined by Five Wounds and Rainbow, sat in a circle in Joseph's big tipi. Joseph spoke first. "It is good that our brothers have returned safely from far over the mountains," he said. "You make our hearts feel stronger, and we will welcome your council. You have seen the signs of trouble in our country."

The sharp-eyed Five Wounds replied, "Coming across the prairie we were threatened by armed men, and on this side of the mountain we saw the bodies of dead soldiers, and are happy that none of your warriors were killed."

The erect and clear-eyed Whitebird, in no way showing his 74 years, now subtly exerted his leadership. "The white soldiers were not strong, and did not show fighting wisdom. We cannot boast too much about driving them away. There are other threats, and we know that Howard will be coming after us soon. I believe that we should go up the river, perhaps to Horseshoe Bend, where we have big country to hide in. They can hunt for us there."

There was more discussion, but no good alternatives. Toohoolhoolzote, fiery as ever, would have preferred to fight, but pointed out, "All of our strength is in our unity, especially now that Five Wounds and Rainbow are back with us." All realized that Looking Glass and his band might not rejoin them. He had taken his people to the Clearwater and, upon learning of the killings across Camas Prairie, had angrily notified Joseph that he was to be left alone. A few of Joseph's band had joined him and were still there, aloof from the rest of the non-treaty bands.

Then Joseph, agreeing with the others, added his thoughts. "Our best protection is within our own country. To the east and the north are Howard and his troops, and others are coming up the Snake River toward Lewiston. To the west is our beloved Wallowa Valley, but there are many settlers there, and they are supported by other troops. If we go to the south, we might soon meet a force coming from the fort down at Boise."

So the decision was made, and the next day before noon the women, with some help from the men this time, had loaded the entire camp onto pack horses and all were mounted and heading up the Salmon River. The growing horse herd, enlarged to over 3,000 by those brought back by Five Wounds and Rainbow, trailed along behind. Before dusk, they reached the great bend in the river; and, because the water was still high, they traveled the extra miles around the loop and camped on its upstream side. From here, sentries would see Howard's troops as they approached from downstream. With the camp located in this safe position, the crafty old Whitebird smiled to himself, for the strategy was his—and he held the field glasses one of the dead troopers no longer needed.

And so the people waited. They had found salmon thronging into a nearby stream, and were now well supplied with fresh fish. For a few days they could stay here in this safe place, resting and feasting and playing, and pretending that this was just another summer expedition. Some of the routines of everyday living, which always help to make life seem normal, were resumed. Though they had plenty of food, indeed, everything edible they owned, they could not resist the abundant salmon, and built fires to smoke some and racks to dry others in the sun. The women began repairing torn clothing and sewing rips in the buffalo hide tipis. The rapid and repeated moves by the bands had not left time for swimming, so Springtime, Wetatonmi, and Running Feet joined other women and their children at a beach by the river. The men had gone upstream, and the women downstream, to find their own private swimming places. For some reason, Little Bird was not interested, and loitered around the tipi.

The women's lodge was set up at a discreet distance from the camp, for this need had also been neglected in recent weeks. Heyoom was there, along with several other women. It was the end of her second day in the lodge, and she rested comfortably on the buffalo robes. The roar of the river from below was softened by the tipi walls, and soon Heyoom became drowsy. But something was missing.

'Little Bird's time starts two or three days after mine," Heyoom thought to herself. "Perhaps she will be here tomorrow." Little Bird did not arrive tomorrow, nor the next day, nor the day after that, and Heyoom left the lodge without seeing her.

Yellow Wolf had found his favorite pinto among the horse herd, and was carefully grooming him. While catching the pony, he had seen Little Bird mount Hawk and ride off along the upstream bend of the river. Only yesterday, Yellow Wolf had again said to Joseph, "You will remember that more than a moon back I asked you for Little Bird to be my wife."

"I do remember. I could not forget such a thing," Joseph said. "But like you and others, my thoughts have been on fighting and keeping the band safe."

"Then do you agree to let me have Little Bird? You know that I have plenty of horses."

"Little Bird is not my daughter, as you know. Heyoom and I have always cared for her and she is to us like our other children. I agree, but the choice is really hers. You are the son of my sister and a family member. There is no reason to talk about horses, or other payment."

Now Yellow Wolf remembered how his heart sang within him. Little Bird would be his wife! Then he remembered the gossip among the women about Little Bird and the young white rancher, also thinking of the day Kirby approached the column as it left Tepahlewam and spoke to Little Bird. "Well, he's just a kid," thought Yellow Wolf. "He has no right to my woman!"

Yellow Wolf finished grooming the pinto, the hooves were clean and bright, the long mane and tail free of all burrs, and the supple bay and white hide glistened in the bright June sunlight. Yellow Wolf rode quickly to his tipi where he brushed his long black hair, plaited in the special ribbons he kept for ceremonies, and dressed himself carefully in his softest buckskin shirt and leggings. Then he remounted the pinto, and was soon approaching the spot where he had last seen Little Bird.

Hawk, needing no guidance, had carried Little Bird more than a mile along the rocky trail, the turbulent, noisy river to the left below them, and to their right, a grassy hillside sloping up to the base of a sheer granite cliff. Little Bird was only slightly aware of the clean smell of grasses and the sweet, almost heavy, scent of the Syringa in full bloom. Trusting Hawk to find the way, her mind had wandered over events of the past few days when the serenity and calmness of the camp were so welcome to all. "A different kind of setting," she thought, "but the feeling is almost like the Wallowa Valley. But we're all pretending as we go our quiet ways, doing what we please. And Yellow Wolf; he also is different, somehow; and once he even smiled at me in that tight-lipped way of his. Yes, Yellow Wolf has spoken to Joseph, but no one has said anything to me. But that is the way of our people, and if I hadn't met Kirby and started thinking of being his wife, maybe I wouldn't think of having any choices."

The trail dipped suddenly into a hollow banked by Syringa bushes at the base of an overhanging bluff. Mosses and ferns grew there, and trailing vines with tiny yellow flowers. Water seeped from a crevice on the bluff, keeping the growing things nourished and green and finally dripping into a crystal-clear pool. Hawk came to a stop, hoping for a drink from the pool. Little Bird slipped from his smooth back, found her own place to drink, then lay down on the grass to gaze upward at the crest of the cliff etched sharply against the arching sky. Soon the scent of the flowers, the somnolent roar of the river, and the soft musical sounds of water falling into the pool brought total relaxation, and Little Bird dozed, her mind drifting back to recent events.

The people of the bands had gathered at a flat place prepared for dancing. The drumbeat was enticing, but the dance had started slowly, almost indifferently, as only a few people began their studied, methodical shuffle around the circle, for some had overindulged at the just-completed feast of broiled salmon and camas and hot bread made from white man's flour; and the tantalizing aromas of these favorite items drifted from the fires. Now the older people form the outer circle, and the young ones move toward the center, taking up the rhythm, placing their feet precisely, each dancer moving independently. Little Bird steps gracefully through the repetitive, almost monotonous, but beautiful routines, not really aware of her own seductiveness, for in recent months her ripe young body has reached full maturity and cannot be hidden beneath the loosely hanging buckskin dress. None of this is lost on Yellow Wolf; and though couples do not touch or join hands in the dance, he moves closer to Little Bird.

The dancers warm to the rhythm as the tempo increases. Some of the older people tire, and move aside to watch. The young women maintain the routine steps, but at a much faster pace, and begin moving in tight circles, while the young men leap and cavort, some having stripped to their loincloths.

Yellow Wolf, still fully dressed, stays close to Little Bird, and she is suddenly aware of his body heat, which increases his man scent and mingles with the pungent odor of his willow-smoked buckskin clothing. She is drawn to his strength and intensity and his obviously admiring eyes, and would like to touch him, but the dance does not call for touching, so she moves alone in the traditional way. But now the buckskin smell increases, which is strange, because he has moved away from her and the dance is over, and the smoky odor is blended with the scent of the Syringa, and the drumbeat is replaced by the murmuring of falling water.

In her sleep, Little Bird has turned on her side; and as her eyes open lazily she expects to see Hawk, but sees both Hawk and the pinto nuzzling each other. Then a shadow falls across her face and she slowly turns, to see Yellow Wolf standing over her, his deep-set eyes gleaming, only a faint smile breaking the eagerness of his lean face.

"Joseph has agreed. You are my woman now."

She starts to speak, and to rise from the grass, but with his slightly raised left hand, the palm down, he motions her to silence, while with the right, not roughly, but firmly, irresistibly, he forces her back down. Then he stands tall again, and in one deft movement removes his shirt. Little Bird watches, fascinated, her breath quickening, as he loosens and drops the buckskin leggings, revealing in full manhood his lean, bronzed body.

With Kirby there had been gentleness, and an awkward, tender kind of fumbling, a little pain, and afterwards they had held each other in a dreamlike glow, peaceful and prolonged, never wanting to part. But for Yellow Wolf this was not a new experience, and it was, like his life, deep and intense, his sinewy body dominating Little Bird's. At first she attempted to resist, but knew she no longer had choices. And though she found herself responding, she sensed the difference without knowing the words: emotional and consuming, but not sweetly fulfilling.

Decisions had been made for her, and together she and Yellow Wolf rode back to the camp. As the bands prepared for the next move, Yellow Wolf brought up two packhorses, which for the time being were enough for his tipi covers, a few buffalo robes, and their other meager belongings. Little Bird on her Appaloosa would lead the packhorses, while Yellow Wolf rode wherever he was needed among the men.

# CHAPTER 11

The Nez Perces quite appropriately called Major General Oliver Otis Howard, "Cut Arm,", for after the battle of Fair Oaks, in the gore and confusion of a hospital tent, a Union Army surgeon had unceremoniously sawed off his right arm and thrown it into a bloody barrel, along with other arms and numerous legs. He had carried high command during the Civil War, and was with Sherman on his ruthless March To The Sea. Later, he had been director of the Freedmen's Bureau, where he was to find new homes and ways of life for liberated black people.

Now Howard was in Idaho, attempting to force a few small bands of rather peaceful Nez Perces from the mountain homelands they loved to the confinement of a reservation which they would hate. And today this commander of great armies, writer of books on military history, and a complete loner, faced the loneliest task ever required of a military leader, especially if his command is small and the men and their wives are well known to him.

The wife of slain soldier Lt. Theller opened the door when General Howard knocked. No words were needed, for his countenance told the story, and she buried her head in her hands, sobbing, "Oh, my husband!"

For perhaps nine months of the year, the valley of Lapwai Creek, where the fort was located, displays little natural beauty. Trees thrive by the creek, but the surrounding hills are sear and brown, their outcroppings of dark lava showing no real loveliness while absorbing heat through the day and radiating it back at night. But in early spring, the landscape comes to life as shrubs and trees along the streams produce leaves and blossoms and the bright green grass on the undulating hills is dotted with flowers. But the beauty was wasted on the people at Lapwai that evening, for they had known and loved the 34 young men who died in Whitebird Canyon.

General Howard can see those men very clearly. It is the same chilling scene, repeated from Bull Run through The Peninsula to Seven Pines and Antietam and on to Chancellorsville, the March Through Georgia, and into the Carolinas; for they are the same young men, blue or gray, those still unburied on Whitebird Creek and those long since buried after all the other campaigns; and all should have been at home with wives, mothers, and sweethearts.

Then he envisions the families of these most recent victims. By now, or within a very few days, all will be aware that 34 are gone but, except for Lt. Theller, not yet named; and some will receive cherished letters written before that terrible day and will continue to live in hope. Then other letters will come, not wrinkled, nor addressed in the scrawled handwriting of their young men, but in crisp, official envelopes from the War Department. And some will look out the window one day, or answer a knock at the door, and see standing before them sober, unsmiling men in military uniforms who try to express the sympathy of the War Department and The President.

Howard's barren quarters with the stern, stiff army cot, small writing desk and straight chair, seemed especially lonely that night. In just two or three days, summer had descended with its sharp heat, and Howard was thankful for the coolness in the evening air as he folded back the olive drab army blanket and stretched out on the dingy sheet, not up to his usual standards. He reflected on his career since Appomattox: remembering that he had been blamed for the failure of the Freedman's Bureau; feeling some pride in his days as Superintendent of West Point, and real comfort in the thought of the many black students attending Howard University in Washington D.C.

Then his insecurities returned as he thought of Perry's failure on Whitebird Creek. In the eyes of the commanders above him, all the way to Sherman, it was Howard's failure, for Perry is an obscure, seldom-heard name. And why, in the light of good military principles, did this failure occur?

---

The night had stolen away and dawn crept through his window, but Howard was not tired; and he arose, to throw himself into a frenzy of action which would reinforce both his personal and military position. Already the local citizenry, newspaper editors, politicians, and some of the military were criticizing him personally. Concentric circles of terror spread from the mountains of the Snake and Salmon Rivers, bringing unreasoning fear to all who were anywhere close to any Indian tribe, whether on or off reservations. At Lewiston, only fifteen miles from Lapwai but a hundred miles from Whitebird Canyon, several dozen volunteers patrolled the streets 24 hours a day, and barricades were built. Far to the north, in the land of the Spokans and Coeur d'Alenes, ranchers banded together, fortifying themselves as best they could. To the west, the Walla Wallas, Yakimas, and Cayuses were also feared, though they had been on reservations for some time. And far to the south, all of the tribes along the Snake River and into the rough Owyhee country bordering Nevada were looked upon with distrust and unreasoning fear.

So on that day, and driven by his own desire for superior numbers, Howard blanketed the country with requests for additional men. Responses included units from Idaho, Oregon, Washington, and California, and a ship bearing troops on their way home from Alaska was stopped at the mouth of the Columbia River and its troops transferred to a river boat headed for Lewiston. Others were started northward from Ft. Boise to apprehend the Nez Perces if they went south, and some military units were dispatched from as far away as Georgia.

During the next few days over this last week in June, Howard received accurate information from various sources. He realized that reports of thousands of fighting Indians were just exaggerations, and that the only identifiable threat lay with a few small bands of Nez Perces somewhere on the Salmon River.

---

Chief Joseph and General Howard had known each other for many years, had sat in treaty councils together, and had felt a mutual understanding and respect. Joseph still carried his respect for the white man, but in recent months Howard had begun to identify Joseph as the leader and instigator in alleged warlike preparations. Howard had been relieved when he knew the bands were camped at Tepahlewam, only a few miles from the reservation. But as reports of the killing forays reached him, Howard again saw Joseph as a villain who was organizing the non-treaty bands, gathering vast stores of weapons, and planning to attack. Were not these recent killings evidence of that?

As word of the rout at Whitebird Creek spread across the country, Joseph's status as a fighting man increased and his very name became fearful to many people. Upon seeing a cloud of dust moving across Camas Prairie, some would say, "There goes Joseph," and their children would repeat that for years to come. And since no one, the military in particular, understood the dynamics of leadership among Indian bands and tribes, the legend grew, and Howard saw an advantage to foster the concept of Joseph as a ruthless military genius. Victory over such a worthy opponent would be sweet, and defeat, should it come, perhaps a little more acceptable to all concerned.

So preparations for battle proceeded rapidly, and a week after the debacle at Whitebird Creek Howard was headed for Camas Prairie, where he would be joined by Perry with some 65 men, bringing his total force to over 400, with more on the way.

All across Camas Prairie fear reigned, and the people were close to blind panic. Since Captain Perry and his exhausted troops had returned from Whitebird Creek, no Indians had been seen on the prairie. But rumors and imaginings were almost as terrifying as reality, and the yelping of a coyote at night or the trill of a bird in early morning sent chills through the hearts of the sleepless citizens. Perry and his men were in bivouac at Grangeville, but their presence brought no comfort to the frightened people, for the aura of defeat hovered over their camp.

Lucas and Kirby continued to live at Brown's Hotel and tried to lend their strength to the local people, working on the fortifications and, along with L. P. Brown, awaiting further word from Howard. Ranchers all across the prairie had vacated their homes and gathered at the fort in Mt. Idaho, and a makeshift one at the Grange Hall on Three Mile Creek. Some farther north had fled to Cottonwood and nearby Norton's Ranch.

Lucas fought the spectral images of dying men, floundering horses rolling into rocky defiles, and the disgraceful retreat from the battlefield to Mt. Idaho. Kirby could not shake the pathetic memory of his father, almost in tears, blaming himself for being useless in the confused and hopeless situation. And the cruel pictures of Jenny rotating slowly on the wagon wheel, while Phoebe lay crumpled across the rock with her lifeblood flowing out—these memories still haunted father and son and they could not yet return to the ranch. So in spite of their uneasiness and resentment toward Ad Chapman, both decided to stay with the volunteers. Now, little over a week since the defeat, word was received that Howard was approaching Grangeville with a strong force.

## CHAPTER 12

There was little happiness anywhere across Camas Prairie. The sky was overcast with low clouds and a light rain was falling. Lucas and Kirby sat in the lobby of Brown's Hotel awaiting the arrival of General Howard and his cavalry, knowing that they had recently passed through Grangeville. This would be their first meeting with the general.

"He only has one arm, you know," commented Lucas. "That doesn't seem to slow him down, though. I heard he helped make peace with Cochise and the Apaches in Arizona. He's also a very religious man, and some say that even in the heat of battle he may suddenly kneel to pray."

"Well, we can certainly use some of that now," replied Kirby. "Perhaps he didn't pray hard enough for Perry and the troops at Whitebird."

Hearing a commotion in the street in front of the hotel, Lucas and Kirby rushed to the door to see Howard and his aides leading the cavalry up the street toward them. Howard, well mounted on a sturdy sorrel Morgan gelding, presented a classic picture of military discipline—a single star glistening brilliantly on the epaulets of his well-pressed uniform, right sleeve folded up and pinned neatly; mouth almost concealed by a moustache and long sideburns flowing into a full beard.

Lucas and Kirby watched as General Howard moved about inspecting the defenses, speaking quietly and compassionately to the injured troopers, reassuring the frightened citizens, and stating he would pursue the war with all available troops. Then he left Mt. Idaho to join the rest of his command, and Lucas rode with him to meet Captain Page of the Walla Walla volunteers.

A few miles west of Grangeville the column reached a point where Lucas could look out across the prairie. There stood the lonely, desolate ranch house beneath the tall pines, whose usually bright, golden-brown bark reflected little light from the gloomy sky. Beyond the ranch he could see the Martin place, and beyond that the leaden blue-gray surface of the lake near Tepahlewam. Both ranch houses were vacant, and he remembered just yesterday seeing Olivia Martin and her daughter Cornelia in Mt. Idaho. Olivia's husband Jethro was somewhere with the volunteers.

Then Lucas struggled to force from his mind the images of Jenny and Phoebe dead behind the wagon, and he seemed to be with them in the ranch house. Both were beautiful and vibrantly alive, Phoebe chattering about her day's experiences at school, then hurrying out to gather the eggs from the henhouse; Jenny moving quickly about the kitchen in her own quiet way, humming to herself as she often did, peeling the potatoes for supper, taking her delicious brown loaves of bread from the oven, their aroma filling the kitchen. What was it Seth Jones had said about remorse, and giving all of your life and all of your love? Did I give all of my life and my love to these women? Certainly to Phoebe. Do I feel a little remorse about Jenny? For all these years have I been sharing part of my love and part of my heart with Mei Ling? That was such a brief thing, but it was the first I had known of real sympathy and compassion and love and understanding. I can't feel guilt or remorse about it. Jenny fulfilled my life, and I have her all the love I had. How could I do more? On the summit Lucas was brought back to reality as the column stopped and Captain Page and Ad Chapman moved ahead for reconnaissance of the Salmon River Canyon.

---

Little Bird had seldom visited this part of the Salmon River but now was enjoying its beauty, sitting with her back against a mossy boulder, the frothy water of Deer Creek rushing past her feet as she looked down the mountainside toward the Salmon River near Horseshoe Bend. The bands had enjoyed almost a week in their camp just above the upstream bend; but as the days passed the leaders became uneasy, for scouts had relayed reports of General Howard and his troops as they moved toward Camas Prairie.

Little Bird reflected on how quickly her people could put aside the concerns of the day, relax and enjoy life. She worried that this easy-going attitude might be fatal. Now she was glad that the camp was on the hill with the Salmon River as protection against Howard's approach.

Since she had been claimed by Yellow Wolf, Little Bird had tried to push away her memory of Kirby. How remote and distant it all seemed; her last sight of him on the prairie, the joy of their lovemaking beneath the willows by the beach, and the inexpressible closeness of their ride up the moonlit canyon. With a feeling of loss, she realized that these memories were growing dim. How could this happen in only a few weeks? Was it the intensity and turmoil of flight, the mind-numbing conflict of the battle?

She rested her head against the boulder behind her and started to relax, but her eyes caught a sudden flash of red on a distant ridgetop beyond the river. Yellow Wolf was waving the red blanket! His signal meant he could see Howard and his troops, and they are close to Whitebird Creek!

---

Lucas watched, thankful that no volunteers had been asked to help, as Captain Perry and several other officers directed the search for the dead troopers. Lucas controlled his feeling of revulsion, thinking that it would have been compassionate of Howard to relieve Perry of the terrible task of searching for his own men, their bodies rotting in the elements for ten days. But the careful search continued, with men covering the hillsides, walking only a few feet apart, steeling their minds, taking only shallow breaths, and some leaving to hide behind nearby rocks where no one could see them be sick.

Lucas was glad he was not close and watched as shallow graves were scooped out of the rocky soil. The pitiful remains, some barely identifiable as human after the coyotes' work, were covered as well as possible and rocks placed on top. Then a stick was driven into the ground by each sorrowful mound and a hat, when one could be found, was hung on top. No one was identified except Lt. Theller, whose body was recognized by Lt. Raines.

Heavy rain was falling, and although Indians were in sight on the far side of the river, it was growing too dark to do anything about them. But they could be a threat, and no one wanted to camp close to the grisly battleground, so all returned up the canyon to camp in the fresh air of higher ground and wait for another day.

During the night the Indians again moved their camp to a safer location higher on the mountain, leaving warriors by the river to wait for Howard's return. Now Joseph, his wives, Running Feet and Little Bird sat together on a flat rock, shading their eyes against the rising sun, and watched the valley far below. As the sun rose higher and drove the shadows from the hollows, they saw the columns of horses moving through the battleground and approaching the river.

"The river is our friend now," exulted Joseph, "for all of those men with their horses and pack mules will have to cross it. Perhaps they do not know about making bullboats, and certainly they have no buffalo hides. Maybe Howard will remember making us cross both the Snake and the Salmon with all of our people and horses when the rivers were even higher."

This was Howard's first trip to the Salmon river, but yesterday he had paid little attention to it or to the surrounding countryside, for he was deeply affected by the burial process and its depressing impact on all of his troops. The soldiers were now spread out along the east bank of the swollen river to look across and see dozens of warriors milling about the hillside, shouting back and forth and occasionally making threatening moves toward the shore as if to cross the river. Howard raised his eyes to scan the mountain beyond them, and was startled. Yesterday, as seen from the slope high above the battlefield, it had seemed like just another mountain; but now, from the bottom of the canyon and with the boiling river at his feet, he shuddered at the prospect of chasing the Nez Perces through such country. The 4,000-foot change in elevation suddenly became real. But it was not just the height—the rocky, bare slopes appeared too steep for safe travel, and to both the north and the south the great mountainside was gashed by the sharp defiles of tributary canyons with rock slides and vertical cliffs.

There was a shout from his men, and Howard lowered his eyes to see the entire body of Indian warriors rushing toward the river, brandishing their arms, shouting, and a few firing. Some of his own men got off futile shots, but the distance was too great and no harm was done.

Since Lucas had moved to the prairie, he had searched the countryside for good horses. His favorite now was a Morgan Thoroughbred gelding which he had perversely named for Vermont and called Monty. Now he led the gelding to the edge of the water for a drink, loosened the cinch strap and tied him in the shade of the willows, then watched as the troops began preparations to cross the river. It was to be a discouraging, and ridiculous process, for the white soldiers and scouts could not make it across the river, and reservation Indians had to swim over to set the western anchor for a rope ferry. But the pulleys didn't work and the effort failed, so the entire command had to be ferried across the Salmon River in rowboats borrowed from ranchers at Slate Creek. The Nez Perces had made this crossing with several hundred men, women, and children, and 3,500 horses in a few hours. It would take one battalion of the United States Army four days.

In the meantime, the Walla Walla volunteers had decided they had more important business at home, and were now traveling back toward Grangeville. Captain Perry and his troops had been dispatched to Cottonwood to obtain additional supplies. Several days earlier, Captain Trimble had made a circuitous trip south from Grangeville through Florence and west to the mouth of Slate Creek, waiting there in case the Nez Perces attempted to retreat up the river. Now he rejoined Howard's main force as they fought the river at the mouth of Whitebird Creek.

---

Some of the people around Mt. Idaho were not happy with having Looking Glass and his band nearby, just within the reservation boundary and close to the Clearwater River. Kirby, restlessly walking the streets and anxious to have some part in the action, overheard the comments of the settlers:

"How do we know that old bastard will stay where he is?"

"Well, we don't. He could just as well move off and attack us."

"That's right. And besides, we need that good land, even if it is inside the reservation. Not only that; I suspect he's sending men to Joseph."

So Kirby was not surprised when D. B. Randall summoned him to the fort and ordered, "Phelps, jump on that big gelding. You know this country, so take that trail over the divide and warn Howard that Looking Glass is slipping reinforcements to Joseph's bands. We think he has sent 30 warriors in the last few days." Kirby, thankful for a break in the tedious waiting, was soon mounted and pushing the black through the rain, past the deserted ranch house, over the mountain beyond, and within two hours had reported to Howard and found Lucas.

"So Looking Glass is providing reinforcements?" questioned Lucas. "I've seen no sign of new arrivals. But I suspect those Indians across the river aren't waiting for more men, and won't stay there long." Kirby replied, "From some of the things I heard in Mt. Idaho, I'm not even sure Looking Glass is a threat."

But Howard saw it differently, and directed Captain Whipple and his men to ride to Looking Glass's village and arrest him. Kirby with his field glasses had been scanning the western side of the river and up the ridge where some said the Nez Perce camp was located. Might he see a trim young woman on a strong spotted horse? His thoughts were suddenly interrupted by a curt command from Captain Whipple. "You there, Phelps! Come with me to find Looking Glass."

Kirby rode with a small group of volunteers led by D. B. Randall, who traveled next to Captain Whipple directing the way toward Looking Glass's camp. They left Mt. Idaho before dawn, and as the sun rose, sat on the crest of a ridge overlooking the sleeping settlement. Kirby noted with surprise the thriving little village, it's plowed fields planted with a variety of vegetables and fenced to keep out the livestock. A few milk cows wandered about or were enclosed in small corrals. Between the ridge and the peaceful Indians the bubbling waters of Clear Creek tumbled toward the south fork of the Clearwater a few hundred yards below.

Now Kirby watched as Bird Alighting, sent out by Looking Glass, splashed through the creek to tell Whipple the people wanted no trouble. Mounted and sitting close to Kirby were several men he had heard lashing out in anger at the Indians, coveting their land, and looking for revenge against those who had killed whites on Camas Prairie. One of them shoved his gun roughly against Bird Alighting's ribs, mistaking him for Looking Glass. Bird Alighting returned to Looking Glass's tipi, but soon came back, again asking the troops to go away. Two Indians then planted a white cloth on a stick between Looking Glass's tipi and the creek. Then Kirby saw one of the volunteers raise his rifle and fire at an Indian. Gunfire broke out among the volunteers all along the hillside, and as bullets struck the tipis, Indian men, women, and children rushed out. They scattered in all directions, their terrified screams shattering the air. Several were wounded and dragged themselves into the brush, and Kirby watched in disbelief and anguish as one woman, carrying her child, plunged into the Clearwater River.Unable to swim in the swift current, both she and her baby were swept downstream. Then both soldiers and volunteers charged down the hillside and through the stream, still firing, and raged among the deserted homes, which were destroyed as the angry men trampled gardens, smashed household goods, and burned tipis. Then they rounded up cattle and hundreds of horses and drove them to Mt. Idaho.

The previous night the Indian leaders had hammered out a plan, though certainly not without dissent. Joseph still argued for a return to the Wallowa, but the other leaders had voted him down. So as Kirby rode eastward with Captain Whipple, Little Bird and some 500 Nez Perces, with all their earthly belongings on pack horses, were struggling upward toward the plateau high above them. There was no trail, and the mountainside was harsh, rugged, and perilously steep. Though the Nez Perces and their horses were accustomed to such terrain, the pressures of flight and the continuing rain were taking their toll, and the going became ever more tedious.

The council decision had been to climb to the plateau, move northward some 25 miles, then drop down, recross the Salmon River, climb out to Camas

Prairie and travel east to where Cottonwood Creek joined the south fork of the Clearwater. From that point, perhaps Howard and Monteith would allow them to go on to the land that they had selected on the reservation. If not, they could move on eastward into the tangled maze of forest along the Lochsa fork of the Clearwater. And were they not well known over there among the Flatheads? Also, the crows and even the whites in Montana were their friends. But this optimistic thinking failed to consider one glaring fact—within the last three weeks the Nez Perces had killed some 60 white people. Cruel treatment and murders of Nez Perces by whites, the violation of truce flags, and self defense, would mean nothing to the aroused and angry American public, and forgiveness by the military would be totally unthinkable. Joseph feared there would be no return to his homeland.

## CHAPTER 13

Joseph settled into his role of guardian and camp chief; and it was an honorable role, for in the Indian way moving the people safely was a respected function, the most important of all. But now his responsibilities were broader as he marshaled the non-fighting men, the women, the children, encouraging them as they loaded the packhorses, soothing their irritations. For all were dispirited and weary, and there was not only his own band, but also those of Whitebird and Toohoolhoolzote, who were not accustomed to acting under a common leadership. And Joseph was everywhere, checking the balance of loads on packhorses, showing quiet gratitude to the women as they helped squalling, tired children onto the horses, easing small squabbles among the bands.

Within two hours all of the mounted people had reached the top of the mountain. Little Bird rode quietly beside Springtime, at times relieving her of the papoose carrier with the sleeping Early Flower, and wondering, with no great concern, where Yellow Wolf might be among the warriors up ahead. A few hours later, their path intersected the trail crossing the plateau above the Snake River and leading eastward down the mountain to the Salmon. White Bird immediately got out his field glasses and, looking down the slope toward the river, from here only a thread in the distance, he saw the cattle which had been left there just a few weeks before. "How fat they look!" he exclaimed. "Let's round up some and take them with us!"

This was enticing to all, for only a few miles back Joseph had directed that large amounts of their food be buried in the ground, as the way was hard, the future uncertain—-and speed might be crucial. And White Bird had seen two groups of soldiers leave Howard's forces above Whitebird Creek and head north toward Cottonwood. One of the companies pulled behind it a Gatling gun. The cattle might become a deterrent, so they were left to graze there by the Salmon River.

Just as the long procession moved northward again, scouts galloped up from the rear to report gleefully that Howard and his troops had not yet finished crossing the river. "Good," replied Toohoolhoolzote. "They are many miles and several days behind us, as slowly as they travel, and by the time they face another difficult crossing of that river there below us, we will be across the prairie at the Clearwater."

He was right, for the bands had traveled 25 demanding miles in less than two days; and as they recrossed the Salmon, Howard's troops were still clawing their way up the muddy, treacherous mountain. Two days into this discouraging pursuit a messenger from Whipple reached Howard to report that the Nez Perces had already recrossed the Salmon, and Camas Prairie again was in jeopardy.

Once across the river, the Nez Perce bands moved eastward over the ridge and camped for the night a few miles from Cottonwood. The next morning, as the still-sleepy camp stretched and yawned, Red Spy, a sentry who had been watching Whipple's camp, galloped in among the tipis. "Two white scouts! One I shot. The other went back to Whipple's camp." Rainbow and Five Wounds, followed by a war party, quickly galloped off to investigate.

From Whipple's camp comes the young and eager 2nd Lt. Sevier Raines, with ten troopers and two civilian guides. Lt. Raines rides valiantly but blindly into an ambush set by Rainbow and Five Wounds. Too late he sees the danger, and tries to lead his men in retreat. Six fall from their horses; seven others, the icy talons of terror clutching their hearts, flee up a nearby hill, where they seek refuge among isolated rocks. But they do not perceive that the Indian who steps into the open is a decoy sent out to draw their fire, and they cannot see into a nearby ravine. Seconds later the Nez Perces rush from the head of the ravine. Lt. Raines, ten eager young soldiers, and three stalwart scouts soon lie scattered among grass and flowers and boulders glistening in the early morning light.

Throughout that day, other skirmishes took place. Captain Whipple barricaded his forces at Norton's Ranch, while the Nez Perces did everything possible to prepare the way for moving their families and their huge horse herd across to the Clearwater. The bands threaded their way between Grangeville to the south and Cottonwood to the north, with troops of soldiers and volunteers in both directions. An advance body of young warriors moved out as a protective screen, guarding the band against the troopers. The rest of the warriors, older and more experienced, covered the flanks and the rear.

Kirby, with D. B. Randall's volunteers, waits at Mt. Idaho, still disturbed over the ridiculous fiasco at Looking Glass's village. Two days pass, and now a rider rushes in to report that the Indians, all of them, are close to Cottonwood and moving eastward. "Mount up!" shouts Randall. "Those troops out there may need help!"

Kirby pounds over the rough wagon road close behind Randall and followed by 15 other ranchers and townsmen turned civilian soldiers. Among them is Jethro Martin, the Phelps' neighbor on the adjoining ranch. Soon Randall sees that the horses are being abused and slows the pace, proceeding at a brisk trot. Now Fate enters the scene, and as the volunteers top a slight rise to look down the long slope to Cottonwood they are shocked to see the screen of young warriors, led by Yellow Wolf and drawn up in a forbidding line across the wagon road!

Randall pauses but briefly, then orders a charge through the line and on to Cottonwood! Kirby, his senses keen, feels warning in his spine, the hair rising on his neck, and a tightness gripping his throat. The line of warriors gives way easily—too easily—and the volunteers gallop through. Now, above the rumble of hoofbeats, come the crash of rifle fire, the whine of bullets, and the seventeen are under vicious attack from their rear by the determined Nez Perces who have closed behind them! Swiftly, relentlessly, the warriors thunder toward Randall and his men. Kirby sees that Cottonwood, two or three miles away, is too far—cover must be found!

Kirby leads the way to the scanty protection of a field of scattered boulders. The sun is well up, mid-morning, and the fight goes on for hours, the warriors pressing the attack. Yellow Wolf rides recklessly, his arrows speeding in among the boulders, seeking the hated enemy. But the answering fire is also heavy, and two warriors are wounded; one, the aging Weesculatat, is sinking fast.

Captain Perry, whose replenished troops are with Whipple at Cottonwood, is the senior officer in charge there, and sees the plight of the volunteers who have come to help; they are surrounded, but Perry refuses to send reinforcements. Is the memory of Whitebird Canyon too bitter, too threatening? Kirby sees the futility, the desperate danger of the weak position, and stays low among the rocks, taking no chances. But the circling warriors are fearsome, and Kirby hears, again, that sickening plop which he first heard when Jenny and Phoebe died behind the wagon—a bullet tearing flesh! And Randall falls, soon is dead.

A little later an agonized cry comes from behind a boulder to Kirby's left, and he crawls there, to find Jethro Martin, his skull exploded, his body twitching, soon quiet. Finally one soldier, boldly ignoring Perry, rushes through the circling warriors, risks his own life to help Randall's men. But it is too late, for Randall lies dead, along with Jethro Martin. Two others were wounded.

Joseph has moved the main body of people south, away from the fighting. Weesculatat's wound is bad, and his life is ebbing, soon he is no more. The screening party withdraws, its protective purpose accomplished, and several hundred refugees with their multitude of horses, never stopping, only detouring, move a few miles south before again swinging to the east, then stream across the open prairie. They are unopposed now, but well-armed scouts still guard their line of march. Tonight they will camp by the Clearwater's south fork. What then?

Kirby, for the second time in a short three weeks, rides the trail of death into Mt. Idaho, needing Lucas' strength and support, feeling the loneliness of a 16-year-old in a cruel grownup world. He watches, helpless, without words to comfort as Mrs. Randall in grief leads away the horse bearing her husband's limp, dangling body. Now Kirby forces himself to the house where he knows Olivia and Cornelia Martin are staying, and is relieved when Seth Jones answers the door, his huge bulk screening any view from inside the house. Seth is Olivia's brother, and with one look at the ghastly burden he ties the horse to a hitching post and turns back into the house, closing the door behind him.

Kirby rides quickly away, feeling some comfort in the familiarity and reality of the black gelding, some shame at abandoning his neighbors, but his stunned mind cannot bear the wails of wife and daughter piercing the heavy oak door.

———

Lucas watched in disbelief as the confused forces under General Howard again attempted to cross the Salmon River. More than a week had passed since the start of the inept, prolonged crossing above Whitebird Creek, and this one was no different. Lacking boats, a failed attempt was made with a long rope attached to a crude raft, hoping that the current would carry it across to the far side. Howard at this time knew that the Nez Perces had crossed the prairie and might be threatening the settlements; what could his small detachments and the almost impotent volunteers there do against them? And now he could not even cross the river which the Nez Perces had crossed so easily a few days before!

There was one poor answer: he must retrace his steps some thirty miles back through the mountains, cross again above Whitebird Creek, and return to Grangeville. That took three more days, making eleven long, frustrating days since he left Camas Prairie in pursuit of the hostile bands. He was desperate and humiliated, and his worn-out men were downcast as they straggled into Grangeville, some infantrymen riding in farm wagons provided by the settlers.

Angry criticism and charges of incompetence came from newspapers and the public in general. "What is wrong with our army?" a citizen asked. "How can a few wandering Indians outguess. outrun, and outfight us at every turn? And this man Joseph—how shrewd and masterful! Howard really has his work cut out for him, opposing a leader like that."

Whipple did not talk to Looking Glass, and the peaceful band was given no chance to stay out of the war. This senseless move, into which Howard was pressured by the white settlers around Mt. Idaho, ended the tranquil days of Looking Glass and his people, for they quickly joined the other bands now camped nearby on the Clearwater. And with Looking Glass went some 50 warriors, perhaps 150 older men, women, and children plus a goodly number from Joseph's band. Also Husishusis Kute, the Paloos chieftain, and a number of his people were now part of the consolidated bands.

So Howard's blunder in sending Whipple after Looking Glass had helped to swell the Nez Perce's fighting forces. And, of course, there were more families to be shepherded and protected along the way. The strong-willed Looking Glass had wanted peace, had chastised the other bands for attacking the settlers, and had been placidly settled on the reservation. Now he was humiliated and deeply angered, and would soon become the war leader of the retreating Nez Perces.

# CHAPTER 14

Lucas rode with the volunteers as they followed Howard's bedraggled troops across the prairie toward Grangeville. The grueling round trip of over a hundred miles, crossing the Salmon River twice, and struggling through the rugged mountains had left Lucas irritable and Monty limping. Within an hour the disorganized group had reached Grangeville, and a few minutes later Kirby rode toward Lucas on the black gelding.

"All of the volunteers here, 45 of us, have elected Ed McConville as our Colonel," Kirby explained, and then he reported on the fight near Cottonwood. The news of D. B. Randall's death, and especially Jethro Martin's, added to Lucas' growing depression. Four new graves in the Mt. Idaho cemetery, and two ranch houses vacant at the edge of the prairie. Is there no end to it? And what of Olivia and Cornelia Martin? These thoughts were interrupted as Kirby proceeded.

"I'm not all that taken with McConville. You don't have the details yet, but the attack on Looking Glass's village should never have happened, and I'm ashamed I had a part in it. At least I didn't shoot anybody. All the Nez Perces are now camped at the mouth of Cottonwood Creek, and there are rumors that McConville plans to lead our group against them."

"I'm not sure I want any part of that," replied Lucas. "Maybe a day or two of rest and some decent food will change my mind. For now, let me get cleaned up, then we'll ride to Mt. Idaho. Maybe we can help Olivia and Cornelia."

Olivia Martin was a tall, handsome woman whose almost regal appearance and confident manner were often mistaken for arrogance—some even felt she was intimidating. But such impressions did not last long, for beneath her sometimes abrasive manner she was warm and gracious. Born to a pioneer family who brought her to the prairie, she had eloped with Jethro Martin when she was 16 and he was 18. Olivia had ridden behind her father's saddle at age one and had her own pony when she was three; by age ten she had gentled and broken her first Morgan filly, which accepted the saddle the first day it was placed on her back and on the second day proudly carried Olivia to the lake and back without bucking.

So through the years her horsemanship had become almost legendary, but it was overshadowed by her love for the prairie people. She knew them all, including the children, by their first names, and quickly sought out and welcomed the newcomers. Her understanding of human frailties and her helping hand had brought comfort and solace to every family in the area.

Olivia's daughter Cornelia was a "seven month baby" which, of course, had caused quite a stir among some neighbors, who covertly counted out months on their fingers. Even Olivia's parents stood a little in awe of their strong-minded daughter and the quiet and unapologetic Jethro, to whom the timing of Cornelia's birth was not important and was never mentioned. Cornelia led a happy, though somewhat isolated life on the ranch, riding horseback in rain, sun, or snow to the country school three miles away. Now approaching seventeen, she was a self-assured young woman and an only child. She had inherited her father's medium, compact build rather than her mother's height, and within the last year had reached full maturity. Coming from her mother, and drawing admiration in any crowd, were Cornelia's jet black hair and china blue eyes.

Olivia Martin and Jenny Phelps had become close friends soon after Jenny and Lucas moved from Mt. Idaho to the prairie's edge. They shared all the joys, sorrows, and burdens of their demanding lives on adjoining ranches, raised their children, exchanged recipes, laughed, cried, and confided in each other; and so developed an inexpressible closeness. But while Kirby and Cornelia grew up and played together as children, they had never felt close.

After Olivia opened the big oak door of Seth Jones' house to greet Kirby and Lucas there were no words for quite a while. They had all been together at the Phelps funeral, and in spite of her own deep sorrow over the loss of Jenny and Phoebe, Olivia's warmth and strength had been a source of help to both Kirby and Lucas as she embraced and comforted them. Cornelia had also brought them solace, and Kirby felt a new closeness to her when she held him and cried on his shoulder.

But today Kirby and Lucas felt they must be the comforters, trying to support these two women who had always lived only a ranch away. Kirby looked at Olivia, not entirely understanding her fortitude during this time of deep sorrow. Slanting sunlight filtering through a curtained window caught the blue-black glints on Cornelia's hair and deepened the blue of her eyes. She looks almost placid, thought Kirby, just like her mother. "And we came here thinking to bring comfort and strength to these two, these women like steel under velvet," Kirby thought.

Not many words were found, nor were many needed, and so the talk turned to practical things. "The Indians are all camped on the South Fork," said Lucas. "McConville thinks they are on the run. Howard is being ridiculed and criticized, but he's a tough one, and will soon be ready to move again. Kirby and I still feel some responsibility to help. Lord knows we have reason for that! We're not highly impressed by the volunteers in general, but we'll see what McConville has to suggest."

"Have you been by the ranches?" asked Olivia. "We feel a real need to get back out there. We have a few good horses here, but the rest of them and our cattle, like yours, are scattered, maybe eaten or driven off by the Indians. What do you suggest, Lucas?"

"The prairie looks safe. It's certainly quiet right now, but who knows when a few young braves may come storming back, just to prove a point. Better not go back out there by yourselves yet. Give us a few days, then we'll know if any volunteers will be following the army beyond the South Fork. Whatever happens, we'll get word back to you."

---

Joseph and Whitebird were feeling good about bringing the bands safely to the South Fork. The fighting chiefs were congratulating themselves on their part in this movement, predicting a safe future, and some saying; "They should be wary of us now. We have beaten them on Whitebird Creek and at Cottonwood, and they should have more respect for our strength."

All spent a peaceful night, but the leisurely breakfast the next morning was interrupted when Sarpsis and Wahlitits raced into camp, warning that soldiers were on the nearby mountain. Quickly the women began gathering their children and household items, while Joseph prepared to move the bands again if necessary. But there was no attack, and it was soon discovered that the men up on the mountain were not soldiers, but civilian volunteers again. Ollokot and Five Wounds led other warriors who formed a ring around McConville and his men, badgered them through the night, stole some of their horses, and by that afternoon had driven them back toward Mt. Idaho.

That night, the exultation increased among the leaders of the bands as they added this victory, casual and minor as it was, to the others of recent weeks. "Now we have five bands, said Looking Glass, "and greatly increased strength. We are stronger than ever!"

Though Looking Glass was confident and boastful, others knew that the position on the South Fork was not a good one, and that Howard would not leave them alone. So while some relaxed and feasted, the rest began caching more supplies which were too heavy to carry. Maybe after a while Howard and the rest might forget the whole thing, and they could return to recover the food and beautiful clothing.

They were too optimistic, though, for Howard had recovered from the stinging humiliation of recent failures. Perry and Whipple with their men had rejoined Howard, and he now had over 400 troops and more than 150 scouts, packers, and volunteers. Ad Chapman was still serving as a guide and Howard was headed for the Nez Perce's camp; but not from the west, as the Indians expected. Chapman had led the army across the river and well upstream from the Indian camp, and all were now headed downstream on the east side of the river along a high plateau. The army had nearly blundered again, for they lacked a good fix on the exact location of the camp. It was discovered accidentally by a lone soldier who rode to the edge of the plateau and looked down. There were the Indians, peacefully enjoying themselves on the opposite side of the river far below!

Though the Indians were much too relaxed, there were some alert eyes and ears, and the camp quickly erupted into action. Some would fight, while others moved the camp and the people away from danger. So as Joseph led the retreat, Toohoolhoolzote led a group of warriors across the river and up the slope to attack; and they stopped Howard's men short for a time. Ollokot, Five Wounds, and Rainbow stayed in camp briefly to protect the people, then joined in the fighting. The steep, barren mountainside was home to the Indians, but hellish for the troops. The one spring on the mountain was controlled by the Indians, leaving the whites panting and thirsty. Little Bird, Running Feet, Wetatonmi, and the other women made grueling trips carrying water up the rocky mountainside to the warriors not close to the spring.

Although the troops finally secured the spring, the battle went on through the night, and into the next day; and for a time, the Indian warriors resisted. But their patience was wearing thin, for they did not enjoy prolonged battles. They began squabbling with their leaders, reminding them that they should protect the people, not risk more lives. Gradually, warriors began leaving the fighting line and returning to camp, while others taunted them, and some called them cowards. The fighting chiefs soon sensed that the warriors left on the mountain were too few, so Joseph, who had joined the fight, hurried back to help the people. But it was too late, for the retreating warriors soon rushed down the mountain behind Joseph. The warriors swam their horses across the river and into the camp, where the confused people were frantically trying to escape. In their panic they abandoned everything—tipis, food, clothing, buffalo robes, fires still burning, and the smell of cooking meat in the air. The soldiers swarmed into the camp, looting and pillaging, probing the recently disturbed earth to find the caches from which they removed the lovely buckskin clothing; some studded with hundreds of elk teeth. Later, these items, the precious handiwork of the Nez Perces, would be sold to traders in Lewiston, and would come into the hands of collectors throughout the nation.

When the retreating warriors rushed down the mountainside ahead of the soldiers, they passed Little Bird and Running Feet, who had been carrying water up the mountain; and the two young women frantically followed them back toward camp, finally reaching the river and swimming across with bullets splashing around them. They ran toward the far edge of camp, fearful lest Joseph's tipis be overrun by the white soldiers and worried about Springtime and her baby. Desperately they raced into the tipi to find Springtime hastily gathering her scattered belongings, and Welweyas—the half-man, half-woman—was helping her.

Now standing alone, this tipi at the edge of the campsite with horses still tethered there, attracted the attention of two greedy soldiers. They were pleased with the loot they were carrying, but they burst into the tipi looking for more. Seeing two attractive young women, and an older one with a baby, they dropped their rifles and their loot and started toward the women. Springtime sprang to her feet, and Welweyas grabbed the cradleboard. The two rushed at the soldiers, pushed them aside, and disappeared into the brush.

"Well, that leaves us the two pretty ones," said the taller soldier as he began to remove his trousers. "You take one, and I'll take the other."

"They both look good to me," said the second soldier, "but I like 'em young." And he lunged at Running Feet.

Little Bird and Running Feet still had the knives they usually carried, but the attack upon them was too fast. Rough hands were tearing at their clothing, muscular bodies pushing them down, bearded, lustful faces grinning over them. Little Bird fought furiously, biting the hands, spitting at the face, scratching the neck, seeking a vital target with her knees. She turned her head once, and saw that Running Feet was quickly being overcome. Then suddenly the weight upon her was released and Little Bird looked up to see a sinewy figure in a loincloth, vise-like hands about the throat of her assailant, hurling his body backward; as he fell to the ground Welweyas' warclub crushed his temple and he collapsed in a quivering heap.

Running Feet's attacker had turned at the sound of his companion's agonized scream, and now leaped through the tipi flap and rushed toward a horse tethered nearby. But Welweyas had grabbed an abandoned rifle, and just as the fleeing soldier reached an upright position in the saddle a bullet crashed into his skull and he toppled off the far side of the horse, his half-naked body rolling and tumbling over boulders, his blood turning to red the frothing water as he floated down Cottonwood Creek.

Welweyas helped Little Bird and Running Feet hastily collect and load their belongings on a packhorse; then, after rescuing Springtime and Early Flower from their hiding places, he managed somehow to find other horses and, turning quickly up Cottonwood Creek, the little group followed the retreating bands. The trail was easy to see, and it appeared that the bands were returning to Camas Prairie.

Four warriors died, and six were wounded, but the Nez Perces had killed 15 white men, wounded 25 more, and escaped with most of their horses and some of their belongings; and now over 800 Nez Perces and their still-large horse herd moved rapidly up Cottonwood Creek. What was their best strategy from here on? They did not feel beaten, but the differing opinions whether to fight or to run threatened their cohesiveness.

Howard claimed a victory. The Indians retreated, didn't they? And that claim was strengthened by the report of one of General McDowell's staff who had arrived at the most opportune time in the course of the battle, a stroke of luck which Howard used to launch a vigorous attack just as he saw that the Indians were beginning to waver. A wire praising Howard had been sent to McDowell in San Francisco, and Howard sent another, announcing his great victory and also praising the Indians for their strong resistance. Joseph again was described as a fierce opponent.

What no one at that time said about the battle at the Clearwater was that Howard could have proceeded immediately to end the war. The Indians were on the run, disorganized and confused. But he let them go. After all, it was almost dark, and they could be followed the next day.

---

Kirby and Lucas watched the canyon carefully. "In spite of all they've done to us, I'm having a little trouble not siding with them," Kirby said. "If Whipple hadn't specifically asked me to take this scouting assignment, I'd be headed for home."

"Whoa, back!" whispered Lucas, pointing down the slope. Soon the canyon bottom was filled with a milling stream of horses moving quickly up the creek, and several minutes passed before the last of them were in sight, followed by the young men who were driving them. Then Kirby and Lucas watched incredulously as hundreds of women and children and their pack-horses filed by, obviously harassed, losing no time, but still moving up the stream in orderly fashion. Another 15 minutes passed before Joseph and the vigorous Whitebird came into sight, accompanied by several women leading horses bearing the wounded. A little longer, and the fighting chiefs began to arrive. All were there, followed closely by the young warriors, still wearing only their battle loincloths.

Almost stunned by this great procession, Lucas had difficulty in speaking. " Never have I seen anything quite like this," he said. "I heard McConville say that he and Chapman were going to lead Howard across the river and attack the Indians from the east. That must have happened, and the troops got the upper hand. But look at these people! Fleeing for their lives, but keeping track of everybody! They're not waging a war. They're trying to get away."

"Wait, Dad. Look what's coming!" Kirby exclaimed. And into sight rode a tall, lean man, leading a horse bearing a woman with a baby in a cradle-board. Behind them came two young women, and Kirby saw immediately that one of them was Little Bird, unmistakable even at that distance, for no other horse looked quite like Hawk.

"I've got to talk to her, Dad!" Kirby said, and before Lucas could stop him Kirby had untied the black, leaped into the saddle without touching the stirrup, and plunged down the hillside. He rode toward the girls and had covered half the distance toward them before anyone heard the black's hooves ringing on the rocks.

Welweyas quickly turned in his saddle, raised his rifle and fired a shot that reverberated between the canyon walls. In the second before Lucas hears the shot he sees the Appaloosa leap forward, crashing against Welweyas' horse, Little Bird's hands moving the rifle barrel upward. Kirby feels the whisper of death as Welweyas' bullet passes by, missing by scant inches.

Now the black has reached the creek, and Kirby urges him across toward Little Bird, who has whirled Hawk and ridden to meet Kirby as he rides out of the water. But her upraised hand, palm out, says "Stop!" Behind the hand is a grim, tight-lipped face smeared with dirt, creased with trails of tears. There is no brightness in the eyes, and her hair hangs in dirty strands, the cleft between the breasts exposed by the torn bodice.

Kirby's uncomprehending mind struggles with this apparition. Lacking the trail of events of the last few hours, he stares in confusion at the blood-stained hand with dirty fingernails; and then, slowly, the hand is lowered and the taunt face sags, but there is no smile. Tears brim the dull eyes, and the stern little chin quivers.

"Why are you here?" Little Bird asks, her voice scarcely audible. "It appears we are enemies now. I saved you from Welweyas' gun, but you must go."

"My mother and sister were killed by your people. But I am not fighting you. Are there no good memories left?"

"My memories are dead. I am Yellow Wolf's woman now. He is my husband."

"Do you love him?"

"He is my husband."

"But do you love him?"

"Good-bye."

Lucas watched from the brow of the hill as the lean warrior and the three women rode on up the trail, and saw Kirby slowly climbing the hillside, the black gelding moving listlessly, lacking spirit.

They did not talk for a while after Kirby dismounted, and then both sought to avoid the pain by talking of immediate and practical things.

"They're heading west, back toward the prairie," started Lucas, "and the army is down there on the river. We'd better hurry and find McConville. The Indians may be heading back to the Salmon River."

As Howard and the volunteers knew, the Nez Perce bands were heading west, but they only rode in that direction for a few miles. Then they swung to the north, traversed a high ridge, and moved back down to the river, where they thought they had friends among the Christian Indians; but those people gave no help, so on their own they crossed the river and made camp on the east side. Looking Glass, now exerting his leadership and supported by the rest of the chiefs, convinced everyone that they must seek safety on the Lolo Trail, that dim, tangled, half-discernable pathway clinging to the slopes of a great ridge between the Lochsa and North Forks of the Clearwater. It traversed the slopes around the high peaks and finally dropped into the Bitter Root Valley of Montana.

The Lolo Trail route was agreed upon, but there were still some hopes, vain as they might be, that the troubles would all go away. So the bands waited on the east side of the South Fork. They knew the wait would not be long, but soon indecision and frustration took over, for to the Indians waiting is not a good substitute for action, and they departed for familiar Camas grounds on the Weippe Prairie. Howard got word that they were moving in that direction, but was too slow again, so the bands arrived at Weippe before Howard left the South Fork.

The constant moving, repeated loss of belongings, the deaths of warriors, and the attack on Little Bird and Running Feet were beginning to tell on the women, and their patient and usually placid natures were wearing thin. But the Camas grounds at Weippe were almost as precious to them as the Camas Prairie. Perhaps there could be a pause here while they dug and ate the Camas and nursed their wounded.

There was some feasting and a little rest, but it was all too brief. There was division also, for a few of Looking Glass's people decided that they wanted no more fighting; so they joined a small neutral band camped by the Camas grounds and said a friendly farewell before starting back to Kamiah on the Clearwater. There they were seized by Howard's soldiers and were sent to Ft. Vancouver. Ironically, this little band, numbering 33, "captured" quietly and with no fighting, were the only prisoners Howard took during the entire war. In his official report he listed them as "hostiles."

Now the final decision about where to go became imminent. "We must take the Lolo Trail," urged Looking Glass. "Our war is not with the white people in Montana, and we will be well received there. Then we can find the Crows, and they may even join us in fighting the whites. If that does not work out well, we can go on to the Land of the Grandmother; 'Victoria,' the people up there call her. It is said that she treats her Indian people better than this country's president in Washington. And Sitting Bull has been there since he and Crazy Horse helped to kill Custer and his men just last summer. We will be welcome there!"

Many of the war leaders agreed with Looking Glass; but Joseph and Ollokot said that the Lolo Trail would take them farther away from home. Looking Glass prevailed, and the council finally chose him as the war leader and guide until they got to the Crow country. So now the five bands prepared to move eastward, the people looking at their leaders with hope, and as much confidence as possible. Though the choice looked like the best that could be made, they could not know how how capricious the winds of fate, how self-threatening their own lack of discipline, and how devious and divided the pathways that would forever separate them.

# CHAPTER 15

Lucas and Kirby were camped with several other volunteers between the South Fork and Mt. Idaho, awaiting direction from McConville. Three days had passed since they saw Little Bird disappear up Cottonwood Creek, and the restlessness and uncertainty about them was becoming an irritation.

"It looks like it may take a few days for this thing to get organized," said Lucas. "Some of the volunteers have gone home for awhile, and there are couriers moving back and forth."

"Yes. I was afraid McConville was going to press me into that service," answered Kirby. "I'm glad he didn't, but I've been worried about Olivia and Cornelia. The Indians are all gone from the prairie now. Let's go find out what's happening back home." And, in less than two hours, they were back in Mt. Idaho, had found the women, and set out to inspect the two ranches.

Stimulated by their release from the gloom still hanging over both Mt. Idaho and Grangeville, the four friends alternately walked, trotted, and cantered their horses westward, and now approached the Phelps ranch house. In the hurried departure a few weeks before, the family had forgotten to lock the door, and it now stood slightly ajar. With some concern, Lucas pushed it open, and all were startled as a few squirrels scampered past them to safety. But there was no apparent damage, only dust and cobwebs, and an oppressive feeling of loneliness.

The women went upstairs to inspect the bedrooms, having first looked at the kitchen. Kirby and Lucas looked over the corrals and outlying buildings, all deserted, lacking livestock. Once together again and ready to mount up, they still could find no words, each struggling with the same thoughts, fearing that the very sound of a voice might frighten away those whom they could feel about them. Reluctantly, they departed.

Still silent, their slowly walking horses sensing their riders' feelings, the group approached the Martin ranch house, rejecting the terrible void left by the death of Jethro.

"What's that to the north?" Olivia asked suddenly. "It looks like smoke—over there near the Fenn place."

"It is smoke!" answered Lucas. Quickly then, as they watched, the thin column of smoke rapidly became larger; and soon, even at the distance of several miles, flames could be seen.

"Whatever's burning will be gone by the time we get there," said Kirby; "but we'd better go and see if we can be of help."

But they had traveled only a mile or so when Lucas raised his hand and stopped the group. "Riders, due north of us and coming our way!"

Almost immediately Kirby cried, “It’s Indians! We’d better get on to the Martin ranch!” The spirited horses leaped forward, and in minutes slid to a stop in front of the ranch house.

“Don’t worry about the house!” shouted Olivia. “Lead the horses right into the living room. Otherwise we may lose them. Cornelia, here’s the key to that closet upstairs where your dad kept all the rifles and ammunition; get them!”

Lucas and Kirby rushed to the front windows and were looking to the north when Cornelia returned with the rifles and ammunition, and busied herself loading them all and handing one to each of the others.

“There’s only three of them,” exclaimed Kirby, “but they’re all carrying firebrands. They intend to burn this house too!”

“We’ll burn them first! Get low behind the windows!” ordered Lucas.

In their frenzied haste the three Indian braves had not seen the four whites. Now they paused, more than a rifle shot’s distance from the house, and could be seen talking together. Then suddenly, almost ceremonially, they ran their prancing horses in a circle, guiding them with their knees, holding aloft in one hand a rifle, and in the other a firebrand. Then they all turned toward the house and, three abreast, began their rush. But only halfway to the house, they again stopped, and a strange thing happened. From behind his saddle, each rider untied a red blanket coat and, in spite of the rifle and firebrand, managed to put on the coat. Then they formed three abreast again, and slowly walked their horses toward the house.

The four inside the house crouched low beneath the windowsills and stared in disbelief. A hot July day, and these people put on red wool coats? But they must come no closer, and at Lucas’ signal, four rifles began to fire. The distance was long, and the first bullets fell short, kicking up spurts of dust in front of the riders, some ricocheting from rocks. In startled confusion, the horses reared and squealed. The riders, having found a hornet’s nest, pulled back to reconsider. Then they raced furiously toward the house, firing at windows, not knowing where the defenders were located, their aim made uncertain by carrying the firebrands. They never got near enough to throw the flaming torches, but one came a little too close, and as his riderless horse galloped away, a bright red-coated mound was left on the prairie grass. The other two riders pulled back out of rifle range and turned away. Soon the red coats became dim in the distance, as Sarpsis Ilppilp and Wahlitits headed back to the south fork of the Clearwater.

The Phelps men and the Martin women stayed at the cabin through that night, desperately hoping for reinforcements and fearful of moving back across the prairie toward Grangeville. No one slept or had much interest in food. The fire they had seen did burn a home; and that fire, plus reports made by Lucas and Olivia upon reaching Grangeville, again brought consternation to the prairie. Olivia and Cornelia, not secure about returning to live at their ranch, went back to Seth Jones’ house in Mt. Idaho. Kirby and Lucas, still feeling some responsibility, reported back to McConville.

## CHAPTER 16

Howard finally decided to cross the river and pursue the bands over the Lolo Trail. "They must not escape again, and they will not," thought Howard. He really had no great enthusiasm for the Lolo Trail, remembering that ten years before a man from Iowa had taken a contract to make it passable by wagons. Nothing was done but a little clearing of brush and small trees, and nature in its relentless way had quickly erased any improvements. The rains, the winds, the rockslides, and the quick regrowth of trees and brush returned the so-called road to its primitive state. Now mazes of tangled, fallen timber blocked the way, and both Infantry and Cavalry must wind their way through such obstacles, fearfully traversing the rocky trail along difficult slopes below the craggy peaks.

---

While Howard reconnoitered beside the Clearwater River, the non-treaty bands moved on toward Montana; but there was conflict. Joseph felt they should capitalize on their successes and again confuse Howard in the Salmon River Mountains. But he again stood alone among the chiefs, the only one who still talked of a return to his homeland. Yes, he could have taken his people and gone, and a few did go back on their own. But knowing that the people on Camas Prairie would gladly hang him, he quit trying to convince anyone. The bands moved steadily up the long slope toward Lolo Pass..

Many of the people had traveled this route before. Rainbow and Five Wounds having come westward on it just a few weeks past. But those had been trips filled with eager anticipation of being with friends and family again. Now they were all part of a procession that stretched for miles, each family shepherding it's own packhorses and the women doing most of the work while the men urged them on and guarded the rear. And this time there was fear—fear of those behind them, and fear of the future.

Within two days the entire procession was deep within the forest maze, often struggling through great overgrown groves too large to circle.

Often riding the horses was too hazardous, and Joseph's family led their saddle horses as well as those laden with packs. Little Bird leads Hawk, the two packhorses trailing behind. "Where is Yellow Wolf now?" she wonders. Perhaps with the rear guard, only worrying about himself and his one horse. Patiently, Little Bird crawls under a fallen log that is too high to climb over, passes the reins across the top of the log, and encourages Hawk to jump. He makes it, and the first pack horse follows, but the second is less nimble, and less courageous, and falters while jumping, falls to one side, and is impaled on the sword-like shaft of a broken limb. Groaning in agony, the horse lunges, enlarging the wound, the weather hardened, jagged limb rupturing blood vessels. Little Bird watches in horror, and tries to help, but it is too late, and the thrashing horse's hot blood spurts out with his final throes. Nothing to do but transfer the packs to another horse and move on.

Up and down the procession others struggle in similar ways, and having cleared the forest they move painfully up the narrow trail, now only a dim mark across a rockslide. Joseph is somewhere up ahead as Springtime rides her mare along the treacherous trail. She fears for the baby, has handed her to Welweyas, who has dismounted and is walking, carrying the cradle-board.

The trail bends sharply into a deep ravine and back out around a sharp, rocky point. Suddenly there is movement in the talus beneath the mare's feet, and she begins to slide, loses her footing, and falls to her left side. Springtime clutches desperately at a small dead tree, and is dragged from the saddle. But the mare is gone. Springtime and Welweyas watch, suffering, as the little horse rolls and tumbles, is finally submerged in the growing rockslide and disappears with it over the bluff; then, shaken and trembling, they pick their way nervously across the slide and hurry to catch up with the rest of the band, while Early Flower continues to sleep peacefully.

Well into this tortuous journey, the pangs of hunger begin to take their toll on both people and animals. At night, memories of the great caches of food left behind them invade the people's minds. They stretch their meager stores and hunt for berries and edible roots, even grass and tender tree bark. Springtime notices that the fullness is gone from her breasts, and her concern for her baby's life increases each day. So, much as they dislike killing horses, they must eat some of them.

Though only nine days in length, the rigors of the struggle through the tangled trees and jumbled rocks of the Lolo Trail were felt by all within the bands. Joseph, especially, showed the stresses on his bronzed face, his eyes sometimes drooping with fatigue. Even Ebenezer limped a little, favoring one leg which had been twisted when he stepped between two logs. And the staunch Heyoom, usually well controlled and stoic, also showed the strain. Now she was carrying the cradleboard containing little Early Flower, giving Springtime a chance to get used to the new horse Joseph selected for her, a proud little roan gelding who handled the trail well. But Springtime was still uneasy after her experience in the rockslide, and while she appreciated the gelding, she felt that he would never replace the nimble-footed mare now lying beneath tons of rocks at the bottom of the Lochsa River.

While the Nez Perces rode southward up the Bitter Root valley, a man whom the Nez Perces had never heard of, Colonel John Gibbon, with a modest force of soldiers, was moving toward them from the eastern side of the great mountains. When he passed through Missoula, he would pick up other men, for a total of no more than 150 soldiers and about twenty officers.

Howard and his forces were just starting from the western end of the

Lolo Trail. Most of the volunteers from the Camas Prairie country and eastern Washington had gone home, having gained very little personal satisfaction and even less appreciation from the army. Ad Chapman still remained as interpreter for Howard, while Lucas and Kirby, somewhat more appreciated by Captain Trimble, decided to stay with the army for awhile. They had not been back to their ranch again, nor had there been any word from Olivia. But the prairie was certainly free from Indians now, and they had great faith in Olivia's ability to watch over both ranches in their absence.

"It would be good to salvage some kind of reputation for the volunteers," Lucas said hopefully as they began the ride up the western end of the Lolo Trail. "Besides, it's obvious that Howard and his forces need some seasoned minds to help support them."

"I'm with you," said Kirby, who had recently told Lucas most of the story of his romance with Little Bird. "It looks like things are over between me and Little Bird. She says she is Yellow Wolf's woman now."

The day Kirby told Lucas about Little Bird, there had been a strange silence, and Lucas' only reply had been, "It looks like you and I are both destined to become involved with heathen women." Kirby had started to ask what he meant, but Lucas quickly turned the conversation to something else.

For the next nine days Lucas and Kirby fought, scrambled, and struggled as the two-mile long column battled its way over the miserable trail. In spite of the help of axmen clearing brush they had many of the same troubles experienced by the Nez Perces just ten days before. What they didn't know was that additional army units were on the alert across the nation, ready to attack the Nez Perces on their own or to join Howard's forces.

## CHAPTER 17

"It's time we find out what happened to our livestock, and clean up those dirty ranch houses," Olivia remarked to Cornelia. "I've had word through one of the returning volunteers that Lucas and Kirby will not be back for awhile."

In characteristic fashion, Olivia was soon prepared and within 24 hours, and she and Cornelia were headed for the ranches, accompanied by two strong Jones-Martin cousins. "We don't need protection, but we sure need help in getting things back in shape," she said to Cornelia, and within two hours the buckboard rattled up in front of the Phelps ranch house. "We'll start here, clean up this place and then lock it up until Kirby and Lucas return," Olivia said. For the next two days she drove herself, Cornelia, and the two young men, setting that place straight. They found some of the Phelps' scattered cattle, brought two bulls and a weak-looking young calf back to the corral, and left one of the young men there to tend them.

In the excitement of protecting the Martin ranch from Sarpsis Ilppilp and his companions and worrying through the night that followed, Olivia had not made a thorough search of her own house. Now, as her young helper tidied up the corrals, mended broken fences, and rode off to look for more stray cattle, Olivia and Cornelia started cleaning up the big ranch house. But a shock awaited them as they opened the pantry door, for there, crouching defensively in the corner among remnants of food was a scrawny Indian boy, perhaps eight years old. He clutched a knife, his lean face grim and fearful. He tensed as if to jump, and Olivia slammed the door in his face.

"Well! What do we do now?" asked Cornelia, more ruffled than her implacable mother. "We leave him right there until our hired ranch hand returns," said the stern-faced Olivia. "This is a job with which we need help." She then calmly locked the door.

When Olivia and the ranch hand reopened the door, the boy was asleep. The knife had fallen from his relaxed hand and was quietly removed. But he was at once awake, again tense and ready to fight, in spite of his obviously weakened condition.

"Cornelia, get some food," commanded Olivia. "I'd just as soon let him starve, but I can't do that." A glass of water, bread and warm soup were placed on the floor in front of the boy. He ignored it, so they locked the door again and walked away, returning an hour later to find the food gone, and the boy looking less combative.

"Somehow he must have gotten lost from his family when they moved across the prairie," said Cornelia. "I suppose by the time he's eaten a couple of times he'll run away. We can't expect any gratitude."

That didn't happen. The boy ate ravenously four times a day and showed no signs of leaving. Then one morning he sat up to the table, and when Olivia, who really didn't want him there, asked if he wanted bacon, it was apparent that he understood her.

"Do you have a name?" asked Cornelia, wondering why she should care. He nodded his head. "Can you tell us what it is?"

"Izhkumzizlakik."

"Ish—-What?!"

"Izh-kum-ziz-la-kik. Means Picket-Pin."

"Picket-Pin? Like a gopher?"

Another nod.

"We'll stick with Gopher."

"Where did you learn English?" asked Olivia.

"Mother was at Lapwai mission school."

"Do you know how to find your family?"

"No. Might be at Lapwai. Been there before."

"This brat is part of the bunch that killed Jethro, Jenny, and Phoebe," Olivia thought. "Why not just let him go, and be rid of him?" Then she heard herself saying, "You're pretty small to make that trip alone. Better wait awhile." There was no reply, so the decision seemed to be made, at least for now. But what to do with an Indian boy who seemed to be increasingly content?

# CHAPTER 18

Across Camas Prairie life became quiet, though certainly not peaceful, for there was still mourning, and it was felt by everyone in this close-knit community. The terrible losses of loved ones had left permanent gaps in extended families and their close neighbors, and all shared mutual comfort and solace, for among such people the bonds of love are as strong as the bonds of blood.

Olivia and Cornelia Martin, drawing support from all around them, coped in their own stoic, private ways, the release of tears coming only when they were alone at Seth Jones' house. But both the mourning and the tears must be put in the past, and the healing of long, hard days at work might help.

"It won't become any easier, Cornelia, and we need to move back home right away," Olivia said. "The Indians are gone for good, so there's no danger there. Yesterday I got this short letter from Lucas, brought by a returning volunteer. He and Kirby are on their way over the Lolo Trail with General Howard. Lucas goes on to say that both he and Kirby are surviving well, but getting more restless every day with the inaction of the volunteers."

"Who knows how long that will go on?" Cornelia asked. "We're here and there's a lot to do, so let's gather all our stuff and move back out to the ranch this week. Why don't we get a Jones boy or two to help us, and stay at the Phelps place for awhile?"

"Good idea. A vacant house and buildings just ask for trouble. Besides, these cool nights lately say fall is near, and we must get ready for winter."

So the work began the next morning with the gathering and packing of everything to be taken. Not surprisingly at this point, Gopher was their best helper, seemingly tireless and quickly understanding what needed to be done. Olivia still harbored resentment, even hatred, for him, but now an irritating worry came into her mind as she watched him, for his presence around Mt. Idaho had not been well accepted. Comments had come to her about "that Indian brat," and "having bad seed around town," and so on. And she had agreed with all of them. Some of Olivia's best friends were resentful, and two or three were open enough to talk to her personally. But she was shocked to hear herself respond, "How would you like one of your boys to be treated if he were lost?" Then she quickly tried to retreat into her comfortable shell of disdain and self-righteousness.

It only took one day to accumulate personal belongings and the few horses they had in Mt. Idaho. Then they trailed across the prairie, the confident Gopher on the spry Morgan gelding, riding proudly beside the Jones boys, one of whom was driving the buckboard. Olivia and Cornelia were out ahead—let the rest of them eat the dust! As they passed the first ranch west of Grangeville, Morty Martin joined them and rode along to help them get settled. The Joneses readily accepted Olivia's invitation to spend the night, but for her and Cornelia it was more than neighborliness. Neither was yet ready to spend the first night alone in the big empty house. Gopher settled quickly and comfortably into a little room upstairs with a window looking out across the prairie.

The stimulation of hard work, and its soothing effect on mind and body was good for the two women. After Olivia was satisfied with the conditions at her place she led the way to the Phelps ranch house. By that evening the Phelps house was clean and Olivia was ready to go back to her own home. "I'd like you fellows to stay here a week or so, maybe longer, depending on what we hear from Lucas. We'll take Gopher and go on back to our own house," she told the men.

Cornelia heard her and thought, "She's still not ready to be alone, and neither am I. But we must both be getting soft, to let this kid worm his way into our lives. He's wise beyond his years, and no wonder. Everybody and everything he knew were lost to him when his family rode across the prairie away from him. Probably didn't even know he was gone till they camped that night; then it was too late to come back."

In the days that followed, the two women drove themselves, seeking through exhaustion an escape from the memory of Seth Jones saying, "There's a body on the horse out there." And both went to bed at night nursing their inborn hatred of Indians, including Gopher.

Then two totally unrelated things began to happen. Olivia could not bear sleeping in the room where she and Jethro spent so many nights, sharing each other's thoughts and bodies. So she and Cornelia, also needing comfort, moved into a room upstairs. From their doorway they could see the door to Gopher's room. Each night after supper, perhaps following an hour or two around the fire, they all climbed the stairs together, and Gopher would look up at them, his eyes like deep pools beneath the glistening black hair which Olivia had bobbed just above his eyebrows. Sometimes tears would glisten in his eyes, and always he would solemnly reach out to touch Olivia or Cornelia, sometimes both, before turning into his room.

Slowly, though still resisting, the two women began to realize that this ebullient little spirit, clinging to the Morgan like a burr as he rode across the prairie with them, eating his meals ravenously, and walking up the stairs with them each night, had become a kind of healing presence.

The second occurrence took place as it did every year, soundlessly, unnoticed by the two women as they rode back and forth between the ranches. Then one evening the sun bathed the mountainside behind the ranch, and Olivia suddenly exclaimed, "Cornelia! The trees!" Their eyes drank in the thing Jethro had loved the most about the fall; for the Tamaracks, not in clumps but as scattered, individual trees, slashed through the deep green of the firs and pines around them, their vivid yellow needles turned orange by the evening light. Each tree blazed like the flame of an immense taper.

"How could we miss it? How did it all happen without us seeing it?" Cornelia marveled. "Dad never missed it, from the day the Tamaracks first showed yellow green until they were pure gold, like they are now." Mother and daughter rode back to the ranch house in silence, sensing and sharing the feeling of peace which had come over both of them. "We've all lost so much," thought Olivia, "but the seasons turn, the cycle of life goes on, and it carries us along."

---

"School starts next week," Olivia said as she started the breakfast dishes, having sent Gopher out to the spring for a bucket of water. "You'd better get together the things you'll need. I've spoken to Miss Henley about Gopher starting school. She's a little dubious, but is willing to give it a try. We'd better ride into town and see if we can find him some proper clothes."

Olivia spoke confidently but was not comfortable, realizing her own capitulation and regarding it as a sign of weakness. "I'll be the oldest student there this year," Cornelia responded. "We know the Cone family will have a first-grader in school, and there are three other real young ones. Gopher's got a long way to go, knowing so little English. Maybe I can help Miss Henley teach him."

The one general store in Mt. Idaho had a few things which Gopher could wear, but the shoppers became strangely silent as the Martin women walked in with the little Nez Perce boy. Most of the people in the store were friends, or at least acquaintances, and all looked hostile. As Olivia removed the money from her purse to pay for her purchases, she glanced up at the clerk, a long-time friend of her family. Olivia started to smile, but in return received only a cold stare and a formal, clipped "Thank you."

"Eliza Randall, what's the matter with you?" demanded Olivia. "And all you other people? I've been in and out of here for years and I've been a good customer! All of you know me and my family!"

"Don't bring that dirty little Indian in here again," responded Eliza, her eyes like slits and her hands trembling. She threw Olivia's change on the counter and turned away.

In consternation and frustrated anger, the two women led Gopher out of the store, untied their horses from the hitching rack, and rode silently out of town, hoping Gopher had not understood the angry exchange.

It was a sober and unhappy Saturday night at the ranch house. Gopher had been quiet and uneasy on their return from town, and had finally walked to the corral, caught the little Morgan, and gone for a ride. There was nothing helpful that Olivia and Cornelia could say to each other, so upon Gopher's return they quietly went to bed, feeling the same little tug at their hearts when Gopher touched their hands and disappeared into his room. Olivia now knew that she must abandon her prejudice and support Gopher. Besides, the women of the area were against her and she loved a good fight.

They couldn't leave Gopher home alone on Sunday, and didn't want to face the coldness at church, so all stayed at the ranch. Olivia tried to dispel the gloom by cooking a big dinner and sending Gopher to the Phelps place to invite the Jones boys over. The trip to town was not mentioned during that day, and again they accompanied Gopher up the stairs and went to bed with Cornelia saying, "Well, I think Miss Henley has a good attitude, and kids are kids—things will go well at school tomorrow."

With a minimal understanding of what school was all about, Gopher rode happily beside Cornelia as they headed east to the one-room school house. Olivia spent the day doing dishes and tidying the house, occasionally wondering how school was going.

Cornelia and Gopher trotted down the lane at about the right time, considering the three-mile ride from school, and took care of the horses. They were soon through the kitchen door, Gopher speaking occasionally in his difficult English, but Cornelia quieter than usual throughout the evening. When they retired to their bedroom Olivia started to question her but thought better of it. "She's trying hard to help Gopher get used to school, and there's bound to be problems. Best to let her work them out."

Breakfast was an unusually silent affair, and Olivia still asked no questions. Gopher and Cornelia again departed for school. The morning chores finished, Olivia had just sat down on the back porch for a rest when she heard horses coming down the lane. Cornelia and Gopher rode by the house, and Olivia watched as they unsaddled the horses, put them in the corral, and came toward her. Gopher looked puzzled, but Cornelia was angry and disappeared into the house without a word. Olivia followed her upstairs to their room, where she found Cornelia in tears.

"Tell me!"

"Only the three of us, only Miss Henley, Gopher, and I were there! Not another student!"

"But why? Those kids all need to be in school! And you offered to help with Gopher, didn't you?"

"Yes. But Miss Henley said that last night a group of parents came to her house and said that if that sneaky Indian brat stays, their kids go."

"Well, we'll see about that!" retorted Olivia, her eyes grim and her chin set in the determined way that Jethro always called her "stubborn" look. "Dick Cone is on the school board, and he only lives three miles away. Some of our other relatives are also on that board. I'll talk to each of them today!" And she was off across the prairie, giving the sleek mare her head, until she reached Dick Cone's house.

Dick was mildly sympathetic and tried to be understanding, but seemed a little evasive. "Olivia, think about the last couple of months. You've suffered a loss as great as anyone, and more than most. And look at your neighbors and some of your relatives, the D. B. Randall family, for example.

And that family that got burned out over by Mr. Fenn's. Sure, the boy lives at your home, and you and Cornelia have come to understand him, but nobody else around here has had that kind of experience. They judge the Indians by their actions, which you, of all people, should understand. Maybe you should talk to other members of the school board, though I'm not sure an order from the board would change many minds."

So Olivia made the rounds, with about the same results from all members of the board. Frustrated and despondent, she rode back toward the ranch from the last interview. "Perhaps if Gopher hadn't come to us I'd feel the same way," she thought. "In fact, for a long time I did feel the same way—that there really aren't any good Indians. Everybody ridicules, don't want to believe that this war started because a young Indian went hunting for the white man who killed his father. And Jethro said once that he knew of some pretty cruel treatment of the Indians down on the Salmon River. Well, I can't change all that, can't have any effect on it now, but the children have to be in school, and it's obvious that they won't be as long as Gopher is there."

So by nightfall Olivia had talked to Miss Henley, who had then informed all the parents she could find, and told the students the next day at school; within a week all were back in classes. Cornelia stayed home for a couple of days, bitter and resentful, but then resumed her attendance. Gopher was puzzled, sensing the women's confusion. He watched Cornelia come and go and stayed out of Olivia's way, not knowing what she was thinking. There weren't enough ways to keep a young boy busy, and Olivia's orderly mind rebelled at his inactivity and her inability to see how it might change.

"I'll teach him myself," she finally told Cornelia as she returned home from school one afternoon. "He may be here quite awhile. We may not ever want him to leave. And every child needs an education. You can help too, Cornelia. You've been in that school for ten years, and you're helping Miss Henley with the first graders. She can't teach you much more, so even if you stay home sometimes it won't matter. And we can certainly help Gopher."

So they got out the old primers, along with the simple teaching aides they had used around the house, and Cornelia brought home from school the alphabet written on little cards.

"It seemed so simple at first!" wailed Cornelia late one afternoon, after the daily session with Gopher had brought mainly blank stares and they had finally sent him out to play. "I never had this kind of trouble learning the ABCs and how to recognize simple words, but I'm starting to see his problem. The few English words someone taught him, or that he picked up on his own, are all about the names of people and places and animals or birds or fish, familiar things. Maybe we should just look for a way to let him go back to the wilds, or take him to his own people."

"A little more patience would be helpful at this time," said Olivia, the patronizing tone in her voice not being missed by Cornelia. "Let's keep trying. Miss Henley felt bad about what happened at school, and would like to help.

Let's see what suggestions she has."

Miss Henley was understanding, and she came to the ranch house and sat down with Olivia and Cornelia, all three looking for ways to bridge the broad gaps between two different worlds, and two languages with absolutely no similarities.

"Between English and German," started Miss Henley, "or between English and Spanish, or even French, you find a lot of similarities, words with the same roots and derivatives, often easy to make the connections. Not so with Nez Perce, or any other Indian language, to the best of my knowledge. He knows a few words of English now, but probably has never seen anything written, since his people have no written language except for a few scriptures translated into Nez Perce. So every new word he hears will be completely new, and will have to mean something in his own experience. He's smart and quick, and with a little teaching and a lot of listening, he'll speak English quite well in a few months. But of course he won't be learning spelling and grammar, just words and their usage to the extent that he hears you folks speak correctly.

"Obviously, we have to keep it simple, but I suspect he'll surprise us all. Let's hold the alphabet and the spelling and the grammar for awhile. But we won't wait too long, because if he gets comfortable with his ability to talk and sees no reason to read or write, he'll never want to do it."

So they began making charts, big pieces of paper with columns to show the animal or the color or the number in the first column, the English name in the second, and space for the Nez Perce word in the third.

For the numbers, the left column showed hands, each with fingers held up from one to five, the second column showing the numerals. For animals or other common things there were pictures in the left hand column and the English name in the second. For the colors, Cornelia cut out colored squares for the left hand column, and wrote the name of the color in the second.

"Now," said Olivia, "he can easily see what our word for each thing looks like in writing, and we'll ask him to repeat it in Nez Perce." Gopher caught on very quickly, and by the second lesson Cornelia had only to start the numbers with one finger, then Gopher went through it himself, naming his five fingers: naqs, lepit, metaat, pilept, paxaat.

Filling in the Nez Perce words, the third column was puzzling, for no one had seen them in writing. So it was all phonetic, and they wrote what they heard Gopher say, making him repeat each word several times.

Gopher giggled when he looked at the pictures of animals, and by the third day was naming each one in both English and Nez Perce:

Grizzly Bear - hahats; Horse - sikem; Coyote - iceyeye; Wolf - himin; Bull - chuslim; Owl - palhockin; Raven - oohqoh; Bird - payopayo; Mountain Sheep- heh-yets.

For the colors, Gopher quickly interpreted:

White- hihhih; Yellow - maqsmaqs; Red - ilppilp; Black - cimux cimuy;

Blue - yosyos.

More charts were made, with more names of common things, and Gopher learned them all quickly. Then they began concentrating on verbs, never failing to use the right word and demonstrate the action as they went about daily tasks. He ate that up too, and soon was repeating the English word for the things he did.

"We're delighted!" exclaimed Olivia at their next visit with Miss Henley. "He's learning everything we give him, and almost demanding more. It seems too easy."

"I agree; it does seem easy," returned Miss Henley. "But I'm not at all surprised. He's so bright; and it's a great satisfaction to him to talk to those around him. And he'll go on this way for a long time, even without any more help from you. But how far will this get him? He's in the white man's world now, and may never go back to his own. We can't let him drift. We must teach him to read and write."

And so began the careful, planned process. They took him slowly, sounding out each letter for him, and showing how the letters and syllables make the word. And they all worked diligently at this for a week, but with little success. Then they tried a second week, and a third, but the results were no better.

"He just doesn't get it," sighed Olivia, puzzled and irritated at her lack of progress with this boy.

"It's probably not that he doesn't get it, it must be that he sees no value in reading and writing, Miss Henley said. "After all, the people he's lived with have no need for it, so he feels no need; and he won't, until he sees what it can do for him."

"Well, we're stressing him, and ourselves too," said Cornelia. "Maybe we'd better back off for awhile, and be thankful for the progress we've made."

"All right, but I'm not giving up," answered Olivia. "This little Indian can't drift along forever."

So they all relaxed and, as the days passed, realized that normal communication with Gopher was becoming easier all the time. Cornelia went back to school on a regular basis, and helped Miss Henley with the younger children. Gopher's sprightly personality and calm temperament, even his very presence, eased some of Olivia's aching loneliness. "In his own small way," she thought, "he's like having a man around the place. I'm glad he's here, and maybe I'm the one who's drifting. He's so eager, wanting to please, doing the chores, never complaining. Right or wrong, his education can wait for awhile."

## CHAPTER 19

The Nez Perce bands rode up the Bitter Root Valley, relishing the familiar territory, still anticipating a welcome by the whites in the valley and their friends among other tribes. Soon they were joined by some old Idaho friends who had been scouting on the Yellowstone with Colonel Miles. They brought a suggestion made by Eagle From The Light, a Nez Perce chieftain who had tired of things in Idaho and had settled among the Flatheads. He urged the leaders of the bands to change direction, move northward through the Flathead reservation, and join Sitting Bull in Canada.

Looking Glass, who only recently had suggested the same route, now squelched the idea, his talk of the fine buffalo hunting over on the Yellowstone still holding appeal for the hunters among the bands. Joseph was noncommittal, almost disinterested. "We are moving away from our homeland, and I see no chance of going back."

The daily marches were short, the grass was tall, the familiar streams glistened in the sunlight, and in some places there were Camas bulbs to be had for the digging. Looking Glass still reveled in his leadership, like a contented pussycat, humoring the people, feeling they deserved a rest. So they laid over for a day, and the neglected women's lodge was again erected outside the camp. As Heyoom made her way toward the old tipi, one of the few remaining from the Clearwater battle, her mind, like her body, was not at ease. Had an entire moon really passed since Horseshoe Bend? The confusion, the continual moving, the shortness of food; and again the thought, "Why is Little Bird not here with me? That woman down at the mission told me what it means to miss these bleeding days, and it looks like Little Bird has now missed two."

The whites in the Bitter Root Valley did not welcome the bands with open arms, saying instead, "We've all heard the stories of Nez Perce depredations in Idaho and the running battles which have led them to our valley. And also there are the Flatheads, who are said to be restive; might they not be willing to join with the Nez Perces, and recruit other tribes as well? Together they could wipe us all out!"

Humiliated by their fears, and frustrated by their weakness, some of the white men joined volunteer groups. Many of the merchants, in spite of general criticism, sold food, ammunition, new canvas and buffalo hides for tipi covers, and provisions of all kinds to the Nez Perces, who were often able to pay in gold. Looking Glass and the other leaders made every attempt to travel peaceably and bother no one, but some of the young men did obtain whiskey, and there were attacks, some thievery, and some burning of homes.

In several cases Looking Glass forced the perpetrators to make amends by paying in horses.

And there were those among the moving bands who did not share the relaxation, the sense of well-being, the belief that the war, and Howard, were far behind them. And some, especially those who had favored going directly north into Canada, worried and looked over their shoulders at night and railed against Looking Glass. Their fears were reinforced and spread to others as they camped one night not far short of the Sacred Medicine Tree. One warrior. a real believer, said to another, "We will see it tomorrow. My father, and his father before him, talked of this tree. And it was there long before their time. And that great mountain sheep horn stuck in the tree, higher than a man can reach—it gives the tree a very strong power. Was there ever a mountain sheep that stood that tall or could leap that high? Perhaps the tree will have a message for us this year."

These remarks, and the strong feeling of spiritual strength and power which surrounded this great Ponderosa Pine worked their spell on the people. Some, including Looking Glass, laughed and ridiculed, but Joseph was caught up in the mystique of it all, for he had seen the medicine tree several times; and his father, old Teukakis, had told him about it. And when near the tree, Joseph had sensed some strange force, almost a loving encirclement, disturbing but comforting, entering into his being, guiding his thoughts.

"Such guidance is needed," he mused. "I have no influence with Looking Glass, and little, it seems, with others. But I must seek greater strength for the things that are expected of me, and perhaps the spirit of the tree can help."

So on this late August night with the wrinkled crest of the Continental Divide looming a few miles to the south, Joseph sits quietly as the campfires turn to embers and the people seek the buffalo robes. Then he leaves the camp, threading his way through the slender Lodgepole Pines, the soft light of the summer moon filtering through the lacy needles and playing capriciously among the streamers of mist rising from the stream.

It is the kind of night and the familiar sensations that Joseph loves—an open glade in full moonlight, where the heat absorbed from the afternoon sun still radiates gently around his legs; with the little hollows shaded by trees and now capturing the cooler evening air as it seeks a lower level. Pervading it all are the mixed scents of pinegum vaporized by the sun and now perfuming the forest, the spice of crushed mint leaves, and the delicate bouquet of wild roses.

Joseph moves on through this night, so much like many others throughout his life, his mind rapidly clearing, relieved of the contentions and concerns of those in the camp, receptive to what he may find ahead; seeing in his mind the Medicine Tree. In a few minutes he reaches the foot of a gently rising meadow, and from there he can see the tree's entire 200-foot height; the rusty bark now dim but reflecting some of the moon's light, the massive trunk with its deep green branches etched sharply against the pale sky and scattered stars.

The moon rests on the crest of the mountain behind Joseph, and its level rays no longer touch the top of the Medicine Tree. Joseph expects the stars to now shine more brightly and the tree to become only a black silhouette. But the stars begin to gleam with a strange intensity, and the tree does not darken. Rather, it begins to glow softly, the brightening cinnamon-brown bark reflecting gold, the graceful plumes of long needles glistening. And around the tree and beginning to engulf Joseph is the same aura of warmth, the same comforting, restful peace that has come to him only once before, on the summit of the mountain above Whitebird Canyon.

"You are troubled, Joseph, and it is time that we talked together again. This tree has a spirit of its own, and in a way I am part of that spirit, as are you and others who are willing to listen."

Joseph feels no apprehension, no fear, only acceptance and joy at the voice of his Guardian Spirit; and he responds, "Your voice and your presence are encouraging, Wyakin, for as the distance from our homeland becomes greater I feel a loss of power, and less ability to look into the future that I may guide my people well. I question the wisdom of the war leaders, and fear for my people. Why are they so willing to follow Looking Glass and the others?"

"It is because they are afraid, Joseph. Their lives of safe, familiar places and predictable patterns have changed. Now there is fear, even the threat of hunger; and danger, at least from the white men behind them. In such times people are always afraid, and will follow the leader who shows the most confidence and seems most likely to provide security."

"Is there no security ahead, or no possibility of going back to our homeland?"

"Joseph, these few little bands are among the last who are trying to remain free. This same Howard who is pursuing you was in the hot deserts far to the south just a few years ago, where he helped to bring Cochise, the great Apache chief, onto a reservation, where he soon died. He and Geronimo, who still rages through the bleak deserts fighting the white man, will always be remembered as the last of the free Apaches. At one time, long ago, they were among the most peaceful of the tribes, but the white men joined with other tribes, and paid them to fight the Apaches, until they retreated to the wildest land and became fierce and warlike and offensive, and known as the most ferocious."

"As the white man moved from the great eastern ocean toward the west, he swept all the tribes off their land, forcing them onto reservations, sending many to Eikish Pah, The Hot Place, far to the south of here. But when the reservations look good to the white settlers, they move in and take the land. Their leaders cannot, or will not, do anything about it. If the Indian makes trouble, his food, or his money, his settlements, or other necessities, are taken away.

"Almost all of your people in this great land, this huge land, have become dependent. It all started with whiskey and guns, for the red man soon became fond of the whiskey, and once he had guns, he could only obtain bullets from the white man. Many of the more compliant chiefs, including some of yours now on the reservation, were given nice homes and receive money every moon from the white man. Then they are answerable to the white man and are of less value to their people."

"Yes, I have seen all of this happen," Joseph said. "But why could we not share the land with the white man? We were willing to do that in the Wallowa country, and the land was marked off and divided. Mistakes were made, the boundaries were wrong, and the white man was not willing to correct them. Why can we not share?"

"Sharing is not the white man's way. He wants it all. He wants a piece of paper that says it is his. It has always been that way."

"But some of the white leaders did seem to understand, and tried to help us in the Wallowa," Joseph said. "Are their voices not heard?"

"Sometimes they are heard, and a few listen, but they are drowned out by the many. Your own reservation, when it was first marked off and was much larger, was invaded by gold miners and ranchers and others; and a few spoke out against it, but towns like Lewiston were established and roads built, and nothing was done."

"Will any of us ever be free again?"

"Not in the way your people think of freedom, for your way of life in which you hunt and fish and gather food from the trees and from the ground requires that you travel freely over large amounts of land. That kind of life is gone and will never return. Though some reservations are quite large, most of them will become smaller. The white man will offer the Indians money for the best parts of their reservations, and most of the Indians will lack the wisdom to see that the money will soon be gone; and they will be left with small, poor reservations and be dependent on the white man."

"Then what are we to do, Wyakin? How can we survive and be happy under these conditions? And what of those people who have already been pushed onto small reservations, or to Eikish Pah?"

"Many of them are only existing, but are not happy and never will be. Many others have long since perished, for their tribes did not survive the white man's wars and the loss of their lands; and their spirits were broken. But for the long, dim future, only those people who will listen to wise leaders can learn how to live in happiness without large amounts of land, or without hunting and fishing. Only those will overcome dependence on the white man. These, of course are the future generations, who must learn to live in this land which is now controlled by the white man—for that will not change. Few of the leaders living today will find such wisdom; their wounds are too deep. Do you understand what I am saying, Joseph?"

"My mind hears and understands, but my heart does not accept, for the wounds you mention are indeed deep. And you seem to be saying that the Indian must give up everything and still be willing to learn to live the white man's way. I do not feel strong enough or wise enough to do that. I sense that our bands are in great danger, though we are told that Howard and his troops are far behind us. I fear our leaders are not careful enough. We are camped tonight just down this valley, relaxed without sentries."

"The danger which you sense is close to you; but it is not Howard, for he is still far away. It is another fighting force, and you must do all you can to warn your people. Go quickly Joseph, and take with you that part of my spirit which will be helpful."

Now the valley was in complete darkness. The moon was far below the crest of the Bitter Roots to the west; stars shown in their normal intensity; and the medicine tree, as it should be at this hour, was a dark silhouette against the midnight sky. Joseph, now lonely and apprehensive, turned and started back down the valley toward the sleeping camp, where he found his own tipi and sought solace against Heyoom's warm body beneath the soft buffalo robe.

During the few remaining hours of the night Joseph slept lightly, trying to find contentment in the familiar warm tipi and the rhythmic breathing of his family. He was awake and up with the dawn, seeking Looking Glass, Rainbow, and others. Yellow Wolf also was restless and ill at ease. Hearing Joseph leaving his tipi, Yellow Wolf followed, and soon both were seated around a fire talking to Looking Glass.

Joseph's voice was urgent as he said, "Looking Glass, I am greatly concerned! I have been to the medicine tree and have talked with my Guardian Spirit. He gave me a strong warning that we are in danger. Howard is far behind, but another force is close to us! I believe we must be on the move immediately, and take greater precautions!"

Looking Glass postured, casually flicked a coal from the fire into the old pipe which he often smoked. "Has your peaceful Wyakin ever told you how to fight, how to organize for battle?" he asked. "Joseph, you are the camp leader, and well respected for that, but I believe your visit to the medicine tree has gone to your head. Our best information says Howard is many days behind us, and we have heard of no other force."

The intense Yellow Wolf leaned forward, appeared to be rising to his feet, and said contemptuously, "Looking Glass, you would do well to listen! Several of us sense the danger around us, and feel the warning of the Sacred Medicine Tree. Your willingness to make short, easy journeys, only a few miles each day, to rest for an entire day, to leave the back trail and the horses unguarded—these things concern us and make us fearful."

Yellow Wolf's rising voice had attracted others, and soon Yellow Buffalo Bull, Rainbow, Five Wounds, Whitebird, and the steady Ollokot gathered around the fire. Some agreed with Joseph. A few sided with Looking Glass, for they enjoyed the relaxed days and nights. But into the circle, unnoticed, had come a lean, wizened little man who, with his few lodges, had joined the bands just a day or two before. Hototo, or Lean Elk, the Nez Perces called him, and he was known to the whites as Poker Joe. His wiry little body was strong and tireless, and on his keen brain there were imprints of every stream, canyon, ridge, and trail throughout Idaho and much of Montana.

"Do not be scornful, Looking Glass," Lean Elk said. "And the rest of you had better listen to Joseph! I understand your love of hunting the game, feasting on the meat, and relaxing through leisurely days. These are the things we all enjoy, but they are a threat to us now, and we must travel with more caution and speed!"

The group was somewhat sobered, but Looking Glass was still the leader, and that day the bands eased their way up the Bitter Root Valley in their contented fashion, moving at a comfortable pace beside the quiet stream, enjoying the crisp mountain air and the brilliant splashes of crimson on the hillsides, where approaching autumn had turned the maples to flame.

They camped that night near a steeply rising trail which wound up the high ridge looming above them, the same ridge which can be traced in its tortuous course from Mexico, through the American and Canadian Rockies, and on across the Yukon to the Arctic. Known as the Continental Divide, its course separates the waters of the Atlantic Ocean from those of the Pacific. Within the next few weeks the Nez Perce bands would cross it three times where it twists along the borders of Idaho, Montana, and Wyoming.

Lean Elk's words still rested uneasily on the minds of some who had heard him speak and their apprehensions increased as they filed past the Medicine Tree that day. Was Howard closing in on them? No, but he had full knowledge of the approach of Col. John Gibbon with a modest but experienced force of soldiers, augmented by volunteers. They were traveling long hours, making up to 40 miles each day, and rapidly drawing closer to the relaxed Nez Perce bands.

This Colonel Gibbon was no Johnny-Come-Lately, for he had earned the eagles on his epaulets in the late months of the Civil War, and scarcely a year before had fought the Sioux in Montana. Though he was fond of his silver eagles, he was human, proud, and ambitious. Perhaps he now dreamed of stars replacing the eagles.

After another carefree night camped in the moonlight the Nez Perces began the ascent of the long western slope leading to the great divide above. It wasn't much of a trail, though it was easily followed through the forest near the base of the mountain; but above that, as the trees began to thin out and timberline was reached, it was merely a dim line of switchbacks across the rockslides. On the summit all paused to look eastward down the mountain to the Big Hole River. Their long-accustomed camping spot sat at the edge of a wide basin along the river, and here they again erected their tipis: 89 lidges in a "V" pointing upstream

That evening a dance was organized. Though most of their usual finery had been lost at the Clearwater battle site, a venerable grandfather now repeated an age-old invitation:

"People, lay everything aside, for we are going to have a dance. Put on your finest clothes and get ready for the dance. People, tonight we shall wear the garments of our dead men from long ago—so everyone must come."

Running Feet joined in the dance eagerly, feeling the excitement, knowing that the eyes of a young man from Whitebird's band were following her movements with interest. Yellow Wolf was not around, and Little Bird sat listlessly with the other women of Joseph's family. The recent relaxed days without stress had brought a degree of calm to her mind, but her body was complaining; feeling a strange sickness, an unfamiliar nausea, and twice recently she had gone to the edge of the camp to vomit—all a new experience for her. But Yellow Wolf did not return, and she did not feel like dancing, though the feasting and the revelry went well into the night.

Eventually the lodges grew peacefully silent, the fires winked out, and the horses, untroubled and unguarded, grazed along the trail leading down from the mountain.

## CHAPTER 20

Lucas and Kirby had been riding with General Howard for several weeks, having reached the eastern end of the Lolo Trail and proceeding up the Bitter Root Valley. Kirby commented, “The word is that Colonel Gibbon has come from Missoula and is pursuing the Nez Perces up this valley. Looks like they will cross over the Continental Divide.”

“That makes sense,” answered Lucas, “and I’m surprised that Howard doesn’t seem more concerned. He’s lolling around camp, while his men bathe in the hot springs just down the valley.”

But Colonel Gibbon wasn’t lolling around. Though he had some insecurities about the size of his force, he remembered vividly what had happened at the Little Big Horn, for he had friends who were close to that action; and of course the recent stories of Perry’s crushing defeat at Whitebird Creek were anything but comforting. But now his troops were close to the western side of the Continental Divide, and he sent Lt. Bradley with some 30 troopers, and some local volunteers to locate the Nez Perces.

“The best thing you can do is stampede their horses,” Gibbon told his troops. “Indians afoot are practically helpless.” Now after a hard climb over the Divide, Bradley and two men approach the Nez Perce camp, crawling through the timber. Soon they hear the voices of women and the sounds of axes, for the women are cutting lodge poles. A scout climbs a tall pine tree, and there before him are the peacefully grazing horses and the Indian tipis. And Bradley sends a message back to Gibbon: “We have found them!”

The morning sunlight dances on the ripples as the stream winds its way through the willows beside the camp. All the bands are there—Whitebird, Toohoolhoolzote, Joseph, Looking Glass, and, farthest downstream, the two Paloos Chieftains, Hatahlekin, and Husishusis Kute. As always, the bands stay together, each family feeling the security of three or sometimes four tipis side by side.

It has not been hard for Looking Glass to convince the people to stay here a few days, replenishing their food supplies, letting their horses regain strength, fishing, hunting, digging the Camas. Through the day Joseph and Ollokot’s wives work diligently along with the other women, cutting more lodgepoles. Late in the day the men return from hunting and all help in preparing the meat. Camas are roasting in the pits, with some of the wives insisting the bulbs must cook all night because that is when they are the best.

The sun sets and the fires come alive. The day’s activities have left everyone with a happy listlessness, their bellies now full and their minds at rest. The evening chill descends rapidly. The little warming fire inside each tipi is welcome, and a friendly darkness embraces the camp. Fair Land has banked the cooking fire in front of Ollokot's tipi and replenished the warming fire inside. Ollokot has dozed off, and Wetatonmi carefully wipes dirt and traces of the evening meal from the face of Jumping Rabbit, her two-year-old son.

Little Bird notices Yellow Wolf remains apprehensive and somewhat distant. But today his hunt has been productive and he is more congenial as he reclines on his bed. "He is careful with his words," thinks Little Bird. "Life with him would be better if he talked more. But perhaps he talks in the right places to the right people, even though it appears he has not had much influence with Looking Glass."

A sudden stirring in her belly interrupts Little Bird's musings. It is not the first time she has felt this movement, and since talking with Heyoom she now knows that there is a baby growing within her. But whose baby? In the confusion and rush and sometimes near panic of the last several months, time has meant even less than usual. Little Bird is not accustomed to the timing of such things, but is aware, though somewhat vaguely, that she cannot be sure about this baby's father.

"Time for another talk with Heyoom," she thinks to herself. Her affection for Yellow Wolf has grown, and now she slides over, shapes her body to his back and hips, and hugs his waist. Yellow Wolf snores softly but does not awaken.

The women's lodge sits away from the camp. Only two women are there tonight, and one of them rests on her buffalo robes, half asleep, savoring her glorious release from pain, her tiny baby boy with his luxuriant black hair nursing noisily.

It is now 10 p.m.by the white man's clock, and the Nez Perce camp sleeps. But over the mountain come Gibbon and his troops, following Bradley's messenger toward the Big Hole River, carrying only a day's rations, each man with 90 rounds of ammunition.

In a few hours they reach Bradley's contingent, and together proceed toward the Indian camp. Now they look down at the silent tipis and the resting horses, totally unprotected, no sentries in sight. Quietly they move on down the hill and, emerging from a protective screen of timber, suddenly find themselves in the midst of the horses, all of them now becoming restive, nervous and nickering at the intruding soldiers. It is a tense moment for the troops, but they ease quietly through the moving herd, which stops on the hill behind them. Gibbon whispers to Bradley, "Exactly where we wanted to be, between the Indians and their horses. Now we will drive these hostiles from their camp." And Bradley deploys his troops the full length of the camp to wait for daylight. They are to attack at the sound of three quick rifle shots.

Sgt. McCarthy, sent ahead by Howard to join Gibbon, sits at the base of a tree a few feet above his squad of twelve soldiers, some of them survivors of the death scene at Whitebird Creek. He recalls that all the odds were with the Indians at that place. "But this time we are in control, in this early-morning hour when people sleep most soundly." Then for a moment, just one brief moment, he wonders if the odds should be so stacked against the sleeping people below. But Gibbon said just yesterday, "We don't want any prisoners."

---

Rainbow pulls the furry buffalo robe closer about his body, grumbling a little at the invasion of cold air as Waddling Duck leaves to build up the cooking fire outside. He knows she will soon return, then sees the quick glow of the fire as she slips back through the briefly opened flap. She giggles as she slides under the big robe and he takes her in his arms. He has been concerned about Looking Glass's easy-going leadership. Now he reflects half-consciously that the danger does seem to be past. His own personal Wyakin has told him that he will not be killed fighting in any battle after sunrise, and morning is almost here.

Five Wounds is awake in the next tipi, but he has no wife to warm his robes or care for his fire, so he shares the tipi with two other single warriors. He is a morning person, always the first out of his bed, eager for the chase, embracing each day, leading the hunting parties. But this morning he is vaguely worried, apprehensive, and more than a little weary of contending with Looking Glass and his stubborn refusal to maintain sentries around the camp.

At the downstream end of the camp Hahtalekin, the Paloos Chief, is also awake, and wonders about his horses. So he leaves his bed and walks quietly through the camp, but he finds no horses and is about to turn back toward his tipi when he hears the sounds of low voices on the hill above him—white men's voices! Quickly he slips back to warn the members of his band and others camped nearby.

From farther upstream comes an aged man, riding a horse kept tethered by his tipi. He is almost blind and the horse carries him toward the hillside and directly into the troops waiting there. A rifle shot shatters the still air, and the old man falls from his horse. Immediately, the three signal shots are fired, but they are drowned out by the barrage of blasts from other rifles all along the hillside. Within seconds the troopers are rushing down the slope and into the sleeping camp, firing first into the tipis, their bullets seeking everyone inside, then ripping open the flaps to fire at any movement.

Cries of terror fill the air, and horses within the camp plunge blindly, their high-pitched, fearful screams adding to the panic. Soon all the tethered horses lie dead, for that is part of the plan. Many of the people, exhausted by the prolonged dancing of the night before, are now shocked awake, spring from their beds. Only a few find rifles in the dark tipis, so they use clubs, knives, rocks—anything that can be found. Bullets, like a great fiery hailstorm, pierce the tipi covers, splintering the shiny new poles. The people who escape from the tents flee toward the willows along the loops of the meandering stream, their only refuge, for the troops are close behind them.

Heyoom and Running Feet, with Springtime carrying little Early Flower, rush from the tipi, seeking escape from the whining, searching bullets. But a soldier near the door levels his rifle and fires, then staggers and falls as a shot from behind him ends his life. Welweyas has found a rifle.

In the panic of the escape Early Flower is lost, but the women cannot go back to find her, and they leap into the stream. They crouch in a deep pool, their heads barely visible above the water, partially protected by the reeds. The morning light has improved and Running Feet, on her knees and downstream from Heyoom, sees a pale red cloud drifting past her in the slowly moving water, her numbed mind at first not grasping it's meaning. Then a thin trickle of fear erupts into horror, and she turns her head to see Heyoom, a growing crimson fountain blossoming in the stream about her, her head sagging, her body already sinking.

Suddenly the other women see Running Feet's face and turn to look at Heyoom. They seize her and hold her above the water, tenderly guiding her body to the nearby shore among thicker bushes on a sloping bank where she will not drown. But soon all know it is too late, and their tears fall into the murmuring, blood-filled water which surrounds them all. The trooper's shot fired in the tipi has done its work, and they are forced to leave Heyoom's still, limp body. Soon Springtime also collapses, unable to walk, even to climb out of the water, for her leg is shattered, and she must be left to hide quietly in the willows. She cries quietly to herself, fearing detection, but her greater fear is, "Where is my little girl?"

Wetatonmi rushes from Ollokot's tipi, followed by Fair Land holding firmly to the hand of Jumping Rabbit. They scurry through the brush, falling suddenly over the steep creek bank as bullets seek them. Wetatonmi hears a plaintive cry, and looks down to see Jumping Rabbit holding up his left arm with his right. His little face is set in pain, threads of flesh hanging around a gaping hole through which light can be seen. Fair Land is no longer beside them. Wetatonmi turns back to find her collapsed against the stream bank, a dark spot on her breast spreading, moving rapidly downward, her blood staining the sand. She must be left behind, for the troops are everywhere. Wetatonmi lifts little Jumping Rabbit and carries him to temporary safety beneath a log bridging a tiny sidestream.

From other tipis no one has escaped, and the desperate hand-to-hand fighting continues. All forms within the tipis look the same to the soldiers, and death comes quickly to many of the women and their little ones. Some women and their staunch young boys stand fighting beside the determined older men. Like angry animals cornered in their dens, they seize any available weapon—a gun not found by a departing warrior, a knife, a club, sometimes a rifle rested from the soldier who attacks them—-and these unexpected, determined fighters delay the progress of the battle. Two of Gibbon's officers are killed, and Gibbon is wounded in the thigh by the same bullet which disables his horse. The battle is not going as Gibbon planned it.

A principle warrior of Looking Glass's band is shot in the head, recovers his senses and goes on to fight, later to be called Wounded Head. The strip of wolf hide with which he ties up his hair is credited with saving his life. In the heat of the battle, Wounded Head's two-year-old boy toddles trustingly toward nearby soldiers, but falls, shot in the hip. His frantic mother picks him up, starts to run, but is shot in the back. Wounded Head, his spirit crushed at the sight of his wounded wife and son, can fight no longer. He leaves the field to care for his family.

In the women's lodge lies the body of a young girl who will never reach full womanhood, will never seek the seclusion of the women's lodge again; and beside her, looking almost peaceful, sits a young mother, her first-born son crumpled at her breast, his head crushed by the swift blow of a rifle butt, the same rifle which first killed his mother.

At the first burst of rifle fire Joseph springs from his bed. He has no weapon but is thinking already of how to save the people. Starting downstream toward Whitebird's camp, he hears a plaintive whimper—the wail of his own daughter, Early Flower. He snatches her into his arms and hurries on to find his helpers, but his child is most important now. As if in answer to his silent prayer Welweyas appears, and Joseph thrusts Early Flower into his waiting hands. He then rushes on, seeking Whitebird. Together Joseph and Whitebird move stealthily downstream to where the camp is quieter, for Hahtalekin's warning has brought greater safety for the people and more damage to the troops who attacked there. And several hundred horses are found. Now there is a chance to move the shattered families to a safer place.

Yellow Wolf, his rifle left behind in the dark tipi, fights fiercely with bow and arrow. The enraged Little Bird is close behind him, her only thought to kill. Yellow Wolf struggles with a burly soldier who comes at him swinging a rifle, clubbing wildly. Yellow Wolf dodges, draws his knife, and thrusts it into the soldier's belly. The rifle is dropped and is picked up by Little Bird. A second soldier raises his rifle, aims at Yellow Wolf, and is shot down by Little Bird. Yellow Wolf now has the rifle and cartridge belt of the fallen soldier and moves on toward the sound of heavier fighting, still followed by Little Bird.

Two figures in red blanket coats rush through the low cover, their rifles barking, finding targets. Then they are separated by the furious charge of soldiers coming toward them. Wahlitits' wife appears as two bullets pierce his body. Another bullet wounds her; but quickly Wahlitits' rifle is in her hands, and she kills the captain who shot them both. But bullets from other rifles find her, and she falls beside her husband. Sarpsis Ilpilp, his red coat a bright, flaming target in the early morning light, charges boldly toward soldiers coming from the creekbed. From down the stream Whitebird's high, piercing voice is heard, clear and strong: "Why retreat? Will we run away and let our women and children be killed? Now is our time to fight!"

And from the other direction comes Looking Glass's challenging battle cry. "Wahlitits! Sarpsis Ilppilp! Now is the time to fight, to share courage! I want to see you killing, for you started this war!" And Sarpsis plunges down the hill, straight into the troops and to his death. Two red blanket coats now gleam in the gathering light, waiting to catch and amplify the rays of a sun not yet risen. And two warriors, who started out to right a wrong, now lie close together in their place of death, no longer invincible.

Waddling Duck holds Small Duck close to her, hoping to protect him as they hide among the thickest of willows. She has not seen Rainbow since the first shots were fired, and her ample body is not good for either running or fighting, so her only choice is to hide. Now in a remote, detached kind of way, she tries to imagine herself back with her Crow family, for their land is not far away. Perhaps Rainbow will now take her there.

Rainbow, among the greatest of the Nez Perce warriors, has fought valiantly, but now he falls among the willows, close to the bodies of other warriors. A bullet has shattered his heart, and he lies in only his loincloth, his unseeing eyes staring at the pale sky above. He had said he could walk among his enemies after sunrise, face their guns, his body no thicker than a hair, and not be killed. But the sun has yet to rise.

Five Wounds stands mourning beside Rainbow's body: "No more will we travel this way, stalk the buffalo, ride our best horses with joy in the dust and frenzy of the stampeding herd. And now I go, like my father and brother, and where the battle is most fierce I shall die, and lie close to Rainbow."

Five Wounds then leaps blindly to the edge of a bluff. The power of his Guardian Spirit, his Wyakin, has left him. His mind is numbed by the loss of his dearest friend, his body no longer protected from the fire of his enemies. He stands plainly visible to entrenched soldiers—and dies in the firestorm of their bullets.

The upper half of the camp is now controlled by the troops, and an order is given to burn the camp. The thick hide and damp canvas covers are hard to light and do not burn well, but hot fragments fall within the tipis where flammable items catch fire. Soon there are smoke and flames and acrid fumes, and the lodge covers begin to drop off in large patches, revealing the naked, bone-white cones of newly-peeled lodgepoles.

The challenging taunts coming from Whitebird and Looking Glass have further enraged the determined warriors and they surge back into the camp, soon driving out the soldiers, who retreat to a nearby promontory where they are besieged by the remaining braves, now fewer in number but well armed with weapons and ammunition abandoned by the troopers.

On the hill the soldiers have dug rude trenches, piled up rocks, and sought logs for shelter, but from the swale below them and from vantage points in trees the warriors' bullets seek them out. The heat has become oppressive, ammunition is low; there is no water, for access to the stream is cut off by the surrounding warriors. The Indians set fire to grass and brush, hoping the flames will sweep over the hill, but the wind changes, saving the soldiers momentarily. Gibbon lies wounded among his men, depressed by the news of Lt. Bradley's death in the early moments of the battle, and Captain Logan's somewhat later. Gibbon does not yet know that it was Wahlitits' wife who killed Logan. Lying near Gibbon is a dead horse, which soon will be attractive as food. Several soldiers lie dead on the hill, and the warriors' bullets find more among the rocks and logs. Many are wounded, some of them mortally, and they cry in pain and uncontrollable fear at seeing their companions die, longing for water to soothe their burning throats. Yet several volunteers, unschooled in military discipline, manage to crawl through the brush undetected and head for home.

While the warriors keep up the siege, Joseph, Whitebird, and many members of the scattered bands return to the camp seeking their families. As they search through the tipis and among the willows along the creek, the full impact of their losses assails them. The besieged soldiers on the hill, though several hundred yards away, are chilled by the tremulous keening of the women; the plaintive wails of the children; and the frenzied cries with which the leaders urge on the warriors. All are mingled in one overpowering wave of passionate anger aimed at revenge. And the soldiers know that the warriors' attack will now be more ferocious.

Most of the people who remain in the Nez Perce camp are wounded, many near death. Many others outside the camp are dead. Little Bird sobs over Heyoom's limp body, the only mother she can remember. "Who now will speak the quiet wisdom so often needed?" she asked herself. "And now how can I know who is my baby's father? Only Heyoom might have counted the moons."

Welweyas is shepherding Ollokot's and Joseph's children. Running Feet, dazed with terror and horror, follows Welweyas almost blindly, carrying Early Flower while he carries Jumping Rabbit, the gaping hole in his arm packed with cattail fuzz and wrapped with a strip of blanket.

Fair Land is grievously wounded, and must be tied on a hastily made rack of willows attached to the long poles of a travois, which will jolt and bump and send shuddering, stabbing pain through her body as the horse drags it over rocks and roots on a trail not meant for a travois. Springtime is in great pain but is tied to her saddle, where she is able to hold herself on despite her shattered leg.

The Paloos bands now look to Husishusis Kute for leadership, for the great Hahtalekin, the defiant and obstinate one who ignored orders to move to the Yakima reservation, has been found dead where the fighting was most fierce.

Looking Glass stands apart from the grieving people, silent and introspective, knowing that greater alertness on his part might have saved them; and a great sadness is upon him, for during the fight his daughter has been killed. He is almost overcome by his grief and remorse, but the rifle fire and war whoops of the warriors bring him back to reality and he returns to the fight.

In the frenzy of the early fighting the chieftains thought that Howard had attacked them, but in lulls in the battle they realize that these officers are different, and word is received that Howard is now approaching with reinforcements. The warriors know that many of the troops are being killed and more wounded, but their first thought, as always, is the protection of the people. While Ollokot, Yellow Wolf, Two Moons, and others continue the siege on the hill, Joseph and Whitebird organize the retreat. They all know they are to meet at a familiar rendezvous spot a few hours up the valley.

But there are so many dead, and so many others wounded! It is a terrible thing to leave behind the torn bodies of family members, for they should be carried along and tenderly buried in places protected from the elements and the hungry animals. But there is not time, and these dear ones must not be left lying exposed to the sun and to the eyes of the white man. So through the sickness of their dread the people search the tipis, finding the bodies there, tenderly moving them. The crudest of holes are dug, and the limp bodies placed within, covered too hastily with thin layers of earth and rocks.

In their panic and terror-driven haste to escape the soldiers' bullets, many of the people plunged over the high bank of the stream beside the camp, where death claimed them. No one now has the time nor energy to lift their shattered bodies back up to the camp level. So all that can be found in the water and among the willows are brought to the shore where there is a long stretch of overhanging bank, undercut by the meandering stream, and here many bodies are nestled into a crude trench. Most of them are women who had no weapons and were attempting to escape with their children. Among them is Heyoom Yokikt, Joseph's first wife, his soft-spoken counselor, his quiet strength. Now the grief-sodden burial party, their eyes averted lest they see too much and remember too long, climb together up the steep bank and collapse the loose rocks and earth over the long row of bodies below.

The soldiers remain on the hill, some of them now eating the dead horse. The warriors keep up their deadly fire, pinning the soldiers in their increasingly desperate position. After a few more hours, the small band of warriors throws a final volley among the huddling troops and races after the remains of the band struggling toward the rendezvous point.

Eighty-nine lodges, family groups camped side by side, and scarcely a family remains intact. It is easy to count the bravest of the warriors who are no more; they are well-known and remembered for their battles against the Sioux to the east and the Bannocks far to the South in Idaho. Rainbow, whose wife Waddling Duck will have to visit her Crow family alone if she ever sees them again. Five Wounds, who would have sung Rainbow's death song for him, but was killed too soon. Wahlitits, who, stunned by a slurring remark and attempting to avenge the death of his father, really started the whole thing; and his valiant little wife, who shot Captain Logan before she died, but could not save her husband. Then there was Sarpsis Ilppilp, who with his cousin-brother Wahlitits, wore with great arrogance the red blanket coats, which did not save either of them.

In addition to the warriors, several dozen wives and mothers and children now lie beneath the rocks and earth and tree roots along the banks of the stream. Joseph would say later that 34 of his people died at The Big Hole, a somber, ironic parody of the 34 soldiers who died on Whitebird Creek.

Little Bird and Wetatonmi, miraculously unscathed by the battle, ride quietly up the valley, attempting to lend their strength to those remaining in Joseph's and Ollokot's families. Springtime sways in the saddle, clinging to the horn, the thick bandage around her leg oozing blood. Running Feet, her mind rejecting the vision of Heyoom in the blood-red water, carries her half-sister Early Flower, who sleeps to the gait of the pony.

In the confusion of the retreat Welweyas has been unable to find a horse, and now walks, carrying little Jumping Rabbit and supporting his injured arm. Little Bird and Wetatonmi keep a close watch over Fair Land, their own bodies sharing the pain imposed by the bumps and jolts of the travois poles. Now there is a brief rest stop, and Wetatonmi and Little Bird quickly kneel on either side of the travois, anxiously bending over Fair Land, peering at her pallid features, searching for any sign of movement. Wetatonmi lifts a limp hand, seeks the pulse of life, then sobs as she places the hand across the still breast.

There is no proper place, no safe place, in this now hostile land where a loved one can be laid to rest. But the women find a sheltered spot, well back in the pines to the side of the trail, and there they gently place Fair Land's body in a shallow trench, wrapping her as securely as possible in a blanket, covering her face carefully. Then they ride up the trail.

The fragmented bands move away, a rear guard remaining to assure that the departing families have time to escape. But a few of the old ones had reached the end of their journey; piteously wounded and all energy drained. They sit down by the trail to die, urging their families to leave them, for they would only be a hindrance.

To the retreating Nez Perces, the illusion that they would find white friends in Montana was shattered, and their dreams of living in peace with other tribes in the buffalo country were dead. From now on they would trust no one, would show no mercy, and would kill when necessary.

And as the reassembled bands repaired torn equipment, cared for their wounded and buried their dead, they ignored Looking Glass. He had left them without protection. Now they looked to the wiry Lean Elk, who knew this country. But even Lean Elk was not entirely confident and while he did assume leadership, both the future and the destination remained uncertain.

## CHAPTER 21

More than 100 miles lay between Howard's forces and the besieged Gibbon when a courier reached Howard to request reinforcement. It then took most of four days for Howard, with a small advance detachment, to reach Gibbon's pathetic camp. It looked more like a hospital, and to the surprise of all, some of Gibbon's men seemed blithely detached from the horrible scene around them, bathing in the creek and washing their clothing, while Gibbon reclined almost leisurely, appearing to ignore his wounded leg.

Had the last three days numbed their minds? Did they now seek to cast off the awfulness of the things that they had seen, heard and done? Surely this must have happened, for they seemed oblivious to their torn and bleeding companions lying unattended, suffering immeasurably in the blazing sun. Five of the command's seventeen officers were dead or soon would be, and some 25 other soldiers and volunteers had fallen under the withering fire of the Nez Perce braves.

Lucas and Kirby walked in silence among the bodies of the dead soldiers, some lying in grotesque positions as if stopped in flight. Others had been stripped of their clothing and ammunition, but none were scalped or mutilated. Soon Howard's main force arrived, among them Bannock Indian scouts, who descended on the battleground like vultures, reading the signs to the shallow Nez Perce graves, digging out the bodies, howling with glee as they raged among the corpses. All that were found were scalped.

Howard watched calmly while the scalps were washed in the clear running water of the stream. When one of his officers protested the grisly scene and the behavior of the Bannock scouts, Howard replied, "This is their way," but he did finally stop them and ordered that some of the bodies be reburied.

Lucas and Kirby moved through the eerie scene in horrified fascination, their senses dazed, unable to comprehend it all. Lucas' mind went back to Whitebird Canyon where he had seen as many or more dead soldiers; but they were scattered over a wider area and there had been no Indian dead, nor mutilation by anyone.

Kirby left the dead and dying soldiers and wandered through the Indian camp, trying to escape from the sights and sounds and foulness of the army camp above him. But there was no escape, and all his senses were more deeply insulted by the sight of the half-buried Indians, the fetid stench of the smoldering buffalo-hides, and the swollen bodies of dead horses. Vainly he tried to mask his eyes, not to see the twisted forms of Nez Perce women and children. And when he finally came to the long, ghastly string of mutilated bodies at the base of the river bank he forced himself to turn away from the hideous scene, realizing suddenly that he might recognize one of them. Then he turned and slowly climbed the hill to find Lucas; but his eyes suddenly detected a glint of white, something partially buried in the loose earth. He stooped to remove the clinging soil, and with a little tug pulled out a dull white strand with a muddy blob on the end. Turning quickly to the stream, he washed away the mud, and held in his hand a gleaming necklace of dentalium attached to a carved shell pendant.

---

Howard congratulated Gibbon on his victory over the Nez Perces, trying to ignore the terrible toll. Gibbon accepted Howard's praise as he would that of others later on, but in his own heart he would always ask, "Why such a terrible result? I notified Howard that we controlled the camp within twenty minutes, and we did clear out the upper part in that time. But the ferocity! The terrible, animal-like ferocity with which all the people fought! And where have they gone?"

The thought was not comforting as Gibbon realized that several hundred Indians, including many of the fighting men, had escaped. "How much have we hurt them? Most of their tipi poles and covers remain here, and in their haste they could not possibly have taken much food. Fall is approaching fast and the nights will be cold." And without admitting it to himself, Gibbon was glad he did not have to continue the pursuit.

The surviving soldiers, many suffering intensely from their wounds, had their own thoughts which would pursue them forever. There was guilt, dissension, and recrimination among the men who had seen or had been part of the killing of women and children.

"We didn't have to do that," one would say. "They weren't really the enemy."

"We surely had to! They were breaking the laws of this nation, or at least their leaders were. And some of those women were fierce fighters."

"That's true, but in the open? And Sergeant, I saw you shoot some of those women who were in the water, up to their chins, hiding behind those scrubby bushes. Two of them came toward me, holding out their little babies, the most appealing, begging looks on their faces. I shook hands with them."

"Well, they were still a threat."

"I know. And Gibbon said to take no prisoners. But I still couldn't shoot them."

So the arguments went on and the guilty feelings remained, and would be there as long as these men lived.

The next day a following detachment arrived, among them two doctors. The dead soldiers had all been buried, or arrangements made to return their bodies. The wounded were cared for and moved off to a hospital in Missoula. Then Howard, his entire force now assembled on the Big Hole River and joined by some of Gibbon's men, took up the pursuit of the Nez Perces. They were on a meandering trail headed south up the river, the Continental Divide looming on their right.

Howard had tried to shut out the horror of the scene at The Big Hole, and to present the calm, objective demeanor of a commander. But now he remembered the friendly encounters with Joseph and Whitebird. They had talked of peaceful things, stability, a reservation for them in their own Wallowa Country. Joseph had pleaded with dignity, and Howard had felt their need. How had it changed? Why was he here now in relentless pursuit, ready to bring death to these same people?

Howard thought of the battle-weary Nez Perces jolting their way over the rocks somewhere ahead; four or five indistinct little bands, a dwindling remnant following uncertain leaders along a bitter trail to nowhere. A light rain was falling. Howard felt the need to pray, and spurred his horse gently to gain a few yards on his following aides. He turned his face to the sky and wept for even a small measure of understanding.

Thoughts of his military companions flooded his mind. All, at first, had worn the blue and had prayed to the same god, as Lincoln had said. But suddenly, many who had so staunchly defended the blue, were wearing the gray:

Robert E, Lee: a seasoned, dedicated soldier, twenty years ahead of me at West Point; fervently religious, thought of everything as being controlled by God. We all thought Stonewall Jackson was the best of Lee's generals, and the two of them together were invincible. Then Howard's mind went dark, for his own Eleventh Union Corps had been ingloriously rolled up by Jackson's master flanking movement at Chancellorsville. And Jackson, riding close to organize a pursuit was shot down in the dust by his own men.

Old Pete, we called him; James Longstreet, best man at Grant's wedding. He and Grant both hoped they'd never meet in battle, but Grant had to put Hancock's Corps out to face Longstreet in the wilderness, and Old Pete, was too much in the thick of it, too close in that dense forest, died in the confused fire of his own men.

That fierce little cavalryman, J.E.B. Stuart, fire in his soul, entirely devoted to Lee, thought no other horse could equal his reb cavalry. But a stern, older Union man, caught Jeb in the open, too close, calmly shot him with a pistol and walked away. Those three shot down while leading, not just supporting. All prayed to the same God. The revered commander, the essential link in the total commitment to purpose, becomes almost an object of worship. But why? The right cannot be on both sides.

Side by side in the mud, asleep to the end of the day.
Tears and love for the Blue, love and tears for the Gray.
Garlanded now at the last, sharing their final bed.
Under the Balsam the white, under the Willow the Red.

## CHAPTER 22

Lucas and Kirby no longer traveled with Howard, because following the loathsome experience at Big Hole they'd had their first major disagreement between father and son.

Kirby had started off by saying, "That death scene back there was too much for me. I can't go on with this any longer!"

"You're going soft!" Lucas said angrily. "Don't forget those people killed your mother and sister."

"I haven't forgotten that! But being here isn't helping any. We stay with Howard but we're never in on the fighting."

"I suppose you're still thinking about that Indian girl we saw on Cottonwood Creek," Lucas said. "Nothing but a little heathen."

"That's not fair, Dad! Besides, she's married to Yellow Wolf now. And you stayed up there with the soldiers while I walked through the camp. You didn't see the dead women and children like I did."

"I saw enough," replied Lucas, his anger beginning to dissipate. "And I guess it was the Bannocks digging up those bodies and scalping them that bothered me the most. I guess I agree we haven't made much of a contribution. And after seeing all of this there really couldn't be much sweetness in revenge."

They walked apart, and it took the rest of the afternoon for them to overcome the bad feelings, the memory of the argument. They came back together, still feeling a strained distance, had a meager meal, and prepared to start home the next morning. With tiring horses and their own listlessness they did not push themselves, and the trip they'd made with the troops in nine days took Lucas and Kirby thirteen. They camped near Kooskia just at sundown, spoke little while fixing supper, and welcomed sleep as darkness descended. "Home tomorrow," was all Lucas said. Kirby mumbled a sleepy reply and rolled over in his blankets.

They rode through the morning hours in silence, relishing the familiar sensations of home, before Lucas finally said, "We should make it to Seth Jones' house in two or three hours. I could stand a civilized bed and some good food. Olivia and Cornelia may be there, but if not we'll see them tomorrow when we get back out to the ranches."

Seth Jones had heard the horses arrive and stood on the front porch as Lucas and Kirby approached. Moving easily down the steps in spite of his ponderous body, he encircled Lucas and Kirby in a great bearhug. He jovially welcomed them into his home, where he immediately served them coffee and asked his wife to prepare an evening meal. Lucas and Kirby welcomed the deep feather beds in one of Seth's comfortable rooms, and allowed themselves the luxury of sleeping late the next morning.

After their first good breakfast in many weeks, and with greetings from Seth to Olivia and Cornelia, they mounted their horses for the ride past Grangeville and on to the ranches. With a mile or two left and the point of a ridge obscuring the ranch house, Lucas recalled a comment made by Seth Jones over breakfast, as he said with a twinkle in his eye, "You've got a surprise waiting for you when you get home."

With the ranch-house in sight, Lucas raised his hand and pulled Monty to a halt. "There's a rider out there among the cattle, and coming this way."

"I'll get out the glasses and see who it is," responded Kirby; and after a quick look said, "The horse looks like that little gray Morgan of Olivia's, but she's not riding it. And it's not Cornelia, either. Too small for either of them. Looks like a kid."

"Well, he's on our land. Let's get out there and see what's going on."

The rider was now approaching at a fast trot, perhaps a hundred yards away. Kirby again had the glasses up to his eyes, and shouted, "It's an Indian, Dad! And that is one of Olivia's horses he's riding!"

Lucas's revolver was out of his holster and leveled, waiting for the rider to come within range. Kirby was still looking through the glasses and exclaimed, "It's a little kid, Dad! Don't shoot!" Kirby wheeled the black into Monty to throw Lucas off balance. The shot went wild, and Gopher wheeled the little Morgan and streaked across the prairie toward the Martin ranch.

Lucas, a little miffed at Kirby's intrusion, reholstered the revolver, spurred Monty into a gallop, and set off in pursuit of the retreating rider, scattering cattle in every direction. Monty and the black, tired from their long trip, were no match for the fleet-footed Morgan. By the time they reached Olivia's house the little Indian boy had disappeared, and a stern-faced Olivia stood defiantly on the front porch.

"Why did you shoot at someone riding one of my horses?" she demanded.

"What do you expect when I see an Indian riding on my land?"

Olivia scowled. "Well, you might have held your temper and asked a few questions before you started shooting!"

But soon the situation became clear to Lucas and Kirby, though not quite believable. Tempers cooled, and Olivia got around to saying she was glad they were back. She explained the situation with Gopher but made no apology.

"Well, come on in, and I'll make some coffee," Olivia invited, and the two men relaxed as they sat down with her at the big kitchen table. After serving the coffee Olivia excused herself, but soon returned with a nervous Indian boy. She said simply, "This is Gopher, whom I told you about."

Kirby was curious and tried to remember seeing the boy around the Indian camp when he went there with Little Bird. Lucas was unfriendly at best, feeling resentful and ill at ease, and thought to himself, "Why should we tolerate this Indian kid around here? I could have shot him, but that would have been a great blow to Olivia, who obviously cares about him. Well, he's living at her place, not mine, and I'll have as little to do with him as possible."

As for Gopher, the sight of the gun, the sound of the shot, and the two riders pursuing him across the prairie had been threatening, and he felt only distrust for the men.

Olivia had commented that Cornelia was away visiting friends on a nearby ranch, and as Kirby and Lucas prepared to leave for their own place, Cornelia came through the big front gate and down the lane toward the house riding Olivia's Morab. Recognizing Kirby and Lucas, she quickly dismounted and strode toward the front porch. Only a few weeks had passed since Kirby had seen Cornelia, but now he wondered when, if ever, he had really looked at her. "This self-assured young lady is not the kid I grew up with," Kirby thought admiringly. "She's a real beauty, but probably still has some of that haughty attitude about her."

Cornelia was now on the porch and embracing Lucas. As she turned toward Kirby, he remembered the day at Seth Jones' house and her head on his shoulder, and now hoped for another hug; but she only smiled and said, "Hello Kirby. I'm glad you're back." Then, sensing something wasn't quite right, she disappeared into the house, looking for Gopher.

As Lucas and Kirby mounted their horses, Olivia asked them to wait, and returned soon with a gunny sack which she tied behind Lucas' saddle. "One of the Jones boys has been at your house part of the time, but you won't find much there to eat. There's some bread, coffee, and bacon in that bag to get you started. Tomorrow we'll help you straighten up the house and put your kitchen in order. And we need to talk more about the cattle. Your other horses are in our pasture, and we'll drive them over tomorrow."

Normally, the homecoming would have been a happy occasion, for this ranch house, though roughly built, had always been a place of warmth and protection, the only secure home either of the two men could remember—Lucas had built it when Kirby was two years old. Both knew that returning to the house for the first night would not be easy, but they were not good at sharing feelings, and silently went about the routine tasks of putting away the food Olivia had sent.

They made a half-hearted tour around the outbuildings and corrals which, lacking horses and cattle, seemed desolate and lonely. Then they ate a simple meal in silence, and at an unusually early hour Kirby climbed the stairs, hearing half-consciously the sound of the one squeaky tread, and went to bed. Lucas at first rejected the thought of sleeping in the room that had always been his and Jenny's, but he finally went to bed in the accustomed place, listening to the almost deafening silence of the vacant house.

The weeks that followed were a blur of dawn-to-dusk days when the Phelps men and the Martin women worked tirelessly repairing the ranch buildings and caring for the cattle. Some of the bull calves had not been cut, and there were older cattle to be dehorned for safety's sake. So each day was a seemingly endless routine of driving in the selected cattle, building the branding fires, roping and tying, the smell of singed hair and burning flesh, the high-pitched bellowing of young calves and the bawling of their anxious mothers, who often had to be driven away from the dust-covered scene. Lucas and Kirby looked on in admiration as Olivia, Cornelia, and Gopher drove in small herds, then cut out individual animals to be roped, dragged in and tied down beside the branding fire.

It was dusty and demanding work, but all thrived on it and most enjoyed it. The closeness of the long, hard days together was a kind of balm that all had needed. The men, of course, did not find the right words, but Olivia in typical fashion summed it up for everyone when she said, "I've enjoyed every minute of it and I'm sorry it's over. We may never again be together for so long or feel so close."

## CHAPTER 23

When the survivors of the Big Hole battle arrived at the rendezvous point Joseph and Whitebird became fully aware of how many were wounded, and how many others lay dead at the battle scene. Joseph had begun moving the people away before Heyoom was killed, and he now shared his agonized grief with Ollokot as both learned of Fair Land's death and her burial beside the trail. All the other deaths were equally tragic to Joseph, and the almost crushing weight of his sorrow increased as each name was tolled. But he joined with Wetatonmi in comforting Ollokot, made the rounds of the other bands to offer his support, and suffered with them through the dreadful night.

By mid-morning of the next day, the inborn resilience of the people had taken over. Their few meager and tattered belongings were loaded on pack-horses and travois' along with the wounded and they were traveling south, knowing that General Howard was not losing any time in his pursuit.

Joseph frowned as he pondered the band's situation. One third of the seasoned fighting men were dead, and perhaps an equal number of women, children, and older men. Many others were wounded. There were no tipi covers left, and many of the people had only the clothing on their backs. As for food, most of their supply had been abandoned. As usual, they would live on what they could dig, shoot, steal, or take by force.

Lean Elk did take over as leader when the bands left the rendezvous, though not with enthusiasm. He was capable of moving the bands, but not sure he enjoyed the role, and was scornful of Looking Glass and his plan to seek refuge among the Crows directly to the east; so he was leading the Nez Perces south toward the land of the Shoshones.

---

The people from both sides of the divide in Montana and Idaho descended on Howard, demanding that he protect them by splitting his troops to cover several villages simultaneously. Howard attempted to meet some of these demands, and the resulting delay cost him time and worked to the advantage of the Nez Perces as they swung around the corner of south-western Montana, heading eastward toward Yellowstone Park.

Howard was not a happy man as he mused to himself about the progress of this so-called war. It wasn't a war at all, really, but just a series of running battles, a pursuit of people whom he had long realized had never really wanted to fight.

Howard thought carefully of the geography he'd soon face. "The Nez Perces crossed over; my scouts saw them and now they're traveling around the outside loop, much longer than the inside bend of the Continental Divide

I'm following. There's a pass over those mountains, only fifty or sixty miles away. If we can move through it soon enough, we might be ahead of them for once in this tiresome war."

But this decision brought great disagreement from those around him, who favored crossing through Monida Pass, much nearer, and falling on the Nez Perces from behind. So Howard summoned Lt. George R. Bacon: "Take your men over Red Rock Pass, and station them to intercept the Nez Perces, who are now headed toward Henry's Lake, and will probably go north over that pass toward the buffalo country. Slow them down, harass them, anything you can; just don't lose touch with them until I arrive." Howard did not need to add that he could tolerate no more mistakes. But, in fact, he himself had blundered again, for the route he expected the Nez Perces to take, and which Bacon was to guard, would not be their choice.

So the bands moved on eastward past the Monida Pass road, frightening citizens along their way, who in turn kept Howard informed of their location. The land they traveled was covered with sagebrush and scrubby aspen on lava ridges, and was not well watered. But soon they came to a clear, beautiful stream coming from the mountains to the north—Camas Creek, it was called. Nearby was Spring Creek, and the two streams together blessed a shallow valley with abundant grass.

The weary people, still tending their wounded on the jolting travois', tired of the crying of their babies, and sorely needing rest, longed to stop here for a day. But that could not be, for they knew that their crossing of the Monida Pass Road would be reported to Howard, who would increase the speed of his pursuit. So, for only one night, they tried to push away their persistent grief, their damaging, oppressive feelings of hate and their desire for revenge. They eased the torn bodies of their wounded off the travois', made the best beds they could for them, and cared for their wounds. At first light they moved on.

Howard did travel south over Monida Pass, found the Nez Perces' tracks, and followed them eastward. At Camas Meadows he camped his forces for the night. Before locating his headquarters on a rise, Howard called his officers together.

"This camp is to be totally secure," he ordered. "The Indians camped here last night and are only a few miles ahead, so we must guard against any possible infiltration. Locate the major units at the corners of a square, the smaller ones in between, and close the gaps with the wagons. Drive all the pack mules into the square and tie the bell mares to the wagon wheels. Your own mounts are to be picketed as usual, close to your tents, and all-night security will be established, by the book!"

The Nez Perce leaders were well aware that Howard and his forces were camped at Camas Meadows, only a short ride away, for their rear guard had seen the soldiers arrive there and start to set up their camp. But suddenly Black Hawk, gritting his teeth as he raised his wounded body slightly from the pallet made for him, spoke up. "Last night at Camas Meadows my pain was great, and I did not sleep. But I had a very clear vision. I saw our warriors go back over the trail to Camas Meadows, where Howard is now camped, and they returned with many horses."

Those who heard Black Hawk speak looked at each other with a glimmer of hope. "Howard and his soldiers are there, very close! Soon they will be going to their tents for sleep. Black Hawk's vision is good medicine. We can drive off their horses! Perhaps if we are stealthy enough we can even kill Howard, and bring great damage to his army."

Nearly thirty warriors took the trail westward toward Camas Meadows as the sky began to brighten behind them, including Looking Glass, Wottolen, Two Moons, Ollokot, White Bull, and the grim-faced Yellow Wolf, now recognized as a warrior for his valor at the Big Hole. Beside him rode his cousin Otskai.

"You must follow the plan, Otskai," cautioned Yellow Wolf. "Do only what we have agreed upon, not some foolish thing, as you sometimes do."

All are quiet, and those on foot are most stealthy, slipping into the big square of wagons and tents, removing the bells from the mares which the mules always follow, and cutting hundreds of halter ropes. The plan is going well! But suddenly a shot is fired—too early and from the wrong direction. Not all the horses and mules have been cut loose. Quickly, mounted warriors storm into the camp, their high-pitched, terrifying screams rending the air. They shoot into the tents, stampede the horses, and soon are assisted by other warriors waiting to help drive the herd away. Speed is essential, but for some reason this herd will not move fast enough, and as daylight brightens it is discovered that most of the animals are not horses, but pack mules, which are not known for their speed.

Struggling to regain their senses, the soldiers leap from their beds, shocked by the thunder of horses' hooves, the rifle shots reverberating among the wagons, the whoops and yells of warriors racing through the camp. But the warriors are quickly gone, and as the sun peeks over the divide to the east, three companies of soldiers take off in pursuit of the fleeing Nez Perces, who are not hard to catch, because the mules are so slow.

Again, their knowledge of this country and the lay of the land favors the Indians, for they are in an area of rough ridges covered with boulders, tall brush, and low Aspens, all good cover. Here the warriors dismount, and are soon joined by reinforcements riding out from their camp. Together they frustrate the troops and encircle Captain Norwood's command, holding him for several hours until Howard rides out to rescue him.

As Yellow Wolf rode back toward camp driving the mules, he wondered if again Otskai's head did not act right. "He is never afraid," thought Yellow Wolf, "and does not hide from the fighting. But sometimes he does foolish things, or has poor timing." And Yellow Wolf soon learned that it was Otskai who fired too soon, and in the wrong place. Perhaps he was challenged by a white sentry and acted too quickly. Otskai made no excuse for his action, and no one censured him.

The public believed Howard's story that only a military genius like Joseph could have broken his security that night, and his report stated that Joseph marched the warriors toward his camp in a column of fours, like cavalry, trying to make the sentry think it was Bacon's party coming back from the divide. But the Nez Perces had no way of knowing about Lt. Bacon, and Joseph was not with the raiding party. So in the public mind the living legend of Joseph continued to grow.

The Nez Perce warriors returned to their camp driving some 150 mules and a few horses. Howard lost three men, and five were wounded. The Nez Perces wanted horses, not mules, thinking to leave the soldiers on foot, so there was some disappointment. But in fact the loss of the mules was a damaging blow to Howard's group.

The next day the Nez Perces moved on east, and Howard's forces, after a day of rest at Camas Meadows, took up the chase. Riding with the soldiers were Bannock warriors under Chief Buffalo Horn. As they passed the place where Wounded Head's little boy and an old Nez Perce woman lay dead, sharp eyes saw the still bodies and two warriors left the trail. A little later they caught up with the rear guard of the troops, and dangling from one lance was a bloody pad of skin covered with long, silvery-grey hair. Tied to the other warrior's lance was a pitiful little black-haired scalp.

Little Bird sat huddled under a ragged blanket, shivering in the chill of the early evening. A smoky fire bought tears to her eyes, and she wiped them out with a grimy hand as she looked across the fire at Running Feet and Wetatonmi. Early Flower, not yet three months old, peeked from beneath the cover of her carrier, resting on Running Feet's lap. Nearby, Welweyas was comforting Jumping Rabbit who was fretful and feverish from the wound in his arm. Springtime lay on a bed of soiled blankets under the one buffalo robe left to Joseph's band from the battle at the Big Hole. She occasionally whimpered, for the grinding pain in her shattered leg would not go away. The crude bandage of torn cloth with a strip of an old blanket over it was soaked with several day's accumulation of dark, blackish-red blood.

"Will we ever stop running? And will we ever have the protection of our tipis, and eat warm food?" Little Bird sighed as she again waved the smoke from her eyes.

"I know it is hard, little one," answered Wetatonmi. "We are all hungry." And she rummaged through the bundles which she carried on her own packhorse, searching for treasured bits of food.

Soon Joseph, having assured himself that the horses and the newly acquired mules were well guarded, returned to the miserable little camp site. More than the eager young warriors, he understood the success of the raid on Howard's camp, thinking that it is good to have the mules, and it is even better that Howard no longer has them.

Joseph, though usually optimistic, was again forced to face discouraging reality: "Most of three moons have passed since we left our homeland. After the Big Hole, when we crossed the divide into our own land, we thought we might find help among some Indian people there on the Lemhi; but Chief Tendoy of the Shoshonis did not want us, for his people are few and fear the growing numbers of white settlers. By stealing and fighting we were able to find food and fresh horses, but what a price we are paying now! Most of that food is gone; we have no tipis, our horses are tiring, and our people are discouraged. There is game in this country, and many big fish in this nearby lake, but we cannot stop to harvest these things. Our scouts report that Howard's men are resting and recovering at Camas Meadows, and we must keep moving."

All around, mothers held their children close, wondering if their shriveling breasts were providing enough milk for the babies. Springtime, in spite of her wound and her misery, nursed Early Flower and worried even more; and through that night all huddled together, taking what little warmth and comfort they could from each other. They tried to remember that in the past, somehow things had gotten better.

Only a short ride east of the camp near Henry's Lake, the long procession of Nez Perces approached Targhee Pass, the place where Lt. Bacon should have been and might have slowed them down enough for Howard to catch up. The trails were narrow, rocky, and steep. Everything was on the pack horses. Most of the badly wounded, the dead or dying old people, and the totally depleted horses had been left behind.

For the third time they were crossing the Continental Divide, and the people knew this land ahead of them—that vast prairie where they had hunted buffalo; the big river beyond; and not far beyond that the Land of the Grandmother. "Sitting Bull and the Sioux are there; they will be our friends."

But between Targhee Pass and Canada they must first cross the jagged, tangled canyons of the Yellowstone country, and beyond them the naked, forbidding plains sloping down to the Missouri, then upward to Canada. Army units were not only behind them to the west, but also ahead to the north, and others were coming from the east.

Lean Elk still led, and felt confident because this was his country; but Looking Glass was restive, and used every opportunity to reassert his leadership. Now Ollokot and Yellow Wolf were bringing up the rear, for there must be no more surprises. Little Bird rode, as usual, along with Joseph's family, leading her own two packhorses. Her belly was still flat, but the stirring within was more frequent. She had not traveled with Joseph's band to this country before, and she now looked ahead across rolling sagebrush ridges and thick lodgepole pine forests to the higher mountains beyond. She couldn't help thinking, "Where in this strange land will my baby be born?"

## CHAPTER 24

The earliest pioneers arriving on Camas Prairie brought with them two things which were easy to carry in their wagons or even in saddlebags. The first were black walnuts or tiny seedlings, which grew rapidly into immense spreading trees with huge horizontal branches, sometimes covering a fourth of an acre. The hard nuts were treasured by everyone, though they had to be cracked with a hammer on an anvil, and sometimes with a rock.

The second were honeysuckle clippings—starts, everyone called them—and they were given to newlyweds and newcomers, so that most every family across the prairie had these delicate pink or salmon colored flowers on trailing vines somewhere on their property. In May their spicy perfume filled the air, never to be forgotten by anyone who spent much time on the prairie.

But now summer was gone, and fall had arrived in earnest. The fragrance of the honeysuckles was only a memory, and the huge, gaunt frames of the black walnut trees stood stark against the lowering sky. Children gathered the walnuts, stuffing them into gunnysacks and dragging them home. Great flocks of ducks and geese rested overnight on the lake, and endless skeins of them could be seen daily, coming from somewhere north of Cottonwood and flying southward over the Salmon river to warm wintering places.

Less than four months had passed since Jenny and Phoebe died, and their terrible loss had been kept alive in Lucas' mind by his experiences with Howard's army. Lucas knew also that Kirby, in his own way, suffered perhaps even more. He was still the little boy needing a mother, the emerging young man refusing to cry. But now in these early days of Autumn both Lucas and Kirby felt a calmness growing around them. They slept soundly through the lengthening cold nights and arose early in the newness of the dawn, leaving tracks in the frost as they walked to the woodlot carrying their saw and axes. There was a soothing in the rhythmic swing of the torso, the tautness of the shoulder muscles, the coordination of push and pull, and the aroma of the pitch as the cutting teeth on the long saw slashed through the yellow wood. The pile of blocks in the woodlot grew, and finally was hauled to the woodshed near the house, where each block was split to fit the fireplace or the kitchen stove.

"Let's hope for a long fall this year. We've got a lot to do," commented Lucas one morning as he mounted Monty, wincing as he settled into the frost-covered saddle, which he had left on the top fence rail instead of in the barn. "I'm not sure having all these cattle is much of a blessing. They seem to take most of our time."

"They sure do." responded Kirby. "And I thought fall was supposed to be the beginning of rest, with the hay cut and the wood in and the branding done. I sure hope it slacks off after awhile."

They took a ride to the Martin place, and soon recognized Cornelia and Gopher riding to meet them. Lucas greeted Cornelia warmly as she rode close enough to give him her usual hug. He was distant to Gopher, who held back a little and looked uncomfortable. Cornelia did not approach Kirby. Hugging Lucas was one thing, but for Kirby something quite different. But she did smile, seeming to Kirby to show a little more interest than usual. She was, in fact, looking at him quite closely. He had removed his hat, and the brilliant sun lit tiny lights on his reddish-blond hair. The brisk ride had brought extra color to his face, and a three-day growth of beard, as yet seldom shaved, now stood out on his ruddy skin. "Well," thought Cornelia, "you're getting to be quite a man!" Then, a little annoyed at herself, she tried to think of him again as the kid with whom she had ridden to and from school for the last ten years.

"We thought we'd check the fence around your haystacks," said Lucas. "That needs to be done before the weather gets cold." Cornelia's deliberate response was well understood by Lucas as she said, "Herbie and I did that yesterday, and the fence is fine." But her comment was not entirely lost on Kirby; this "Herbie" stuff sounded a little too cozy. Lucas broke the short silence. "Let's ride on over to your house Cornelia. We haven't seen your mother for a few days. I need to talk to her about getting ready for the winter, possibly finding more hay for all these cattle."

Olivia Martin had found a warm spot on the south-facing porch just outside her kitchen door, protected from the chilly wind blowing from the northwest. She pondered her daughter's future. "She's over seventeen now, and still involved with grade school stuff, helping Miss Henley. Nothing wrong with that, but it mustn't hold her much longer. She's ready for high school, but she'd have to go to Lewiston. She's ready for that, but I'm not. Herb is totally gone on her, but she can't see him. He's probably not strong enough for her anyway; she'd probably dominate him. Kirby might be the one, but so far shows no interest. Something strange about that distant look in his eyes.

"Then there's Gopher. How have I let him creep into my heart? Full of life, never worries, always helpful. And what's his future? I can't keep him here forever. No one accepts him here, and life on the reservation sounds pretty grim to me; but so does being without him. Yet it may be the only answer, and if we're going to take him there we should do it before winter sets in."

Then Olivia thought of Lucas—big, burly, always dependable Lucas. "I've known him now for fifteen years, since the very day he and Jenny started building their cabin and later the ranch house. In all that time I don't think he ever spoke a cross word to Jenny or the children. Seth thinks he's a great man, and it's sure a comfort to have him nearby."

Olivia's wandering thoughts were interrupted by the sound of horse's hooves as Gopher and Herb Jones rode by the house toward the barn. Gopher spoke English well enough now to talk about the essential tasks of the day, and Herb had gradually come to accept him as a working partner, a tireless, skilled rider, almost a peer. But sometimes, especially when they rode far enough north to see Cottonwood, Gopher seemed to withdraw, sometimes not speaking for an hour or more. It was during these times that he tried to uncover the buried memory in the blank space in his mind. There was his father, Two Moons and, riding nearby, Ollokot and Yellow Wolf and Little Bird, and all around him the strained faces of the other people, in hurried but organized flight across the prairie.

Then suddenly an extra horse, entrusted to Gopher to lead, suddenly bolted in fright from a rattlesnake, jerking the lead rope from Gopher's hand. They were near the edge of the eastward-moving procession, and the wild-eyed horse ran toward the south, with Gopher in pursuit. Just as Gopher was out of sight of the other people, his pony stepped in a badger hole, somersaulted, and threw him over its head. The fleeing bands moved rapidly away.

There was no sense of time, and only the most hazy memory of wandering without direction, stumbling, falling, wanting only to rest. Then finally a ranch house, an unlocked door, protection from the chill of the night, a dark closet and later the sound of voices, and strange white faces. And every so often, there were more white faces, also strange, and most of them angry looking, even threatening.

"Gopher, let's go home," he heard Herb say, and together they rode back to the Martin ranch, where there was good food, a soft bed, and mostly friendly faces.

# CHAPTER 25

As the retreating Nez Perce bands moved up the Madison River into Yellowstone Park, William Tecumseh Sherman, now General of the Armies, became one of the park's visitors. He had learned during his visit that the Nez Perces were approaching from the west, and was heard to say that their superstitious minds associated the geysers and hot springs with Hell, so they certainly would not enter the park.

At best, Sherman's opinion reflected his scanty knowledge of the mind of the Nez Perces, perhaps of Indians in general, for now, on a bright, late-August day, the bands were well within the park, camped on a small stream that would become known as Nez Perce Creek. A short distance above its confluence with the Fire Hole River, many Nez Perce women and children relaxed in the warm water. The day was cool, and steam drifted upward from the surface of the Fire Hole, warmed by the boiling springs upstream. Farther down the river, the young men and boys had found their swimming spot. Content and soothed by the swirling warmth about them, the women chatted.

"It is almost like a dream," murmured Wetatonmi. "We have run so far, and so long; and it would be good if this peaceful place could be our home for awhile."

"Never can I remember being so hungry, or feeling so tired." answered Little Bird. "I feared that some of our people were near starvation. Except for the first few days after the Big Hole, we have never seemed so weary, or so discouraged. But this chance to rest, to bathe, to feast on the elk the men have killed, has revived our spirits. Perhaps we will even have time to tan some of those big hides."

That night, with scouts out in all directions, the camp slept less fearfully. The threat of Howard was still there, though they had more lead on him than they knew, for after resting a full day at Camas Meadows his own exhausted troops had almost mutinied when he rousted them out at 2 a.m. to pursue the Nez Perces. Then Howard, somewhat shamed, paid closer attention to the deplorable condition of his men: short on blankets, clothing, shoes, in need of better horses; terribly crippled by the loss of the pack mules driven off by the Indians.

So Howard rode north almost 100 miles to Virginia City, where he personally bought the clothing, food, and fresh animals so needed by his troops. While there he was subjected, again, to the sarcasm of aggressive frontier newspapermen, who said he should be replaced. The criticism of his superiors was even worse, and his old friend General Sherman telegraphed him that he should pursue the Nez Perces to the death, but if tired he should give the command to a younger, more energetic officer.

The Nez Perce bands dared not rest for long on the Fire Hole, and they moved on, though in a casual, disorganized kind of way, drifting out of camp late in the morning in small family groups. The Lodgepole pines through which they traveled were incredibly thick, often requiring the women to search for trees spaced widely enough for loaded horses to pass through. Each family cared for its own horses as they moved upward toward the plateau, where they were finally able to look toward the southeast and see the broad, blue expanse of Yellowstone Lake.

Yellow Wolf and other vigorous young men ranged far to the north and northwest, well down the Yellowstone River, suspecting danger in that direction, always on the alert. For a short time, Lean Elk was disoriented in the heavy forest of the high country. Then Yellow Wolf captured a prospector out looking for his horses, and he was pressed into guide duty. The man liked the Indians and stayed around for awhile, helping them with the pack animals, and no one attempted to stop him when he finally left the camp on his own. But it was from his reports, plus those made by Army scouts and by citizens who encountered the far-ranging Nez Perce guards, that Howard became aware of the approximate location of the fleeing Indians.

Lean Elk had his bearings now. Looking Glass and others had traveled through this country before, and they knew that in order to reach the plains and move toward the Missouri River they had only three choices. Army units coming from several directions were commanded by young, vigorous officers, several of whom had fought the Sioux in these same locations. They knew the escape routes also, and were now systematically bottling the Nez Perces up.

In a council of the chiefs, Looking Glass emphasized their need for help from other tribes: "Just a few years ago I helped the Absarokas, the Crows, or Bird People as they call themselves, and they were able to defeat the Sioux war party that was upon them." So he departed for the land of the Absarokas to enlist their help. The bands moved on slowly, waiting for Looking Glass to return, hoping for help from the Crows. Camped at a fine meadow on the upper LaMar River, they again went hunting, mended clothes and tents, dried some meat, and waited.

"I did talk to the Crow chiefs," Looking Glass said upon his return, and by his solemn face the assembled chiefs knew that the news was not good. "They were friendly enough, and seemed to remember that we had helped them in the past, but the best they would promise was not to fight against us if they were around when the battle started."

Then Looking Glass reported more threatening news: a large force of troops, some 360 men plus Crow scouts, were on the Clark Fork River. This was Colonel Sturgis, who had been sent to watch that fork of the Yellowstone. Sturgis' position took care of one possible escape route for the Nez Perces. And to the north on the main Yellowstone River was Lt. Doane, also accompanied by a large number of Crows. Two of the three escape routes were now guarded. And unknown to the Nez Perces, Major Hart was to the east of the park guarding the Shoshone river, the last exit.

Clearly there was danger to the east. Sturgis with those 360 men and the Crow scouts. And now new evidence had arrived from the sentries that Howard's advance party was closing from the west.

Joseph wanted to go north immediately, but Looking Glass objected. "It would be best to climb onto the divide, where we will have some choices," he said. "If the Clark's Fork is well guarded we can go south to the Shoshone and down to the Big Horn. The way you have chosen, Joseph, will almost certainly involve more fighting. We must not lose more people."

The two strong-willed chieftains could not agree, and so Joseph started northward, while Looking Glass moved to the southeast toward the top of the Absaroka Divide. Maybe they would all meet again, perhaps somewhere far out on the plains.

Yellow Wolf and a small band of scouts thundered up the Yellowstone River, having just burned a cabin near Mammoth Hot Springs. Rounding a sharp bend in the river, they were faced with the leaders of Joseph's band.

"Soldiers are following close behind us!" shouted Yellow Wolf. "They now know where we are, and other soldiers will follow them. We must turn back up the river!"

Joseph realized it would be best to get back with Looking Glass and the other bands, so they turned east along a trail they knew from hunting trips in the past. As if by instinct, perhaps more by chance, they found Looking Glass on the rocky, high divide at the head of the creek they had followed. Together, the reunited bands moved forward to the rim of the upper Clark's Fork River, its jagged, thousand-foot-high walls warning of death as they carefully skirted the narrow gorge which yawned to their left.

"The canyon is too deep, too dangerous, and there seem to be no trails which we could follow to the river. We must continue along this ridge bordering the canyon. Perhaps farther down we will find a trail that is passable." Lean Elk spoke boldly, but with a resolution he did not feel, for he sensed the growing threat to his leadership, the apparent willingness of the people to forget that Looking Glass had once failed them.

---

The Clark's Fork River canyon to the north of the Nez Perce bands opened onto the plains within a few miles; and just over the divide to the south ran the Shoshone River, perhaps twenty miles away. Colonel Sturgis had been ordered to watch both these rivers but was apprehensive about the adequacy of his force and the distances to be covered. His scouts were finding nothing, and Sturgis was uneasy, so he sent out a reconnaissance squad. They saw, or imagined, horses in the distance. Were they real? Were they decoys sent out by the Nez Perces to fool Sturgis? Or did Sturgis mention the horses in his final report to ease the criticism of his blunder?

Behind the Nez Perces as usual, Howard was camped beside the

Yellowstone River. From his scouts' reports, he now knew the Nez Perce's path from the upper LaMar valley over the Absaroka Divide. His main force was too slow, so he moved on ahead with the cavalry, lightly supplied and on their best mounts. A few days later they were on the Clark's Fork drainage, where the white scout S. G. Fisher overtook them. There they met prospectors who had recently talked with Colonel Sturgis. "Now we are making progress. I know where Sturgis is!" exulted Howard. And he sent a courier to Sturgis: "We are moving fast; will join you soon." But Nez Perce raiders killed the courier before he reached Sturgis. Fisher, however, was optimistic: "There is no opening left for the Nez Perces to wiggle through. They must now fight!"

High on the ridge above Clark's Fork, Nez Perce scouts watched Sturgis' forces move to the south toward the mouth of the Shoshone. "Are they really gone? Are they only exploring? Will they be back? It does look like our way is now clear out onto the plains, but there is no time to lose, for more troops are coming from behind. There is no easy way down, so we must take the one poor choice."

But before leaving the high ridge to plunge into the rock-strewn canyon, the Nez Perces planned an evasive strategy: "Ride your mounts, lead your packhorses. Drive the loose herd around this meadow and it's boundaries. Make many tracks over a large area, and we can confuse the troops when they arrive, at least slow them down." Then into the narrow, sharp-walled defile, little more than a slot, a seemingly impossible route that would later be known as Dead Indian Gulch, the warriors forced over 2,000 squealing horses, most of them gashed and bruised by sharp rocks, some collapsing under broken bones which left them groaning and struggling, to die at the bottom of the deepest crevasses. But the herd helped to some extent to clear the way for the people coming behind with their saddle horses and pack mules.

Little Bird, Running Feet, and Wetatonmi followed Joseph and Ollokot down the plunging gully, finding no real trail, threading their way in single file among the sharp-edged slabs and boulders, wondering if they might follow the others which through the years had littered the jumbled canyon bottom. Joseph still rode Ebenezer and kept close track of Joshua. Springtime, depleted but recovering from her wound at the Big Hole, remained thankful for the agile little roan gelding. Hawk Who Rides The Wind was strong, in spite of bruises and cuts from the broken tree branches and sharp rocks through which they had traveled.

Little Bird felt some comfort in the presence of Yellow Wolf, who rode just behind on his pinto. All the horses, like the people, showed the stress of the long journey, now well into its fourth month, for the rest stops where there was good grass and plentiful game to kill had been too few and too short. Little Bird wondered why at this moment she should count Ebenezer's lean ribs as he rounded a turn ahead of her, and be distressed at his gaunt thighs and protruding pelvic bones. There had been little time to worry about personal matters over the past few weeks, but now she thought of the baby within her, and for some strange reason wondered about the dentalium necklace that she had not seen since the Big Hole battle.

After two or three miles of the hellish journey down Dead Indian Gulch, the Nez Perces reached the main floor of the Clark's Fork canyon, and soon were at the river's mouth. In spite of the report that Sturgis had moved south toward the Shoshone, the Nez Perce held up the procession until the area had been completely scouted. But Sturgis was gone, and there was no one else to be seen. The way was now open; the bands could move across the plains toward the Missouri River.

The next day S. G. Fisher, along with part of Howard's troops, arrived at the place where the Indians had disappeared. No Indians there, of course, but Fisher was not long confused by the maze of tracks, so he led the way down the forbidding canyon, which seasoned soldiers declared the worst they had ever traveled. Then they followed on down the Clark's Fork, nursing their bone-weary horses, wondering why they were here. Sgt. McCarthy, whose memory of this ridiculous war went all the way back to Whitebird Canyon, mused that the grueling route through the wilds of the Salmon River was not as bad as this one.

The West Virginian who had had his first doubts at the Big Hole again pushed his loyalty aside for a moment and said to a companion: "Why do we continue chasing these people? they are no real threat to America! I have heard they are trying to get to Canada and join Sitting Bull. Why not just let them go?" The answer would have been clear to Sturgis, remembering his son's death at the Little Big Horn, and to the most other traditional military men. Certainly the people on Camas Prairie would not say, "Let them go." But, s expressed by newspaper editors in the area, the army had blundered all the way through and the Indians were winning. "The Nez Perces are again on the move toward freedom. We hope they get there." And to many citizens across the nation Joseph was fast becoming a gentleman, the peerless commander who continued to defeat the army and lead his people away: Moses vs. The Pharoh.

Sturgis, well aware that he had ridden away from the Nez Perces as they were coming down the Clark's Fork, was thoroughly humiliated and asked Howard for another chance by taking his relatively fresh men and horses in pursuit of the hostiles.The next day his well-armed and augmented forces were off down the Yellowstone River. The Nez Perces fled down the river, leaving behind them the destructive Dead Indian Gulch—the trap from which S. G. Fisher had said they could not escape. Worn out by several months of running, the depleted people with their struggling horses and mules, many no longer of much value, followed the north bank of the Yellowstone. They did feel a little more at ease, for no troops had been seen for several days.

## CHAPTER 26

"I'm not sure I should be going to this dance at all," Olivia commented to Cornelia. "Jethro has been gone less than four months, and some people will think it's not proper for me to be seen at a social event. And I can't stand going out even once more in that black dress I've been wearing to church."

"Mother, people can't expect you to go on mourning forever. They regard me as an adult too, and I'm sick of these somber clothes."

Olivia watched as Cornelia turned the chicken frying in a pan on the stove and checked the progress of cookies in the oven. "Well, I think you're right, but let's not make the transition too fast. Why don't you wear that deep rose colored dress, and I'll wear my dark green velvet. Nobody should complain about the styles, and the colors aren't vivid."

Cornelia proceeded with the chicken and the cookies while Olivia made bread and butter sandwiches and brought apples from the thick-walled, insulated storage cellar just outside the back door. The two women were assembling lunchboxes for the social to be held in early evening, before the dance scheduled at the Grange Hall on Three-Mile Creek.

"Everybody we've known for years is looking forward to this dance, you know; and I must admit I'm kind of excited about it. It's been rather dull each year in makeshift places like school houses and new barns. Now it's nice to have the Grange Hall, which will hold a much bigger crowd," Olivia went on, as she assembled the various items for the two lunch boxes.

Cornelia finished the chicken, took the cookies out of the oven, and set both out to cool, then she helped Olivia as they finished the fancy boxes—known as "baskets"—and all the women vied with each other in making them beautiful. Cardboard boxes from the store were saved, covered with crepe paper, fancy ribbons, dried flower arrangements, sometimes even stuffed birds taken from old hats. Each unmarried girl worked hard at this project, devising ingenious ways to let her favorite beau know which basket was hers, hoping he would out-bid others at the auction and have supper with her.

"I'm not much excited about it," said Cornelia. "It'll be the same old crowd. Herb will have his spies out, probably that sneaky little sister of his, trying to see what my basket looks like and report back to him. I'm glad he's gone for the day now, or we'd have to be hiding this stuff from him."

"Well, how about Kirby? You could find ways to let him know when your basket comes up for sale."

"Mother!" Cornelia almost shouted. "How obvious do you want me to be? I admit eating with Kirby would be a lot better than with Herb, but I'm not entirely sold on that either. And yet, who else is there?"

"I agree there's not a lot of choice. Maybe you're spending too much time with that bunch of little kids at school." Olivia had thought again, recently, about sending Cornelia to high school in Lewiston, and she thought of casually mentioning it now. But she wasn't ready to face the days and nights alone, so she pushed the thought away and helped Cornelia into her dress.

It had been a long, tiring day for Lucas and Kirby. After caring for their horses, both felt like settling down around the fire for the evening rather than heading for the dance at the Grange Hall.

"But if we stay home," said Kirby, "we'll have to fix supper here. There'll be that basket social before the dance, and those meals are usually good. Besides, we've been almost like two hermits since we came back from Montana. It's time we got back with our old friends."

Lucas agreed without great enthusiasm, and within the hour they were approaching Three Mile Creek where it splashed happily among the alders and willows above the Grange Hall. They turned down the creek and soon had their horses tied to the hitching rail in front of the hall, among numerous other mounts. Beside the building, closer to the creek, was a variety of buggies, hacks, and buckboards.

"Looks like this will be a record crowd," said Kirby.feeling his spirits rise. "Let's get in there and find ourselves a likely looking basket."

As Lucas and Kirby entered the hall, the auctioneer was slowing down, and only two baskets remained on the table. Spying the Phelps men, the auctioneer swung into his routine again. Lucas had seen Bob Cone sitting with Olivia and knew her basket was gone, so he bid on the first one offered. No one outbid him, and Miss Henley, the school teacher, smilingly approached, took him by the hand, and led him to a table.

Herb Jones had watched carefully, and though his spies had brought him no useful information he now knew, as did Kirby, that the last basket belonged to Cornelia. As the bidding started Kirby mentally counted the meager supply of coins in his pocket. But he kept raising the bid, five cents at a time, reluctant to spend everything he had. When Herb raised the ante to three dollars, Kirby glanced at Cornelia, saw the pleading look in her eyes, and bid his last two bits. The shock on Herb's face showed that he had shot his wad, and Cornelia came to the table smiling thankfully at Kirby, picked up her basket, and they sat down to eat.

Olivia sat inconspicuously, close to the far wall, well away from the platform where the band was assembling. A distant cousin, Bob Cone, who had ridden some thirty five miles from Slate Creek on the Salmon River, had purchased her basket. They had eaten quietly, and he was now beginning to show the fatigue from the long day's ride. When he greeted Olivia earlier in the evening his eyes had widened and he had murmured his appreciation. Few women, and certainly no man, could have ignored her beauty. Her princess-style gown of deep green velvet, was a study in subtle understatement. The full-length mutton chop sleeves were trimmed with lace about her wrists, and served to broaden her shoulders and accentuate her height. Lace also encircled the high collar, and at the last moment before leaving home she had pinned on her favorite gift from Jethro, a cameo brooch. The gown hugged her waist, and the flaring full-length skirt was gathered to form soft pleats which rippled in shades of green.

Some of the women in the crowd whispered to each other that the style was too young for her, or that the dress was too showy for this occasion. But all knew that the dress had been made for her by the best seamstress in Lewiston, and three 90-mile trips each way on horseback had been required just for the fittings. Olivia, who had wondered about the propriety of coming in the first place, had ended up defiantly dressing her best. Not that she wanted to attract a man—after all, who was there?

Cornelia, on the other hand, had accepted her mother's suggestion and put on her deep rose taffeta. The puffed sleeves made her look a little taller, the bodice was cut appropriately low and emphasized her tiny waist. The voluminous skirt was worn over small hoops, and rustled with every step.

Lucas and Kirby had done all they could, but though they were wearing their best and had shined their shoes they felt no match for the Martin women. But both enjoyed dancing and watched as the band assembled: two violins, a banjo, an accordion, and a square grand piano, imported from Austria by way of Portland, and the pride and joy of the Charity Grange.

Olivia and Cornelia had talked late in the afternoon while preparing their baskets. "What shall we do about Gopher? Many would not welcome him at the dance, and of course he'd feel uncomfortable," said Olivia. Cornelia thought a moment before answering. "He's very self-sufficient and almost seems to enjoy being alone. Let's just feed him a good supper and leave him here." So they did that, cautioning him to be careful about the fire, and went on their way. Gopher ate his supper and settled down in a big chair before the fireplace, thoroughly content, as loneliness was not part of his life. He dozed a bit, and heard only faintly the low rumble of thunder, realizing that it was some distance away.

The prairie people loved all kinds of dancing, but the Polka was usually used as a warm-up, since it was less formal than the Square Dance and Virginia Reel, and the band now swung into one of it's favorites. Newcomers to the prairie always stood in open-mouthed amazement when the Seth Joneses danced, and tonight, as usual, they were first on the floor. He resembled most of all a large, floating balloon with legs, and he never missed a step, regardless of how fast or how intricate the dance might be. His pert little wife, of average size, danced merrily around him held at arm's length by his rotund belly. Some said his waist measured sixty-four inches.

It was the custom, without being asked, for each woman to dance the first dance with the man who had bought her supper basket. Olivia, still a little self-conscious about possible criticism of her being there at all, accepted Bob

Cone's hand, and they managed the polka. As a third cousin, Bob was an eligible suitor for Olivia, and that thought was not too deep in his mind, for his own wife had died a few years before. At first sight of Olivia this evening, regal and lovely, he had caught his breath suddenly; and an almost forgotten, warm glow swept over him.

Four squares had now been formed, and Seth Jones had turned from dancer to caller. He was known throughout the area for his knowledge of the square dance movements, and his booming voice resounded throughout the hall. Kirby and Cornelia had danced the polka together, and were interrupted once when Herb Jones cut in, but then Kirby took Cornelia back. Now they were in one of the squares, and Kirby, though less proficient than Cornelia, was enchanted by her grace and precision, and, with her help, followed the dance easily. Now Seth directed the dancers:

Honor your old-fashioned girl,
Hold her close, swing and whirl,
Then promenade that ring.
Meet your maid and promenade round,
Like a jaybird walkin'' on frozen ground.
Do-sa-do your corner girl, go back home and swing and swirl,
Swing the girl like dear old Daddy said,
Allemande left with the ol' left hand,
Partner right and right and left grand,
A right and left around the ring,
While the roosters crow and the birdies sing.
Head gents swing your maids, take those girls and promenade
Just half-way 'round that ring.
Right and left through, right up the middle,
Hurry up boys, keep time to the fiddle.
Your left-hand ladies chain, all four ladies
Chain across the hall,
Chain right back again, don't let 'em fall.
Promenade this new little girl, she's just like the girl
That married dear old Dad.
Chicken on a fence and possum on a rail,
Take your honey and away you sail.
She's that gal from Mt. Idaho City,
Golly Gee, now ain't she pretty!

Cornelia's hoop skirt bothered Kirby at first, but soon he ignored it and seized every opportunity to hold her close, thrilling to her warmth, the subtle scent of her perfume, the swell of her young breasts. They danced most numbers together, rather breathless and feeling a new, disturbing closeness. The building's frame of heavy timbers vibrated in time with the music and the motion of the dancers, and none heard the rumble of thunder overhead.

Gopher, having returned from the kitchen after finishing off the last of the fried chicken, was dozing again in the big chair. He had heard the thunder at least twice, but ignored it. Now he was abruptly awakened as a dagger of light flashed through the window, and an ear-splitting explosion, a splintering, bursting crash seemed to tear apart all air and all objects about it. Gopher cowered for a few seconds, fearing a repetition of the terrifying light and sound; then he realized there was a different kind of light, and hurried to a window where he could look out toward the barn.

The giant Ponderosa Pine had stood for two hundred years before Jethro built the barn beside it, and one of its first branches, itself a foot in diameter, extended horizontally above the roof. The lightning bolt, in a fraction of a second, had coursed through the tree, shattering the huge trunk and cleaving off one half. As that half fell, the mammoth branch, laden with pitch and flaming blue-white, pierced the roof as if it were paper; and the glowing shaft shot fire into the dry Timothy hay, igniting the entire haymow and roof structure.

Gopher remembered Olivia and Cornelia driving away in the buggy pulled by their favorite team of matched Hambletonians, but he knows that in the barn are other horses, secure in their stalls where Olivia and Cornelia have been grooming them for the fair to be held soon. Gopher hurries to the kitchen door, and off the back porch into the slashing rain which has come with the lightning. The house and barn are deliberately built far apart, to prevent the spread of fire at a time such as this, and the 100-yard distance seems forever as Gopher races through the mud, slipping and falling, recovering his feet, intent on reaching the barn in time. He remembers when some of his father's best horses were tied in a shelter which caught fire, how wild-eyed they were, and how some, even when rescued and led away, attempted to run back into the flames.

Gopher struggles with the heavy door through which the horses must be led to safety, for the wind is blowing against it; but he forces it partially open and blocks it with a rock. The smoke is thick now, even on the ground floor of the barn, and he hears the horses' terrified screams, their high-pitched whinnies, the sound of stomping and kicking as they lunge about in their stalls. First he finds Olivia's Morab and the Morgan gelding which is his favorite. They know him, and the fire is not so threatening at that place, and he leads them out of the barn to a corral far enough away that they will be safe, and there he ties them.

Now he runs back to the barn, and as he rushes through the door he steps on small fires burning on the floor as patches of flaming hay fall from the haymow through cracks in the ceiling. The other horses are frantic now, for the smoke burns their nostrils, stings their eyes, and their tears run down. These are larger, more powerful horses, and Gopher knows instinctively that they are about to cross the quivering line between terror and mindless panic. He takes one horse at a time, hurrying to the closest fence where it can be tied safety. The floor is hot on his bare feet as he leads the last horse through the barn; a falling swatch of burning hay lands on his shoulder, but he shakes it off and stumbles on. With the horses all out Gopher wonders about the saddles, and scurries to the tackroom where they are kept. The ceiling above is on fire, and he can reach only the saddles closest to the door. The saddles are too hot to touch, but he manages to wrap saddle blankets around the horns of two of them. Together they weigh as much as he does, but he drags them out into the rain and lets them drop, succumbing to his exhaustion, sitting in the mud.

In fascination he watches the high vault of the barn collapse into the interior. All is a mass of flames, almost too hot to tolerate from fifty yards away. Then he rises to his feet and walks toward the corral, feeling for the first time the searing pain on the soles of his feet. There is a bridle hanging on one saddlehorn but it is too big to fit the Morgan—the halter rope must do as a rein. When he tries to swing the saddle up his arms do not work right and his hands fail to respond. Nor does he have the strength to mount bareback, so he leads the horse over beside the fence, which he uses as a ladder, and climbs on. Then he urges the little gelding toward the Grange Hall.

The revelry of the dance is now at its peak. All the adults have danced several times and many are tired. Some men have repeatedly gone outdoors to nip at the jugs, and a couple of city dudes from Mt. Idaho have shared their hip flasks. But the crowd is generally orderly, and all feel the closeness of friends about them. Children are asleep on piles of coats or on the floor beneath the tables. The band plays valiantly on, but the tempo begins to drag. Seth stops calling, and the couples stop dancing as they feel a cold draft about their feet and look toward the open door; finally Olivia, relaxed and talking comfortably with Lucas, looks that way also. The band has stopped playing, the room is entirely silent, and all eyes are on a small boy standing in the dark opening, his hair disheveled, a thin wet shirt clinging to his shivering shoulders, water dripping from his mud-streaked pants across his bare feet and onto the floor.

The silence is broken by a muffled scream as Olivia rushes to the door, kneels before Gopher, and hugs his rain-soaked body to the bodice of her velvet princess gown.

## CHAPTER 27

Yellow Wolf saw them first, hundreds of them in their well-ordered columns, flagstaffs fluttering the company pennants, and teams pulling two howitzers. And there also were Indian scouts, too far away to identify, but he knew they were Crows and Bannocks, perhaps a hundred of them—after the horses again!

Joseph saw Yellow Wolf's signal: "It is time to move the people!" White Bird and Welweyas responded quickly to Joseph's command, while Yellow Wolf and the rear guard raced to join the fleeing bands. Other warriors, with Looking Glass, formed a protective line across the mouth of the canyon. With a minimum of commands from anyone, the people moved on, though with less speed than usual, for their horses were weary and many of the remounts worn out.

"Some will have to be abandoned," said Joseph. "We will make them useless by cutting one foot on each horse; then all will be limping and neither the army nor the Indian scouts can use them."

The valley of Canyon Creek hardly deserved to be called a canyon. The trail was rocky and brush-laden, but it's rimrocks were high enough for good surveillance, and there the warriors took refuge behind rocks and fired carefully, deliberately, conserving their ammunition. The people hurried through the canyon to seek a camping place beyond, knowing that they had killed several soldiers and wounded many more; and at the rear the sharpshooter, Teeto Hoonod, carrying his fifteen-pound long gun, retreated slowly, skirting the high rimrock, sniping at any soldier that moved in the valley below.

Again, Howard arrived at the scene of the battle after the fighting was over. Other forces joined him there, but though they brought some supplies with them, food was so low that it was necessary to kill and eat wounded Indian ponies. The next day, Howard sent his cavalry ahead with Sturgis, who continued the pursuit for 150 miles. Then he simply gave up, informing Howard that he was not gaining on the Nez Perces, his supplies were almost gone and he was moving farther away from resupply every day: "It is a helpless pursuit, and I will stop before my horses are completely destroyed."

Sturgis soon changed his mind about quitting, however, and rested on the Musselshell River, waiting for Howard to catch up. The Nez Perces moved to the north, toward the crossing of the Missouri River and Canada. "We must avoid those mountain ranges both to the east and to the west," said Lean Elk, who was still leading. "I have always found good grass, plenty of buffalo, elk, and antelope in Judith Basin."

During the forced marches of recent weeks, the desperate and harried people had had little opportunity to observe the usual routines of their lives. The needs of the women were essentially ignored, and no woman's lodge had been set up since the night they camped on the Firehole River. Among the struggling women was a young widow, now terribly alone because not only her husband, but also her mother and mother-in-law had died at the Big Hole. Her belly was big with her first child, and while other women of her band usually watched over her, their own troubles now held their attention. She had struggled for a week or more, disturbed by the occasional flow of blood which she did not understand. Now she dropped out of the procession and took shelter in a grove beside the trail while the people moved on.

The sun then stood high in the heavens—midday—but it sat on the western horizon when the baby boy was born, and the delivery had left her exhausted. Soon the sun was gone, and the evening chill crept in as she lay huddled in the grove, the still-slimy little baby held to her breast beneath her light cloak.

The lonely mother—Fair Dawn, she was called—spent the night there beneath the trees, instinctively sensing the need to rest and conserve her strength. The people were now miles ahead of her, and she was without food. The bleak plains, devoid of camas or kouse, familiar nuts or berries, stretched away from her in all directions. Soon she must find food, and she was desperately thirsty.

As Fair Dawn arose to move on, hoping especially to find water, she realized that the spongy umbilical cord still stretched from her body to her baby. She had not helped with a birthing, and was confused about what to do, so she did nothing, only walked on to the north, hoping to find some kind of help. After a mile or two she felt a sudden gush of fluid, and then contractions like she might be having another baby, so she lay down on the ground and soon was relieved of her placenta. But it was still attached to the baby. She had seen other babies, tiny newborns, with the little stubs attached to their bellies and knots tied in them. So, lacking a knife, she lifted the baby, bit the cord in two with her teeth, tied a knot in it, and walked on.

The people had eaten well and had plenty of water while camping in Judith Basin, and Fair Dawn's breasts were full, so she thought her baby would be well fed. But the first day became the second, which merged into the third and that into the fourth, while the nights grew increasingly colder; she had found no food and drank only the dew from leaves each morning.

By the end of the fifth day she began to feel faint, and on the seventh day her eyes did not focus properly. She stumbled more often and realized in an abstract way that she was seeing things that really weren't there. During the morning of the eighth day she simply lay down beneath a tree, where darkness closed over her.

The jolting and swaying of the travois was disturbing her sleep, though the litter beneath her was comfortable, and the buffalo robes were delightful. She was warm and realized that her mouth was no longer dry, nor did her stomach feel so terribly empty. After a few hours the sound of horses' feet and the jolting of the travois stopped, and she was lifted off and carried into a warm tipi where someone laid her baby on her breast.

By the look of the things they used and wore, Fair Dawn knew she was with the Crows, and by their actions and the familiar sign language common to all tribes she learned quickly that these people meant her no harm. "Had they not been friendly, they would have left me out there with my baby to die," she thought.

Months passed, during which Fair Dawn and her baby thrived and became almost content with the Crows. It was not so hard to forget her own people, for most of those close to her were dead; perhaps she would just stay here. But there was talk among the Crows: "If the white agent discovers that she is not one of us, but a Nez Perce, she will be returned to her people. And where will they be then?"

## CHAPTER 28

Olivia and Cornelia cried out in anguish as they helped the still-shivering Gopher into dry clothes before the fire and discovered the extent of his injuries. Kirby was close to tears, and even Lucas, visibly moved, brushed his eyes with the back of his hand.

In the dim light of the kerosene lamps at the Grange Hall, and with wind and rain blowing through the door, Gopher had appeared to be only drenched and tired, so they hurried him into Olivia's carriage, where they wrapped him in a blanket. Lucas drove the carriage as they headed back toward the ranch while Kirby followed on the saddlehorses. The rain was still torrential, and the normally small streams that must be crossed were threateningly high and rolled rocks against the spokes of the carriage wheels. The banks of the streams and the steep pitches along the road were slippery with mud, and the Hambletonians struggled.

They reached the Martin place without accident, and as they approached from the north could see beyond the house the luminous glow from the heap of embers which once was the barn. At the Grange Hall Gopher, almost incoherent, had said only, "Fire in barn. Horses all right." But now the barn was no more and the once-huge Ponderosa Pine, the ageless sentinel of this ranch, was only a ghostly, blackened snag. Tearing their eyes from the riveting fascination of the huge mound of glowing coals, they scanned the barnyard to see two saddles lying in the mud, and farther away, at a safe distance from the fire, their beautiful horses, heads hanging low and rumps tucked as the rain streamed off them.

Wordlessly, they entered the house, and now the tears they might have shed over the loss of the barn or in joy at the safety of the horses could not be held back, for as the stiff, muddy trousers were pulled over Gopher's feet he cried out, and all saw that in his haste to reach the barn and save the horses he had forgotten his shoes, and the hot plank floor in the tackroom, even the soil outside the barn, had seared his feet, and they were a mass of deep blisters, the skin hanging loosely. Then they looked at his hands, and saw only raw flesh, with dirt-encrusted lines running across the palms, for the saddles he had dragged from the tackroom had cooked his hands, and some of the skin would be found on the halter rope of the little Morgan he had ridden to the Grange Hall.

All the home remedies known to the Martin and Phelps families, and the help of the doctor in Mt. Idaho, were required to save Gopher from the infections that invaded his hands and feet and threatened his life. Olivia and Cornelia nursed him constantly, rolled countless yards of cotton cloth for dressings, and perhaps most importantly, helped to keep up his spirits. Everyone else said Gopher would never make it; and if he did he would never use either his hands or feet, and would never ride again. But the thought of not riding again never entered his mind.

In the earliest days of his recovery Gopher cried like any young boy, but only during the most painful processes, and never for very long. The experience was not entirely new to him, for he had seen his sister stumble into a fire in the dark, and with only the simplest of care she had limped about the camp, been carried piggy-back by older children and lifted onto her horse. But she walked again. Weeks passed before Gopher could use either his hands or his feet, but on the day that he realized he could grasp the bridle reins he demanded his little Morgan.

They lifted him into the saddle, tucked his padded feet under the skirting rather than in the stirrups, and from that day he was back helping with the cattle and running errands for Olivia. The fires of October had smoldered to gray on the hillsides, and November was well along before the daily demands of caring for Gopher began to diminish. By that time Cornelia had taken over most of his care and Olivia's days were filled with supervising Herb and the other helpers with the cattle. Friends from nearby ranches had helped with the winter wood supply, while Lucas and Olivia directed hired hands in obtaining hay from as far away as Cottonwood, hoping the supply would be adequate for the winter.

A temporary lean-to shelter had been built immediately after the fire to protect the horses from the fall rains and all the horse equipment, including two new saddles, was now stored in the woodshed close to the house. Within a week after the fire Olivia and Lucas had talked about a new barn and had agreed she should rebuild on the old foundation.

"The mill at Mt. Idaho has a good supply of lumber available now," Lucas advised. "However, the heavy timbers are quite expensive. Since there's plenty of timber right here on your own land, you'll save by using logs for the posts and beams, even if you have to hire help for it."

"Sounds reasonable," responded Olivia, "but there's a lot to do on the foundation. I'm reluctant to accept more volunteer help, and I can stand the expense of new timbers."

Then both remembered what had happened on the third day after the fire when, in the dimness of the late October dawn, men began to gather from all directions. Lucas and Kirby, the instigators, were the first to arrive; others came from within the great arc extending from the breaks of the South Fork on the east to Rocky Canyon on the west. A few even came from the Salmon River. They came on horseback, driving buckboards or pulling flat sledges with wooden runners—stone boats they called them—which slid easily across the prairie sod. Some of them were already loaded with rocks picked up along the way, for everyone knew that much of the foundation of the burned barn would need to be replaced. By the end of the day the charred timbers, unusable rocks, ashes, and rubble had all been loaded onto the stone boats and dumped in a gully at the base of the mountain. Some had brought cross-cut saws with which they felled and cut up the charred snag of the ponderosa.

After the tired men had started home, well-fed by the huge meal prepared by Cornelia and Olivia, the two women walked out to sit on the five-foot-wide stump of the pine tree.

"How Dad loved this barn!" said Cornelia. "And you did too, Mother, sometimes I think almost as much as the house. You both had your own way with horses, and were always so comfortable caring for them." Olivia agreed, adding only that "we can replace the barn, but not this tree." And as she looked down at the massive stump on which they sat, she reflected that it was by far the largest of a number of such denizens scattered for miles along the base of the mountain.

"These trees thrive under just the right conditions," Jethro would often say. "The right altitude, at the right latitude, just enough rainfall, lots of sunlight; and this stretch bordering the prairie is ideal." Then sometimes he would muse that this tree was big even before anyone came to Camas Prairie, and may have been here when the first colonies were started on the East Coast. Sometimes Jethro even personified the tree, saying things like, "This old guy keeps things in perspective around here."

"Well, they're both gone now," thought Olivia, "but they'll always help me to maintain my perspective."

Gopher was helping Herb Jones and a couple of his cousins finish the foundation for the new barn. The Hambletonians were getting a workout as they pulled the wooden-runnered stone boat across the prairie grass. Gopher rode one horse and controlled the reins of both as they moved from spot to spot, where the cousins rolled on selected rocks. The sun was moving longingly toward rest in the featherbed of clouds on the far side of the Salmon River, and long, ghostly, shadows, thin counterparts of men and horses, walked beside them as the last load of rocks was pulled toward the barn site. The women had supper ready, and the tired young men ate without much talk. Herb not only was tired, but a little depressed, because he had again failed to obtain a seat next to Cornelia.

"It's just not possible for me to thank you people enough," said Olivia, subduing the wonder in her eyes as she watched Gopher manipulate a forkful of food with a hand hard to rotate and fingers that did not grasp well. "Some day I hope I can pay you adequately, and I'll greatly appreciate your being here early tomorrow morning when the dray wagons bring the posts and beams from Mt. Idaho. As Lucas says, those big rascals are expensive. We ship-sawed them from our own timber for the first barn; that was when most of you were just kids. But it was, as always, hard, slow, man-killing work, and I won't see anyone go through that again."

There was no response from the young men, and Olivia, presuming they were just tired, failed to notice the glances that passed between them.

They got up quietly and left the table, to mount their saddle horses and head home. Herb would spend an hour or two around the house with Gopher, helping him with his reading, then he would bring in the wood to keep the fires going through the evening. When the barn burned, it robbed Herb of his cozy little bunk area next to the tack room. Olivia had come to realize how much she relied on him since Gopher was disabled, and especially Herb's great patience in helping with Gopher's recovery.

So she put him in the guest room, explaining carefully that this was temporary, and she had something else in mind. The next day, Olivia summoned the best carpenters from among the cousins, and within two days they had enclosed one end of the back porch, where three walls, a window, and a door, now provided a comfortable room for Herb. Now he was close to the house but not inside it, which would not have been considered proper with the young Cornelia living there; and it was only a few steps to the pump in the back yard and to the door of the woodshed. Keeping the house supplied with wood and water was easy, and Herb loved the entire arrangement.

During the afternoon that Herb and the cousins were finishing the foundation for the barn Lucas had ridden over for a final inspection. He had been in the old barn many times, and Olivia's memory of it's construction was detailed, so together they had made a sketch of the foundation, and Lucas had helped the young men lay out the big rectangle on the ground, following the lines of the old foundation. Today he had made a final check to be sure the low foundation walls were level and there was a place to set each of the large posts that would be delivered tomorrow morning. "It will be a little slow," he had told Olivia, "with just me and Kirby and Herb and one or two carpenters. But within a couple of days we can have the main framework up and braced. The rest has to go up from there, of course, and if the weather doesn't favor us we'll wait until spring to enclose it and put on the roof."

"Well, the foundation looks great," said Olivia. "We counted two or three times, and agreed on the number and sizes of the posts and beams. I sure appreciate your taking care of that order over at Mt. Idaho. I presume everything's fine." Lucas agreed that everything was in order, and mounted Monty for the ride home. Olivia turned toward the house, remembering vaguely the glances exchanged by the young men after dinner. "Now Lucas had that strange twinkle in his eye. I'm being left out of something here."

The sun was barely up when Olivia and Cornelia walked out to await the arrival of the dray wagons bearing the posts and beams. Herb was puttering around the new foundation, and Gopher sat quietly on the Morgan gelding. His feet were still tender, and he as yet walked very little. Then Lucas and Kirby rode up, along with a couple of the Jones cousins, and all looked toward the east, watching for the big wagons. Olivia had brought a large pot of coffee, and sat it along with cups, sugar and cream, and freshly baked cookies on the stump of the pine tree. After a few minutes someone shouted, "There's the wagons!" And all watched as the wagons drew nearer. But as they started up the lane and approached the waiting foundation, a strange silence took over. It was broken by Olivia.

"There are no timbers!" she shouted, and hurried over to the driver. "Why are you bringing lumber? We ordered posts and beams!"

The driver looked a little puzzled, and pointed to Lucas. "There's the man who placed the order, and here's the bill of lading. See for yourself." And he handed it to Olivia, who confirmed with a glance that it was all lumber, plus nails and spikes and cast iron plates. Then Olivia looked at Lucas, whose face was blank. But the younger men were grinning. Feeling herself on the outside of some kind of a circle, she challenged Lucas, half-angrily, "Lucas, what's going on? Why did you buy this lumber? We can't start this barn without posts and beams!" Lucas gave no answer, but was looking beyond Olivia, who realized that another wagon had arrived. A grinning Morty Martin sat on the seat, along with his wife Jenny, and on the wagon behind them was a neat stack of a dozen or more newly peeled posts, all uniform in length and thickness.

"Now look to the east," said Morty, and Olivia turned to see other wagons approaching, each of them carrying it's load of carefully selected posts of a specific length, or long beams for a particular purpose, and they kept coming, the same people with the same buckboards and stone boats, who had helped clean up the burned out barn. Those from the flat prairie had not personally brought anything, since they had no timber, but had joined in with those closer to the mountain in cutting the posts and beams.

The early excitement had died down. Olivia in wonderment had walked among the wagons with Lucas, who pointed to each load: "Nine-foot posts to support the ceiling above the stalls. Twelve-foot posts for the higher walkway down the center of the barn. Sturdy beams sized to span from post to post. Long posts to support the high-pitched roofs. Skinny poles for rafters to receive the roof sheathing."

"All the pieces are here," thought Olivia, realizing why Lucas had been so searching and so detailed as they discussed the construction of the barn. Her thoughts were interrupted by laughter and a shout.

"Look what's coming!" And all looked eastward to see a strange contrivance approaching the Martin ranch. But it was not heading directly for the front gate. Instead, it had made a long swing to the north, starting perhaps a quarter of a mile to the east. Now the swing was almost completed, and soon Seth Jones, driving his prize team of black Percherons, arrived at the gate. Chained to the bed of his wagon in such a way that it could swing freely but not move forward or back was one end of a sixty-foot-long Tamarack, it's newly peeled trunk gleaming. Some forty feet back the slender trunk rested on the crossbeam of a set of front wagon wheels which had been removed from the rest of the wagon. The wagon tongue was suspended from the tree trunk in front of the wheels.

"No one but Seth Jones would come up with a rig like that!" laughed

Lucas, as Seth made a long, clean sweep to the left in order to bring the tree close to the barn site. He was greeted with cheers, good-natured laughter, and a lot of questions.

"How did you get it down out of the timber and onto the wagon?"

"How did you get it around the curves, and over the gullies where the road crosses those little creeks?"

"Why didn't you put the front end on your stone boat, and drag it?"

Seth took all this ribbing with his usual good nature, and then explained: "Every barn needs a good ridge pole, the slimmest, tallest Tamarack that can be found. In New England it's called a Larch, and makes the finest spars and masts for ships. I had my men cut it on that north slope this side of Grangeville, where the trees are all close together and skinny and tall. They dragged it out on the prairie before they peeled it, and we came on level ground, all the way. Yes, I could have dragged it behind the stone boat, but that would have scratched it all up."

There was more laughter, but it was all mixed with admiration and appreciation for the compliment Seth paid his sister by bringing her the cleanest ridge pole that would ever be installed on any barn on the prairie.

Teams of two men each had been assigned to cut, peel, and deliver a certain number of timbers of approximate length and diameter. Lucas, who had served as architect for this building, now became the construction foreman, and he knew where every timber was to be placed. The assembled crew included the prairie's best sawyers, carpenters, and axmen, and all had brought their tools. Crosscuts whined, as posts and beams were trimmed to exact length and the ends hewn to precise dimensions to fit when joined. This careful work took several minutes for each timber, but within an hour the frame began to take form, and by lunch time the shape and size of the building could be seen: 36 feet wide, 50 feet long, on each long side a 12-foot bay, nine feet high. But the center bay, also 12 feet wide, would be 12 feet high, for here Olivia would begin the breaking and training of the colts; and from the ceiling would be suspended pairs of halter ropes with snaps to be attached to the rings on a halter.

"If he can't get his head down he can't buck," explained Olivia. On the beams above the bays would be nailed the planking, making a floor for the second story containing the hay mow. Rooms would be enclosed there to serve as a bunkhouse for hired men, for Olivia was looking to the future.

By evening, the basic framework of posts and beams had been fitted, carefully squared, diagonally braced, and firmly joined with iron plates and big spikes. At proper intervals tall posts had been set to support the roof structure; beneath that would be the mow, in which would be stored the meadow hay which was always Olivia's choice for her horses.

"A good day's work," sighed Seth Jones, arising from a pile of logs. Everyone understood why he did not engage in physical labor, and they also listened to his advice.

"How about the ridge pole?" questioned one of the young Joneses. "It has to be there before we can put on the rafters."

"Far too late in the day to start a job like that," asserted Seth, and Lucas nodded in agreement.

"Tomorrow the Henleys will be here, and they're the experts on derricks and scaffolding and stuff of that sort. And I'm glad, because it's no small job; it takes real skill to put a ridge pole like that in place."

Gopher was mobile and comfortable on horseback. Herb had helped him onto the Morgan, from where he had watched the arrival of the wagons and the beginning of the construction. It was exciting at first, but he had no real part in it and his interest began to lag. Lucas asked him to ride to the Phelps ranch and bring back a large augur, which would be found hanging on the wall beside the door in the workshop. That had taken over an hour, and by the time Gopher returned the women had opened the big baskets of food they had brought and dinner was set up on plank tables beneath the wide spreading branches of the walnut tree.

Gopher sat inconspicuously beside Herb, not entirely comfortable, for this gathering of white people included some of the antagonistic kids he had seen at school a few months back, and their parents. With dinner over, and the children having explored all the corners of the ranch buildings, they were becoming bored, and so was Gopher.

"It's going to be a long afternoon," thought Cornelia, and she organized a baseball game to keep the children occupied. Then she realized that Gopher was left out, for as yet he could barely walk, much less run, and his hands could not grasp the bat. "But he can ride, and most of these kids brought their own horses." she thought. So a race course was set up, and all of the women, along with the men not occupied on the barn, joined the children to watch the race.

"You've rigged this race, Cornelia," chuckled Olivia, speaking quietly to be sure no one else could hear. "You know very well that none of the ponies, or even some of the better horses these kids rode here have a chance against Gopher on that Morgan."

"Of course I know that," smiled Cornelia. "And most of the other adults here know that also. But the kids don't, and they'll have fun. Besides, Gopher needs something to boost him right now."

They raced in four heats, with Gopher winning his by a full length. The other three winners were older boys well up in their teens, and Olivia recognized two of the mounts she knew had been sired by one of Ad Chapman's stallions and some of Seth Jones' mares. "Some competition after all," whispered Olivia to Cornelia.

Gopher's three opponents were all on good horses, which Olivia was sure the young riders had wheedled their fathers into letting them use for this race. "And there's the one that will give Gopher some stiff competition," she whispered. "I know that horse, and he's half Thoroughbred." The crowd was excited now. Men came down from the barn building and all gathered on both sides of the finish line at the end of the rough half-mile oval. “A Jones, a Henley, a Cone, and a nine-year-old Indian kid who can’t even walk,” Olivia mused, half aloud, as she watched Herb help Gopher into the saddle, wrap the reins around his calloused hands, and tuck his feet between the leathers above the stirrup.

Olivia and Cornelia knew that the little Morgan, shorter and not as fiery as the lean half-Thoroughbred, would not look good at the start, might even get away last; and at the end of the first fifty yards he was two lengths behind. No whip or spurs were needed, and it was soon seen that the Morgan was gaining ground. He was flat out in long, powerful bounds, encouraged by the sound of Gopher’s voice, who could not stand in the stirrups but was stretched low against the horse’s neck, his face lost in the flowing mane.

At the quarter mile Gopher had gained a full length on the Thoroughbred and was a neck ahead of the other two horses. Added to the strength of the Morgan, Gopher had another edge: he was thirty pounds lighter than any of the other riders. These advantages began to tell, and with only a furlong left the Cone boy on the Thoroughbred could hear the Morgan’s deep, rapid breathing and see his head out of the corner of his eye. The Thoroughbred’s lead was only a nose, and that’s the way the race ended. The crowd was wild; all were cheering, some were laughing, some were crying, and there was no telling which horse or rider had been the favorite.

The Cone boy knew he had come far too close to being beaten riding his Dad’s vaunted Thoroughbred—and by an Indian kid on a short-legged Morgan. He accepted the congratulations of his family and friends, and felt real admiration for Gopher, but kept that to himself. Lucas, Kirby, Cornelia, and Olivia gathered around, along with several of the Jones and Martin boys as Herb helped Gopher off the Morgan. Seth Jones was generous in his praise and Miss Henley, the school teacher, had tears in her eyes as she embraced Gopher. But many in the crowd, though they may have been cheering for Gopher at the end of the race, looked down their noses at Miss Henley’s show of emotion.

Eliza Randall, who had shunned Olivia and Gopher in the General Store, looked on in arrogant silence and said nothing. Some of the horse lovers in the crowd looked at Olivia’s horses, safe in the lean-to shelter, and silently gave thanks for the little Indian kid who was there when the lightning struck. As for Gopher, he was his usual happy self. Racing had always been part of his life, and no one spent much time congratulating the winner or worrying about coming in second.

The Henleys arrived bright and early the next morning with all the needed equipment to extend a derrick above the level needed for the ridge pole, hang their big block and tackle, and hoist one end of the long, slender pole into place; then they repeated the process on the opposite end of the barn. By noon the roof structure was firmly joined and it was time to install the long, skinny poles that would serve as rafters. By evening of that day most of the roof sheathing was on, and as the sun set, big bundles of thick cedar shakes waited on wagons on both sides of the building. They came from the shadowy side canyons along the forks of the Clearwater where, amidst the ferns and cool greenery beside the creeks, men with long crosscuts spent their days "making cedar". A tree might be six feet thick on the butt, and require an hour or more to be felled. Then it was made into fence posts or reduced to blocks the length of shakes. From such blocks the shakes were split, each one falling off at the resounding blow of the mallet on the thick-bladed splitting froh.

"I've been back in those cool draws and watched them make cedar." said Lucas. "It's a peaceful place to be, and the cedar smells like no other wood around here. Expensive to have them bundled up and hauled by wagon all the way to Mt. Idaho, but there's nothing better, and they'll be on that roof after most of us are gone."

Three days of hard, willing work, and the quiet, unpretentious love of family and friends. No one hesitated when asked to help, for all had volunteered to build other barns or houses, and some had buildings built by these same people. And some day, for whatever reason, it would happen again.

Lucas smiled at Olivia, and from a package he had been carrying under his arm he unwrapped a bronze weathervane.

"How appropriate," murmured Olivia as her hand moved over the smooth, polished contours of a running horse. And when the last shakes were nailed in place, Lucas climbed the steep roof and attached the weathervane to the ridge pole, where it rotated freely in the slightest breeze, the horse always facing into the wind.

The scent of the aromatic cedar hung in the evening air, as it would for years to come. The freshly peeled posts and beams gleamed softly and, forty feet above, the sixty-foot-long ridge pole supported the slender rafters as they formed the vault of the cavernous hay mow. Ten feet of the ridge pole extended beyond one end of the barn above the big doors that could be swung open at haying time when the pulley attatched to the outer end of the ridge pole would be used to lift the big forks of hay from the wagons into the haymow.

Many of the families across the prairie had helped to build the barn and had seen Seth Jones deliver the ridge pole, and within a week or two everyone else had heard the story. In later years when newcomers came to the ranch, perhaps to see Olivia's horses, someone would take them to the second floor of the barn and point up past the great mounds of hay to the ridge pole, and tell the story of how Seth Jones hauled it on two wagons—well, really a wagon and a half—when he brought it to his sister Olivia in the fall of 1877.

## CHAPTER 29

Rifle Pit
Cow Island
Sept. 23, 1877
10:00 A. M.

Colonel Glendinnin
Ft. Benton, Montana Territory

Chief Joseph is here, and says he will surrender for two hundred bags of sugar. I told him to surrender without the sugar. He took the sugar and will not surrender. What shall I do?

Michael Foley

When the Nez Perces crossed the Missouri at Cow Island, a few warriors visited the army supply dump, where they took what they wanted. They then made their way into a nearby ravine hidden from the soldier's rifle fire and rejoined the bands.

The next day the bands moved on northward, encountered a train of freight wagons, killed three teamsters, and took provisions. Now, with meat from Judith Basin, the Cow Island supplies, and those from the freight wagons, the Nez Perces were well supplied. But food was not enough, for the long months of running had almost depleted the horses; even those taken from the Crows at Judith Basin were weary and limping. Alternating periods of near starvation and heavy feasting when food was available had sapped the people's strength. Hurrying was not to their liking, so the ruthless Looking Glass, ever watchful but biding his time, now moved in to displace Lean Elk.

"You are pushing the people too hard, Lean Elk," Looking Glass charged coldly. "Look at the horses and the people! They need rest, and time for their bodies and minds to readjust. We have always found buffalo in this country, and will certainly find some in the next day or two. There's a storm coming in, and that storm will slow Howard's pursuit." The nonchalant attitude of the people made Looking Glass' words very attractive, and their memories again were poor. So they listened, and Lean Elk gave in, saying, "All right, Looking Glass, you can lead. I am trying to save the people, doing my best to cross over into Canada before the soldiers find us. You can take command, but I think we will be caught and killed."

Ignoring Lean Elk's warnings, the council of chiefs agreed to let Looking Glass reassume the leadership; and the bands resumed the leisurely pattern of travel. The warriors ranging ahead of the procession killed several buffalo along Snake Creek on the northern side of the Bear's Paw Mountains, a familiar place where the Nez Perces had often camped before; Tsanim Alikos Pah, the Place of the Manure Fires, it was called, for the ground everywhere was littered with buffalo chips, easily available for cooking fires.

Here they rested, well supplied with water, protected from the sharp northerly winds, now occasionally spitting snow; and they rapidly replenished their supply of buffalo meat and saved the big hides to make robes. The gaunt horses gained weight as they fed on the abundant buffalo grass, and their tender hooves began to heal and toughen again.

"Life is good now," all thought. "We have outdistanced Howard and are well supplied with things we have taken from the white man; and with this big supply of buffalo meat we can face the winter. And best of all, the Land of the Grandmother is only two, possibly three days ride ahead."

Little Bird had felt insecure when Looking Glass rested the leadership from Lean Elk. None of the other leaders had protested, and this added to her uneasiness. "Why is their memory so short? Why do not Ollokot, Joseph, Wottolen, and the other strong leaders protest this change? Only White Bird has expressed any opposition."

She had started to speak, but held her tongue, for disagreement by a woman was unthinkable. Now, though it was almost mid-morning, Little Bird lay in Yellow Wolf's lodge listening to the sounds of people moving about the camp, smelling the already fetid odor of the hides taken from slaughtered buffalo, relaxed and listless, lacking her usual compulsion to start the day. A growing breeze whispered across the barren hills and mingled the smell of burning buffalo chips with the stench of the hides.

White Bird's voice cut through the morning air. "We must move on. Sitting Bull is only a two-day ride to the north." Then followed Looking Glass' soothing, persuasive reply: "No hurry. Enjoy the fires here away from the wind, finish your morning meal." Little Bird groaned inwardly, resenting the urgency in her bladder that pushed her to get up. She arose heavily, wrapped a blanket about her, and moved down the gully past several families who were partially packed for the day's trip. Across the creek on the rise of the hill she saw movement among the herd as other people caught their horses. "Perhaps Hawk is there," she thought, and walked in that direction, realizing vaguely that she had seen little of Yellow Wolf through the night just passed and the day before. "He is probably scouting the back trail. He and Ollokot and a few others like them do not wait for Looking Glass to give orders for our safety."

Having found a place to relieve herself behind the brush in a small gully, she soon felt better and moved toward the horse herd. She saw Hawk, called to him, and he came at a trot. A few days of rest with plenty of water and grass had returned the sparkle to his eyes and the spring to his steps.

Yellow Wolf watched from a rise north of the camp, ignoring the snowflakes that drifted on the gathering wind. To his left and slightly behind him he was aware of people catching horses, tying on the packs. Looking across the little valley where the camp lay, he could see the ridge that rose above it to the south, and beyond that the broad sweep of the dry, rolling hills, bleak under the dull autumn sky and blending with the gray horizon. Less than an hour before Yellow Wolf had heard the urgent warning of a rider racing in from the south: "Buffalo running! Soldiers are coming!" Back from the camp had come Looking Glass' reassuring voice, slowing down the people: "Buffalo are always running somewhere. Take your time, feed your children."

But now as more of the people found their horses and continued their packing, Yellow Wolf's Wyakin blessing began to assert itself, that part that had always said, "You can hear whatever you want to hear at great distances," and at first it was just a rustling in the wind, only a slight trembling in the earth, like the faintest far-distant thunder, barely heard but ignored. But soon the sound could no longer be ignored, though as yet no one but Yellow Wolf could hear it. He turned again, probing the far distance, sensing the power in his eyes, and there he saw several dark blue bars, barely discernible in the dim light. And though he heard the increasing sound, the meaning of the dark, moving bars was not yet perceived; but suddenly the bars became a long blue band stretching from east to west as columns of four spread to form a skirmish line.

Then to Yellow Wolf's left and on a higher ridge much closer to the camp appeared a rider wheeling his horse, waving the blanket: "Soldiers are coming! They are almost upon us!" Yellow Wolf's eyes swept the camp, where many people now responded to the sentry's warning. Joseph was not in sight, still behind the little ridge, not yet aware of the danger. At the edge of the horse herd Yellow Wolf saw a flash of white, then discerned dark spots on a horse's white rump: Hawk! And Little Bird leading him! The frenzied activity increased as more people rushed toward the herd to find their pack horses, load them, and prepare to flee.

Almost 3,000 hard hooves drummed the earth like continuous thunder, louder than hail on tipi walls, as more than 600 mounted soldiers spurred their excited horses toward the camp. Yellow Wolf watched as the approaching blue band quickly projected an evil claw from each end, clutching hungrily at the camp; and above the deafening roar of the pounding hooves came crackling volleys of rifle fire. Then he turned to see the eastern claw encircling the camp. Many of the people were packed and moving, some escorted by young warriors. Joseph lifted Running Feet to a pony's back, slapped its rump with his quirt, mounted his own horse Ebenezer, and, along with many warriors returning from the horse herd, rushed back toward the camp. Other warriors had reached the heads of gullies and small sandy ridges, digging in, facing the higher ridge to the south, returning the soldiers' fire.

Yellow Wolf soon realized that these were not Howard's men, for they were more vigorous and more precise. And with them were not the Bannocks and the Crows, but scouts from the Cheyenne and the Sioux, and some of them, leading that eastern claw, had helped to drive away many of the Nez Perce horses. No, this new force was directed by Col. Nelson Miles; he had underestimated the distance to the camp when starting his charge and many of the horses were tiring, but he still hoped to overcome the camp in one devastating onslaught. And he might have succeeded, except for the determined Nez Perce warriors crouched low behind those small ridges, half buried in the protecting sand. Their fire was chillingly accurate, but so were the soldiers' shots. Many, both white and Indian, looked into the eyes of death.

When Colonel Miles received orders from General Howard to pursue the Nez Perces, he assembled a formidable force of over 600 well-equipped men. Among them was the Seventh Cavalry, which only a year ago and not far from here had lost more than 200 men, along with George Armstrong Custer. Now Miles threw the Seventh directly at the Nez Perces. It's commander, Captain Hale, was killed instantly, and a second officer was mortally wounded. Two other officers were seriously wounded, and the Seventh was almost annihilated.

Captain Carter also charged the camp, but was beaten back with the loss of one-third of his command. Devastating numbers of officers were killed within the first thirty minutes, picked off individually each time a Nez Perce warrior heard one of them give a command. When Lt. Eckerson, dripping blood, rushed back to Miles to say that he was, "the only damned man of the Seventh who wears shoulder straps left alive", Miles stopped the frontal attack and settled down to siege the encircled village. It was a wise decision, for of the 125 men in the Seventh Cavalry, 53 were already dead. Mounted infantrymen augmented the Seventh Cavalry, and facing both units were not more than 80 Nez Perces, who fought them to a standstill.

The Nez Perce resistance was fierce, and their deadly accuracy took a heavy toll, but there was also much confusion. Three Nez Perce braves near the border of the camp were mistaken for enemy scouts, and Husishushis Kute calmly shot all three. Another Nez Perce warrior, in the dim light of a blustery day, thought he saw a Cheyenne scout. A shot rang out and the man fell dead; but it was not a Cheyenne, for dying there was Lean Elk, he of the keen mind and determined spirit who had led the people well, but was defeated by their capricious nature and the wiles of Looking Glass.

Throughout the first day's fighting Yellow Wolf, along with other warriors who had attempted to reach the horse herd, was outside the circle of soldiers surrounding the camp and watched as Cheyenne and Sioux scouts shot both Nez Perce warriors and women. Amidst furious and frenzied fighting, Yellow Wolf led a foray against a company of infantry attempting to break through to the camp, and not more than twenty Nez Perce warriors drove back some sixty soldiers.

Now with the wind heavy with snow and burning with the flash of guns and the odor of black powder, Yellow Wolf longed for the times of peace when his people had seldom been required to fight. Then as the tide of battle worsened, he looked about him with despair. Soldiers were coming from every direction and there was little hope left. He must fight or die. He raised his rifle to the sky and shouted, "Here in this lonely place I will die! I will die for my people, and for our homes, though they are far away."

As Joseph slapped the pony and watched it carry Running Feet into the storm, he was almost trampled by the retreating horse herd, and knew he must return to the camp to fight, for Springtime and Early Flower were there. He had caught Ebenezer, but had no rifle, so with a prayer to his Wyakin he plunged through the thickest of the battle, guns exploding on all sides and bullets tearing at his clothing. Ebenezer was wounded but Joseph reached his lodge unharmed, where Springtime handed him his rifle. Through that afternoon the furious battle continued, and several warriors were killed. Then soldiers charged into the camp, killing yet others, and Joseph stood with his men to form a defensive wall, fighting hand-to-hand. The soldiers were driven back to their main line, leaving their dead behind.

The snow grew heavier as the fighting continued. The resourceful women and their children burrowed into the banks of the ravines like badgers, using anything available—sticks, knives, cooking pots, their bare hands—and they soon had caves deep enough to protect them from the storm and the stinging missiles of death from the hill above them. They had only small fires, for the willow wood was gone; the buffalo chips, sought beneath the snow by numb hands or bare feet, were damp, and only smoldered. The dead and wounded lay everywhere. Hungry, terrified children whimpered. The chill air quivered with the high, keening wails of the women, while one mortally wounded warrior began, with his fading breath, to sing his death chant, and was joined by others.

During that first day and through the night fifteen Nez Perce men and three women were killed. Crumpled in a small ravine, the falling snow now obscuring his face, was the one closest to Joseph's heart—Ollokot. He had perished in the withering fire of Cheyenne scouts and soldiers who appeared suddenly above the rim. And not far from Ollokot lay the "cross-grained old growler," the obstinate, unyielding Toohoolhoolzote, whose spirit would now soar above the high plateau between the Salmon and Snake rivers. Others died that day, and the remaining chiefs, reduced to only three—Joseph, Whitebird, and Looking Glass—faced a grim prospect as all but a few of the horses were gone. Sitting Bull was two or three days away, and they had no reason to believe he'd be coming to help. Several hundred soldiers surrounded them, and both Howard and Sturgis were approaching with additional forces.

Having deliberately left her bed, Little Bird was better clothed than most of the people. Searching for their horses, many had left the camp without shoes, and some were almost naked, having planned to lead their horses back to be loaded. Some carried bridles only, and few had saddles. With the danger now terrifyingly real, Little Bird improvised a single rein using the thong about her waist, looped it around Hawk's jaw, and with some difficulty pulled herself onto his bare back. Then she was engulfed in the frantic throng of women, children, older men, and a few mounted warriors, all hoping they were headed north but confused by the sudden attack. The gray sky didn't allow the sun to shine as a guide. None had ever crossed into Canada before, and no one knew the exact location of Sitting Bull's camp, but now they thought only of survival as they hurried away into the blowing snow.

The departure had been confused, lacking Joseph's usual leadership. Very few people had completed loading their horses, and both their departure and their progress were disorderly. Small clusters became lost from the others and wandered aimlessly. Little Bird found herself part of such a group, and moved with it through the storm; all hearing behind them the sounds of rifle fire and the heavy booms of the cannon with which Miles' men were hurling exploding shells among the cowering people in their dugouts. Little Bird pitied the people about her, especially the children, half-dressed and without moccasins, riding behind their mothers, their bare, shivering arms clutching waists for security and warmth.

Little food had been loaded on the horses, and many of the people had not eaten breakfast. Now as the night descended the pangs of hunger overtook them, and they shared precious morsels. Not daring to build fires, they huddled together, sleeping in the snow without blankets, holding their horses' reins, for to lose their horses would almost certainly mean death. And as darkness shrouded them, their thoughts turned back to the camp, imagining the now-cold body of a relative they might have helped to bury. Then in spite of their gnawing hunger weariness prevailed, and they slept in sheer exhaustion and the hope of shutting out the bitter memories.

In the thin gray light of dawn Little Bird awakened to the whisper of a feathery coldness about her face. Hawk stood nearby, his head drooping, the blanket of snow making him pure white. Little Bird suppressed her nausea and arose to give whatever help she could to the troubled people around her. Then the group moved on, trusting the man who had assumed leadership to take them to Sitting Bull. The next day they were saved by Nez Perce warriors who overtook them. the warriors had a better sense of direction; and soon they built a fire, that most wondrous comforter to those who wander in cold and loneliness. Soon they were joined by other refugees, and the men in council determined to move on as rapidly as possible to find Sitting Bull. Then great fortune! A buffalo was killed and all feasted hungrily. As they came closer to Canada they encountered a friendly band of Chippewa who gave them more food and provided them with essential things. Most welcome of all were new moccasins for frozen feet!

All about them, though unseen and not sensed in the whirling snowstorm, were more travelers. Some lacked determination and turned back toward the camp, for surrounding them was the white, silent nothingness. But why return to the camp? The sound of guns, the moaning of the wounded, the stiffening bodies of loved ones, their tortured faces now hidden beneath the merciful shroud of snow. But there were live people there also. So in the night they crept back between the sentries, who in their own loneliness had gathered two by two, leaving gaps in the picket line. This same ease of filtering through the lines had caused Joseph and Looking Glass to recruit volunteers whom they sent northward in the hope that Sitting Bull would come to their rescue. But the messengers encountered a band of Assiniboins and were all murdered, for the Assiniboins wanted the army to know they were not assisting the Nez Perces.

## CHAPTER 30

In at least one way Colonel Nelson A. Miles had something in common with Colonel Gibbon, who had commanded at the Big Hole: the silver eagles on his epaulets no longer satisfied his ambition. He had stars in his eyes, permanent stars. "They will be so much brighter," he fantasized, "than those temporary stars which were replaced by these eagles at the end of the Civil War." Upon orders from Howard, Miles had moved rapidly toward the Bear's Paw, correctly calculating the route the Nez Perces were following. "No more shooting at deer or antelope, or anything else," he told his troops. "The Nez Perces don't know we're coming, and must be given no warning! We will roll over them with our first charge!"

Though the Nez Perces were severely damaged by the initial attack, it was even more devastating for Miles' forces. So he completed his encirclement of the camp and settled down for a siege. "It's obvious that for the Nez Perces the end is in sight," he said to his officers. "We saw some of their fighting men head north, along with many of the people. Those remaining have little food and can't get more, for we now have them surrounded. They can get water, but only at night. And we have over 500 soldiers left, with adequate supplies and an unrestricted line of resupply."

Miles knew that General Howard, Colonel Sturgis, and several hundred additional men were approaching from the southwest, but Miles' compulsive ambition and desire for a permanent star compelled him to end the conflict. Miles also had a second motivation: his wife was the niece of General William T. Sherman. Both she and her uncle would bask in the glory of this victory!

After the initial crushing attack, both the army and the Nez Perces spent the first dreary night caring for their wounded and bury their dead, many of whom lay exposed to rifle fire and could not be retrieved safely. So the Indians and their attackers shivered through the darkness, the Indians a little better protected in the deep holes they had dug, for they knew about buffalo chips and had fires, which the soldiers did not. And twenty percent of Miles' command were now dead! In the light of dawn with snow still falling, firing became a contest of sharpshooters, who found few targets among their entrenched and wary opponents. As the day wore on, Miles' determination to force an early surrender became stronger, so he put up a white flag and called for Joseph.

The name "Joseph" retained the same encompassing, collective kind of meaning it had acquired on Camas Prairie, in newspapers and army records, even at the Cow Island crossing, when the message "Joseph is here," was sent by a private who had never seen him. So now Miles recognized Joseph as overall leader and asked for a conference. Joseph consented to talk with Miles, and at first it seemed they might make progress, for it was clear that the army had the upper hand.

But then Miles decreed, "You must surrender all of your guns." Joseph drew back and said, "No. We live on wild game. We must keep at least half of our guns." And he turned to return to his people.

This war had really started when Ad Chapman, scouting for Captain Perry, fired on a white flag party at Whitebird Canyon. Now another white flag was used as a truce for the attempted peace talk between Miles and Joseph. And there in the snow-swept, bleak plains of far northern Montana the truce flag was again violated as Miles seized Joseph, had him hobbled, rolled tightly in a blanket, and left with the mules. But the young, naive Lt. Jerome wandered into the Nez Perce camp, just to look around while the white flag was up, and was immediately seized by Yellow Bull.

"Kill him!" shouted the fierce young warriors. But Wottolen, always the steady one, along with Yellow Bull said, "No. We now have some advantage. They won't harm Joseph as long as we have this officer."

The Nez Perces were deliberate in treating Lt. Jerome well, and when Colonel Miles learned of this he retrieved Joseph from the mule corral, took off his hobbles and let him walk back to his people. The siege continued for three more days, the Nez Perces hoping that Sitting Bull would come to their rescue, and Miles fearing that possibility. So when on the fourth day a cry went up, "Riders coming from the north," the army units frantically prepared for a defense. But soon it was seen that no mounted warriors were approaching, but rather a herd of buffalo. With snow encrusted on their arching humps they did look like horsemen at a distance. The Nez Perces were downcast, and the army was jubilant.

Finally Howard arrived with a small advance detachment; he had heard nothing from Miles for six days, and found him well in command of the situation. Howard approached his former aide, but was rebuffed by Miles. This Howard ignored, understanding well the driving ambition of career officers. So he expressed his appreciation to Miles, and asked him to finish the work so well begun. Howard was accepting and gracious, and Miles was relieved and delighted. But Howard's men felt he should have the honor, and expressed their resentment openly: "After all, we have struggled for three demanding months! Now comes another bunch out of their snug compound down there at Fort Keogh. After an unchallenged march of less than two weeks, they charge in here at the last moment to end the war!"

These arguments had little effect on Howard, for Miles had been very close to him during the Civil War. Miles would be allowed to accept the surrender, a fact which was of course quickly known by General William. T. Sherman, and was influential in Miles' future promotions. He would become Chief of Staff, and a few years later, be promoted to Lt. General, with three permanent shining stars gracing his epaulets.

Before Howard's arrival, the remaining warriors and the three band chieftains—Whitebird, Looking Glass, and Joseph—had some hope of reaching Sitting Bull. But then suddenly Howard was there, and soon his main force would arrive and overrun the camp. Though the chieftains saw the futility of further resistance, they would follow the Indian way and not necessarily agree; each of them, and each individual, was still free to act on his own. Joseph lamented his people roaming the bleak land, suffering from the cold, possibly freezing, while at the battle scene children were crying with hunger in the clammy dampness of the pits. It was for them that he would surrender.

But Looking Glass, remembering his bitter experiences with Howard at the Lapwai council, spoke of him as a man of two faces and two tongues, saying, "Joseph, if you surrender you will be sorry, and in your sorrow you will feel rather to be dead than suffer that deception. I will never surrender to a deceitful white chief." Then Whitebird, oldest of all the band chieftains and old enough to be Joseph's father, repeated his declaration, "I have never known a white man to honor an agreement." He had already decided to take his people on to Canada.

After this exchange Joseph, along with several warriors, crossed over the lines for one last talk with Miles and Howard. Looking Glass lay in one of the exposed rifle pits, talking with other warriors, when one suddenly said, "A warrior is approaching on a horse. Perhaps it is a Sioux, come to help us." Looking Glass leaped to the bank above the rifle pit, took one look, and turned to tell his friends that it was only one of their own riders. But an army sharpshooter had seen him. All heard the sucking plop of the bullet that tore Looking Glass's skull apart, and he fell dead among his friends.

White Bird and Joseph now remained as the recognized leaders and neither of them could know that after this day they would never see each other again; nor could they imagine how great the fragmentation and how weary the ways now facing their people.

During the final talk between the Nez Perces and the army staff Howard, having acceded to Miles and still in possession of his fatherly feeling toward him, stood back while Miles proceeded with the negotiations. The Nez Perces did not fully trust Howard. Miles sensed that fact and told Joseph and his warriors that Howard would soon be off on another campaign, and would probably forget this situation. "Then I will take you to a safe place. In the spring you can return to your homes."

Joseph, though knowing that the people could fight no more, never agreed that he or anyone else had sought the surrender. "I did not say 'Let's Quit;' they did!" he declared, as he started the short ride to Howard and Miles. Joseph, his head bare, his unkempt braids hanging loosely, his blanket dirty, his buckskin leggings stiff with mud, rode a strange horse, for Ebenezer had been driven off or killed during the battle. Though he had not said, "I quit," the sickness of defeat was in his heart, and sadness settled over him.

But he held himself erect and proud, as the waiting officers had hoped he would and could now report that he did. For The Army does not fight face-less bands of Indians or second-level leaders; it fights ferocious, indomitable chieftains who, when finally overcome after the bravest of battles, surrender with great dignity.

Howard's aide, Lt. Wood, stood with the assembled officers as Joseph approached. Looking on was Ad Chapman, he who had fled to Lapwai as soon as fighting started on the Salmon River, to be employed as a scout by Howard; he who had fired upon the white flag party at Whitebird Canyon and later boasted about it, and had outrun the other volunteers as they fled up the mountain away from the battle. Now he watched as Joseph solemnly dismounted, walked to General Howard, and held out his rifle. Howard refused the rifle, and motioned Joseph on to Miles, who accepted it.

Then Joseph began to speak. Ad Chapman interpreted and Lt. Wood took notes. No one knows exactly what Joseph said that day, for Chapman, a rough-hewn rancher with little education, may not have really understood the full meaning of the words; and the speech, as reported, was filtered through the fertile, creative mind of Lt. Wood, and rewritten before being published. But certainly Joseph spoke of the things that were in his heart: the depth of suffering he shared with his wandering people and his desire to take them home; his bitter feelings over the loss of so many; the memory of his dead brother Ollokot; his need to find his family and rest with them. And then he ended his speech, referring to the time, establishing a day and hour in a way that perhaps only the Indians present fully understood:

"From where the sun now stands, I will fight no more forever."

---

Those Nez Perces remaining in the camp thought all the horses were gone, and they were nearly right, for the Bannock and Crow scouts along the way had taken many. The army had captured 600 the first day of the battle and given many to the Cheyenne and Sioux scouts. And the people who fled toward Canada had taken some horses with them, few of which would survive the trip.

And now the warriors, sad and downcast, formed a pathetic line as they walked toward Miles to surrender their weapons. Women and children followed them, and were treated well by the soldiers, for there were warming fires and plenty of food. There was much posturing, some joviality, and attempts by the army officers to be magnanimous with their captives. "No more battles, no more wars," they would say. "Plenty of rest, good food and water from this time on. I have lost brothers, but they are also your brothers, and those you have lost are mine."

That night Whitebird assembled the remainder of his band and led them away toward Canada, making well over 200 souls who were now struggling desperately through the snow, seeking Sitting Bull's camp.

"Yellow Wolf, your mother and my daughter are wandering in the cold," Joseph said. "Find them and bring them back." Yellow Wolf quickly obtained a warm blanket, placed his short rifle inside his leggings and wrapped two cartridge belts around his body. "I refuse to go with the people controlled by the soldiers," he said. "I will walk past the guards, and if they try to stop me I will kill them."

Howard and Miles agreed the Nez Perces they now controlled would spend the winter at Fort Keogh and in the spring they would return to Idaho, just as Joseph understood when he surrendered the remnants of the bands. So the disheveled, downcast people, dependent on bare necessities provided by the army, were assembled on the plain near the camp. Those who could ride were provided horses, until recently their own but now loaned to them by Miles. The wounded and the weak were loaded into wagons, where brush and grass had been placed to protect them, however slightly, from the jostling and bouncing of the stiff wagon beds. In this way the despondent captives moved toward Fort Keogh, reversing the route which Miles had traveled to defeat them.

Howard met them at the Musselshell River, again talked briefly about sending the Nez Perces home the next spring, but expressed some concern that the plan might be vetoed by a higher command; so he boarded a steamboat and headed for Chicago to talk to General Sheridan. Miles was doing his part, and upon arrival at Fort Keogh he helped the Nez Perce prisoners establish a comfortable camp on the south bank of the Yellowstone.

## CHAPTER 31

The sun, which had been seen dimly through low, broken clouds was now lost beyond the Salmon River. Olivia, Cornelia, and Gopher sat before a fire which dispelled the evening chill and had barely settled themselves in comfortable chairs when there was a knock on the door. Olivia opened it to greet Lucas and Kirby, their sheepskin collars turned up around their ears. There were the usual warm greetings, with neighborly hugs all around, except that Lucas did not hug Gopher. To Olivia's surprise, Cornelia hugged Kirby, but released him quickly, and both Olivia and Lucas saw Cornelia blush. She showed no indifference, but a new kind of shyness, a sense of expectation.

Kirby understood, for in the final moments of the last dance at the Grange Hall, just as Gopher arrived and while the crowd watched the forlorn figure at the open door, he and Cornelia had found a secluded spot behind the coatrack, where they kissed, and lingered and kissed again, and neither was sure who had started it all. Now they composed themselves and sat down by the fire as Lucas brought out a bedraggled newspaper from the inside pocket of his coat.

"Morty Martin brought this copy of the Lewiston Teller when he came back from the valley with his draywagon yesterday. The most interesting story in it tells of the surrender of Chief Joseph and the Nez Perces at a place called Snake Creek in the Bear's Paw Mountains of northern Montana. It quotes part of an account by Col. Nelson Miles about his subduing the hostile Nez Perces, and accepting Joseph's surrender. Miles! Who is this Miles? And where was Howard? He isn't even mentioned! Sounds just like Colonel Gibbon marching in at the Battle of the Big Hole before Howard got there."

The next day the weekly delivery of the Lewiston Teller arrived in Grangeville, where copies could be bought at the General Store. It carried added details about the Nez Perce surrender and Miles' great victory. But what caught the attention of everyone who read the surrender account was one short paragraph: "It is reported that Colonel Miles and General Howard, who was finally present for the surrender, have agreed that the Nez Perces should be held at Fort Keogh through the winter, and then returned to Idaho."

That message—the Nez Perces are coming back to Idaho—spread rapidly . Among readers of The Teller, in excited conversations on the street, and at every public meeting, the smoldering hatred flamed again. There were posturing, ragings against an insensitive government, vows to recall the volunteers and begin active training and of course, the threats. "They shall not be returned here, and if they are, every one of them will die! Keep your weapons ready at all times, and a goodly supply of ammunition. In the meantime, we will call upon the Territorial Governor, and send the strongest of messages to our people in Washington. There shall be no repetition of the hell we went through last summer!"

In Oregon's Wallowa Country there was also great consternation. "We must go immediately to the state capitol and talk to the Governor! We came by this land fairly and squarely, under established Federal Law, and will not have Joseph, or any other Indians, living anywhere near us!"

So, with an eye to their own political futures, representatives from both states listened carefully and took the necessary actions. The return of any Nez Perce to any part of Idaho or Oregon must not be allowed!

After the news of the Nez Perces' defeat and the rumor that they might be returning to Idaho, Olivia again became concerned about Gopher's education, for each day she saw evidence of high intelligence, a rapidly increasing vocabulary, and a better understanding of the words he heard spoken. Once more, she talked with Miss Henley about bringing Gopher back to school.

"I don't see him very often," replied Miss Henley, "but when I do I observe all the things you mention, and I'm willing to try again. Let's plan on this coming Monday." But on Saturday morning an apologetic Miss Henley rode up to Olivia's door. "I told the children at school that Gopher was coming back. They didn't say much; their reactions were guarded at best. But within an hour after school let out five parents descended upon me, and all were adamant: "If Gopher comes back to school our children stay home. And don't try this again or the school board will hear from all of us, and more!" Gone were Olivia's hopes that time and familiarity, and especially Gopher's heroism in saving the horses from the fire, might have changed some minds; the parents now seemed more determined than ever to exclude him.

With the heaviest of the fall work behind them, Lucas and Kirby had relaxed a little. Now, feeling guilty about loafing, they let their minds wander. Kirby's was back at the Martin ranchhouse, and he felt a glow as he remembered Cornelia's embrace—warm, but quick, attempting to look casual without much success. For this excitement, this growing awareness of Cornelia, often came back to him at odd times and places. And then would come the conflicts: "Why are these feelings so different from my memories of Little Bird, those quiet, peaceful, almost idyllic times that finally exploded and were blown away by violent events? Why does it all seem so remote now? But when I am close to Cornelia, our feelings are real, and in the present; nothing remote about them. So what do you do now, Phelps?" And that afternoon he saddled the black and rode toward the Martin ranch.

Lucas still struggled with his own thoughts: "More than fifteen years since I last saw her! And yet, unpredictably, those vivid images return—Mei Ling's face, the sweetness of love in her eyes, her trim, slight, figure, the blue-black glint of lamplight on her hair." Then his guilt would shame him. "I should have risked my life trying to find her in that dark river!"

And while Jenny's soft smile, her innate dignity, her total devotion to him and to Kirby and Phoebe still lingered, she had become a vignette, a shadowy memory, sweet and sustaining but without excitement, fire, or passion. At the recent dance at the Grange Hall he had overheard a conversation not meant for his ears: "Lucas needs a woman, though of course he's proper enough to not show it this soon after Jenny's death." Lucas had thought it a natural enough conclusion, and realized the need was there, even as he approached fifty years of age. Then he thought of Olivia, beautiful, queenly, strong Olivia, always in control: "She doesn't appear to need another man, yet she's ten years younger than I am, in her prime as an adult woman. When I'm close to her it's easy to sense her passion, also controlled. Too soon to think about whether she could be my wife, though it's the most logical thing in the world and probably is in the minds of many people on the prairie. We have common interests, adjacent ranches, two old friends jointly managing a growing herd of cattle. When I really think about her she's a very exciting woman; but it takes more than common interests, and the excitement should come without having to think about it."

---

There was no apparent reason for Kirby to arrive at the Martin ranch at four o'clock on an autumn afternoon. He said he was just riding by, at which Olivia smiled inwardly, cordially invited him in, and saw his quick glance around the living room, and up the stairs, obviously looking for Cornelia. Herb Jones came in to speak briefly with Olivia, gave Kirby a quick "Hello," then retreated through the kitchen door. Cornelia had not heard Kirby arrive, but saw him when she was halfway down the stairs. She hesitated momentarily, then came on down and greeted him warmly.

"I was just riding by," Kirby repeated. "I had to check out some things over by the lake." Then he asked Cornelia if she would like to take a ride. She nodded, almost giggled, and turned back up the stairs to change. Kirby headed for the barn, and by the time he had the Morab saddled Cornelia was waiting. Kirby felt strangely shy, and wondered why his mind should be on the details of the new barn.

"Supper will be ready about 6:30," called Olivia as Cornelia and Kirby rode by the house. "But don't hurry. It'll wait."

Only Herb Jones was unhappy about this development, and he went to his secure, private room on the back porch. Kirby and Cornelia rode across the prairie as the fading sun cast long shadows behind them, and there was only the muffled sound of the horses' hooves on the prairie grass. They had ridden together hundreds of times, to school and back, to the villages, and sometimes the three miles across the prairie at Olivia's request to invite the Fenns for Sunday dinner. All these rides had been business-like, for obvious reasons, so both had always been relaxed. But this ride was different, for as casual as Kirby had tried to make it appear, it was clearly planned.

The sun rested on the crest of the dim, far-away Blue Mountains, like a great red orange with a golden halo, when they reached the lake. They had ridden in silence, aware of each other but shy and expectant, avoiding crowding the horses together. It was one thing to be caught up in the closeness of the dance at the Grange Hall, but quite another to be here on their first date. Kirby remembered rides to this same lake with Little Bird, feeling natural, unaffected, relaxed, and that last night together when they had ridden up the moonlit canyon. Cornelia remembered their closeness at the dance, wondered why she couldn't feel that way now, and was confused at her own shyness, thinking, "This is not the way I really am!"

As the twilight deepened, Kirby and Cornelia circled the lake, then started back toward the Martin ranch. So far they had not spoken, and now Cornelia said, "Three miles to supper," and that broke the ice. During the homeward ride they relaxed, looked directly at each other, and talked, but only of safe subjects.

Olivia had made Kirby's favorite food: roast beef, steamed carrots and mashed potatoes and, of course, brown gravy. Sitting nearby on the kitchen counter were two fresh-baked apple pies. As they ate all were comfortable except Herb. Gopher chattered, enjoying his increasing vocabulary, and Olivia appreciated the not-so-shy glances exchanged between Kirby and Cornelia and thinking to herself, "Do they think they're fooling anyone, sitting close together like that, Kirby's left hand and Cornelia's right under the table? It's a good thing she's left-handed, so she can keep eating."

Cornelia walked to the corral with Kirby, and leaned against a fence-post while he saddled the black to ride home. Night had fallen, and a few starts were glittering. The best Kirby could come up with as he prepared to leave was, "Guess it's time to head home. It'll really be dark by the time I get there." But while he gathered the reins in his left hand, and was about to reach for the saddle horn, Cornelia touched him on the arm, and as he turned, her arms were about him and she kissed him fervently, holding back nothing, her lips lingering and caressing his mouth as she felt him respond. Then he was holding her very close, and they kissed again. Finally she pushed him gently away. "This thing is going too fast. I need time to think." Kirby released her and swung into the saddle, but before he rode away he bent down, tipped up her face, and kissed her very softly one last time.

The first major snowstorm of the year came during the second week of December. The wagons were pulled into the sheds for the winter and out came the bobsleds and fancy cutters. Lucas had a big bobsled and two sturdy Percherons which could pull it with an average load; if the load was very heavy Monty and the black were harnessed in tandem in front of the Percherons.

Olivia had no bobsled, since Jethro and Lucas had worked together a lot and shared Lucas' sled, but she had a beautiful cutter, sleek and shiny and painted red. It comfortably held four people, and the Hambletonians, stimulated by the cold winter air and blowing frost from their nostrils, could pull the cutter at an exciting speed, sometimes fast enough to be dangerous when

Olivia let them have their heads.

In spite of heavy storms the prairie wasn't snowbound, though the draymen were thinking twice about trips over Cottonwood Butte and on down to Lewiston. On Christmas Eve, many of the same people who had helped to build the barn arrived for Olivia's annual Christmas party. All were either in their big, comfortable bobsleds riding on soft hay or cavorting across the meadows in their fast cutters. The Salmon River Canyon usually had little or no snow and was no place for sleighs, nor was the trail over the mountain, so Bob Cone arrived on a tired horse, having stayed overnight in Whitebird and ridden all day through the fourteen miles of snow over the summit.

Lucas and Kirby, as usual, had helped Olivia and Cornelia decorate the house. A ten-foot fir tree gleaming with candles stood before the big windows, and the scent from the tree, as well as freshly cut boughs, filled the house. Several loved faces were missing from among the prairie families on this first Christmas following the Nez Perce War, and those who felt the losses most deeply also had the greatest appreciation for family and friends around them.

Olivia and Cornelia were dressed in the same gowns they had worn to the last dance at the Grange Hall, and were beautiful and gracious hostesses. Kirby and Cornelia had progressed to where they held hands openly, though tonight Cornelia was too busy to give Kirby the attention he wanted, which brought Herb Jones a little satisfaction at least. Lucas felt a new kind of warmth as he watched Olivia greet the incoming guests, then supervise her helpers in preparing and setting out her Christmas buffet. Once that was done Olivia seemed to relax, and Lucas moved closer to her, only to become suddenly aware that she was enjoying the attentions of Bob Cone. That went on through the evening, with Olivia staying close to Bob, though polite to Lucas. "Well," thought Lucas, "Slate Creek is thirty miles away. Bob won't make many trips over that mountain with the snow getting worse every week."

On the prairie the snow was almost as bad as on the mountain. Fierce winds blew the snow into great drifts, which in many places covered the fenceposts. The wagon roads were lost beneath the white bleakness, and the trip to Grangeville or Mt. Idaho became almost impossible. So they stayed home, relying on the hay in their stacks and mows for their livestock.

During the bright days following the first two or three snowstorms the Phelps and Martin families rode between their ranches with little difficulty. But by the middle of January it was obvious that the snow would soon be so heavy and deep that the horses could not travel through it. So by nailing thick planks in a V form to the front of their stone-boat and piling on rocks for extra weight, the Phelps men created a snowplow to which they hitched the Percherons and started toward Olivia's ranch. It took most of the day to make the three miles, and the horses were almost too tired to move, but they now had a trail, not wide enough for the bobsled but just right for Olivia's cutter.

Then when the major storm had passed, there came a shining week of blue-crystal beauty when the prairie was all soft contours sparkling beneath the brilliant sunlight. On such days Olivia would hitch the Hambletonians to the cutter and drive Herb and Gopher to the haystacks, or she and Cornelia would race over the hard-packed trail to the Phelps ranch, peeking between woolen mufflers and stocking caps, the horses breathing out clouds of vapor to drift on the freezing air.

Kirby now had a standing invitation at the Martin ranch and was there often. Sometimes it was late when he started home, and Cornelia, with Olivia's blessing, would ride halfway with him in the starlight, or with the moon sprinkling the snow with jewels. On one such night, when the brilliance of the moon dimmed the stars and they already had kissed several times, Cornelia turned her horse to ride home and found herself facing Kirby and very close to him; she leaned toward him as he reached out to embrace her, and the horses, feeling the shifting of weight, moved together. They held each other closely for a long time, not speaking lest words might drive away the magic. Even more kisses seemed unnecessary because both knew that there would never be anyone else.

---

Lucas Phelps and Olivia Martin between them owned over three thousand acres of prairie land. This was all pasture and hay land, but they also had access to public land not yet deeded to anyone on the mountain to the south of their ranches. Olivia had fenced the west boundary of this land and Lucas the east, with each fence beginning about a half mile up the mountain and running to the north property line, where a third fence ran from east to west to enclose the five square mile rectangle. Now it was all covered deeply in snow, not necessarily a record, but becoming a threat.

"I've seen it like this before, but I don't think we're in real trouble yet," said Seth Jones, who had ridden over from Mt. Idaho on a narrow trail kept open by ranchers along the way. "We had one much like this in 1863, and we made it through. Of course, there weren't nearly as many cattle to worry about then."

" I hope you're right," replied Lucas. "This cold weather takes a lot out of the cattle, and they just naturally want to eat more. We've started conserving the hay, and some of them are starting to look a little lean."

During the following week the weather moderated. The sun shone brightly, the temperature was above freezing during the day, and all agreed that probably the worst of it was over. Then came a Chinook wind, not strong but persistent and warm, and the snow began to settle and was soft on top. But suddenly the Chinook stopped, and within a few hours an Arctic blast dropped the temperature to ten below zero.

"Mother!" shouted Cornelia, "Come to the window! What has happened?" Olivia came and stood beside her, to look out on a world turned to ice. A "silver thaw," Jethro had called it once, when the soft snow following a Chinook suddenly froze. Olivia and Cornelia stared, unable to believe their eyes, and went downstairs and out through the front door. In wonder they looked slowly around the great semicircle of the prairie, shading their eyes against the glistening surfaces. When they walked toward the front gate they slipped precariously on the inch-thick ice. As the women re-entered the house through the front door Herb Jones and Gopher came in the back, discarding their heavy coats. Olivia, through the kitchen window, noticed their weary-looking horses tied to the corral fence.

"I've never seen this before!" Herb exclaimed. "When we went to check on the cattle part of them were gathered around the haystacks, but while it was warm the last couple of days a bunch must have wandered off, tired of hay, I guess, and looking for anything sticking up through the snow that they could eat. Then came this ice, which wouldn't support them, so their feet broke through and their knees were cut with every step. Gopher and I could see them across the prairie, and picked the easiest route to where they were stranded. We drove them back, but they still suffered. Our horse's legs are in bad shape, but at least the cattle are back by the haystacks. I suspect they've learned to stay there." Olivia hurried toward the corral, thankful a path had been cleared, and on into the barn to find the necessary lineaments and medications to treat the horse's cut legs.

It was still possible to ride the trail between the Martin and the Phelps places, icy and hard as it was, and soon Lucas and Kirby arrived. "I've seen these silver thaws before, and they don't usually last long," said Lucas reassuringly. "A day or two of sunshine and the ice is gone. Besides, it's almost February, and this winter weather should be slacking off soon."

For the next three days it looked like Lucas was right, for the ice did melt, the snow was only crusty in the early morning, and the sun shone brightly. But on the morning of the fourth day the sky was dark and heavily overcast. As Lucas glanced to the east, there he saw the blackest of the clouds. With growing fear, he remembered his first year on this ranch, when the worst snowstorm of the year had roared out of the east, rather than from the northwest as it usually did. That one also had followed a Chinook wind.

He sent Kirby toward their haystacks. "Be sure all the cattle are close in. Give them extra hay today. Also, the Percherons were out tramping through the snow yesterday. They need to be in the barn." Then Lucas pushed Monty across the plowed trail to the Martin ranch, where he found Olivia taking the same precautions.

It was mid-day when the snow began falling, and it seemed like an ordinary storm, for by suppertime only two or three inches had accumulated. But at ten p.m. when Kirby started toward the barn for his evening check on the horses, he stepped off the back porch into knee-deep snow. And at the Martin ranch Herb Jones returned from Olivia's barn caked with snow. "We've got plenty of hay in the barn for the horses, but the stacks for the cattle are getting low," he said. "And the cattle will only take so much of this fierce wind before they do something crazy."

All that night and into the next day the wind blew. The falling snow decreased, but the 34 inches which fell in 24 hours was all moving horizontally from east to west and forming huge drifts. Kirby and Lucas felt insecure about the Martins and decided to ride to their ranch over the trail, which in places was swept clean down to the bare ice but in others was covered with drifts six feet deep. And soon both riders and horses were plastered with solid snow, barely able to see, numb and almost stiff, like slowly moving marble statues. They saw that the cattle had reached the breaking point and done "something crazy" as Herb had put it when, half-way to the Martin ranch, they encountered the first steers drifting before the storm, tails to the wind, their bodies encrusted. Following them were the usually patient mother cows, now confused and fearful. Their calves, dwarfed by the snowdrifts, moved blindly, searching for wind-blown pathways.

"We've got to get to Olivia's fast!" shouted Lucas, barely heard through the howling wind. "All the help we can get may not be enough!" And they hurried on, urging, and at times even spurring, their horses through the huge drifts. Lucas reflected that the year before they had removed the line fence between his property and Olivia's, sharing the range, but now giving the Phelps cattle farther to drift unimpeded.

Olivia became aware of the drifting cattle when she glanced out her living room window and saw the dim, ghostly figures of cows moving across the front yard. She hurried to report this to Herb, and was throwing on her coat when Lucas and Kirby arrived at the back door. About the same time Morty Martin and his two sons rode in through the storm. They had few cattle and all had been brought into the corrals, but they had seen Lucas' herd, like phantoms in the dimness, gliding past their ranch house.

"They're all on the move!" exclaimed Morty, and Olivia glanced at Lucas, trying, not too successfully, to control her anxiety.

"In less than an hour some of them will reach the west line fence and start piling up against it," Lucas said. "Once it breaks they'll surge right on, and in this blinding storm they'll plunge over the rim of the canyon. Right now they're wandering aimlessly, looking for ways around those big drifts, so we may have time to get ahead of them. The main trouble is, they're spread out from north to south, a long front to cover, and somehow we've got to turn them back toward the mountain."

In less than five minutes all were mounted, their slickers snapping in the wind, half-closed eyes peering through the driving storm. They rode toward Olivia's northwest corner, hoping they had time to encircle the slowly moving cattle and turn them to the south. Seven men and two women, having agreed on their plan and to ride as teams: Lucas with Olivia, Kirby with Cornelia, Gopher with Herb, Morty Martin with his two boys.

Through the fierce quartering wind, hunched in their saddles, trying to protect their faces, they followed Morty and his boys in close file as he searched for the wind-cleared patches. A few cattle were seen heading directly west, and the Martins turned them south.

"It looks like we're ahead of them," shouted Morty as they reached the fence line. "Let's ride back a couple of hundred yards north along the fence, then the nine of us stretch out from west to east and ride slowly close together, heading south. Lucas and Olivia stay next to the fence line. The boys and I will take the east end of the line. These critters will follow their leaders, and they're the ones we must turn!"

So the slow sweep was started, the horses shaking their heads, protesting as the howling wind blew ice particles into their eyes, the riders with arms held up against the blast. Morty and his sons, at the far end of the line, were the first to see cattle approaching. They fired a few shots and shouted, futile as that seemed, and whipped the snow-covered backs with short bullwhips. At first it seemed that the plan was working well, for the three Martin men had deflected several dozen cattle, and the riders closer to the fence had forced them to complete their turn toward the south. At times Lucas and Olivia, closest to the fence, were in fear of being caught between the cattle and the barbed wire. But they forced the growing herd a few yards away from the fence, and the other horsemen pushed them from behind.

Then came disaster! Lucas and Olivia were suddenly confronted with a virtual wall of snow-covered cattle directly in front of them. Some of the cattle, led by two old bulls, had reached the fence ahead of the riders. Everyone could hear the squealing of the barbed wire through the staples holding it to the fenceposts as the confused cattle crowded against it. The posts began to lean and would soon be flattened. Even through the storm, Olivia recognized the nearest bull as one of the best that had been driven up from the Salmon River, and she shuddered as Lucas calmly drew his pistol, shot that bull in the head, and, leaning from his saddle over the quivering carcass, shot the second. Their great bodies now formed a barrier over which the smaller cattle could not climb.

Through the laying on of whips and the firing of pistols, Olivia and Lucas started moving the cattle past the two dead bulls and others that had been trampled or suffocated. The sweep continued, and it appeared that most of the cattle were now ahead of the riders. Olivia and Lucas continued riding the fence line, close enough to see the posts, thankful that it gave them bearing and directions. The cattle ahead of them would follow the hillside to the left, and she and Lucas must do the same.

A sudden gust increased the intensity of the wind, enveloping Olivia and her horse in a swirling cloud of snow, and she closed her eyes. Lucas, riding a few feet behind Olivia, saw the cloud coming and raised his arm to cover his face. Then suddenly the capricious wind slackened, and dimly he saw the heavy post at the end of the fence. Thinking that Olivia had suddenly turned downhill, he glanced in that direction. The open, gradual slope was bare! In horror, he rode close to the edge of the bluff, and saw there the horse tracks in the clinging snow and heard faintly from below the high-pitched, agonized whinny of Olivia's Morab screaming in pain, then only silence.

Turning back quickly to his left, Lucas moved downhill to intercept Kirby and Cornelia, motioning them to follow him, sensing the terror in their faces as they saw him alone. In a matter of seconds they had circled back to the right and were at the base of the cliff, where they found the Morab, crumpled among jagged lava boulders, the body still, the head twisted grotesquely, the eyes staring sightlessly.

As her horse had hit the rocks and somersaulted, Olivia was thrown free and catapulted some 20 feet through a thorn bush, which undoubtedly saved her life; but she landed at the base of a rock against which she struck her head. When they found her she lay motionless, looking very small. The thornbush had torn off her hat and woolen scarf, and her dark hair contrasted vividly with her pale features, now deeply slashed and bleeding from the hard thorn spikes. All feared she was dead, until Lucas detected a pulse and shallow breathing.

Kirby hurried back to intercept the others. "Forget the cattle! Olivia is hurt!" He led them all back to where she lay. There was some shelter among the rocks and small trees where they found Olivia, and they placed her on a slicker out of the wind, with someone's coat and another slicker over her. It appeared that the storm was almost over, and some of the cattle, as hoped, were wandering about the lake basin, while others had found shelter in the timber nearby.

"The Morab is dead, and we can't move her on a horse anyway," said Lucas after talking with Morty Martin. "It's protected enough here to be of some help. Somebody build a fire. Gopher and Cornelia, stay here with me. The rest of you make your way back to my ranch, hook the Percherons onto my bobsled, and bring it back. And leave a canteen and some of that lunch from your saddlebags here with us."

It was six hours before Kirby, the Martins, and Herb Jones returned with the bobsled, having beaten their way to the Phelps ranch and followed their own tracks back. Olivia was barely conscious and groaned weakly while they improvised a stretcher and moved her into the back of the sled. The trip back to the ranch was faster, for the wind had died down and the sleigh on it's way from the ranch had already broken a trail. Lucas had sent Kirby ahead to find a doctor—Grangeville, Mt. Idaho, anywhere—to be brought to the Phelps ranch. But the doctor did not arrive until three hours after Olivia had been put to bed at Lucas' place.

"She has a severe concussion at best, possibly a skull fracture," the doctor reported. "Her right collarbone and arm are both broken, and I will cast those as well as possible; collar bones are hard to manage. It's going to take awhile, and Cornelia, you're going to be the nurse; I'll teach you everything I can about taking care of your mother. She'll be laid up for several weeks."

Olivia was alert by the second day and, with her fierce determination, sat up in bed on the third. On the fourth day she asked Lucas, "How about the cattle?" Because of the way he hesitated she sensed that all was not well, and she was right; for the previous day Lucas, Kirby, Herb, and Gopher had ridden out to appraise the losses.

"They'll all be loafing around that big basin, even though there is little food," asserted Lucas. "They're pretty exhausted." So the four riders continued on toward the lake, but once close to the shore they began to feel uneasy. The cattle weren't in the timber, and the men rode back down and circled the lake. No cattle, but plenty of tracks, and all leading to where the gate lay in splinters. They rode down the canyon trail to the snowline, where they could see the river. Below them where the canyon opened out and there were bunchgrass-covered hillsides they saw some cattle feeding, and across the river were others.

"We think one or two of those bulls you brought from the Salmon River led them back home," said Lucas despondently, having told Olivia as much as he could. "I figure over two hundred went down that trail." Everyone was shocked and discouraged except Gopher, for to him such happenings were almost routine.

Olivia's injuries did not keep her down for long, nor would she accept confinement to the house. But she was limited in some ways, and did not try to ride for several weeks, so Cornelia had to drive the cutter and later the carriage. Olivia had stayed at Lucas' house, cared for by Cornelia, for most of two weeks. During that time Lucas came to a new and deeper appreciation of her enduring courage and constant concern for everyone around her. And one night after an evening spent by the fire, when she had said good night and painfully climbed the stairs, Lucas looked at Kirby and saw reflected in his face what both now realized: "this woman belongs here with us."

# CHAPTER 32

The debilitating, summer-long flight from Idaho had been the worst of all periods in the life of the Nez Perce bands. During that time there had been fear, anxiety, and hunger—stressful times broken only by a few stolen days of relaxation when they all pushed away reality.

In the desolate, wearisome months and years to come, they would look back, as people have always done, and compartmentalize their memories, putting aside those sealed cells containing terror and fear, cherishing with happy nostalgia the ones that held better memories. But now the people moved hopelessly, through an alien land that bore no familiar markings or comfortable camping places. It was devoid of all feelings, except those of cold and pain and hunger and misery and sorrow. A few traveled alone, dependent entirely on their own resources. Others moved in groups, people from various bands; and included in one such group was Little Bird.

The last to leave the Bear's Paw battleground with White Bird were some 200 more, including Ollokot's wife Wetatonmi. In all, perhaps 300 were headed for Canada. The rest were with Joseph and Colonel Miles, carrying in their hearts the promise of a safe camp for the winter and return to Idaho in the spring. They were less stressed than those headed north, for the troops were with them and provided food, but all watched with sorrow as their now reduced horse herd almost vanished when Miles rewarded each Chyenne and Sioux scout with his pick of five ponies.

Yellow Wolf moved through the desolate land, riding a good horse and better equipped than most in the procession, for he had planned his departure, had a good rifle, and was comforted by the weight of one full cartridge belt slung over his shoulder and a second around his waist. Though he had seen Little Bird with Hawk shortly before the first group left the camp, he had not thought of her for the last several days. Now as he rode she came into his mind. His heart sang when he cautiously approached an Indian camp, and saw among the people Little Bird, and Running Feet, Joseph's daughter, as well as some of his cousins. And there was his mother, Yikyik Wasumwah, who had been crying. "I heard that you were dead," she said, "that someone had shot you." But he answered, "Perhaps I will die from sickness, but never by the gun. I will not die that way!"

Yellow Wolf rejoiced at finding his mother and Running Feet. "Perhaps it is not loyal to Joseph," he rationalized, "but I will not take them back to him, for the soldiers now have him in charge, and he must do as they say."

So for two more days Yellow Wolf rode on with the little band, searching through the storm. And on the third day they saw unfamiliar

Indians approaching, and one threw the sign which said, "What tribe?" The answer went back, "Nez Perce. Who are you?" And the happy, hoped-for sign was returned, "The Sioux."

The men smoked together and one Nez Perce signed, "How far?" and was answered, "One-quarter sun." Then the Sioux led the way, one riding ahead to carry the news to the camp, from which people came to welcome the wanderers. Little Bird and Running Feet looked on in wonderment as their exhausted people rode toward the Sioux tipis. Some say there were 2,000 Sioux camped there, their many lodges scattered for miles along a small canyon. The Nez Perces were well received by the Sioux, who cried openly, sharing in the suffering, quickly providing warm clothing and moccasins to replace the torn blanket fragments wrapped around frozen feet.

When White Bird arrived, Sitting Bull rode out to meet him, his attending braves having handed him his ceremonial war bonnet after he mounted his horse. The bonnet, a hindrance to a man on foot, now stretched in all it's magnificence from Sitting Bull's head to below the horse's belly. Around Sitting Bull pranced six of his finest race horses, and clustered about him were his proud warriors, some of them veterans of the Little Big Horn and never defeated in battle. Looking up at all this splendor were White Bird and his people, many on foot, half naked, clothing in tatters, faces grimy and hair disheveled. But their heads were held high. The great Sitting Bull dismounted from his splendid pony, listened to the story of the Nez Perces' final battle and forced surrender, then led his warriors in weeping and wailing, showing their grief and sharing the loss, the final breakup of the last free-roving bands of American Indians.

The arrival of the Nez Perces was not a surprise to the Sioux, who knew that many refugees were on the way, and they followed the plan to which all had agreed. Little Bird watched as Sioux women approached the huddled, insecure people, and each Sioux woman walked away leading one Nez Perce person, or sometimes a mother and her child.

"You are all well settled in your lodges," Sitting Bull had said at the council when the impending arrival of the Nez Perces was discussed. "Most of you do not have room for an entire family, but each of you can handle one person. Provide them what they need and treat them as part of your family. Perhaps later when we all know them better, when they are able to take care of themselves, they can be reunited as families."

Without any need to throw or receive the signs in which they were not proficient, Little Bird was led away by one Sioux woman, Running Feet by a second, and Yellow Wolf's mother by a third. Yellow Wolf was approached by a solemn Sioux warrior; they exchanged signs, then walked up the canyon to a tipi. The same casual selection took place with all the Nez Perces, and only by chance were any two housed close to each other. Some were taken for several miles, and many were mercifully placed on horses for their bleeding feet and depleted bodies no longer supported them. Thus, on a cold day of early October 1877, these splintered survivors of the non-treaty Nez Perce bands were welcomed by Sitting Bull and his people who, in spite of their apparent prosperity, were also refugees.

In their temporary homes, warm and well fed for the first time in many weeks, the members of Joseph's family had their own thoughts. Running Feet worried about Joseph, for she had not seen him since he sent her off into the storm. Yellow Wolf's mother, not entirely comfortable with the older squaw with whom she was housed, wondered about Yellow Wolf, and was thankful for his obvious vigor and her knowledge that he was a survivor. Yellow Wolf, resting on a buffalo robe in the tipi of the strong, quiet Sioux warrior with his one wife and no children, was more comfortable than he had been for months. He was good at exchanging the signs, and communicated readily with his host. He thought briefly of Little Bird, and remembered with satisfaction that she looked better than any of the other women he had seen. "She will always get along," he thought. Though his basic needs were well satisfied—the new clothing, the warm tipi, the good cooking of the Sioux squaw—Yellow Wolf was already thinking about ways to leave this foreign place and return to his own land.

Little Bird was placed in the tipi of a handsome warrior with a pregnant wife. The decision to lodge Little Bird here was a mistake, for from the day of her arrival her beauty was apparent. At the first opportunity she had carefully washed her hands and face, waited until the warrior was absent from the tipi to wash her body, put on the buckskin dress given to her and encircled it with an intricately beaded belt for which the Sioux were famous. She began to feel better, and after she had combed her long hair and carefully redone her braids her loveliness seemed to spring forth. None of this was missed by the pregnant Sioux wife watching from the opposite side of the tipi, nor by her tall, powerful husband when he returned from the hunt that day. Little Bird, her physical needs satisfied and unaware of any disruptions her presence might bring to the tipi, felt again the ever-present concern: "Is it here among strangers that my baby will be born?"

---

General Howard had doubts about General Sheridan's approval of his plans to send the Nez Perces home, so he hurried to Division Headquarters in Chicago, where he would try to change Sheridan's mind. Sheridan had earlier decided against Fort Keogh as a wintering place: "For these Indians? Too expensive, supply lines are too long. Besides, there's a lot of furor out west. The people of Oregon and Idaho are edgy. Two or three other tribes out there are restless. Why risk sending Joseph back home to stir up more trouble?" So Sheridan, with Sherman's approval, ordered that the Nez Perces now at Fort Keogh be sent down the river to Fort Lincoln at Bismarck, North Dakota; "And perhaps, we should send them on to Fort Leavenworth, Kansas, where they will be comfortable until a permanent decision can be made."

Howard was by no means happy about all of this. " But after all," he would say defensively, "Joseph surrendered all the people who remained at the Bear's Paw at the time of their defeat, and White Bird later nullified any promises I made by fleeing to Canada." Colonel Miles, on the other hand, though arrogant and hungry for promotion, would try to keep his word and return the Nez Perces to their home land.

Joseph surveyed the campsite which he and his people, with the help of a detail of soldiers sent out by Miles, were attempting to make livable. Miles meant well, but had to admit that this collection of rag-tag Indians presented a real challenge. Springtime, having survived the ordeal of the leg shattered at the Bit Hole, limped quietly about, helping other families. Early Flower, now almost four months old, was the most peaceful person around as she slept on her cradle board hanging from a tree limb. Only six days had passed since Miles ushered the Nez Perces into Fort Keogh with his own Fifth Infantry Band playing, "Hail To The Chief." Some of the people lining the riverbank were from the little village developing nearby, and would later honor the Colonel by naming the town Miles City.

Ad Chapman was translating for Miles now, and as they approached Joseph, Miles was apologetic: "Not my doing, but I have received orders that we must again be on the move. We will head on down the river tomorrow, or the next day at the latest." As Chapman interpreted this report, Joseph and his people stood in stunned silence. "On down the river. No mention of returning to Idaho. White Bird was right. Miles seems to be trying, but when will we ever find a white man who will keep his promises?"

Sherman's self-fulfilling prophecy—"They must all be killed, or become paupers"—long since applied to scores of other tribes, now settled with chilling finality over these Nez Perces on the Yellowstone River and their splintered companions far to the north with Sitting Bull.

## CHAPTER 33

Eight hundred miles separated Fort Keogh from Bismarck, North Dakota, and slush ice was forming rapidly in the Yellowstone River. So Miles, in usual fashion, acted quickly to move these people before the river froze solid from shore to shore. The able-bodied were easy to handle, and Miles mounted them on the scant remnants of what was once their own horse herd. But how to move the sick and wounded, and those who must care for them? Many of them will never survive that long horseback ride.

Then Miles remembered that tied to the riverbank were several large flatboats which had been used to bring to Fort Keogh from ranches far up the Yellowstone winter supplies of vegetables, meat, butter, and other produce. "They could not be dragged back up the river," thought Miles, "so we bought them for a song. Now I know why." He immediately began recruiting boatmen familiar with the river and soon was loading the boats with Indians.

On one of these boats was assembled as motley a crew as ever sailed. The oldest of these was a wiry, robust man called Daytime Smoke, whose ease of movement and apparent vigor belied his 72 winters; but the most unusual thing about him was not his overall physical appearance; it was his hair and eyes. For the hair was not white, nor was it the dark salt and pepper mixture common among old Nez Perce men; rather, it was a sandy gray, and in some places could be seen hairs that were almost blond, or at least a light brown. And Daytime Smoke's eyes, as could be seen if one lifted the wrinkled, drooping eyelids and looked closely, were not deep brown like those of other Nez Perces. They were a kind of blue-gray, some might say smokey, which could have had something to do with his name.

With Daytime Smoke, though more often mixing with the other passengers, was his gregarious sixteen-year-old granddaughter, who looked very much like other young Nez Perce women but whose hair was not quite black and whose eyes were only light brown. She was called Iltolkt, and she had a baby not yet named. While Iltolkt's genes for hair, eyes, and skin color left her looking much like the rest of her people, the inheritance of her baby was another story; for in this fifth generation the baby, now six months old and fair-skinned, gazed with definitely blue-gray eyes from beneath abundant and noticeably blond hair.

Commanding this crew and this unusual craft was a vigorous 25-year-old frontiersman named Fred Bond who described himself modestly as "tall, dark, and powerful, and of true English blood." He was also a romantic, and while he was not illiterate, his speech and writing might be described as colorful. Now he appraised the rest of his erstwhile crew:

One squaw, in a grubby, loose-hanging buckskin dress and leading by the hand a boy of two or three years whose left arm had been seriously wounded. There was a feeling of power and vitality about this woman which the boatman knew would be helpful when the going got tough on the river. A second squaw carried with one hand a cradle board, it's protecting flap pulled down over the baby's face to shield her from the cold wind. A solid kind of person, Bond thought. There were three other women, two wounded warriors, and several young boys. Bond wondered why the boys weren't riding with Joseph, and decided they had been sent along to help with the operation of the boat, and for that Bond was thankful.

Then Bond's eyes turned back to old Daytime Smoke, with his sandy-gray hair, to his granddaughter Iltolkt, who was not vividly dark of hair or eyes, and to the blue-eyed baby with the lovely blond hair. And to himself he expressed the obvious: "'The old man had a white father."

Bond organized his crew in ways that would make the trip go well, and he appointed Daytime Smoke as its director, naming him Chief George Washington. Then he issued this new chief a rifle, because he knew he could be trusted, and carefully informed all on board of their assigned duties. It soon became apparent that Welweyas, whom Bond identified as a muscular and exceptionally strong woman, was capable of a kind of sub-chief role, and this role she accepted readily, moving nimbly about the boat, now helping with the oars, again pushing hard with a long pole to help free the boat from sandbars. Sometimes she even relieved Bond on the big sweep at the back of the boat with which it was steered. Soon Bond also noticed Welweyas' subtle and kindly influence with the women and children on board. The boat moved along rapidly, for Bond had responded to Miles' challenge and offer to reward the boatman who arrived first in Bismarck. As the crew settled in to the long days on the river, Daytime Smoke relished his new position, quite unaware that his father, Capt. William Clark, had once floated down this same river, remembering the Nez Perce maiden with whom he had shared a tipi beside the Clearwater River in Idaho, when he and Capt. Meriweather Lewis were leading their expedition back from the Pacific Coast in 1806.

It was in the very early days of the voyage, indeed within the first few hours, that Bond recognized the nubile Iltolkt as a creature of rare beauty with interesting possibilities for him in the course of the journey. He had heard Daytime Smoke call her by name, but Bond could not possibly pronounce it, so he called her Viola, for in exactly the right light, when she opened her eyes wide, perhaps in surprise, Bond could see, blended with the brown, the deepest shade of blue violet, which only a romantic Englishman would have noticed. And Viola was indeed a lovely person, standing out in this crowd like a shining light. Her dress was of fine white deerskin, and she kept her cheeks tinted with pink rouge. Bond, in his journal, said when she was teased, "You could see the youthful blush raise through the Erythrite polish on her dimpled cheek." Her desire for adornment took some bizarre turns, one of which was that she plaited into her long hair a dozen or more five-dollar bills. She was to Bond, "A picture of true wild human nature."

Food supplies on the boat were adequate but dull—rice, beans, flour, and hard bread. But Daytime Smoke, with his rifle, proved to be a good hunter. Each day toward late afternoon the boat would be tied to the riverbank and all would go ashore to relax, stretch themselves, and care for their personal needs. Daytime Smoke, whom all now called Chief Washington, would go hunting along with the boys. He sometimes shot a deer or an antelope, while the boys were more successful with their homemade bows and arrows at killing rabbits or squirrels, and occasionally beavers, whose roasted tails were savored by the people. There were berries, often in great abundance, and sometimes the boat would be anchored beneath overhanging bullberry bushes while the people feasted.

When Bond first organized the crew he was understandably stern, for at that point he was not certain how to manage them, but his concerns vanished as he watched every one do the job assigned and move easily into a daily pattern. He developed a paternalistic, almost fatherly, feeling about his diverse crew, and what had started out as a job became a personal responsibility, a kind of stewardship, though in his own rough way he would not have used those words.

Though Bond was aware of the increasing anxiety and fears that clouded the people's minds, he could not fully comprehend the continuing impact of the long flight, the repeated battles, the detachment from reality that was felt by all. And those feelings increased on the broad expanse of the icy river. The indecision of the military high command forced them to lay over at Fort Buford where the Yellowstone joins the Missouri, and there, housed in rough huts, they were scorned by the camp followers, while some of the soldiers cast lustful eyes on Viola, to whom Bond loaned his knife "to protect her honor." At the Mandan Indian villages the Nez Perces were forced to defend themselves from the openly hostile residents, who showered them with rocks. Bond managed to evade them, though other boats were overturned. And added to these new troubles was the Nez Perces decreasing confidence in Miles and Howard and the entire power structure above them. They had no understanding of how it worked, but desperately needed to trust it, for they sensed that on that structure their future and their very lives depended.

Bond looked for ways to offset some of these fears, so with Chief Washington's help as translator, his own crude English, and much sign language, he talked to his crew, and wrote in his journal:

"After tying up for the nights and our feast was over, I would explain to my people about our head chief, 'Great Father', at Washington D.C., how they held consol's there to run so large white nation, the city where the people lived so thick they would fight for space to live and air to breath; the great iron horse that had the speed of a hundred ponies but lived on wood and water, and how many sun it would take this iron horse to reach Washington D.C. Washington would help me translate and by signs my people understood. We seat there and talk till the moon would throw it's silver rays on the frozen river mist on the driftwood. All then would be hushed when Washington gave a prayer."

Beyond Fort Buford, Bond's boat proceeded rapidly down the Missouri. Speed was now even more essential, for the slush ice was turning to heavy blocks. But Bond and his crew knew the race was won, and he would receive a handsome prize.

Though trains were common by this time, the Nez Perces had never traveled far enough from their homeland to see one, and they were terrified by the Northern Pacific engines in Bismarck: the screeching wheels, the ear-piercing whistles, the blasts of steam, the clatter and rumble of the huge driving mechanisms; and added to all these were the welcoming rifle salutes by the military, a sign of impending death to the Nez Perces. Bond recorded that his people "set up a moaning chant, no doubt their death chant."

Waiting in Bismarck for the other flatboats and Miles with the overland procession to arrive, Bond had plenty of time to tour the little town with Daytime Smoke and Viola. They were fearful and almost in shock as Bond helped them push their way through the three blocks crowded with noisy and boisterous miners, gamblers, trappers, rivermen, scouts, Sioux and various other Indians. Bond in his exhilaration described the scene:

"There was law and order because there was no lawyers. Great respect was shown to the gentler sex. Every person was more or less jolly because money was plenterful and each person was robust and strong, for the week had not yet appeared."

While Bond and his two wide-eyed companions were eating breakfast, a band struck up the "Star Spangle Banner," and they watched as Miles and Joseph approached, followed by the soldiers guarding the Nez Perces who had ridden from the Bear's Paw. Once in the town, the soldiers formed a hollow square around the Indians, whose fame had preceded them. The admiring townspeople, enthralled perhaps by reading Joseph's speech as published in the Bismarck Tri-Weekly Tribune, rushed through the town and into the hollow square. Laughing, shouting, bearing delicious food, they proceeded to feed all of the assembled Indians, as well as the soldiers.

Miles and his staff were feted at a banquet, but the citizens of Bismarck—most of them, it seemed—were more interested in Joseph, and they staged an event and issued an invitation still unmatched in American Indian history:

Bismarck Tri-Weekly Tribune, November 21, 1877

To Joseph, Head Chief of Nez Perces

Sir: Desiring to show you our kind feeling, and the admiration we have for your bravery and humanity as exhibited in your recent conflict with the forces of the United States, we most cordially invite you to dine with us at the

Sheridan House in this city. The dinner will be given at one and one half p.m. today. Before the dinner, a reception will be held in the hotel salon.

The curious townspeople, including overdressed and intensely attentive women, greeted Joseph effusively. The picture taken of him that day was the best ever made, and sold well throughout the nation. Through all of this adulation Joseph was his usual quiet self. Some said that at one point he murmured sadly, "When will the white man ever learn to tell the truth?"

Bond, with the money from winning the flatboat race and more won in gambling halls, bought Daytime Smoke a new shirt and took Viola shopping. But she sat forlornly on the sidelines at the ball, for the shoes he bought her were too big to dance in. The ladies had a reception, at which Viola was overwhelmed and, "dazed at the splendor." Bond and Viola stayed up all night, seeing the sights of the town and gambling.

The next day the sad Indians, many of them weeping, were loaded onto trains, for by Sherman's decree they were to be moved on to Fort Leavenworth, Kansas. Bond went with Viola to the depot, but was not allowed to help her board. He gave her a note as he turned to leave, and it said, "After you have learned to read English you can find me near the headwaters of the two mighty rivers that flows toward the risen sun." A crowd of townspeople, still stimulated by the experiences at the reception and cherishing their memories of Joseph, came to the depot to see the Indians off. One of the women, remembered only as "The Belle of Bismarck," kissed Joseph on the cheek. Then came the clatter of wheels, the hiss of escaping steam, and the blast of the whistle as the train pulled out of the station, slowly gaining speed, bearing dispirited people toward places they had never seen and could not envision.

Fred Bond never saw any of the Nez Perces again. But he was remembered by one small group, for in his own way he had been a softening influence during a terrible time, when he tried to ease their adjustment to a bleak future. Ironically, he ended his story by writing, "I turned my face towards the evening sun to join once more the winners of the golden west." Perhaps as the years passed he watched for Viola among the little bands of Indians he encountered there on the morning side of the Rockies, along the '"two mighty rivers that flows toward the risen sun."

## CHAPTER 34

The Sioux were not in Canada by choice, and they were refugees as surely as the Nez Perces; for Sitting Bull, leader of the Strong Heart Warrior Society and Chief of the Teton Dakota, had bitterly opposed the U.S. Troops invading his hunting grounds in 1864. Then he made peace with the white man but, like the non-treaty Nez Perces, refused to move to a reservation. Just over a year ago he had joined with Crazy Horse of the Oglalla, said to be the greatest of Sioux tacticians, and together they annihilated Custer's forces on the Little Big Horn River.

Sitting Bull retreated to Canada, while Crazy Horse remained in his own Sioux country, where he was pursued and forced to surrender by, of all people, Col. Nelson A. Miles. Now Crazy Horse was dead. He had been promised limited freedom and was shot by his own guards, who said he was trying to escape. The future for Sitting Bull and his people was anything but secure, but perhaps his memories of the struggles of the many Sioux bands made him willing to accept this new liability in the form of the Nez Perces.

Sitting Bull had chosen his refuge well, for he was close enough to the buffalo country to go south for hunting, though he faced the risk of more battles with the U.S. Army. And he had the flexibility of moving farther to the north to make detection and pursuit more difficult for the forces of the Queen, who were not very happy to have him there. Winter came early to this country, and by mid-October, at the latest, the permanent snow arrived and did not melt before April. At times fierce, howling blizzards roared down from the north, sweeping the rocky plains and redistributing the snow. To at least partially escape these storms, Sitting Bull had located his camp in a narrow, meandering canyon where the tipis had some protection.

Nearly a month had passed since Yellow Wolf caught up with Little Bird, Running Feet, and his own mother and traveled with them until they were met by Sitting Bull's warriors. The assignment of individual Nez Perces to Sioux families was so efficient and happened so quickly that Yellow Wolf and Little Bird were immediately separated, and lost track of their tribesmen. Little Bird settled down, warm, comfortable and well fed in the tipi of the imposing Sioux warrior and his pregnant wife. But her mind was not at ease. Increasingly she felt isolated from her own people, no one of whom she had seen since the arrival. The Sioux couple made no attempt to teach her the signs, and she longed for the sounds of her own language. Now into the fifth month of her pregnancy, she felt her baby stir frequently, and her body had acquired that ripening glow that comes to most expectant mothers. She was deliciously attractive, and each day became more aware of the admiring glances of her host and the sullen jealousy of his wife.

On an early November day, when the sun shone dimly through clouds hanging low above the canyon walls, Little Bird took advantage of the freedom of movement allowed and walked up the stream, passing many tipis on the way. She had gone farther than usual this trip, and was suddenly delighted to hear, in her own Shahaptin tongue, her own name, "Payopayo Kute!" and she turned to see Wetatonmi running toward her. They laughed, and embraced each other, and their tears ran down, almost overcome by the joy of hearing the sweet sounds of their own language, which for a little while they had been denied.

"Have you seen Two Moons? Or Wottolen? Or Black Eagle?"

"No. I'm not even sure how many of them arrived here. I did not see them with White Bird's band as we traveled," answered Wetatonmi. "Have you seen Yellow Wolf or Running Feet?"

"Not since the day we arrived, for they were taken away quickly, as was Yellow Wolf's mother. Are the people in your tipi good to you?"

"Yes. But I am not good at the signs. It seems that the men understand this thing the best. And it is hard, not understanding what the people say, why they laugh, why they sometimes look at me curiously, though not unkindly. Perhaps they do not trust us."

"I wonder about that, and do not have a good feeling in the tipi where I live." Then she told Wetatonmi about her fear of the Sioux warrior.

The feeble sun was behind dense clouds and the daylight was almost gone when the two women turned back toward their own lodgings. "Now that I know where you live, I will come to see you often." Then Wetatonmi returned to the tipi with eight children, and Little Bird to the one where two babies were yet to be born.

Yellow Wolf was more comfortable in all ways than the other isolated Nez Perces, for he used the signs well, and talked at will with his hosts, and they laughed a lot. He went hunting with the Sioux warriors, who soon recognized his great strength and energy and his skill as a hunter. On their first trip south, stopping just short of the border, they did see a few buffalo and killed three. But on the next trip, though they ranged far to the southwest and put out scouts who watched while they hunted below the border, they found few buffalo and only got one; and that night as they returned home Yellow Wolf realized for the first time that this land was no longer a place of abundance.

What he was not yet fully aware of was that farther to the south, along the railroads that now bridged the continent, a terrible thing had been happening because the white man had discovered the value of buffalo hides. Professional hunters plied their bloody trade, some slaughtering hundreds of buffalo each day, often leaving the meat to rot on the plains. And on fancy railroad trains nattily dressed "sportsmen" shot countless buffalo from the observation platforms of parked parlor cars while their stylishly attired ladies sipped their drinks and applauded. Within a few years such hunting would destroy some thirty million buffalo, and the major source of food, clothing, warm beds, and shelter for the Plains Indians would be gone forever.

The impact of this devastation had long since been felt by the tribes who followed the buffalo, including Sitting Bull and his people and now affecting their guests, the Nez Perces, for this land contained little other game.

Some say the destruction of the vast buffalo herds was part of a deliberate plan to starve into submission the Plains Indians. It warked, but only after long, bitter, and costly war. For to the Indians the buffalo were more than an economic necessity; they were part of life itself, a spiritual presence essential to peace of mind. and throughout the central and southern plains, as the herds disappeared, the Indians, angered and confused, believed they may have offended the spirits, and that the reek of rotting buffalo carcasses further insulted them. So they held ceremonies, trying to placate the spirits and bring back the buffalo. Then their great loss, along with continuing white atrocities, set them on the warpath. More than ten years were required to subdue these fierce tribes, break their spirits, and crowd them into Indian Territory along with many others.

With the disturbing scarcity of buffalo still on his mind, Yellow Wolf wandered up the canyon and encountered Wetatonmi, and she told him where to find Little Bird: "By the bend in the canyon, where that little stream comes in from the east. It's that small tipi next to the large one where the woman's mother lives." The tipi described was on Yellow Wolf's way back to his own lodging, and he walked quickly in that direction.

Little Bird's host, Running Fox, had gone hunting, but it had not been a good day. The one deer which he had stalked and was sure of shooting eluded him and he returned home feeling cheated and unhappy with himself. His wife had lounged about the tipi all day, petulant and resentful, remembering how Running Fox had looked across the tipi at Little Bird just before he left for his hunt. Running Fox walked up the canyon, approaching his tipi, while Yellow Wolf was still some distance away. Little Bird was dozing when Running Fox stepped through the tipi flap to find no food cooking and his wife gone. But Little Bird was there, half asleep, and Running Fox moved toward her, quietly discarding his heavy hunting coat.

He stood over her, admiring the fullness of her body beneath the tight buckskin dress. Little Bird in her half sleep sensed his presence and opened her eyes as he discarded his shirt. She gasped in fear, and he was upon her, covering her mouth with his hand lest her cries be heard through the tipi walls. But she writhed and turned, and in desperation bit his hand.

When Yellow Wolf fled the Bear's Paw campground he carried not only his rifle and ammunition but also his kopluts, his war club. This fearsome weapon, capable of crushing a skull with one blow, Yellow Wolf had always used in battle. Because it was sacred to him he carried it everywhere, and now it was concealed beneath his shirt. As he stood before Running Fox's tipi, about to knock on the flap and stand back respectfully until invited in, he heard a piercing scream. Recognizing Little Bird's voice, Yellow Wolf leaped through the tipi flap, the wicked kopluts in his hand, to find the lusting Sioux warrior kneeling over Little Bird, one hand about her throat, the other, a fist, ready to smash into her face. In his excitement, and because of Little Bird's cries, Running Fox had not heard Yellow Wolf enter the tipi, but he turned at the Nez Perce's challenging cry and sprang upright to meet him. Leaping nimbly to the side, Running Fox grasped his lance and rushed at Yellow Wolf, who twisted suddenly, evading the sharp lance point. Then Yellow Wolf was upon Running Fox, there was a dull, sodden thud as the kopluts descended, and Running Fox slumped to the floor. His body twitched momentarily, then lay still.

Yellow Wolf rushed to Little Bird, took her in his arms, and tried to comfort her. "We must leave this place! I fear the man is dead, and the Sioux will kill me!" Little Bird arose awkwardly, grasped Yellow Wolf's hand, and they turned toward the tipi door, meeting head-on Running Fox's pregnant wife, who screamed in terror and rushed back to her mother's tipi. The screams had alarmed the neighbors, and a crowd quickly gathered. Strong, angry men seized Yellow Wolf before they knew what had happened. With his arms bound, Yellow Wolf was led to one of Sitting Bull's sub-chiefs where, in great anger and excitement, a solemn council was convened. "This Nez Perce has killed one of our strongest warriors," someone said. And the council proceeded toward a decision that would mean torture and ultimate death for Yellow Wolf.

Occasionally within an Indian band there was a respected, almost revered woman, a kind of matriarch who sometimes sat in council and whose word was always respected. Such a woman was Graceful Swan, the mother-in-law of Running Fox, and it was she who intervened with the Sioux council. For soon after Little Bird's arrival in Running Fox's tipi his wife had started complaining to her mother. Graceful Swan had listened, and had visited the small tipi, where she observed Little Bird's beauty and the obvious glances of her son-in-law. Though her daughter wailed loudly, tore her hair, and defended her husband as is the way of wives, the wise Graceful Swan could see what had happened, and so informed the council. The council listened, and spared Yellow Wolf's life.

Sitting Bull and his council had from the beginning planned to bring the Nez Perce families back together where they could live in their own way and speak their own tongue. The death of Running Fox, the only case of violence between a Sioux and a Nez Perce within the camp, convinced the Sioux council that now was the time to reunite the families, and that was done.

The Sioux had plenty of buffalo hides for tipi covers and extra poles cached in a dry cave in the canyon. Tipis were quickly set up for the Nez Perce families and they came back together, rejoicing at the sound of their own unique tongue, the ease of communication without exchanging signs, their own ways of making their beds, caring for their children, cooking their food. Running Fox was quickly forgotten by all but his pregnant wife and his regretful mother-in-law—he had violated a basic law of his people and had paid the price. Yellow Wolf, now even more highly respected, continued to associate with the young Sioux men, while the Sioux women were helpful to the Nez Perce wives and taught them some of their skills.

The oppressive grip of winter settled over the Sioux camp, where the people were often cold because firewood was scarce. As the dreary days passed the Nez Perces yearned for the protective canyons of their own land, where the kouse and other edible plants would soon be sprouting on the warm south slopes. And as Yellow Wolf had feared following the last meager hunt, the rest of the Nez Perces soon sensed: they, along with Sitting Bull's people and other Indians living nearby, were faced with famine. Each Nez Perce person and each family had their own thoughts, and discussed them quietly as they waited for the signs of spring. And many thought of the routes and the means by which they might return to their homes.

# CHAPTER 35

Fort Leavenworth! Joseph had heard those words repeated by soldiers as he and his people were loaded on the train at Bismarck. Now several passenger cars, the least desirable ones available, moved toward the south, strange and terrifying noises assailing the people's ears along with the choking smell of coal smoke and the blowing cinders which stung their eyes. And it was cold on this late November morning, though none of the warmly dressed trainmen worried about the faulty heating system in the cars.

Joseph moved from car to car surveying the condition of the people, almost 400 of them, some from each of the five bands. Each had been strong and complete when it left Idaho, but now diminished by the terrible losses along the way. Only a few of White Bird's people, who in the confusion had not fled toward Canada with him, were on the train.

And Joseph was among theses people the surviving young warriors. 'No one calls them chiefs,' he thought, 'but they were the strength of the fighting forces, the ones who made the quick plans, took the right action, and carried out the battles. There is Yellow Bull, my good friend of White Bird's band. Yes, he did lead the second foray to the Salmon River and helped to kill many whites, touching off the war; but he has been a great strength in all our fighting. How I miss Yellow Wolf and Running Feet! He said he would bring her back, and I believe he found her and that she still lives. But I really could not expect him to return and face surrender. He said many times, "I will die first!" and perhaps he will.'

Springtime sat on a grimy, worn plush seat, her cradleboard beside her. The army had provided enough food for the people, dull and unappetizing as it was, and now Springtime lifted her five-month old girl from the cradleboard and opened the blouse given to her by a woman in Bismarck. Early Flower seized the exposed nipple and began her breakfast. Springtime, thought about those left behind; and Heyoom came to mind. "She taught me much and I came to love her, though I was the second wife, and not highly regarded. What will life be like with Joseph now? He is so intense, so strong in his heart and so determined, demanding that the government people treat us well and that they take us back to our home."

The memories of Bismarck, the brass band, the smiling people bearing delicious food and gifts, remained in the minds of the people and had been of some comfort as they rode the rattling train toward Fort Leavenworth. But now those good memories were entirely erased as they prepared to occupy their camp site, for it wasn't on the good dry land close to the military post, where there might have been more feeling of protection and less of isolation.

It was on a now frozen swamp, with a brackish lagoon on one side and the fast-flowing, muddy Missouri on the other. Here, with the skimpiest of their own belongings, in the tents and with the meager equipment provided by the army, they prepared to spend the winter, still regarded by everyone, from Sherman in Washington to Capt. George Randolph at Fort Leavenworth, as prisoners of war.

While winter remained, these enduring people, now among the world's experts at survival, faced each day in their own determined ways. They had seen as bad or worse before, though one white observer said that the spot must have been selected for the express purpose of decimating the Indians. So they cooked the unfamiliar food provided, shivered together at night in their drafty tents with little firewood, and always went beyond the outer borders of the campsite for their toilet needs.

Then came the inglorious spring! The frozen ground melted, the earth beneath the tents turned soggy, and the entire camp became a quagmire. It was now impossible to keep anything or anybody clean, and the people lived in filth. As the sun warmed the lagoon there arose myriads of mosquitoes, and with them came not only their incessant droning and stinging bites, but also malaria, a new and debilitating disease to these people. The army protected it's own personnel, but provided no quinine for the Indians. "Our people are sickening, and we are helpless to do anything for them," Joseph complained to Captain Randolph, who could not or would not provide any real assistance. Springtime and all the women were ever more careful in caring for their children, but all became sick with malaria.

The spring months blazed into summer and the desperate Joseph and Yellow Bull could only watch as more of their people sickened. Women wailed as their newborn babies died. Old Alahoos, who had so carefully recorded the names of dead and wounded in the battles, was no longer with them, but someone kept track for the sake of tribal history; and the army kept it's own cold, impersonal records. Within six months 21 of the people had died. No one recorded the number of newborn babies, but not one remained alive.

Technically it was not legal for the Nez Perces to be held as prisoners of war indefinitely. The Commissioner of Indian Affairs ignored that detail and issued his own report: "But for their murders of whites, these Indians would be sent back to the reservation in Idaho. Now, however, they will have to be sent to the Indian Territory. This will be no hardship to them, as the difference in temperature between that latitude and their old home is inconsiderable."

The Commissioner's insensitivity was on par with that of most citizens as he blithely made a judgment based on the single factor of temperature, obviously lacking any knowledge of the lovely mountains where these people had lived. Those who visited the Nez Perce camp at Fort Leavenworth were appalled, one physician saying that one half could be considered sick, and all were "affected by the poisonous malaria of the camp."

A second observer compared conditions to the "horrors of Andersonville," that foul repository in Georgia for Yankee prisoners in 1864 where 13,000 men died and were buried in mass graves. Now the emaciated Nez Perces, most of them seriously ill, were again loaded into railroad cars.. Three more children died before they reached the Quawpaw reservation. After a long ride in open wagons they found that conditions there were no better than at Fort Leavenworth. They were forced to camp in the open without shelter, their tipi poles having been left at the railroad station. There was still no quinine to ease the effects of the malaria, and they often went as much as ten days at a time without any kind of medication. In three months 47 more were dead.

Joseph was desperate, saying, "I think very little of this country. It is like a poor man. It amounts to nothing." He complained to everyone he could find, and did attract some attention in the form of a visit from the Indian Commissioner, who traveled with Joseph almost 200 miles to the Ponca agency. There they found fertile, well-timbered country, as enticing as any in the Oklahoma Territory at that time. "Surely," said The Commissioner, "Joseph and his people will be happy here, especially when he comes to accept the fact that he is not returning to Idaho." The Commissioner was also a politician, noting in his report that, "The present unhappy condition of the Indians appeals to the sympathy of a very large portion of the American people." And he made arrangements for Joseph to travel to Washington, D.C. to visit with no less than President Rutherford B. Hayes and Secretary of the Interior Carl Schurz.

Joseph and Yellow Bull did talk to President Hayes and Secretary Schurz; but the meeting was brief, for to them it served no public purpose. It was more important that the people see Joseph and Yellow Bull, as they had seen many other Indians brought to Washington D.C. And, of greatest importance, these Indians would see the power and the glory of the white man as they traveled across the land, and especially here, in his great camp with its huge lodges beside the Potomac.

A large crowd awaited Joseph in eager anticipation, as all knew his reputation. For more than a year these people had read newspaper accounts of this mighty warrior, this underdog who had become their hero, this red Napoleon, this military tactician perhaps unexcelled throughout history. And his surrender speech! How it had thrilled their minds and prepared them to hear more—this time directly from the mouth of Joseph himself; much better than a speech translated by the Army before appearing in the Bismarck Tri-Weekly Tribune. This speech would be published in the distinguished North American Review, but how accurately it would reflect Joseph's actual words and real meanings is hard to say.

Joseph and Yellow Bull were awed by the size and opulence of the great hall where Joseph was to speak. Chapman named the hall for them, calling it Lincoln Center, and Joseph remembered his Wyakin had mentioned the words of the man Lincoln: "If I live, this accursed system of robbery and shame in our treatment of the Indians shall be reformed."

Joseph pondered what might have happened if Lincoln had not been killed. Would he, alive rather than dead these last 13 years, have made things better for our people? None of those who followed him had helped much.

The people had come to hear Joseph, and they were well prepared for the occasion. Good, solid citizens, many of them Senators and Congressmen from states which fifty years earlier had solved their Indian problems by helping to create the Indian Territory. So this audience could now be deliberate and objective about Indian matters, for the Indians were all gone from their states or safely tucked away on small reservations and seldom seen.

Joseph's appearance, his bearing, his manner of speaking and the things he said—all were what the audience expected. He spoke a few lines, then waited patiently while Chapman translated. The speech took two hours, but no one in the audience thought of the time.

At one point Joseph spoke with passion; "Some of you think an Indian is a wild animal. This is a great mistake. I will tell you about our people, and then you can judge whether an Indian is a man or not. Yes, some of our young men did start the fighting on the Salmon River and killed white people. But that was in retaliation for wrongs done by white men." Then he spoke bitterly about the white man's making war on women and children, something his people could never do because, "We would feel ashamed of so cowardly an act."

"I could not bear to see my wounded men and women suffer any longer; we had lost enough already," Joseph said in speaking of the surrender at the Bear's Paw. "Colonel Miles promised we might return to our country; he could not have made any other terms with me at that time. I cannot understand how the government sends a man out to fight us, as it did Colonel Miles, and then breaks it's word. Good words do not last long until they amount to something. Words do not pay for my dead people. They do not pay for my country. They do not protect my father's grave. Good words will not give me back my children."

Then Joseph challenged the audience, and indeed, through them, the nation. "I know my race must change. We cannot hold our own with the white men as we are. We only ask an even chance to live as other men live. We ask to be recognized as men. We ask that the same laws work alike on all men. Let me be a free man—free to travel, free to stop, free to work, free to trade where I chose, free to choose my own teachers, free to follow the religion of my fathers, free to think and talk and act for myself—and I will obey every law, or submit to the penalty.

"Whenever the white men treat the Indian as they treat each other, then we shall have no wars. We shall be all alike—brothers of one father and one mother, with one sky above us and one country around us and one government for all. Then the great spirit chief who moves above will smile upon this land, and send rain to wash out the bloody spots made by brothers' hands upon the face of the earth. For this time the Indian race are waiting and praying. I have spoken for my people."

The audience that night was conditioned not only by the attitudes of people in the eastern part of the country who no longer faced the real problems of dealing with Indians. Some of them idealized the plight of the proud and dignified Indian overcoming the terrible odds imposed by the encroaching white man. It had not always been this way, for following the fury and bloody action by Indian-hating presidents, especially Andrew Jackson and William Henry Harrison, there had been guilt and soul-searching and personal struggles among some to justify what they saw happening to the Indians.

In 1845 this fervor, this almost sacred quest, was glorified when John L. O'Sullivan wrote of, "the fulfillment of our manifest destiny, to overspread the continent allotted by Providence for the free development of our yearly multiplying millions." So cleansing and sanctifying, so subtly religious in it's implications! It was quickly spread through the public press, from pulpits, and by politicians and helped to ease the consciences of those who had qualms about the treatment of Indians, and many, had they been asked if the word "divine" appeared in O'Sullivan's declaration, would quickly have answered "Yes."

But now, Joseph's speech was loudly applauded by the people assembled in Lincoln Center but it brought no real results. Instead, he and Yellow Bull returned to the Quawpaw reservation to face another move, far to the southwest.

# CHAPTER 36

Spring had come early along the Mississippi, starting when Joseph and his people floundered in the sticky mud, battled mosquitoes and dysentery and suffered terribly with malaria. But far to the north in Saskatchewan other Nez Perce refugees awaited the signs of spring. Though it was already mid-April, the days, and especially the nights, felt like February and ice still clung to the creeks. The horses, now lean and bony, were confined to the canyon where there was no food, and it was necessary to take them out to the wind-blown ridges to find a little dry grass.

Yellow Wolf helped the Sioux warriors with the horse herd, and often saw Hawk, who looked better than most; perhaps he could make the trip back to Idaho. The horse which Yellow Wolf had ridden from the Bear's Paw battle-field was also with the herd. "He is one of the few remaining of our many horses," thought Yellow Wolf, "but he does not look healthy." And in Yellow Wolf's mind the yearning and the planning for the long trip back to Idaho and Oregon became ever stronger.

On a blustery morning when only an occasional ray of sunshine broke through the clouds, Little Bird hurried to find Wetatonmi, who shared a tipi with Running Feet and Yellow Wolf's mother. "I was in pain during the night, and my mind was uneasy," said Little Bird. "Perhaps it was the strange food we had last night. The Sioux eat different roots, and make their pemmican with different berries than we do." Wetatonmi smiled, asked a few questions, and then said, "Your time is near. When the pains start again send someone to get me and go to the women's lodge at once!" Yellow Wolf seemed to be aware of his coming fatherhood, though it was not a big event for him. Babies were being born all the time, nothing for a man to get excited about

The day was well started when the baby was born, and a few hours later Wetatonmi, as she had been taught by Heyoom, hung the embilical cord up to dry. Then she returned to Yellow Wolf's tipi and informed him that the baby had been born but that Little Bird would be in the women's lodge for a day or two. The next morning, since this was a casual event in Yellow Wolf's life, and he could not approach the women's lodge anyway, he again went beaver hunting with his Sioux companions. But during the day, as he relaxed beside the pond, he reflected that it would be good to have a son. "Colonel Miles said we would all be returning home, and somewhere out there I can teach that boy to hunt something much more exciting than beavers."

Yellow Wolf was busy with his Sioux friends for several days, and paid no attention to the baby. Then, on a bright morning a week or more later, when the sun shone directly on the east-facing tipi, Little Bird lifted the flap and held the baby up for Yellow Wolf's inspection. The tipi was warm now and the baby was not swaddled; it's hair was exposed and it's eyes wide open. Until now even Little Bird had not looked at the baby so closely and in such good light, and Yikyik had been changing its wet clothing. Now she could see very clearly, as could Yellow Wolf. They saw the small, delicate body; the almond colored skin, the light brown hair; the eyes that were closer to gray than to brown and in the morning light could even be called blue.

Yellow Wolf did not speak, nor did his face display any emotion. He quietly turned, lifted his kopluts from where it hung on a tipi pole, and slipped the carrying thong over his head. Then he added his two ammunition belts, picked up his rifle and warmest coat, slung an extra pair of moccasins over one arm, and left the tipi, walking back toward the lodge of his Sioux bachelor friends. "It's a girl, and it's not mine!" he fumed, recognizing in the eyes and hair of the baby a blond young rancher on a tall black horse. "Well, I'll be going that way before long, and I'll find him there around Tepahlewam."

# CHAPTER 37

"More than two snows have passed since we left our homes," Joseph lamented to Husishusis Kute as he and Yellow Bull rode along with Ad Chapman. They had covered well over a hundred miles, and almost a hundred still remained before they would reach the site on the Ponca Agency which they had agreed to several months before. "Our people are still weak and sick, and someone dies every day," continued Joseph. "But perhaps there on the banks of that river called Chikaskia things will be better for our people."

But things were not better. The people were still housed in tents, had no medical care, and food was always short. The canvas tents became ragged and rotten from wind, rain, and sun, and provided very little protection. Slowly a few homes were built, though after almost two years only 18 families were living in houses. Then came the encroachment of settlers, arrogantly moving onto the land, stealing the Indians' cattle, interfering in their everyday lives. They came in increasing numbers, with greedy eyes on beautiful land they said was too good for a bunch of Indians. And in these attitudes they were encouraged by government officials at all levels. The rigors of frequent moves, poor diet, constant stress, the dreadful effects of unfamiliar diseases, and isolation from all things familiar to them, brought a deep spiritual despondency which could not be pushed aside. Nor was it helped much by the provision of better housing, food, and tools, which finally arrived after more discouraging delays.

And the deaths continued. Of some 500 who had left the Bear's Paw battle site, only 300 were still alive. Among those who lingered and weakened and whose spirit seemed to drift away was Springtime, the only one of Joseph's wives to reach Indian Territory. Their daughter, Early Flower, born at Tepahlewam and now in her fourth year, was also depleted, and one day Joseph found them both on the riverbank, apparently resting peacefully in the shade. He tried to awaken Springtime, but she did not respond to his soft voice nor to his touch. So he took her hand to help her to her feet, but the skin was cold, the hand and arm limp and heavy. Joseph dropped to his knees, weeping, and turned toward Early Flower, who lay beside her mother. She too seemed to be sleeping, but he knew she would not awaken. The place where Joseph laid Springtime and Early Flower to rest left him no feeling of peace. "The government has bought this land for us, and they say it is ours, but we do not claim it for our own."

---

Lt. General Miles, now Commanding Officer, Department of the Columbia, had for years pressed his appeals for the Nez Perces through his superiors and wrote to President Hayes:

"I still adhere to my opinion that to punish a village of people, many of them innocent, is not in accord with any law or just rule, and I therefore recommend that that portion of the tribe not charged with crime be allowed to return to their reservation."

Joseph's still was determined to return his people to their homeland, and his fervent pleas persisted. To one group visiting the Nez Perces in Indian Territory Joseph said:

"You come to see me as you would a man upon his deathbed. The Great Spirit above has left me and my people to their fate. The white men forget us, and death comes almost daily to some of my people. A few months more and we will be in the ground."

Throughout the nation, people were listening and helping, among them the Indian Rights Association and the Presbyterian Church, who urged that the Nez Perces be returned to the mountains. C.E.S. Wood, General Howard's former aide, having resigned from the army, became Joseph's staunch friend and began a vigorous campaign to enlist the support of humanitarians throughout the country.

The exiled people continued to die, as they had from the earliest days of the long journey. The Indian Agent who had watched almost 200 captives die said, "The tribe, unless something is done for them, will soon be extinct."

# CHAPTER 38

"I knew when Yellow Wolf left the tipi he would not be back," Little Bird said to Wetatonmi as they sat in the April sunshine. "But I do not feel any loss. He was never harsh with me, but I did not seem to be part of his life. The Sioux have been good to me and life has become almost happy, almost peaceful. It is said that Yellow Wolf is getting ready to start home, and that several of the strongest of our men will go with them. But I will not travel with them. In my own time I'll go with those who choose to go with me."

"Some say that the army from across the border is trying to get White Bird to return home," remarked Wetatonmi. And that rumor was true, but he was never to return to the United States. His friends would later learn of his death when, as a medicine man, he treated the two sons of another Nez Perce medicine man. Both boys died; and both when asked, "Who are you?" had repeated White Bird's name, "Payopayo Hihhih." The boy's father shot and killed White Bird, believing it was his power which killed the children, for this was the accepted law of retaliation.

Little Bird watched as Yellow Wolf joined the first group of Nez Perces preparing to start back to their homes. The late spring sun was warm, and the restlessness which had begun during the winter was now stronger in all of them, especially Yellow Wolf. In some way Joseph had gotten word to all the exiles to surrender and join him, and members of his band were willing to do that.

So the strongest 30 young men prepared to leave, among them Necklace, Hoof Necklace, Tabador, and Yellow Wolf. With them were Yellow Wolf's mother Yikyik, Joseph's daughter, Running Feet; and several children. They knew the way would be long and hard, and there would be those who would try to kill them if possible; and they made a solemn agreement: "Trouble will not be sought, but trouble will be found by any who may seek it. We will live off the land, which is our right, for we gave up much when we left our homes and made this long journey to Canada."

Always, when they encountered white settlers, the Nez Perces offered friendship, but it was rejected by the whites unless they could see that they must provide food or horses in order to protect their own lives. At times of great danger one man in the group with a particularly strong Wyakin would smoke his pipe, whereupon a thick fog would arise and cover the refugees. They would steal through it, escaping from their current enemies. Sometimes a dream saved them, gave them forewarning of imminent danger, allowing them to outsmart and overcome the enemy at hand, or to escape undetected.

Finally they left the Bitter Root Valley to cross over into their own

Clearwater country. All would have known, of course, if any member of their party had been killed, but in the daily struggle for survival only Yellow Wolf, the most intensely involved of all, appreciated the miracle. "Not one is dead or lost! We are all here alive in this familiar place and Lapwai is not far away; perhaps we will find friends there."

Hoping for acceptance, they found only rejection, and were separated. Yellow Wolf's mother, Yikyik, Joseph's daughter, Running Feet, several other women, and the children were taken to the reservation at Lapwai. The rest, lonely men yearning for their homeland, traveled up the long slope to Camas Prairie, planning to cross over the mountain onto the Salmon River. But the ranchers on the prairie and along the river soon learned that some of the Nez Perces had returned, and everywhere the wandering people traveled they were attacked; and all but Yellow Wolf, Tabador, and Ten Owls returned to Lapwai, where they surrendered.

It was mid-July, and at the end of a dusty day a tired Gopher rode toward the lake for a swim. As he rounded a grove near the lakeshore he saw three horses drinking. Nearby were three Indian men with their moccasins off bathing their feet and washing the dust from their hands and faces. Tears came to Gopher's eyes, for he saw that these were some of his own people; then one of them stood and turned toward him, and he cried out with joy: "Hemene Moxmox!"

Yellow Wolf, hearing his name called in Nez Perce, though hardly believing his ears, ran to Gopher and embraced him. Ten Owls and Tabador joined them and all laughed and talked rapidly, the men eager to learn how Gopher had come to be there, and Gopher in turn asking many questions about his family and where were these men going. To Yellow Wolf and his friends it was apparent that Gopher was well cared for and content. Their journey to the Salmon river and perhaps beyond would be hard and perilous. It was best to leave Gopher on the prairie with the good white woman.

The years of fighting, wandering, near-starvation and rejection were wearing away at the hearts of Yellow Wolf and his two friends, and they thought that perhaps in their real homeland they would find some feeling of peace again. So they rode up the Salmon river to Deer Creek, looking for the cache which had been hidden more than a year before. But that had not been a familiar trail and erosion had worn away the signs, and because their minds were now dulled by loneliness and despair they could not find the cache.

They left the place feeling forlorn and dejected, to travel across Toohoolhoolzote's country. Like the domains of Looking Glass and Whitebird through which they had recently passed, this high, pine-studded tableland, lacking any human inhabitants, seemed desolate, almost forbidding; and they rode in silence, hurrying over it, then plunging down the steep, rugged slope to the Snake River, climbing over the great mountain to the west, and descending into the canyon of the Imnaha. "How remote it all seems," thought Yellow Wolf. "Can it be that only one snow has passed since we followed this same route?"

Tabador and Ten Owls were not of Joseph's band, and did not like the hot August sun in the valley of the Imnaha, but they stayed with Yellow Wolf as he led them over the next divide to Joseph Creek. They reach the creek's mouth, where they took refuge in the cool cave where Joseph had been born. But when Yellow Wolf wanted them to go with him up the Grande Ronde and into the Wallowa Valley they declined, for they were lonely for other friends, and started back toward Camas Prairie.

Yellow Wolf wandered on alone, eating the roots and berries familiar to him. Once he killed a deer, dried its meat, then moved on upstream. He found some solace in the sights and sounds and sensations of the land, but he was discovered by white ranchers and only his alertness and skill in covering his tracks saved him from capture. Then one morning as he awakened deep in a grove where he had hidden with his horse and had built no fire, he noticed the aspens above him were turning to gold. Winter was fast approaching, and he must prepare for it. So he turned downstream to follow the Grande Ronde to the mouth of Joseph Creek. Along the way he passed the small villages of shallow pithouses, their timber frameworks bare and gaunt, lacking the grass mats which made them warm and dry winter homes. Unused for a year, they showed signs of deterioration; and over them hung a cloud of loneliness.

Yellow Wolf had some concerns about using the cave as a wintering place, for it had only one entrance and he might be trapped inside. Then he realized that there were no signs of cattle and horses nearby, that the white settlers did not bring their herds so far downstream for the winter. He would take the chance. And during the autumn months he caught salmon from the late run, dried them over a low fire, pounded their flesh and stored it in their skins. It was too late for Camas and Kouse but there were still abundant berries, and he made pemmican by mixing them with the fat and meat of an elk he killed on the ridge above the cave. Soon the nights grew chilly and he knew that snow had fallen higher up, but would not bother him here. Each day he rode the dun gelding along the streams, maintaining vigorous activity for both himself and the horse; he would rest for an hour or two while the horse filled up on the bunch grass, then walk back to the cave.

In this way Yellow Wolf spent the winter, realizing in his loneliness that he must honor Joseph's request to all of his people to join him wherever he might be. "And besides," he thought, "I still have a score to settle with a young white man up on the prairie."

---

In Canada, Little Bird watched her fragile baby grow, worried because during the winter the horses had been reduced to eating willows, and finally to gnawing on the bark of larger trees. Hawk's ribs could be counted; his hip bones protruded, and his thigh muscles were gaunt. These concerns helped Little Bird decide that she would not start home this summer, but would wait until her baby was older, more able to make the trip. As for Hawk, Little Bird would cut the abundant grasses of summer and hide them in large crevices in the canyon walls, to personally feed him when food became scarce again. Wetatonmi continued to drift, making no decision about her return to Idaho. "Ollokot is dead," she said. "While we have had reports that Joseph and the rest of the people are in Indian Territory, no one has mentioned Welweyas or Jumping Rabbit."

So together Little Bird and Wetatonmi spent the spring and short summer in the Sioux camp, watching small groups of their people leave for Idaho. They had no way of knowing that many of those journeys would be aimless and meandering, with some of the travelers finding refuge with friendly tribes while others were captured by the army, to be taken to Lapwai or to be with Joseph in Indian Territory.

---

Following the blizzard that swept the Phelps and Martin cattle down Rocky Canyon, the temperature on the prairie plunged to forty degrees below zero. Most of the ranchers had smaller herds than Lucas and Olivia, and had gotten them into shelter before the storm struck. And for three of these bitter days and even colder nights, no one ventured farther than to their barns to check on the livestock. On the fourth day, as Lucas and Kirby dressed before the fire which they had kept burning all night, Kirby stepped to the window to look at the thermometer hanging outside, exclaiming, "It's 10:30 a.m. and still twenty-five below!"

"At least it's warmed up a little," said Lucas, "and I think we should ride across the prairie. The horses can use some exercise, and by the time we're ready to go maybe it will only be twenty below!"

The sun was bright and there was no wind, but they still needed their warmest clothing. As they approached the line fence, they saw pathetic mounds and knew that each one covered the body of a cow or a calf or a steer.

"Look, Dad; over by the fence! There are three cattle still alive!" Lucas saw three steers standing like statues, their heads low, hides totally encrusted with snow; and as the two riders came closer both felt an almost eerie sense of apprehension. They saw no movement, no twitching of an ear, no slight swinging of a tail. Soon they realized that these were indeed statues, that as the storm subsided and the temperature dropped, these critters, tails to the wind, heads down, feet planted, were chilled first by hypothermia which stiffened their legs, then by the deepening frost which stopped the flow of blood and finally froze all tissues. Now they stood—three solid, ice-filled carcasses that would not fall until someone tipped them over or warm weather unlocked their joints.

Lucas and Kirby stared at the ice-shrouded steers, unwilling to believe. Then they rode slowly northward, counting dead cattle as they went, returning past the three frozen statues to the mouth of the canyon, assessing their total losses. "With last year's calf crop, there were possibly 375 head," said Lucas. "Nearly 75 are dead here on the prairie, and some perished as they went down the canyon. But others quickly moved below the snow line and into those warmer side canyons, where a lot of them will survive. They aren't going anywhere, although some may cross back over the Salmon River. There's dry bunch grass down there, and they're better off than fighting the cold up here. Besides, they'd further deplete our hay supply. They'll get along, and the grass will turn green sooner down there than up here on the prairie."

In spite of the record storm in February 1878, one such as no one on the prairie could remember or would ever forget, spring came early, and by the middle of May the grass was good. The blue blush of camas blossoms appeared in the low wet places, and flowers dotted the hillsides. But on the Phelps and Martin ranches the broad expanses of pastureland were lonely, and both families felt desolate. The only cattle which had been seen were dead ones, and the repulsive job of disposing of the carcasses had left them all depressed.

"It's time to get a bunch of those cattle back up from the river," declared Olivia on a bright May morning, and by that evening the cowboys were ready, along with Cornelia, Gopher, and Olivia, still limited by her weak arm and shoulder but determined as ever. This time Lucas and Kirby were also part of the crew. The cattle were scattered, for water was plentiful and the grass was still good on the hills. Some were reluctant to be pushed across the river and up the rocky trail, so it took two trips, with time in between for other work, and June was nearly gone.

"If there are any more left in those gullies and thorn thickets, they can stay there," Lucas said, and Olivia agreed. Gopher had worked right along with the older cowboys during these roundups, for he was now a year older, his feet and hands were fully recovered. He rode the sturdy gray Morgan like the expert he was, and worked as hard as anyone at the branding.

## CHAPTER 39

For both the Sioux and the Nez Perces in Canada, famine made survival increasingly difficult. As her second year in the camp wore on, Little Bird's restlessness increased. But she did not regret her decision to remain through the winter, for her baby girl, whom she had named Camas Blossom, was now thriving. She went regularly to the small side canyon where she had devised a corral for Hawk close to her cache of dry grass. In spite of the hard winter, Hawk looked strong, and Little Bird thanked her Wyakin for the inspiration to store the extra food. "I am sure now that Wetatonmi will not go home with me," reflected Little Bird as she returned from the corral. "That is her choice, but I must join some of the others."

In the weeks that followed Little Bird gathered her scarce personal belongings and carefully hoarded morsels of food; but even as the late April sunshine melted the snows, and time for the departure was fast approaching, the supply was pitifully small. She moved quietly among the Nez Perce tipis, listening carefully but talking little, learning which of the people were eager to start the trip home. Several agreed to form a party, and she notified Sitting Bull's sub-chief, Strong Heart, who informed the council that more of the Nez Perces would be leaving the camp. Sitting Bull agreed to provide them with horses. All knew that Little Bird had a good horse, and she was thankful for him. On a warm morning in early May the party assembled, and Little Bird bid a tearful farewell to Wetatonmi, who had been as a sister, and her only confidante within the Sioux camp.

Mitaat Ooquoh, named for the three ravens seen by his mother a few days following his birth, was the leader of the little party of fifteen, which included his wife, Ilppilp Wahyakt, who wore the red necklace given to her by her mother. Little Bird admired this couple, both of whom had seen more than fifty snows, as well as their strong son of twelve winters and their precocious daughter of thirteen. Three Ravens was among the best of the buffalo hunters and had traveled to northern Montana several times. He knew the ways, and that the rugged mountains and steep canyons of the Yellowstone country should be avoided.

As the party traveled southward, crossing the border and the Milk River, Three Ravens swung to the west of the Bear's Paw battlefield, avoiding the evil memories that lingered there. They continued to the south, crossed the Missouri, and started up the long slope to Judith Basin. It was a long, demanding ride, and the supply of food doled out meticulously by Red Necklace grew smaller each day. But fortunately the warmer weather made the rodents active, and a few rabbits were shot during the day or caught in snares during the night. Then they had the great fortune to encounter and kill several antelope, and later they found buffalo. Their food supply was assured, at least for a time.

Three Ravens, using the young warriors of Toohoolhoolzote's band as scouts, was always alert for army units. Fortunately, most of them had been sent south to help subdue the few remaining Indians, including the Bannocks, along the Snake River plains. So the homeward-bound Nez Perces were not threatened by soldiers, though they barely missed being detected by one small unit. Toward the end of a long day's march one of the scouts returned, and with him rode two refugees, the object of an army detail sent out by the Crow agent, who had learned that Fair Dawn, a Nez Perce, was with the Crows and said she must be sent back to her own people; so she fled the Crow camp.

Fair Dawn, since leaving the fleeing Nez Perce bands to bear her baby, had spent almost two years with the Crows, never seeing any of her own people, and hearing only the Crow tongue, which she had not yet mastered but in which her little son Blackbird was already quite fluent. Now Fair Dawn almost fell from her horse to be among her own people. She lifted Blackbird from the saddle, placed him beside Camas Blossom and was joyously embraced by Little Bird, Red Necklace, the other women, and even some of the men. Little Bird remembered her own happy reunion with Wetatonmi, and understood Fair Dawn's almost delirious joy at the precious sounds of her own Nez Perce language as she listened and laughed and babbled around the campfire and ate buffalo meat cooked in the Nez Perce way. Camas Blossom and Blackbird, now asleep, had both been puzzled while playing, for she was still struggling with a mixture of Sioux and Nez Perce, and he spoke only Crow. Fair Dawn also was a little confused, for even after two years the Crow words stumbled about in her mind and sometimes got in the way of the Nez Perce phrases now being spoken so rapidly around her.

Days blended into weeks, and June was gone before Three Ravens completed the journey across Montana, having stayed well north of the Yellowstone country, skirting the Big Hole River valley and the cloud of misery and death which hung over that place. He had dropped down onto the Bitter Root River, and led his tiny mixed band over Nez Perce Pass and into their own land.

"The waters running to the north and those running to the south are very close together here," said Three Ravens, for with Nez Perce Pass behind them they had crossed the tiny headwaters of the Selway fork of the Clearwater, climbed over Green Mountain, and skirted the great shoulder of Magruder Mountain.

They descended into the valley of the Red River, following the trail downstream to Elk City, which they skirted lest they be detected by white settlers there. Their minds and hearts told them they were home, for the Red River soon joined the south fork of the Clearwater, and after another day's travel they would only have to go up Cottonwood Creek, cross the northern end of Camas Prairie, and descend into the Lapwai Valley.

---

"Lucas! Kirby! Get your guns! The Nez Perces are back on the prairie!"

Morty Martin's strident voice, out of character with his usually calm nature, resounded through the Phelps ranch house where he had swung open the door without knocking. As Lucas came running from the kitchen after an early breakfast, Morty hurriedly added that McConville again was calling up the volunteers and all were to head for Tepahlewam. "Word has been received that a band of Nez Perces is approaching from the Salmon River. We must stop them!"

Lucas saw no way to avoid being recalled this time, and quickly summoned Kirby. Together they joined a small, excited body of volunteers on the shore of the lake, where the zealous McConville commanded, "Spread out across the base of the mountain! Cover the trail that comes down from the south. We will allow no Indians back on this prairie!"

It was not a long wait, and soon the armed citizen-soldiers could see a column of riders following the winding trail down through the timber and approaching the edge of the prairie. The volunteer line, as instructed by McConville, drew back on both sides of the trail to let the Indians through, and then surrounded them. Each man, his rifle raised and cocked, rode toward the center, and the circle closed around the huddled group of Indians. Flushed with their victory, paying little attention to the condition of the people they confronted, the volunteers at McConville's order herded the hostiles toward Grangeville. "Notify Captain Falck down at Lapwai, and he can take care of this bunch," exulted McConville. "None of them will get away from us!"

Captain Falck had already been informed by telegraph of the impending arrival of these Nez Perces from Indian Territory, and he met the prairie defenders at the outskirts of Grangeville, where his calm, firm manner soon cooled their tempers and they were able to look closely at their captives: 29 bedraggled, tired people, mostly women and children, riding worn-out horses. They were led by James Reuben, a missionary who had traveled from Lapwai to teach them in Indian Territory and had led them home. "The government has approved the return of these defeated people to the reservation, and assured them safe journey," stated Captain Falck. "It is now my responsibility to escort them on to Lapwai." And with this cowering party which had so aroused the valor of the volunteers were Welweyas and Jumping Rabbit.

It was autumn again by the time Olivia's injuries were entirely healed. In the meantime she had tried to convince everyone that she was perfectly all right, though both Lucas and Cornelia still noticed a slight hesitation when she grasped the saddlehorn and swung onto her horse. The impact of not feeling physically whole and not entirely in control had made her edgy and less receptive to Lucas' renewed interest and advances. And the loss of their cattle hadn't helped any. Also, there was Bob Cone, who made several trips during the course of the summer and each time pressed his suit more fervently. All this attention was really more than Olivia wanted, for she was still dealing with the romance between Cornelia and Kirby. She was convinced that it was moving far too fast, remembering her own passion at age 16 when she and Jethro had eloped and ridden all the way to the County Seat to be married.

Kirby and Cornelia were blissfully unaware that they had any problems, though of course Cornelia could not ignore her mother's less than subtle comments about her behavior and the dangers of becoming too intimate. Lucas was more than a little irritable, and quite impatient. "After all," he complained to himself, "I've known this woman for 17 years now. She knows most of what there is to know about me. She most certainly is aware of my intentions."

Bob Cone, on the other corner of the triangle, would reflect as he made the long ride back to Slate Creek that things had really gone quite well, and then the vast reaches of the Salmon River country would close around him and he would become absorbed with his horse herd, and content with his peaceful existence.

In this rather prosaic pattern the fall and winter passed, and it was again spring on Camas Prairie. On a warm night in late May, when moonlight filtered through the branches of the walnut tree, crickets sang their persistent songs, and the air was heavy with the fragrance of honeysuckle, Olivia, in her robe and bare feet, walked through the open kitchen door to the back porch. She had made no sound, but there were sounds to be heard, and they were coming from the porch swing to her right. There were rustlings, whisperings, and murmurings. Kirby's low voice had a note of urgency and Olivia heard Cornelia's half-hearted protest. It was obvious that the couple on the porch swing were well beyond quick hugs and short kisses and, in spite of her dislike of the spy role, Olivia cleared her throat loudly and said, "Cornelia, perhaps you had better come in the house now."

Cornelia anticipated Kirby's next visit, resenting her mother's intrusion, and Olivia waited her out, hoping that the trust developed over 18 years, and especially their closeness since Jethro's death, would prevail. Cornelia was not a pouter, nor was she about to be apologetic, and within 24 hours she and her mother were chatting about everyday things; so upon Kirby's next visit Olivia, sure that the young couple must have discussed marriage, approached the problem head-on.

"Are you two thinking of a wedding?" she asked. Whereupon Kirby answered "Yes," and Cornelia quickly added, "As soon as possible!"

Though Olivia had never admitted it openly, the hurried informality of her own marriage had always bothered her and she wanted something quite different for Cornelia. But planning a nice wedding would take a lot of time and thought, and for once in her life she realized her need for advice and help from someone else. And then there was the matter of protecting these two kids from each other until September, when the wedding was to be held. She had sat them down and said in her own blunt way, "You two have got to keep your hands off each other. I know that won't be easy, but I believe you can do it until September."

"I do understand the whole situation," Lucas assured Olivia, still not quite believing that she had come to him for advice. "You will need help planning the kind of wedding you have in mind, and there probably isn't anyone here on the prairie who can make the kind of dress you want for Cornelia," he said.

Olivia was reassured by Lucas' calm response to what she considered a crisis and answered, "That's true. While Seth Jones and his wife may be of some help with the wedding, we will have to go to Lewiston to have the dress made." "Perhaps that will help kill two birds with one stone," offered Lucas, "because it will take at least two trips for the fitting, and a third one to bring home the dress. You've got a sister there with whom you can stay each time, and stretch out the visits to show Cornelia the sights of Lewiston, such as they are. You can take up most of the month of June that way, and I'll have Kirby busy here. How does that sound?"

"Good! And I just remembered something. Bob Cone mentioned on his last visit that the work with his horses and cattle is getting heavy and he needs some help this summer. Kirby obviously could use the extra money. Maybe you could manage to get him down to Slate Creek, perhaps for the entire month of July. So the blissful couple looking forward to a September wedding were being protected by a plan of which they were totally unaware, and Olivia, as she rode back toward her own ranch, reflected again that she did not like elopements, hurry-up weddings, and seven-month babies.

---

It was early June when Yellow Wolf decided it was time to start for Camas Prairie. Though there was never much snow at the mouth of Joseph Creek, he was worried about the dangerous river crossings such as those of two years before. But the rivers were only moderately high and he crossed both without difficulty, riding up Rocky Canyon in the twilight; and as darkness settled over the prairie he and the dun gelding were hidden in the timber above the Phelps ranch.

The routine of the work with which Lucas was keeping Kirby busy was an advantage to Yellow Wolf, for it involved fixing a stretch of the line fence extending up the mountain not far from Yellow Wolf's hiding place. After two days watching Kirby come up the mountain in the morning and go back at night, Yellow Wolf on the third morning was hidden in a grove close to the fence, the deadly kopluts in his hand, as he exulted, 'I will give him warning, a chance to fight, but he will not escape me."

Kirby felt stark terror at Yellow Wolf's cry and the hideous glare of hate in his eyes as he waited, half-crouched, the kopluts raised above his head, his long-awaited lust for revenge twisting his face. But terror quickly turned to action as Kirby gripped the hammer with which he had been nailing staples and lunged at Yellow Wolf, eluding his first rush and twisting sideways so that the kopluts was only the whisper of doom as it passed his ear and brushed his shoulder. Then Kirby's foot caught in a projecting tree root and he fell, knowing in that instant that he indeed faced death.

While waiting in the timber through the two long days and three chilly nights, during which he had only a small supply of water and cold food, Yellow Wolf had sought the comfort of his Guardian Spirit. The promises had been renewed—the keen vision; the gathering of distant sounds no one else could hear; detecting the scent of animals he was hunting, or enemies while they were far off. But there had also been a caution from his Wyakin, an admonition to kill only in support of his band or to protect his own life. And now as he stood over Kirby and again raised his kopluts there came to his mind, as if from his Wyakin, or perhaps from Joseph, this question: "Why are you doing this? Little Bird chose this man, which was her right." Then a weakness came over him and the weight of the kopluts drew his arm to his side; he spat contemptuously at Kirby and turned back toward the grove to find the dun gelding. Then he rode south toward Lapwai.

Kirby lay on the ground for a long time, trying to absorb what had just happened. He had last seen Yellow Wolf the day the bands fled from Tepahlewam toward Cottonwood Creek, and only once before that; but this was a different Yellow Wolf. He was haggard, fierce, and hollow-eyed. Kirby had scarcely recognized him. He finally picked up his hammer and went back to the fence, but was so shaken he was unable to work. He returned to the ranch house, where he told Lucas only he didn't feel well, and needed to rest.

---

"Yellow Wolf, we do not want you Dreamers disrupting our peaceful Christian life. President Grant assigned this reservation to the Presbyterians ten years ago, and we have been faithful in helping the missionaries to overcome the degradation in which we have always lived."

Yellow Wolf listened to the young, neatly dressed Nez Perce minister whom he had known since childhood; then, controlling his rising anger, he replied, "We took different trails many years ago. You know that I have been to Canada and back. But now I am tired; tired of running and fighting, tired of living in fear and loneliness. So I am going to see the agent and surrender peaceably. Maybe he will send me to Eikish Pah to be with Joseph."

"Well, don't expect any sympathy from Monteith. He is a good Presbyterian who was picked by our leaders and readily appointed by the government. He doesn't like Joseph, or Whitebird, or any of you wild people."

The news that Monteith was still agent disturbed Yellow Wolf, but refusing to show any sign of weakness, he turned silently and proceeded to the agency office. There he was questioned by an officious underling, refused to give any reply, and was kept waiting for two or three hours before Monteith condescended to talk with him. The discussion did not go well, and it was apparent that Monteith was seeking retaliation. Then, surprisingly, Yellow Wolf was saved by a detail of soldiers, who took him to see the young Post Commander, Captain William Falck.

Captain Falck questioned Yellow Wolf in detail, got straight answers, and cleared up some misinformation about what Yellow Wolf and the traveling band had done to white settlers and others before reaching Lapwai. "You must also tell me about the horse and saddle you stole over beyond the prairie, for which you could go to prison for several years. I do not want that to happen."

Yellow Wolf told how he had been attacked and almost killed, and had taken the horse in self defense in order to escape, but later returned it. Captain Falck accepted that explanation. So Yellow Wolf was returned to the guardhouse, where he was kept for several days, secure in Captain Falck's statement that it was only for his protection against the schemes of Monteith.

After a week had passed, Yellow Wolf heard the doors being opened, and in came his old friend, Tabador. They shed tears of joy, and Tabador told of his troubles, and wished that he had stayed in Oregon with Yellow Wolf. "But we are here now, together again," said Yellow Wolf, "and I believe Captain Falck will send us to Indian Territory." And the next day Tabador, Yellow Wolf, and several other Nez Perce men started the long, tedious journey, south to the Snake River plains and into northern Utah, where they boarded a train which took them to Oklahoma.

There was a great commotion among the exiled Nez Perces along the Chikaskia River as an army detail arrived, herding before it a small, disconsolate huddle of weary people, some almost unrecognizable in their nondescript clothing, gathered in various places along their wandering routes. Among them was Yellow Wolf, lean and haggard and with an absent, hollow look in his eyes. The memories of kind treatment by Captain Falck at Lapwai had faded during the long trip, replaced by longing for the land which he now believed he would never see again. Joseph embraced him and shared his tears and took him to his house. Yellow Wolf lacked the will to speak that night, and for three days was in a kind of stupor. Joseph, though his mind was full of questions, allowed Yellow Wolf his privacy.

In a few days, Yellow Wolf and Joseph talked together. It seemed they could never stop, for there were so many questions about family and friends and events in their far-flung meanderings, and with much sadness each recounted the deaths along their separate ways. Yellow Wolf listened sadly to Joseph's account of the loss of all the newborn babies, most of the old people, and many others. Among the most recent of the old ones to die was Hahlahtookit, the 74-year-old son of Capt. William Clark, known to Fred Bond on the flatboat as Daytime Smoke.

Yellow Wolf, in his own stoic and determined way, found life livable in

Indian Territory in spite of its hardships, and spent much time with Tabador. "It is bad news that I bring you," said Joseph a few weeks later as he entered the house where Yellow Wolf sat cleaning his rifle. "I have just come back from the store, where I learned that Tabador is dead." The shocking news almost overcame Yellow Wolf, for he had seen too much of death and now must face it again; the loss of a close companion with whom he had traveled and fought and hunted, who was near his own age and, next to Joseph, his dearest friend. But why? And how? Here in this place where there is no more fighting? Soon he learned that Tabador had gone to the store, where he bought a bottle of whiskey, and someone in the house where Tabador had been drinking told Yellow Wolf the story:

"He had an old cap and ball pistol, you know. Always carried it in a worn-out holster or stuck in his belt. I had a few drinks with him, and then he went into another room, where I heard him rocking back and forth in that creaky old chair. Then I heard the shot, and rushed in to that room, to find him on the floor. You remember that he always carried his pistol with a cap in place, ready to shoot. It looked like as he rocked the pistol fell from the holster onto the floor and went off. The ball tore away the top of his head." Joseph, who had known Tabador as a boy, was as stunned as Yellow Wolf, and said only, "The white man's whiskey has won another victory."

Life wore on in the Indian Territory, with the people struggling to care for their cattle herd and improve their little farms, while prevailing upon the government officials to provide more homes, for there were no materials with which they could build any themselves. Ad Chapman was there with them, but now he had a Modoc woman as a temporary replacement for his Umatilla wife, who was still back in Idaho. Joseph maintained his unceasing efforts toward returning the people to their homeland, and across the nation there was increasing interest, and some positive action, toward that end.

# CHAPTER 40

"It is good to be back in our own land," said Three Ravens to Little Bird as they moved along the south fork. "But I wonder how we will be treated when we reach Lapwai."

Little Bird's reply was slow and deliberate, for in spite of her youth she understood how things worked at Lapwai. "A few will be treated well, perhaps those from Looking Glass's band, and maybe that one mother with her boy from the Paloos area. But those who were most active in the fighting and those of the Dreamer faith will be shunned."

The next day Three Ravens led them to the prairie, across Lawyers Canyon, on to the northwest and down Lapwai Creek. That evening they camped within sight of the agency.

While they were finishing breakfast they saw a horse loping toward them, and soon someone shouted, "It is Welweyas!" And another exclaimed, "And Jumping Rabbit is with him!" So they had a happy little reunion, and hugged Jumping Rabbit and inspected the big scar on his arm, and all smiled at Welweyas, for they knew that he had saved Jumping Rabbit's life. Then, with some fear, they followed Welweyas to the agency office, knowing that the decision as to where they could live rested with Monteith. But on the way they met the same young Presbyterian minister who had railed against Yellow Wolf, and he singled out and preached to those within the group whom he perceived to be great threats because several were Dreamers.

Soon it was apparent that this diverse group of heathens would not be well received, but they rode on to the agency office where, after a long wait in the hot sun, Three Ravens was finally received into the presence of Agent Monteith. The reception by the agent was cool and conducted in a threatening atmosphere, and again Captain Falck was required to provide protection. He did not use the guardhouse this time, but gave Monteith very firm direction to leave these people alone, and to instruct the missionaries to do likewise. "I will not send these people to Indian Territory." said Falck. "There are too many Indian people there already, and steps are being taken to bring the Nez Perces home."

Three Ravens and his wife Red Necklace were in their declining years and, of all within this small group now being treated so coldly, carried the greatest longing for their homeland. "We would rather be there," Three Ravens thought, "staying alive by our old ways and hunted by the white man, than to be here where our own people shun us."

So Three Ravens convened his own council, calling on the wisdom which he sensed within the group: His 12-year-old son Little Bear, who had turned from boy to man on the long trip from Canada; Eagle, one of the young warriors from Toohoolhoolzote's band; and Welweyas, whose selection would have been a surprise to some, but not to this little group, for all of them now appreciated his strength and compassion. Then, not unprecedented but still unusual, he included Little Bird among the council members, for he had come to know her as mature and wise beyond her years. And finally he chose Swan Woman, the aged, wrinkled, woman of Looking Glass' band. "No one has ever included two women on a council," he realized, "but no one will ever know of this but us."

Three Ravens had quietly watched the diverse group during the arduous trip from Canada, and realized that the fires of adversity had aged them, and made them capable of great vision, which would be required for the plan he had in mind and for which they would be totally responsible when he and Red Necklace were no longer with them; now as he thought of the group again he realized that, collectively, they represented all of the non-treaty bands now sadly fragmented, some still in Canada, many in Indian Territory, others wandering alone, never to be united again.

So before this embryo council, few of whom fully understood the import of the decisions they must make, Three Ravens laid out the rudiments of a plan for survival, and all prepared to cross Camas Prairie and return to the Salmon River country.

---

"The winter was hard on the cattle, but we'll manage," said Lucas as he and Olivia sat watching the herd. "We do need some new blood in the herd, and I've talked with some people over at Cottonwood about getting two or three new bulls, some good Hereford stock from England."

Olivia suddenly realized that she had been ignoring Lucas, so she leaned toward him, smiled and touched his hand. "The cattle are important to us," she said, "but right now the most important thing is to get these kids married, and there's a fair amount of work to do. The dress is finished, and Cornelia is beautiful in it. I think we'll have the wedding at my house rather than at the Grange Hall. We'll need to have a rehearsal, and possibly some adjustments to the plan after that."

"Yes, you showed me the dress, and I can imagine it on Cornelia. Well, the kids are settled down now, sort of, and Kirby will soon be back from Slate Creek. That's been a good experience for him."

The next week Kirby did return from Slate Creek, showing the maturity of hard work during the two months he had been gone. On the day after Kirby's return, Olivia and Cornelia arrived at Lucas' house, bringing part of the food for a big dinner. Lucas would provide and cook the steaks.

"Kirby, where did you get this lovely necklace?" exclaimed Cornelia as she walked toward him from the entry closet where she had found the dentalium necklace hanging on a nail, and was now wearing it. Kirby started to reply, but stopped with his mouth open as he saw the necklace, the pure white carved shell gleaming against the darkness of Cornelia's blue blouse. The sudden shock was only momentary, and Kirby, hiding his surprise, answered simply that he had found it at the Big Hole. Cornelia said, "May I wear it for awhile?" In spite of his reluctance, Kirby said, "That's all right with me."

"Come in, Reverend Henley!" exclaimed Olivia as she met him at her door the next day. "We really appreciate your riding out here for the rehearsal. You've performed enough marriages that we could have simply shown you where to stand and you could have taken it from there, but I'm sure it will go better because you are here today."

"I'm glad to do it," replied The Reverend. "Besides, I needed a good ride in this beautiful autumn weather. And it's nice to see the new barn again, with the sun shining on that bronze weathervane up there."

In her orderly way, Olivia had already decided where everyone would stand, where the minister would be, and how Cornelia would come down the stairs to take Seth Jones' arm and proceed over to face Kirby, where Seth would give her away in Jethro's absence. So they went through that routine, with a crestfallen Herb Jones standing in for Seth, who had not made the extra trip for the rehearsal. Cornelia was a little breathless, and Olivia, wanting to avoid bustle and confusion, sent Kirby and Herb out to set up tables beneath the walnut tree, where the reception would be held the next day.

All had relaxed, and Olivia was putting out cider and doughnuts when there was a knock on the front door. Cornelia went to open it—and was face to face with a strange young Indian woman in a rumpled buckskin dress. Like a camera, Cornelia's mind recorded sharp images: the faint smile on the full lips, now parted as if she were about to speak; clear, though slightly smudged, skin which did not hide the solemn beauty of the finely chiseled features, so unlike Cornelia's stereotyped idea of an Indian face; the totally black hair, drawn back to reveal a strong forehead and held neatly in two long braids; the deep-set, almost mesmerizing eyes, brown like the depths of a shaded pool where dark, mossy rocks absorb most of the sunlight. And in the eyes Cornelia saw sorrow, but little joy; sadness, and dignity, and premature wisdom. The wrinkled, greasy buckskin dress escaped notice, for it could not conceal the fullness of the slim body, the ripeness of the firm, unhaltered breasts, the delicate flair of the hips, the overall strength and vitality of this lovely woman.

"They call him Gopher, there at that ranch," Welweyas had said, and from the way he described the location, Little Bird knew it was not the Phelps place. Now she stood on the Martin's porch before Cornelia, about to ask for Gopher, but as she started to speak her eyes fell on the white carved pendant and the dentalium strands around Cornelia's neck. It was obvious to Cornelia that this woman had seen the necklace before, for now she reached out to touch it. Cornelia drew back, and at that moment Kirby, having heard a commotion in front of the house, jumped up on the end of the porch and slid to a stop almost between Cornelia and Little Bird. He instantly took in the whole scene: Little Bird, who had turned to look at him; to his right, tied to the front gate, the unmistakable Appaloosa named Hawk; and sitting comfortably behind the saddle, an almost-blond little girl. A few yards beyond Hawk were other Indian people on horses.

The sounds on the front porch had attracted Olivia and Lucas, who now came to stand behind Cornelia. They saw Kirby's eyes riveted to the little girl sitting on Hawk's back, not thirty feet away. Lucas' mind was suddenly back in a meadow by a grove more than two years before, when he had seen this girl, and Kirby, and that horse. The realization that shone in Kirby's eyes was reflected in the minds of all watching, for they had seen the yearning, the almost imperceptible movement to reach out, to touch, as Kirby and Little Bird looked at each other. Slowly, Cornelia, her face stony and unsmiling, removed the necklace, handed it to Little Bird, turned and disappeared into the house.

Unnoticed, Gopher had come to stand behind Lucas and saw his own people on horses beyond the gate. Kirby, a look of panic in his eyes, started through the door to follow Cornelia, but was stopped by Olivia. "Let her go, Kirby!" Little Bird turned and started back toward Hawk, and Gopher followed, running past her to greet Welweyas and the rest of the waiting people. And there was his aunt, Red Necklace, and she held him to her ample bosom while her tears streamed into his tousled hair.

Olivia watched in consternation, torn by the sudden rush of disturbing events: a heartbroken daughter behind her in the house; the agonized-looking Kirby as he recognized the Indian child, and now Gopher being embraced by a tearful woman, probably a relative. "He is like one of my own," sobbed Olivia to herself, "and before this day I thought I could tolerate Cornelia being gone from the house because Gopher would be here with me. Now it looks like I may lose him too, probably forever."

Gopher did go with Little Bird and Red Necklace, riding double behind Three Raven's 12-year-old son. And as they rode away, Olivia realized that he had taken nothing with him. "He left as he arrived—with nothing. Except that now he is with his own people. And where can that possibly lead him?"

Cornelia locked herself in her room, and a confused, dejected Kirby rode home with Lucas, who was no happier. Olivia slept not at all that night, the awful stillness of the house beating about her ears, for Cornelia had refused to open her door. But she was equally concerned about Gopher, and in the faint light of dawn she was riding toward Tepahlewam, mounted on a mare which had replaced the dead Morab and leading Gopher's little gray Morgan gelding. Behind the saddle hung two saddlebags filled with clothes, shoes, gloves, food that Gopher especially liked; and tied to the saddlehorn was a bulging gunnysack containing more of the same. As the sun's first rays warmed her back, Olivia tied the gray Morgan to a tree beside the sleeping camp and rode back to her own ranch to see what she could do for Cornelia.

In the pre-dawn dimness when all others slept and only a dog or two barked, Three Ravens had led his newly-formed council and the rest of his little band away from Lapwai without official permission, as no Indians were supposed to be roaming across the prairie or into the Salmon River country; it was mid-morning before anyone knew they were gone. When the alarm was spread Captain Falck ignored it, and when the aroused volunteers again thundered up to the Phelps ranch house to inform Lucas that more hostile Indians were crossing the prairie, he made no reply. And all those who had been at the wedding rehearsal remained silent. As for Three Ravens and Little Bird and the others with them, they simply disappeared, and were never seen on Camas Prairie again.

No one outside the immediate Phelps and Martin families ever knew what really happened the day of the wedding rehearsal. Herb Jones had gone from setting up tables to feeding horses in the barn. The Reverend Henley, having consumed too much cider, was headed for the privy about the time Little Bird knocked on the front door, and by the time he and Herb returned to the house, Cornelia was in her room and Gopher was gone. So people around the prairie heard only that the wedding was postponed and that Gopher had gone back to live with some of his family. Seth Jones thought he could worm the truth out of his sister Olivia, but when he tried, first asking about Gopher, he could see the deep hurt in her eyes and went no further.

"There will be no wedding!" was all Cornelia said when Olivia first talked to her. And when Olivia used all of the usual arguments, such as, "We're all human," and "These things happen," and "They were just a couple of kids," Cornelia remained silent, obdurate and unwavering. Then Olivia reached into the depths of her private life, asking Cornelia if she knew she was a seven-month baby, pointing out that at barely sixteen years of age she had run off in the night with Jethro Martin. Actually, Cornelia had known the truth for several years because, entirely by chance, she had found her parents' marriage certificate and subtracted it's date from her own birth date. "But that was something quite different, just a mistake by rebellious teenagers," she rationalized. "I can't stand the thought of being married to an almost-squawman, the father of a bastard, half-breed child.'

Olivia took the situation as a challenge, determined that in some way she would change Cornelia's mind and the marriage would eventually take place. And it did, though it took two years, during which time Cornelia went to a high-school program conducted in the Grange Hall. Kirby continued to help with the cattle on the prairie and spent several weeks each summer working for Bob Cone at the Slate Creek ranch, while Olivia procrastinated and made excuses to herself and repeatedly postponed the decision about marrying either Lucas or Bob Cone. It wasn't the lack of suitors that finally changed Cornelia's mind, for there were several eligible and attractive young men in the high school, and one she had met at Lewiston. Nor was it her mother's wisdom and persistent counsel; it was simply that Cornelia had found no one she considered Kirby's equal. She eventually gained a great deal of wisdom and understanding on her own, and finally forgave him. Besides, she loved him deeply, and they had a quiet wedding in the ranch house with The Reverend Henley officiating but without benefit of another rehearsal.

The marriage of Cornelia soon forced Olivia to make her own decision. Not surprisingly, it was another dance at the Grange Hall which helped her make up her mind. Though it was the same setting, this dance, a few months after Kirby and Cornelia were married, was quite different. To begin with, Bob Cone was not there, and Lucas and Olivia drove to Grangeville in his buggy in the soft twilight of a May evening, while Kirby and Cornelia chose to ride two of the fast horses.

In Bob Cone's absence, Olivia danced almost every number with Lucas, sensing his increasing ardor and relaxing comfortably with her head on his shoulder. Then in the pale light of a moon not yet full, they took almost two hours for the six-mile drive to Olivia's ranch. It was late, and at the door Lucas kissed her passionately and again asked her to set a date for their wedding. She did not reply directly, but gave him a second warm kiss, and did not ask him in, saying only, "I still need a little more time." Lucas drove home more briskly, believing now that it was, indeed, only a matter of time. Olivia, before dropping off to sleep that night, murmured to herself, "What a dear man! And in a way I do love him. But something is not quite right, and I'm afraid it's with him rather than with me, which is scary."

Three days later, before Olivia had again seen Lucas, Bob Cone made one of his regular visits, was positive and charming in his unpretentious way, and when he again asked Olivia to marry him she answered, "Yes!" The next day they were married by the Justice of the Peace in Mt. Idaho, with Kirby and Cornelia standing by as witnesses, and by sundown they were halfway to Slate Creek.

Lucas learned of the wedding the next day when Kirby rode over, knowing that this abrupt turn of affairs would be a shock to his father. While the hurt did show on Lucas' face, there was something else which Kirby couldn't quite read. Kirby stayed for a couple of hours and had supper with Lucas and Herb. Then Lucas rode a mile or two out on the prairie with Kirby before returning home. "I've had her pretty much to myself for the last three or four years and didn't make those long rides like Bob Cone did," he thought. "I love her and always will." But he didn't get to the point of asking himself, "Why am I not disappointed?"

---

Bob Cone sometimes said laughingly, "I'm up to my ass in horses," and it was obvious to Olivia that there were a lot of them, and that they were good. "I started out with the best grade mares I could find," Bob explained, "and the best stallion I could afford, but I only had one, a fine Morgan, which I still have, incidentally. I knew that my best market would be the Army Remount Service, and they want quality and prefer Morgans, or Morgan-

Thoroughbreds to get taller horses. The foals I was getting looked good, but they weren't quite up to army standards and there weren't enough of them, so I got that big Thoroughbred stallion over there in the other corral, and as fast as I could afford it I bought top-quality Morgan and Thoroughbred mares. Now the foals from the Thoroughbred mares are by the Morgan stallion, and vice versa; and the army is happy with the results."

Olivia looked around her in wonderment and had to agree that it had worked very well as she saw the beautiful mares feeding in the pasture between the house and the river. "I don't see that this many horses would come up to your—as high on you as you infer," said Olivia with a twinkle in her eye. And Bob explained that only the best of the pregnant mares were kept here on the home ranch.

"We're very careful with these choice mares. And besides, the herds have gotten so large that there isn't enough pasture down here. The rest of them are in the high country, some to the east of us toward Florence, others in the side canyons, and many along the headwaters of the Little Salmon River in those big, grassy meadows. In fact, the little town up there is called Meadows." And Olivia recalled Jethro mentioning that settlement. Then she felt a thrill of anticipation as Bob went on: "You got here just in time, in the middle of September, because in the next thirty days we'll be rounding up the horses, driving part of them over to the Weiser River to meet the Army Remount Service, and bringing the rest down to winter pastures." And then he added, "Winter comes early and stays late in those high valleys of the Little Salmon."

The next several days were full of hard work and orderly preparation for the fall roundup of the scattered herds. Olivia reveled in the joy of it all, selecting her personal equipment, and happy that she could take two of her own best horses. In spite of her 42 years, she moved quickly and deliberately, and Bob marveled at her apparently endless energy. He frequently said to himself, "How could I be so lucky?"

At supper the evening before their departure Bob said to his nephew Marty, a saddlewise 22-year-old, "I'd like you to ride up Slate Creek again as usual. You can take one of the other boys with you. Bring back those yearlings and older mares, and if the grass looks good partway up the canyon you can leave some of them there. We can bring them down later." And the next morning Bob and Olivia headed up the Salmon River toward Riggins, each leading a packhorse.

The next week was among the happiest of Olivia's life: long, exhilarating days of hard riding, gathering in scattered herds of horses which to most people would have looked much alike but to Olivia were all new, and all beautiful. At times she felt a slight shadow of guilt, wondering if it was entirely right to be so happy with a second husband. "But it's been four years," she thought. "Jethro and I had it all, and Seth would be proud of me because I have no reason to feel remorse." And in the intimate, quiet moments on the trail, Bob would often try, and usually feel he had failed, to let Olivia know how deep was his love and how great his fortune to have shared the lives of two strong, sensitive women.

Within a week the gathering was complete, and all the three-year-olds had been cut out into a separate herd. "These are the ones for the army," said Bob, admiring the sturdy, tall Morgan-Thoroughbred geldings. "The two-year-olds are not yet strong enough, and lack the necessary endurance." Then he turned to one of the ranch hands, saying, "You ride with Olivia and me while we take this herd to the remount station." The other riders needed no direction, for they had been through this cycle before. They started downstream, trailing the yearlings, the two-year-olds, and twenty or thirty mares which had foaled early; those foals were strong enough to make the long trip and now frisked across the meadows with tails held high and manes flying, covering extra miles each day. At the end of the first day traveling south Bob and Olivia stopped pushing the herd, and let them spread out to feed along the banks of the river, now much smaller as it meandered in loops through the broad valley.

"We'll travel west over that low divide to the Weiser river, and on down to the remount station," said Bob, then he added proudly, "There's over a hundred strong geldings in that herd. We've taken as many as a hundred and fifty down there at times, but never brought one back yet. The army only buys the best." Olivia came to understand and love this orderly cycle: the turn of the seasons, the annual trips with the horses, the growing, improving herds. And one summer evening, as the jagged shadows of the peaks on the far side of the river swept up the meadows toward them and enveloped the porch where they sat, she said to Bob in wonderment, "I can hardly believe that I'm part of all this."

Olivia's choice of Bob Cone, their unceremonious marriage and early departure for his Slate Creek ranch, had seemed hasty and inconsiderate to many of the people around the prairie. She had soon realized that there were some loose ends, and immediately after the first horse roundup she had returned to the prairie, feeling a little apologetic toward Lucas and wanting to discuss things from a business standpoint. "We've shared the cattle without any formal arrangement except the brands. We've also shared the pastureland which is deeded to each of us, without any fence, and you'll need to decide what to do about that. Now I'm giving the Rocking M cattle to Cornelia and Kirby, and will expect a twenty-five percent share of the profits each year. The Martin land will remain in my name for the time being. Eventually, of course, Cornelia will inherit it."

Then Olivia surprised everyone when she said to Lucas, "I have something for you," as she led the way to the barn, where she and Bob had stabled their horses, along with a third one which they were leading when they arrived the day before. And she led from a stall into the broad central aisle a lean-limbed gelding, almost seventeen hands high, a deep, glistening chestnut sorrel with a red mane and tail. "I've noticed that Monty is showing his age," she said, as she handed the lead rope to Lucas. "And besides, you can always stand another good horse or two around the ranch."

Lucas cleared his throat and looked around the circle of friends and family, but could not speak. There were tears as all admired the magnificent horse, knowing that this was Olivia's way of telling Lucas that she was sorry, and would always love him.

When Olivia and Bob left for Slate Creek the next morning, the reality that she was no longer part of their daily routine finally came home to Lucas, as well as to Kirby and Cornelia. It wasn't something that could be expressed, and no one tried, but all sensed that for a time at least they would feel less stability in their lives. And even Lucas, though he would not have admitted it, realized that decisions would be a little more difficult now.

Lucas admired the big chestnut, and especially appreciated how superbly he was trained, but he felt a little reluctant to bring this new horse into his barn, as if in a way he was turning his back on Monty. So he continued to ride both Monty and the new horse, which he named Oliver but soon called Ollie.

"You will be a grandfather in August!" Kirby proudly informed Lucas as they were branding the new calves a few months after Olivia and Bob's last visit. "Cornelia just saw the doctor in Mt. Idaho yesterday, and is feeling generally well in spite of morning sickness." The word grandfather was a bit difficult for Lucas to accept, for he did not think of himself as being old at 54. But the distance from Vermont, though he seldom thought of it as home, the long separation from his family, stern and uncaring as they had seemed, and the feeling of remoteness from his roots had always burdened him. Now he could hope that the Phelps name would be continued. His life merged with the seasonal routines of calving, branding, putting up the hay, maintaining the ranch buildings, keeping the cattle healthy, improving the vitality of the herd by purchasing young heifers or an occasional new bull. Kirby proved himself very proficient in these same things, and the two ranches, operated essentially as one, continued to prosper.

Lucas to some extent had fantasized that Herb Jones would always be with him, and Herb had given no other indication; but in the course of one week in early June Herb had come home late at night three times. Lucas, always hesitant about inquiring into private matters, though realizing that something different was going on with Herb, said nothing. "Yes, she was my school teacher. And she's four years older than I am," Herb said almost defensively when he finally told Lucas that he had been seeing Miss Henley. Things had gotten serious. "She's a fine woman," asserted Lucas. "You couldn't do better. And don't worry about the age difference. What is she? Twenty-six? Twenty-seven? You're both still young." So in September there was a second wedding at the Martin ranch house, with the ceremony conducted by the same minister and Lucas acting as best man. Cornelia graciously hosted the short reception that followed, feeling relieved that Herb was finally married.

# CHAPTER 41

Olivia had barely started back to her ranch on the morning after the disastrous wedding rehearsal when Three Ravens arose from the bed where he had been sleeping among the trees near the lake, for his destitute little group had no tipis. He saw the sturdy gray Morgan gelding tied nearby, admired the fine, almost new, saddle and knew that the horse must have been left there for Gopher. The rest of the camp was soon awake, and Gopher ran quickly to his favorite horse. He would have taken it back to Olivia had not Red Necklace said, "It is a gift from a dear friend. And such a gift we do not return." And Gopher rode the Morgan proudly.

Seeing the joy on Gopher's face, and the pride he took in his horse, Three Ravens let him lead the way over the mountain south of Tepahlewam and down Whitebird Canyon. Tahmonmah, the people called this place, the only home most of White Bird's people could remember. Now Three Ravens, Red Necklace, their sturdy son and girl-woman daughter rode along the stream and through the campgrounds which they had left more than two years before and had not expected to see again. Then all continued up the Salmon River, crossing to the west side just below Horseshoe Bend to save the extra miles of riding around the big loop; and as they approached the mouth of Deer Creek Three Ravens raised his hand as a sign to stop, turned, and spoke:

"We have had a long day's ride and we will camp here," he said. "When the sun rises we will ride up that mountain, and each of you is to have your horse equipped to pack everything possible back down. We are going to the cache which our people left two winters ago, and in the place I am taking you to live we will need everything the horses can carry."

Most of the work of filling the cache, as well as camouflaging the site close to this little-used trail, had been done by the women, and among them on that day had been Red Necklace, who for years had roamed this part of the canyon with White Bird's band. So she led Three Ravens to that place and said, "We dig here."

When the bands had passed this way two years before, they were following a plan to confuse Howard and his forces in the wilds of the Salmon River mountains, and they carried on their packhorses everything they owned: old weapons no longer useful against the rifles of the white man; extra clothing, ceremonial garments and paraphernalia; buffalo robes; extra carrying bags of grass or leather; and lots of food. Though the Nez Perces were in flight the pursuing soldiers were on the far side of the river, so there had been time to construct a good cache. Now Three Ravens and Red Necklace supervised its opening, and were gratified at the condition of the contents.

Red Necklace began removing the food and handing parcels to each individual. As shirts, dresses, leggings, and other clothing items were removed, Red Necklace gave advice to each person as to what would be most useful, and cautioned against being greedy and trying to carry too much. The ceremonial items were dear to the hearts of many of the onlookers, for each represented a particular event from the past, recalling memories of people now dead, or wandering in unknown directions. Red Necklace conferred with Three Ravens, and though they disliked making decisions for others, they chose a few cherished items which they thought were meaningful to someone in each band, and left the rest behind.

Three Ravens had left the weapons to the last, and now he began lifting them out of the cache, starting first with two beautiful, short horn bows, the sight of which brought tears to the eyes of those of Joseph's band. Not more than two or three of the young men watching were yet strong enough to pull one of those bows. But they were a part of their heritage, so he gave one to Welweyas and another to his own son. More useful were the bows of red cedar, for they would last indefinitely and were less susceptible to damage by moisture.

Each man in the group was given at least one of those, along with fine arrows fashioned from serviceberry limbs. All of the stored bowstrings of twisted deer sinew were taken out, along with arrowheads meticulously chipped from flint or more often basalt, the most prized ones of obsidian.

The packhorses were all loaded and each saddle was hung with a variety of bags and loose items suspended by thongs. As a final act, Three Ravens drew out a stack of buffalo robes, and one was lashed to the top of each horse's pack.

A thin sliver of sunlight had glimmered above the eastern horizon and barely kissed the high plateau to the west as Three Ravens led the procession of heavily laden horses up the twisted trail, away from the Salmon River. It had been eighteen hours since they had left the cache and, except for a brief rest and a cold meal as they hid in a dense thicket near the Salmon River, the little group had been moving steadily. Now Three Ravens tugged gently on the rein and spoke softly to his pinto, who needed only the slightest signal to stop, for he too was nearly exhausted. "Most of the trail is behind us," said Three Ravens as the people gathered around him in a tiny meadow beside a stream, "but the hardest part is still ahead. It is not so long, but very steep. We must walk, and lead the horses." So after another short rest, more cold food, and deep drinks from the creek, Three Ravens led the ascent of the ridge which loomed above them. The sun had not yet touched the slope up which they struggled and it lay in semi-darkness, the coolness welcome to both people and horses as they climbed over granite so smooth that the horses' hooves made no marks and left no trail.

More than an hour had passed when Three Ravens came to a halt, and the worn-out people drew up beside him. All murmured in surprise and delight at the scene before them. They had ridden into the light of the morning sun and saw a gracious valley, brightened by a splashing stream which erupted from the base of a cliff to the east and disappeared over a precipice not far to the west. "How beautiful!" murmured Little Bird as she slid from Hawk's back and helped Camas Blossom down to stand beside her.

"But the valley is quite small," protested Red Necklace. "It is not big enough for us. It has little grass, and is surrounded by steep, rocky hills like the one where we stand. We are far from any hunting country, and that stream down there is too shallow for salmon."

Three Ravens smiled indulgently, saying, "You must have patience." Then he added, "This is not the place," and led his tired horse down a slope that was almost as steep as the one just climbed. The weary people followed him to the narrow, grassy meadow, but as they proceeded upstream some raised their eyes in question, obviously perplexed, and none could understand Three Raven's quiet nonchalance as he rode to the very base of an immense wall of granite which seemed to grow from the valley floor. Sheer, smooth, and lacking any fissure or crevice, it loomed above the uplifted eyes of the people who stood, craning their necks, trying to see the top.

As her neck and eyes grew tired, Red Necklace turned to Three Ravens, the impatient question on her half-scornful face said, "Where do we go from here?" Three Ravens turned to his left, rode a few yards to a dense clump of wild cherry growing tightly against the rock, and there he dismounted, saying to Welweyas, "Help me here." Together the two sturdy men pulled aside the closely grown limbs to reveal a cleft in the granite, hardly wide enough to admit a horse, it's top so low that riders would have to dismount. Through this small opening the people walked, each leading a horse and carrying part of the load when the horse could not squeeze through with a full pack. What was thought to be a cave proved to be a dimly lighted tunnel.

It took awhile for eyes to adjust to the darkness, then the tunnel ended, the light quickly improved, and the people could see that they were riding at the bottom of a cleft between two soaring walls, so narrow in places that those horses bearing packs could barely pass through. The walls appeared to rise forever, and there was no direct sunlight. Seldom could the sky be seen, for the walls in places were tilted and seemed to close overhead. The thin, dark passageway was also long, and ominous time passed before Three Ravens rounded a slight bend and Red Necklace, riding just behind, saw him raise one arm to shade his eyes. She too was momentarily blinded as she rode into full sunshine, but as her pupils closed and she could see again she gasped in disbelief at the scene before her.

Some 800 million years ago, the land which the Nez Perces now called home rested on the old North American continental plate. Slowly, over many millions of years, a great rift split that plate, and a new ocean basin began to form. The future site of the Salmon and Snake River canyons lay on the west coast of North America and the Pacific Ocean broadened, stretching, reaching endlessly westward, primordial and uninhabited.

Many more millions of years passed before other huge rifts began to open in the North American plate, some of them thousands of miles in length; and at one such rift another ocean appeared, at first just a narrow gulf, which grew wider as the plates on opposite sides drifted apart. The North American plate moved westward, away from the enlarging Atlantic Ocean, and headed for it's inevitable collision with the Pacific plate. As always happens in such a collision, the heavier oceanic plate dove beneath the lighter continental plate, and some of it's crusts were scraped off and jammed into the westward-moving continent above. The terrible forces of the collision compressed the western edge of the continent along what would someday be the border between Idaho and Oregon. And as the incomprehensible power of the collision fractured the continental edge, immense pieces were forced upward, pushed over each other, and rose to form a new range of mountains along the coastline. The coast, of course, did not remain there, for the Pacific plate continued to dive under the continental plate, adding immense quantities of rock to the coastline and thus extending it westward. One such addition consisted of fragments from far out in the Southwest Pacific They were small continents, perhaps similar to Australia, and chains of volcanic islands, not unlike the Hawaiians, some of them surrounded by lovely coral reefs teeming with life. The primitive west coast of North America received, and still holds to its bosom, the rocks of those enchanting desert islands and the fossils of those exquisite coral reefs. Those whose eyes are trained to see such things may still look at them along the Snake and Salmon rivers where Idaho meets Oregon.

It was the results of some of those cataclysmic changes which greeted the eyes of Three Ravens and Red Necklace and those who followed them out of the claustrophobic, narrow slot through which they had traveled. To the people's left but a half mile away stretched the north wall of the canyon, a great, blank, unbroken barrier some five miles in length and reaching over 2,500 feet into the sky. And to the right, its base obscured by trees, loomed the south wall, as high as that on the north but different in that it had fractured so that its several pieces sat at slight angles to each other, creating delightful coves. From these recesses ran small streams, draining the massive mountain above. But what the people failed to see immediately was that the south wall did not stand straight; it was tilted at a slight angle, perhaps only five degrees, but in its height of over a half-mile this angle became important, for the overhanging cliff shaded a verdant strip of land some two hundred yards wide.

So entranced were the people by the overall beauty and majesty of the canyon that they did not yet see all its details. But Three Ravens and Welweyas soon perceived that this canyon was impenetrable, except by the narrow trail through which they had just entered; and that trail could be guarded very easily by one man in a commanding spot and supplied with adequate weapons, or simply by blocking the opening with boulders. What Three Ravens and Welweyas did not perceive, or at least did not admit to themselves, was that they and their people also had only one way to leave the valley, and for that reason could become prisoners within its walls.

Night was falling and the air became chill, so the people unloaded their horses and turned them loose to graze in the meadows along the stream. Then they found shelter in the protection of a cave at the base of the north wall, where the sun had warmed the rocks, and there, feeling secure in their isolation, they fell into a sodden sleep. Tomorrow they would explore their new home.

## CHAPTER 42

Chief Moses was big, burly, and always talking. He sat in his tipi among his five wives and magnanimously greeted Otskai and his two Nez Perce friends, offering them whiskey, which they refused.

"It is good to hear from my old friend Joseph," said the effusive Moses. "I have feared for his safety these last eight years."

"Joseph is strong and well, in spite of the sorrowful life in Eikish Pah," replied Otskai respectfully, "and he sends you this token of the friendship between you."

Then Otskai waited, somewhat awed by the obvious position of this strong leader of the Wenatchee, Chelans, Okanogans, and others on the Colville reservation. Moses did not respond immediately, and Otskai solemnly handed him a leather-bound bundle which, when Moses opened it, revealed a headband of otter fur adorned with eagle feathers and the white, black-tipped tails of ermines. "It was obtained from a Cherokee chieftain in Eikish Pah," said Otskai. And Moses understood the meaning of this thing: a symbol worn long ago by a Cherokee chieftain in Georgia, obtained at a worthy price by Joseph, a Nez Perce in Oklahoma, and sent to his friend Moses near the Columbia in far-off Washington. It had traveled almost from sea to sea.

After the men had smoked, Otskai got around to the purpose of his visit: "Joseph knows that many white men in Idaho are waiting to kill him, and also that if he goes there he will lose all chances of ever returning to the Wallowa. So he asks to come here and live with your people. He has great respect for you, and will never try to replace you as Chief. Of course, if you die before him he will willingly become Chief here."

Moses drew deeply from his pipe, held the smoke, and exhaled slowly, to watch the tiny rings of smoke rise toward the tipi opening, thinking to himself, "Joseph and I have been friends for many years, and he will be no threat if he comes here."

So Moses said he would welcome Joseph and his people, and Otskai returned to inform Joseph, who was embroiled in more conflict with white agents, who were now preparing to move the Nez Perces back to their homes.

"Two weeks is not enough time for us to gather all our cattle and sell them at a good price," complained Joseph to the impatient Dr. Faulkner, a special agent sent to direct the movement of the Nez Perces from Indian Territory to the Northwest. "You are forcing us, just as Howard did when we left the Wallowa country with the rivers at flood stage."

But Faulkner had a job to do and was insistent: "A deadline is a deadline, and we will depart on May 21," he declared, ignoring the fact that the Nez Perces had been here in this place for six years. Why the hurry now?

In spite of the long days of hard work, trying to meet the enforced deadline, the people visited the graves of their relatives and wept over them, thinking also of the many others, 200 or more, who had died in this forbidding land. Here in this little graveyard by the Chikaskia River was the most pathetic place of all; almost a hundred little mounds, some bordered by small rocks, a few with sticks or boards driven into the ground, but all unmarked. They covered the wasted bodies of tiny babies who had been poorly nourished before birth.

"At least we were able to bury these dear ones, and we know where they are," mourned Joseph to Yellow Wolf, "and we had time to bury them in our own way." But he could not bring himself to speak of Ollokot, Heyoom, Rainbow, Five Wounds, the intrepid little Lean Elk, or the many others, dead in so many places between Idaho and Saskatchewan. Where and how were they buried, if at all?

Joseph's decision had been made—he would go to the Colville reservation to be with Moses, and most of his remaining band would go with him. Dr. Faulkner was adamant, refused to extend the deadline, pushed the people, and their cattle and horses were sold to white interlopers and other Indians at giveaway prices. At first light on May 21, 1885, they hurriedly dismantled their camp, and part of them were loaded into wagons while the men and many of the women slogged all day through the mud and steady rain toward Arkansas, Kansas and the train that would rumble and rattle toward the Northwest, day and night for five days.

"A lot of people want Joseph dead," Captain Baldwin of the Fifth Infantry warned Dr. Faulkner while the train was stopped in Pocatello, Idaho. "I represent General Miles and feel responsible for getting Joseph and his people safely to Wallula Junction in Washington. Several indictments have been issued accusing Joseph of murder, and I am informed that a U.S. Marshal will be boarding here to arrest him. We must keep this train, and all these people, moving westward!"

There was confusion, confrontation, and delay while the train sat through most of the night, but Faulkner was insistent, and by daybreak the train was ready to move. But just as it was gathering steam there was a commotion on the platform, and up the steps to confront Faulkner came the U.S. Marshal, wearing his star and backed by two subordinates, each carrying a sidearm.

"You are to turn Chief Joseph over to me," commanded the Marshal. "I have here a warrant for his arrest for murder." Dr. Faulkner and the Union Pacific agent stood their ground. "I am Dr. William E. Faulkner, Special U.S. Agent, with authority and responsibility to deliver these Indians to reservations as assigned by the Indian Bureau and backed by the U.S. Army."

The Marshal was unimpressed and ordered his two deputies to draw their weapons, pushed Faulkner and the railroad agent aside, and strode into the car containing Joseph, Yellow Wolf, and others of that band. The Marshal had never seen Joseph, but he had a picture, and the muscular, solemn, six-foot Indian who rose to greet him was without doubt the man he was seeking.

"You are under arrest for murder, Joseph, and are to come with me," ordered the Marshal, moving up to stand between his two deputies, who stood with their weapons leveled. Then all three were suddenly aware that a second man had quietly come to stand beside Joseph, and that behind him had gathered other grim-faced Indian men. But it was Yellow Wolf's eyes, glowing, penetrating, transfixing, which drew their attention away from Joseph and seemed to rivet them to the floor. All three stood for several seconds as the terrible eyes threatened them, then slowly the Marshal drew back, hoping his men would shoot but fearing the result of bullets in this crowded car. But he gave no order to withdraw, and the deputies felt the urgency of their sworn duty.

To Faulker, to the Marshal, to Joseph, to the deputies, and to all the others looking on, the action of the next split second seemed to occur in slow motion. The deputies saw Yellow Wolf's hand slide beneath his belt and sensed somehow that his eyes were no longer on theirs but rather on their guns. The eyes, in their intense concentration caught the flicker of a constricting trigger finger, then came a ripping sound, followed by two sharp cracks as Yellow Wolf's kopluts was torn out of his shirt and crashed in lightning succession against the hands of both guards, whose pistols flew in opposite directions, clattering against the windows of the coach. The deputies bellowed in pain, grabbed their crushed hands, and fell backward against the Marshal. Then, as Joseph stepped aside, Yellow Wolf and several warriors charged the three U.S. Officers, pushed them onto the steel platform between the cars, and threw them bodily down the steps.

The agent signaled the conductor, who passed the message on to the engineer, and the idling, grumbling train, impatient and bloated with its full load of steam, gave off great hissing blasts, ground its screaming wheels, and moved westward out of Pocatello.

Once across the bleak Snake River plains in Idaho Territory the train started up the tortuous grade beyond Baker, Oregon, toward the Blue Mountains. Joseph looked to the north, and saw the slopes leading to the great crest of his beloved Wallowa Mountains.

Wallowa! The name and the place had become an obsessive passion in Joseph's mind, to some extent beyond reason, for the permanent home of his people during eight months of the year was really the lower valleys: Joseph Creek, his birthplace; the Imnaha River, the Grande Ronde, the rocky beaches of the Snake River. But the Wallow Valley with the placid river winding through; green, bathed in mild sunlight, surrounded by the mountains was a haven from the radiant heat of lava cliffs in the low valleys. But most important, it had become a symbol, an always accessible refuge which, until a few short years ago had never been denied. Joseph thought of it now in the way the Norsemen thought of Valhalla: a place of rest for the soul. How many Nez Perce souls dwelt there now?

Over Oregon's Blue Mountains, down to the Columbia River, and upstream to Wallula, just below the mouth of the Snake River; there waited Charles Monteith, who had replaced his brother John as Agent at Lapwai.

"It is my responsibility to separate you into two groups, those for Lapwai, and those for Colville," announced Monteith dogmatically; and all sensed that attitudes at the Lapwai Agency had not changed much.

There was no question as to Joseph, Yellow Wolf, and their closest followers. They were headed for Colville and refuge with Chief Moses. Yellow Wolf would say later that the deciding factors for the rest of the people were: "Cut your hair, agree to be Christians, and you can go to Lapwai. Keep your hair and your wild ways, your Dreamer faith, and go to the reservation at Colville."

And so it was done, with very nearly half the people going in each direction. Joseph and his group went on up the Columbia by train to Spokane Falls, then west by wagon some 60 miles to the Colville Reservation. The Lapwai group went east by train to Riparia, then up the Snake River by boat to Lewiston; from there they walked over the hills to Lapwai.

In the eyes of the government, and to those people who had worked for and watched their return, the Nez Perces were home. "But home is not a place or a feeling imposed by someone outside the family," Joseph thought as he traveled. "We Nez Perces lost our real home years ago when we gave up our identity and were driven from our land."

---

"We do not want you here. You are wanderers, murderers and thieves, just like that old drunkard Chief Moses," stormed Solaskin of the San Poils, where Joseph and his people had been left to face a bleak existence. Without decent shelter or food, and scantily clad, they had again been thrust upon settled tribes who resented them.

"My old friend Moses and his people are not far from here, and the message he sent to us by Otskai said he would welcome us," said Joseph to the surly white agent, who was glad to see these bothersome Nez Perces move anywhere.

"Moses and his people welcomed us at first," lamented Joseph, "but these Nespelems rebel against Moses, and scorn us. We have been here now for almost two years without any good horses, only those puny ponies we won from gambling with the Nespelems. The government has not sent us the seeds and farming equipment it promised, and it would not do us much good, for most of the land is rocky and poor, and the best is already occupied by these resentful people, who certainly will not share with us."

Yellow Wolf was happy enough with the Nespelems. Yes, it would be nice to go back to the Wallowa, but that possibility seemed remote, and life was not bad here. He tried to encourage and support the despondent Joseph, who now ignored the house built for him by the government, and lived in a tipi.

And though life was tolerable for some of the people, the ever-present feeling of humiliation and dependency stayed with Joseph, and he could not push it from his mind. "We raise a pitifully small amount of food," he thought to himself, "and though the fish and the deer and the elk are real food to us and very welcome, along with the berries and roots, these things are not enough to keep us from starving; so we continue to depend on the government for our very lives."

# CHAPTER 43

"I was here just once before," said Three Ravens to Welweyas as they set out to explore the walled valley. "That was when I was a boy of only ten or twelve winters. One of the older boys dared me to come with him up that steep, rocky face, and we came through the opening in the cliff, but only a little way into this valley."

But Three Ravens did not describe the apprehension he had felt on that first visit, for he knew even as a child that though this place had been known to White Bird's band for generations, it was to be avoided. The few that had gone there had reported strange feelings, a sense of some threatening presence; and had come to believe that even talking about it might bring danger to their people. But it had been hard for the young boys to keep still about the huge animals they had seen.

So Three Ravens had thought long and deeply, and sought the help of his Wyakin before deciding to seek refuge here. He did get some comfort from his Wyakin, who reminded him that this was a most secure place. So Three Ravens had decided there was no better place to hide. As for the bad omens and tales of strange animals, he would face these things in his own mind, tell no one else about them, and see if they were really true.

Three Ravens and Welweyas stood in front of the cave at the base of the sheer granite wall that soared above them. There was no trail leading down to the valley floor, so they picked their way around large granite boulders and through tangled brush to the broad meadow, and there they caught and mounted their horses for the day's exploration. When he had first looked into the valley the day before, Three Ravens had realized that this was a place of splendor, and quite large, though he could not really envision its extent.

"Let's cross the creek, and ride to the base of those cliffs on the south," said Three Ravens; "then we will ride east, and see how large this valley really is." As they rode they were increasingly impressed with the beauty about them, and by the time they reached the south wall they realized that this valley was more than a white man's mile in width. Though it was now midmorning and the sun was well up in the sky they rode into shade while still some 200 yards from the base of the cliff; for the great slab tilted to the north and here in its shadow was a kind of sub-climate, with luxuriant grasses, ferns, and trees that were different from those growing on the valley floor. On this early fall day the shady glens were almost cold. They had gained a little elevation, climbing to explore the sunless nooks where little streams seeped from the base of the mountain. Now they moved back down to the valley floor and rode eastward, soon encountering a bend in the creek, which wandered in great loops through the meadows.

It was a feeling which neither could describe to the other, nor would they have tried even if the words could be found. It started as an uneasy sensation which detracted from the placid beauty of the day and grew until it said that something was wrong. Three Ravens had felt it first, remembering his brief experience here some 40 winters before, and for a while he had tried to push it aside. Now he felt threatened, and glanced furtively at Welweyas, trying to read his expression. But Welweyas kept his eyes to the front, struggling with his own feelings, denying his fear, searching his mind for reasons.

The two riders had left one loop of the stream behind them and now approached a second, the stream itself hidden by trees to their left, when suddenly Three Ravens stopped his horse, reached up and pulled down a leafy branch to look at it more closely.

"I do not know this tree. Have you seen one like it?" he asked, the apprehension in his eyes now showing clearly. And Welweyas shook his head, "No." Then they rode on through tall grasses which brushed against their knees, and Welweyas pulled off the strange-looking heads, holding them up before Three Ravens, and both realized that this grass was something entirely new to them.

They were still pondering these strange things when they heard in the gully below them a change in the sound of the water and, moving through the trees, they were faced with what appeared at first to be a logjam over which the water roared into a large pool below. Riding on upstream they soon saw that it was not just a logjam, for the end of each log was uniformly tapered, and bore the even, regular toothmarks of beavers. Though no longer common through the Salmon River country, a beaver dam of itself was not remarkable. But now, as they circled the end of the dam and gazed out across the pond behind it they again looked at each other, and their puzzlement was increased, for this was no ordinary dam of fifty or a hundred feet in length.

This one stretched for a quarter of a mile across the valley, where it was connected to a ridge extending out from the far wall; and the logs which formed the main structure of the dam were not the usual three or four inch aspens or alders; they were twelve or fourteen inches in diameter, and the two Nez Perces saw that behind them on the hill stood the sharply incised, conical stumps of the many trees which had become part of the dam. And these trees were also entirely strange. Dotting the placid pond were the lodges, not the usual little mounds standing two or three feet above the water and perhaps six feet wide. These lodges stood seven and eight feet above the water and were at least ten feet wide; it was obvious that they were the tops of log igloos standing fifteen to eighteen feet high and resting in at least ten feet of water.

Still unwilling to openly express their fears, and seeking reality in the things about them, the two Nez Perces rode up the grassy margin of the pond, and in a little while Welweyas, riding ahead, raised his hand cautiously and said, "Do not move. There is a big animal among the trees; I think it is Ha'hac, a grizzly bear." But the animal moved across their path, shuffled down the bank dragging its plank-like four-foot tail, slid into the pond, and was gone—a beaver as big as a bear!

"Nothing we have seen holds any danger, but they are all part of these strange feelings," said Three Ravens. "But this is where we have chosen to live, and we must see more of it—how big it is, and what there is here for food." So they rode on for more than an hour, and agreed that this valley was at least five miles in length. The stream beside which they had ridden, Three Ravens called Skookumchuck, and they now looked at its major origin, a cascade-like spring erupting from the base of the granite wall which enclosed the eastern end of the canyon. Small brooks flowed from the cool, shaded nooks beneath the overhanging south wall and enlarged the stream as it flowed westward. "This stream pours out of the canyon wall beside the Salmon River," explained Three Ravens, "and runs across the trail before falling into the river. No one pays much attention to it, because all they see as they look up from the trail are those sheer cliffs. I think no white man has ever been here."

After crossing the valley to the north wall, they started back downstream, keeping their horses in a steady running walk to cover the five-mile ride to the cave while there was still daylight. Soon they came to a huge rock-slide which forced them to move out on the valley floor. It was no ordinary slide, for its immense, jumbled boulders sloped upward a thousand feet to the base of the smooth granite face looming above; and the slide extended far down the valley. Then suddenly as they rode around a massive boulder Three Ravens and Welweyas saw quick movement ahead as several graceful animals sprang from the edge of the grassy meadow and leaped nimbly up the rocky slope.

"He'yets!" exclaimed Welweyas, hardly believing his eyes, for the agile mountain sheep ewes leaping over the rocks were the size of a large buck deer, and their gently curving spiked horns were two feet long. Even the lambs, only a few months old, were larger than the adult ewes the Nez Perces usually saw along the Salmon River. Then, as the amazed men gazed upward they saw on a pinnacle near the top of the slide a great ram, etched against the granite cliff. They stared in wonderment at his heavy, immense body, as large as an elk, and at the huge ribbed horns, with their full, graceful curl, cover two feet in diameter and glistening in the late afternoon sun.

The two men stood speechless, not willing to accept the things they had seen this day: the strange trees, the exotic ferns, the unfamiliar grasses, a beaver as big as a grizzly bear, mountain sheep ewes as large as a muledeer buck, and now this ram, three times the size of any they had ever seen before. They remembered, too, the slow-moving creature they had seen disappearing into a hole in the meadow. It rolled and shuffled as it walked, and they thought at first it was a badger. But a badger as large as a tall dog?

Three Ravens and Welweyas would never understand the things they had seen, and did not try to find the meaning or express it to each other. Had their little band upon entering this valley been thrust backward through the dimness of countless millennia to the days when giants walked the earth? Had this little valley, these few square miles, remained essentially unchanged, except for the on-going erosion of wind and rain and cold and heat? And had its very isolation, the totally favorable environment, the absence of competitors and disease, preserved these plants and animals in their primitive size and form?

The animals which Three Ravens and Welweyas had seen during the day, though startling, were not threatening, but the day was not over. "We must get back to our people," said Three Ravens anxiously as they proceeded along a dim trail at the base of the north cliff. "None of the animals looked fierce, but there may be others which are dangerous."

And they had gone only a short distance when they saw, leading down toward the meadow, a trail of blood, and on the flat surfaces of the rocks, bloody pawprints, like those of a dog but much larger. Then they heard the fearful wailing of their people from the cave, not far ahead, and they hurried to the opening, where they met Red Necklace and Little Bird and Gopher, and all were weeping and could hardly talk.

"It appeared suddenly at the mouth of the cave," sobbed Red Necklace. "It was black, and stood tall enough to look right into my eyes. And it seized little Blackbird in its huge jaws and turned to carry him away. Gopher and the older men returned from hunting just as the thing—it was like a huge wolf—was carrying Blackbird out of the cave. Eagle had one of the horn bows and shot, but only wounded it. The others attacked it with rocks and clubs, and it dropped Blackbird and ran away."

Three Ravens hurried to the back of the cave where Fair Dawn was cleaning the ugly wounds on Blackbird's arms and chest, sponging his already feverish forehead with cool water, and looking for ways to keep him warm, for in the excitement no one had put wood on the fire and it had died down to gray-white ashes. Three Ravens threw small sticks on the fire, knelt beside it, and blew on the coals until flames arose. Then he assigned his son and Gopher to keep the fire going and organized a party to find additional wood to last through the night. The next morning he talked to the group.

"Welweyas and I have seen that this is a beautiful valley, with plenty of game, and probably fish in the stream. But already a wolf has attacked us; there may be more like him, and perhaps other vicious animals. We must protect ourselves and prepare for the winter. We will build a rock wall across the front of this cave, and a corral for the horses, for they also are in danger. Without guns, our greatest protection while in the cave will be fire, which all wild animals fear, and we will have to guard the horses at all times. The food we have may last through the winter if we are very careful, but we must also hunt, and that means much practice with the bows, and making more arrows."

Three Ravens said nothing about clothing or sleeping robes, but Little Bird, Red Necklace, and the other women knew that soon these needs must be faced, for such things could no longer be obtained from the white man or from other tribes.

"We will use the face of the cliff for one side of the corral," Three Ravens explained to the other men. "And now we must have logs and poles for the other three sides." Then he assigned the strong warrior Eagle, with the horn bow, to stay at the cave, to protect the women and keep the fire burning. The rest of the men rode across the valley to the timbered, shady glens to find poles. Here their lack of any kind of ax or saw became real; they were forced to find small trees which had fallen or had perhaps been cut by a beaver and not yet dragged into the pond, and a few were even stolen from the top of the beaver dam. Then the long poles were dragged by the sweating, grunting horses across the mile-wide valley, where they formed three sides of a crude corral.

A few days later they saw the crippled wolf limping into the timber, and he was not alone. But they must satisfy their growing need for fresh meat, and hunted cautiously, always close to their horses should they need to flee from the wolves. The young men's skill with the bows and arrows had increased and though they missed some shots they managed to kill two mountain sheep ewes, for the sheep were not yet fearful of man. The beavers were more wary, and always scurried back into the pond before the hunters were close enough to shoot them. It was old Swan Woman from Looking Glass's band who solved this problem, for she remembered her people catching beavers around the ponds on Clear Creek. "You need to use snares," she said, and showed the young men how to make them. And in this way they caught three beavers.

All feasted hungrily on the fresh mountain sheep meat roasted over the fire, welcoming the change from the dry jerky. The roasted beaver tails were good, though most of the people preferred the mutton. They didn't like the smell of the beaver meat, but proceeded to dry it for the winter. Then with Little Bird, Fair Dawn, and the younger girls looking on, Red Necklace and Swan Woman began the tedious process of tanning the sheep and beaver hides.

"We must remove the hair from these sheepskins," said Swan Woman, "for we will make leather of them." And she hung each of the hides over a smooth pole leaning against the wall; stretching the hide over the pole, holding it between her knees, and grasping a large sheep rib, she began scraping against the grain of the hair. Then she handed ribs to the girls and young women, and all took turns at the hard work of scraping the hair from the hides. Once that was done, the hides were turned over and their inner sides scraped to remove all the flesh and fat.

"These big beaver skins will make fine, warm robes!" exclaimed Swan Woman, "So we must leave the fur on them." Then she brought out five wet leather bags in which the brains had been soaking overnight, saying, "Each animal's brain is about the right size to tan its hide." She placed each brain, mixed with a little water, in a newly-made willow basket and showed her helpers how to stir the contents to make a thin, grayish paste in which each hide was placed to soak until the next morning.

"Now the work gets harder," said Swan Woman as she tied one end of a hide to a large upright log and attached a two foot long stick to the opposite end. Grasping the stick with her two hands, she used its leverage to twist the hide, grunting a little as the hide became tight and the water dripped from it. Then Red Necklace and Swan Woman showed the girls how to knead and scrape the wet hide with a flat rock, holding the lower edge with their feet and stretching the hide upward toward their bodies. It was time-consuming, tiring work, for each hide had to be scraped at least two hours before it became soft and supple, and there were five hides that required this treatment.

Now a long, narrow pit was dug in which Swan Woman built a fire of dry wood from beside the creek, the closest thing to willows she could find. When the fire no longer flamed, green wood was thrown on to produced a heavy smoke, the skins were hung over a low rack above the pit and smoked for an hour or two. Great care was taken to avoid burning the fur on the beaver skins, and they came off the rack warm and supple, and big enough to cover a child; even an older person with knees drawn up could sleep beneath this luxurious beaver skin robe. The large mountain sheep skins were soft but surprisingly strong, and the leather would be useful for many purposes; but like the beaver skins they would forever carry the odor of the wood smoke, though it would decrease with time.

Except for Red Necklace, Swan Woman, and Three Ravens, the tanning of the hides was new and strange to all in this little valley which they now called He-Yets Pah, The Place of the Mountain Sheep. Little Bird thought this over and realized, "We have gotten so much from the white man that we younger ones have lost our skills and our ability to use the things around us." And she eyed the beautiful, reddish-tan sheepskins hanging on a crude rack nearby, thinking of the need to replace her own decrepit buckskin dress, and to make new winter clothes for Camas Blossom.

Such matters were heavy on the minds of all the people, and Three Ravens called the council together to talk about facing the winter that was close upon them. "We must kill more mountain sheep as soon as possible," he declared, "both for their meat and for their skins."

All agreed that another sheep hunt must start immediately, and that they had a little more time to get the beavers because they did not migrate. So again leaving the women with a good fire and one warrior with a horn bow, the men and boys set out the next morning after mountain sheep. Again they were successful, and by late afternoon were headed back toward camp with mountain sheep dangling across the saddles of six horses. It was then that they again saw the wolf, slipping silently through the timber not far from the trail. All armed their bows with arrows, and Welweyas, carrying the horn bow, moved to the front of the column. The wolf was very lean, and still limping, but soon disappeared, so they relaxed, thinking that their numbers had discouraged him.

But this was a desperate wolf, for his wound had sapped his strength and cut his speed and endurance so that he could no longer catch a healthy mountain sheep, or even the slow-moving beaver he had tried to surprise in the timber near the pond. Now as the trail swung close to the trees the waiting wolf suddenly charged, his hunger and blood lust aroused by the scent of the dripping mountain sheep carcasses. His course toward one of them was slightly behind Welweyas, who turned swiftly as he heard the throaty growls and aimed the powerful horn bow; but the arrow missed. The arrows from the other bows were smaller and less effective, and in one bound the wolf was among the horses, raging, snarling, leaping, and so menacing that the men feared for their lives in spite of their weapons. Quickly Three Ravens drew his knife and cut the thongs so that one mountain sheep carcass fell to the ground; it was immediately seized by the wolf, who easily dragged the heavy body into the brush.

The shaken men looked at each other with terror in their eyes, hardly believing that the vicious black wolf was so huge. His broad head was almost level with Welweyas' chest, and when he snarled he revealed interlocking canine teeth over two inches in length. His body was more than six feet long, and even with one hind leg badly disabled he had almost carried a 200-pound mountain sheep. As the silent men rode back toward camp, they remembered that just a few days before someone had seen a second wolf with this one. How many wolves were there in this small valley?

Fresh meat and a growing supply of both sheepskins and jerky raised the people's spirits, and within the week they went beaver hunting. At the end of the first day's hunt they returned home with four, but that night a storm swept over the plateau and the temperature in the valley plunged almost to zero. The need to greatly increase their wood supply now became critical, taking all their time for several days; and when they again went after beavers they found the pond completely covered with ice, and saw only the round domes of the lodges in which the beavers would spend the winter.

The reality of winter was soon upon them, for they were virtually prisoners of the wolves and isolated in the cave, which was uncomfortably small for twenty people. They thought longingly of the warm, sheltered canyons in the lower valleys where they could move about at will and where they had spacious longhouses or individual family shelters beside the streams. Here they seldom ventured far from the cave, and if they did every available man and weapon was required for protection. The horses became increasingly worrisome, for they were confined to an enclosure of not more than an acre, where there was no food. Some meadow grass and the most tender of branches from the creekside had been stored before the storms came, and were rationed carefully each day, but lasted only a few weeks. Then the horses, guarded by all the men, were led to the meadows, where they expended their energy pawing for grass and finally resorted to eating the larger tree branches and gnawing on the trunks.

Little Blackbird struggled for survival, his body grievously infected. Swan Woman had some remedies in her medicine bag, and she made poultices of roots. She also found spiderwebs in the dark corners of the cave, and to these she added water to made a thick paste which she spread on Blackbird's wounds. She was sure his arm was broken, and fashioned a crude splint of stiff willow limbs covered with soft mountain sheep skin. None of these measures brought protection against the invasive hordes of bacteria left in Blackbird's body by the jaws of the wolf, and soon after the first winter storm the little boy died.

The ground was frozen and covered with snow, and was too lonely a place for any grave, so they wrapped the wasted body in the softest buckskin and laid it in the narrow V where the roof of the cave met the floor. There they also placed Blackbird's primitive little toys, and sealed the burial vault with a rock wall. Though the Nez Perce people did not dwell on death, Fair Dawn's period of mourning was prolonged, for the little wall of clean new rock was a daily reminder, and there was no escape from the crowded cave. Camas Blossom, not understanding what had happened, grieved for her playmate, and tried to comfort Fair Dawn.

Three Ravens, Red Necklace, and Swan Woman had realized before the snows came that confinement within the cave would bring depression to the people; and while it could not be entirely avoided, it might be relieved by keeping their hands busy. So the three elders had gathered all manner of materials for making the things they knew would be needed.

Three Ravens had already used some of the horns from the mountain sheep ewes to make wedges for splitting wood. With the help of Welweyas and the older warriors, who had seen such things but never made them, they scoured the rocky bars beside the stream to find hard stones the right size and shape to make pestles for grinding and several large, flat rocks with slightly concave surfaces which could be used as mortars.

At first it had appeared that their supply of arrowheads might be adequate, but many had been lost by inaccurate shooting and inexperience, a few even in practice, and some during the encounters with the wolf. There had been some good flint, and even one piece of rare obsidian, in the cache, and Three Ravens had placed these materials in his bag. As he searched for similar materials here in He-yets Pah he longed for just a few hours to gather obsidian on the John Day River, but that was far away, beyond the Grand Ronde in Oregon. He saved all the mountain sheep horns, knowing that the women would make the smaller ones into spoons and ladles, and dreamed that the huge full curl from the big ram they had killed might make a horn bow.

Red Necklace and Swan Woman had also been busy gathering materials. The greatest need would be for clothing, and that required tools for sewing, and they must have better utensils for cooking. So they had gone first, as always well protected by armed men, to the brush beside the stream, where they found long, whip-like limbs, something like willows, and they gathered these to be woven into baskets. None of the trees were familiar, but some of them did have pitch oozing from their bark and this was collected to seal the baskets and make them watertight.

During the butchering of the mountain sheep they had kept various bones and now selected the hardest of the small ones for awls, to bore holes along the seams of clothing in order to draw through the slender thongs which would make the seams tight.

The days grew shorter, and the forest beneath the overhanging cliff on the south side of the valley was always shady and cold. But for a few hours each day the sun warmed the south-facing plaza in front of the cave, heating the rock wall, which gave back part of its heat at night after the fires died down. The cave was too dark for fine work, such as chipping arrowheads, sewing sheepskins, or pecking with a small, hard rock on a softer cylindrical one to form a handle for a tool; most of this work was done during the sunny hours in front of the cave.

The pitch-lined willow baskets proved their worth, for they were good for boiling meat, a welcome relief from jerky or even fresh meat cooked on the coals; and one basket, containing water mixed with ashes from the fire, was used to soak the sheep horns which were laboriously fashioned into spoons and ladles.

In this way, the long winter wore on; and while most of the people were busy part of the time, they began to chafe under their confinement and lack of physical exertion. Even lovemaking was at a great disadvantage in the narrow confines of the cave. This was not important to Three Ravens and Red Necklace, or old Swan Woman, and to Welweyas, now some thirty years old, it was still a matter of confusion. But to the two young warriors from the lower Salmon River, and to both Little Bird and Fair Dawn it was a different matter, and increased their irritability. And then there were the teenagers, including Gopher and Three Ravens' daughter, for the fires of youth were beginning to smolder within their loins.

By the end of February, while snow still covered the valley and before any edible roots were obtainable—though no one knew what to look for—the older women began to realize that the constant diet of meat was not a good thing. The dried serviceberry cakes, like candy to the lonely people, were all gone now. There was some dried kouse left, and several planks of camas which, when boiled, provided variety. But how long would it last? And what replacements for these foods could be gathered under the lustful eyes of the wolves?

## CHAPTER 44

Olivia and Bob Cone trailed more than 50 three-year-old geldings along the Little Salmon River, but there was no anticipation in their eyes, for it was late September and they were traveling in the wrong direction.

"These, as usual, are prime horses," the Captain at the Remount Station had said, sitting like a ramrod on his own mature Morgan. "You've always brought us the best, and they've served the army well, but things are changing rapidly. The Indian Wars in the west are all but over; the Nez Perces are subdued and scattered in several directions, and all the tribes along the Snake and Columbia are on reservations. The Bannocks down on the Snake River plain were pacified last year, and that little band of Apaches under Geronimo is still wandering back and forth across the Mexican Border; but that's a long ways away, and the army gets its horses from someone down there. So Miles has told us to stop buying, and all we need this year are not more than fifty of your best, to replace the old ones we've sold off."

Olivia had seen Bob set his jaw and hesitate before answering and she had almost cried, for during the five years since she had first made this trip with Bob they had never driven any horses back home. By now she knew by heart the history of the ranch and the pedigree of practically every horse on it. The Captain had done his best to soften the blow without breaking military demeanor, but there were no good answers; and the next morning they had started back up the Weiser River to cross the divide onto the Little Salmon. That night they stopped at the cabin where the river plunged into the gorge.

"We probably have the best herd of Morgan and Thoroughbred stock in the West," lamented Bob as they lay awake in the dark. "I suppose I should have anticipated that someday the demand by the army would drop off. So where do we look for a market now? In spite of the growing population on the prairie, they're not looking for many saddlehorses. Actually, they'll need workhorses more. Of course there are still some packhorses being used, but mining is dropping off also. And can you imagine any of these beautiful animals carrying packs?"

"Of course not!" responded Olivia, almost in tears. "And we have so many horses! Not only those fifty or so three-year-olds out there in the meadow, but a lot of two-year-olds and yearlings back in the side canyons. And down at the home ranch and on the meadows nearby are all those pregnant mares. All told, we've got somewhere around 250 head. You just don't suddenly turn off the production line in this kind of operation."

The next morning they proceeded down river, leaving a few three-year-olds in each of several side canyons, along with younger horses that were to winter there, but they still had 30 three-year-old geldings when they reached Slate Creek.

"The horses will still be here when we get back," said Bob, attempting to be lighthearted about the whole matter as they started down the river toward Whitebird, "and we need to see our friends and family on the prairie. Marty and the other boys can cover things at Slate Creek while we're gone." And by noon of the third day they stood on the front porch of the Martin ranch house, waiting to surprise Cornelia and family. They were attacked joyously by Olivia's four-year-old grandson and two-year-old granddaughter, both of whom considered Bob their real grandpa, and called him Papa Bob; their other grandfather was Papa Lucas.

The get-together at the Phelps ranch should have been an entirely happy affair, for it included not only the Martin and Phelps families, with the two grandchildren dominating the scene, but also the Seth Joneses, who had driven over from Mt. Idaho. Morty Martin and Jenny were there too, along with Herb Jones and Geneva, now obviously pregnant. Olivia and Cornelia had talked quietly soon after the Cones arrived, and maneuvered to have the party at Lucas' place. "He's just not himself," Cornelia reported. "Seldom smiles, and spends a lot of time just riding around, up to the top of the mountain, or down Rocky Canyon. He's got us all worried. Maybe having the family there will cheer him up." And when Olivia took Kirby aside to talk with him, he said simply, "I'm worried sick."

Cornelia and Geneva had collaborated on the supper, and it was superb. Everybody savored it, including Lucas, as the aroma of the big beef roast, the glazed ham, and the apple pies filled the house. All relaxed, enjoying the delicious meal, and no one was talking much. Olivia and Bob had mentioned only casually the declining horse market, but now, as Seth Jones buttered his third roll and started to raise it to his mouth, a thought suddenly struck him, and he said, "Bob, I just remembered something, though it may not be of any help to you. Ad Chapman is back from Oklahoma, you know. He's still in the horse business, and just returned from a trip to the Palouse country. He tells some interesting stories about the growing demand for draft horses on those rolling wheat fields. Yes, I know they're totally different horses than yours, but the supply over there is far short of the need. Importing the kind of horses they really want is very expensive. It might be worth a trip to look it over; it's unique country."

The party ended on a happier note, and Lucas seemed more cheerful. And that night, as Olivia and Bob lay in the big bed in her former room she mused, "I've never been beyond the Snake River to that Palouse country, but I do know that some of the best Appaloosas come from that area. Let's ride over there. There are no big demands at Slate Creek right now." And three days later they had made the long trip, northward across the prairie and down the rocky ridges, to Lapwai Creek, then down the Clearwater and up the totally bare and very steep hills north of Lewiston. Two or three hours later they sat on the crest of a knoll gazing at a seemingly endless succession of knobby, steep-sided, grassy hills stretching from east to west and fading into hazy blue on the far northern horizon. Not a tree of any size was to be seen, but the grass was luxuriant, and small streams meandered through the little valleys, appearing to go nowhere.

"If ever I've seen horse country, this is it!" exclaimed Olivia, and they rode on to the northwest to find the farmers who needed a particular kind of horse to till the huge wheat fields, plant the wheat, and harvest the grain.

"Those big Percherons and Clydesdales are no good here. They're clumsy on these steep hills and bump each other in the turns," one of the farmers said. "We use hitches of twenty-four, even forty, horses at a time to pull our combines. The big horses just don't work well in such numbers. What we need are horses that weigh around 1,400 pounds, not 1,900 or 2,000, like the Percherons and Clydesdales. Cleveland Bays are great, but there aren't many around and by the time we get them here they're far too expensive. Our breeders do have a plan underway, but it takes time." Then he led them over a small ridge and pointed to a unique contrivance.

In the swale below was a pond of water surrounded by a rather strange corral. It had only two rails, but both the top and the bottom rail were higher than usual. In the corral was a fiery Thoroughbred stallion, who raised his head and snorted as Olivia and Bob rode toward him. But he had more important things to snort about, for even as they watched, a small Appaloosa mare, apparently an Indian pony, ducked her head, slithered under the bottom rail, and was immediately mounted by the stallion. Bob and Olivia were puzzled as to how this fit into the plan for obtaining the right-sized farm horses, and they asked the farmer, who said, "Talk to the breeder."

"That mare you saw, and a lot of others like her that sneak into the corrals around the area, will produce foals that will weigh a thousand to eleven hundred pounds," began the breeder.

"But they're not big enough, are they?" questioned Olivia.

"No, they're not. But this is only half of the plan." And he led them up the swale to a second corral, which contained a big Clydesdale stallion with shaggy white feet and a wide blazed face. Here the bottom rail was a little higher, and the breeder explained: "When the mares from that Thoroughbred stallion and that skinny Appaloosa mare come into this corral they mate with that Clydesdale, and the resulting foals are just what we need. The problem, of course, is that it takes at least seven years before we have a mature horse of the right size, ready to start training in the big hitches. We've been at this for several years now, but we can't keep up with the demand for horses to produce all the wheat on the land now under cultivation, much less the new farms that are being broken every year."

Olivia and Bob rode back to the prairie, amused and astonished at this rather intricate process of producing farm horses. Both wondered how it could help them, with two hundred fifty head of Morgans and Thoroughbreds, all several hundred pounds too light to meet the demand in the Palouse area. It was Olivia who finally saw the light, and exclaimed, "Bob! We're halfway there! We're years ahead of those breeders in the Palouse area. We have all these mares of just the right size for the second cross—all we need now are big Percheron and Clydesdale stallions! Seth Jones and Ad Chapman have several of those, and can get more easily. In three years we'll have our first crop of two-year-olds, the right size and ready to train. And even better, they can use not only the geldings but also the mares, which the army never wanted."

Bob was silent for at least a minute, marveling again at this woman and the way her mind worked, and a little irritated that he hadn't seen the solution himself. Then he said quietly, "It will work, and we'll do it." Both realized that agreeing on the plan was one thing; putting it into action was another, for it would mean moving over 250 head of horses from the wild canyons along the Salmon River to Camas Prairie, which was hard work; but it also would mean leaving the Slate Creek ranch and their life on the river, which would tear their hearts.

Seth Jones was enthusiastic about the new plan, and agreed readily that he and Ad Chapman could find the big stallions. Then he added, "You may also be putting yourself just ahead of the demand for similar horses around Camas Prairie, for a lot of wheat fields are being plowed and planted here, and the prairie farmers also will need more horses."

The next morning Bob and Olivia bade a reluctant and tearful farewell to the grandchildren who clung to them, to Kirby and Cornelia, who wiped away their own tears, thinking of the time and the miles between, and finally to Lucas, in whose eyes they could again see returning loneliness. Then they started for Slate Creek, cantering quickly over the soft prairie grass and onto the rocky trail that would take them over the mountain, down Whitebird Creek, and up the Salmon River. The decision was made and there was excitement in looking forward to the new venture and again living on the prairie. But there was a vague uneasiness, felt by both but not shared, a kind of foreboding of events beyond their control.

---

As the first winter in the cave was softened by February thaws, Swan Woman sat quietly in her own impassive way, observing the potential couplings among the young people of the group and worrying that they might develop too rapidly. With the help of Three Ravens and Red Necklace, and even Welweyas, she managed a kind of segregated sleeping arrangement, hoping to delay the inevitable. It was not the eventual new babies she was concerned about, it was the health of the babies; for in Looking Glass' band she had been a kind of genetic watchdog, keeping track of who had married whom, what bands they were from, the closeness of their blood relationship, which couplings would be safe and which should be avoided. It was not enough, for example, to say that an Esnime girl from Upper Slate Creek could safely marry a Salwepu boy from the Clearwater River above Kooskia, for there had been many marriages between those two bands in the past, as well as others far removed, and that meant that a man in one band might be, and often was, a first cousin, or cousin-brother, of a woman in another band whose daughter was the object of his son's affection. Swan Woman knew, and it was widely accepted, that marriage of first cousins was taboo; that a second cousin marriage should be avoided, and marriage of third cousins was, at best, frowned upon. So she had carefully analyzed what she knew of the relationships between families of the marriageable young people, and had discretely asked questions to fill in the genealogy when she was not sure.

She knew by now that Red Necklace's thirteen year old daughter would not make a suitable bride for one of the young warriors from Toohoolhoolzote's band, for their parents had been first cousins. Nor should Gopher marry a girl from Joseph's band, though Red Necklace's daughter would be a good bride for him. Swan Necklace saw other suitable couplings, one of which would allow a safe marriage between Welweyas and Little Bird or, for that matter, Welweyas and Fair Dawn, for Swan Necklace knew of no relationship harmful to either pairing, except that Welweyas and Fair Dawn might possibly be third cousins, and that was not for sure.

As the oldest person among the cave dwellers, the wise Swan Necklace was well aware of the stigma which had long hung over Welweyas, and until very recently even she would never have thought of him as a potential husband for anyone. But since Welweyas and Jumping Rabbit had joined this refugee band at Lapwai almost a year before, Swan Woman and the others old enough to remember had barely thought of, and never uttered, the 'half-man, half-woman' slur formerly applied to Welweyas; and none could fathom the torture which had wrenched his mind as he assumed the full male role and abandoned the female. But the older ones were well aware that he was now different, and although Welweyas could not analyze the change, he knew somehow that it had started when he left the buckskin dress somewhere in Indian Territory; with his closeness to Joseph as a strong helper in moving the bands; and with his continuing commitment as a foster father to little Jumping Rabbit.

Swan Necklace had not actively thought of Welweyas and Little Bird as a couple, but perhaps as she aged she had become less sensitive to what was going on. Little Bird had become increasingly aware that Welweyas used or created opportunities to be close to her, to help her with the harder work, and to be sure that she and Camas Blossom got their share of the best food. But it was more than these personal kindnesses, for when the trail was difficult or the work the most demanding, or when danger was imminent, Welweyas was always there in the midst of everything, doing more than his share. He was steady and dependable, and his continual nurturing of Jumping Rabbit, and the obvious love between them, warmed Little Bird's heart. As it would be with all of the couples who came together in this place, there was no family from whom permission could be obtained, no gifts to be given or received, and no ceremony of any kind. Quietly and without comment or announcement Welweyas helped Little Bird and Camas Blossom move their sleeping robes and meager belongings to the corner of the cave where he and Jumping Rabbit slept. Little Bird had known Welweyas as long as she could remember, and was sure that there had never been a woman in his bed. So she was patient and cooperative, and he was inept but gentle, as she had known he would be. And both knew that life within the confines of this crowded cave would now be more bearable, and the smokey walls no longer seemed oppressive.

The signs of approaching spring brought no relief to the crowded, hungry people; though the sun had melted the snows on the rocky bluffs, the mountain sheep were still high in their warm glades, and ice still covered the beaver ponds. The good food collected during the autumn days was long gone, and the people were reduced to eating tiny daily rations of dried camas and kouse.

The horses had become pathetically lean as the store of meadow hay disappeared and the willow-like trees were gnawed down to stubs. The wolves were a constant threat, and could be kept at bay only by fire as long as the wood supply lasted, but it was almost gone. More arrows had been lost or broken, and few produced to replace them, so that the people felt increasingly vulnerable. So all stayed close to the cave, carefully stretching the wood supply for both warmth and safety, and waiting for spring. In desperation, Three Ravens decided they would kill the least useful horse, and all feasted on the stringy meat. The women wrapped the brain in a piece of sheepskin, carefully scraped the flesh side of the horsehide, and stored both in a cool crevice until conditions seemed better for tanning.

When the snow receded from the base of the cliffs, leaving a broadening band of meadow grass which slowly turned green, the women searched for familiar plants; but there was neither kouse nor camas here, and all they found were the tender tops of a plant which looked like their own wild carrot. It needed to grow for awhile, but when they tried it it was good, though not a real substitute for the carrots they had known.

Fortune did smile briefly as the ice on the beaver pond became rotten and the rising sap reddened the tree bark; the tiniest of tender buds began to appear on the trees, the beavers became eager to escape their winter homes, abandon the waterlogged branches stored there, and cut fresh ones along the shoreline. Some young beavers had forgotten the hazards of the past summer and three were killed by Welweyas and Gopher, who were elated by their success. But while dragging the beavers across the valley toward the camp they were again forced to fight off the big wolf, still suffering the pangs of a hard winter, and he robbed them of one of their beavers.

"I remember those beautiful gardens we had on Clear Creek, before the soldiers drove Looking Glass and all of us away," mused Swan Woman as she sat in the sun before the cave looking across the valley, now almost completely clear of snow, and greening rapidly. "It would be so good to have gardens here; but we lack seeds, and the sod is so heavy. We had white man's tools, even a plow or two, on Clear Creek, and that made it easier to prepare the soil."

She pushed the thought of the garden aside, and went to help with the tanning. But a day or two later she was back looking at the meadows and thinking about the gardens. "Corn, and beans, and squash! Some melons would be so good!" Then a commotion among the horses caused her to glance down at the corral. More than an acre, three sides surrounded by poles, the fourth enclosed by the sheer wall of the cliff, and suddenly Swan Woman realized that there was no sod, and no green grass, within the corral.

"There's our garden spot!" she shouted. "The horses have broken it loose with their feet and fertilized it well. Move the horse corral!" The men, who had just returned from hunting and this time had brought home four mountain sheep, were awakened from their afternoon nap, and quickly heard her story:

"We have a spot well prepared for a garden. All we need to do now is to move two sides of the corral and enclose a new piece of grass. But this time make the long side longer, and next year we will have a larger garden spot." The men agreed that it could be done, but raised the question of the seeds; it was Red Necklace who answered.

"Many times I have seen white men along the Salmon river planting gardens about this time of year. The biggest ones are at Slate Creek. Someone must go there and get seeds."

"The trip over the big rocky ridge and down to the river is long and hard," warned Three Ravens, "and those who go must be young and strong. There is danger in being caught, so there must be a plan to avoid detection. Welweyas, I want you to make the first trip, and take one of the warriors with you. Leave your horses hidden near the top of the big ridge. It is safer and faster for you to go by foot over those smooth, steep rocks on the other side. When you approach the gardens at Slate Creek, find places to walk in the horse manure so that it will be difficult to trail you with dogs. And one thing we must all solemnly agree on, and you must swear to now: If one of you is ever caught, your lips must be sealed. No matter how you are threatened, or even tortured, you must tell no one the way to this place."

So Welweyas and Eagle prepared for the trip, agreeing that they should leave early, hide their horses as directed by Three Ravens, sleep overnight a safe distance from the Slate Creek ranch, and by daylight the next morning be concealed on the hillside where they could watch the activity around the gardens and make their plan. The trip, as planned, went well, and by noon of the second day they had watched two young men with bags of corn slung over their shoulders methodically stepping off the distance between each hill, digging a small hole, and dropping in the seeds. After three round trips they were back at the big gunnysacks full of cornseed from which they filled their shoulder bags. And that's what Welweyas and Eagle were looking for. The afternoon sun was hot, the ever-present flies were pestering them, and they longed for a drink from the nearby creek; but all they could do was wait. Finally, just before sundown when the two workmen left their pouches beside the big gunnysacks and headed for the ranch house, Welweyas said to Eagle, "You wait here. It will be safer if only one of us goes after the seed. I hope to make two trips, and bring back loads big enough for each of us to carry to the cave. If things go well on the first trip I will try on the second to enter the barn and look for other kinds of seeds."

"Suppose there are dogs," commented Eagle.

"I am prepared for that," said Welweyas, patting the ample bag of jerky on his belt.

Welweyas skirted the border of the cornfield, walking on the grass and through the bushes, leaving no visible tracks, and arrived at the big sacks of seed just before the sun dropped behind the mountains. Returning quickly to where Eagle waited, he left the first bag of corn and retraced his steps, this time by-passing the corn seed, walking through the manure-covered corral and entering the barn. There he found baskets of squash and bean seeds, and some he believed to be melons; with these he filled the bag in which he carried the jerky. Elated at his success, he was just leaving the barn when he heard a low growl and turned to face a large, surly-looking dog, his head down, his tail up, suspicious of this stranger. Welweyas stopped immediately, spoke softly, but did not look directly into the dog's eyes. His hand moved slowly into the bag at his side, and he pulled out a piece of jerky, slipped it into his mouth, and chewed vigorously. The delicious aroma was too much for the dog. He dropped his tail, his ears went back, and saliva began to drip from his mouth. So Welweyas tossed him the jerky and began to chew on another piece. After the dog had eaten a second piece of jerky another dog appeared through the barn door and joined in the feast. Welweyas left most of the jerky and proceeded back to Eagle's hiding place with the second load of corn, as well as the bean, squash, and melon seeds.

Swan Woman and Red Necklace—indeed, all at the cave—were delighted with the seeds. The men flip-flopped the pole fences as directed by Red Necklace, and all began clearing rocks from the old fertile corral, further loosened the soil with digging sticks, and planted the precious seeds.

The squashes and beans did well in the fertile soil of the original corral, producing a large crop. But the planting had been two or three weeks late for the corn and the melons; the corn produced small ears and the melons did not ripen.

"We must plant earlier next year," declared Swan Woman, "and that means we must obtain the seeds this fall; for by the time the men can get over the big mountain after the snows have melted it is almost summer, and too late for planting."

So it was decided that a fall trip must be made to obtain next year's seeds, and this time Welweyas and Gopher would go..

"There will be no one planting at this time," explained Welweyas, "but they may be harvesting the corn, so we must, as before, have time to watch from our hiding place and be sure they have gone in to eat their evening meal before we slip into the cornfield. And we need a little time in the barn while there is still light. Our women very much need shovels and other tools. We may see the dogs again, but they are no trouble." And he reached into the pouch at his side, brought out two pieces of jerky, slipped one into his mouth, and handed the other to Gopher.

"Well, almost half the crop is in the barn," said Marty, as he and two of the ranch-hands pulled to a halt before the big barn door, their wagon heaped high with the golden ears of corn. Inside the barn sat two other cowboys, not entirely happy with the boring job of shelling corn. But all felt satisfied with the day's work, and while the other men headed for the back porch of the ranch house to clean up for supper, Marty unhitched the team, removed their harnesses, and hung them on the big pegs just inside the barn door. Then he heaved a satisfactory kind of sigh and headed for the house.

Olivia and Bob sat comfortably with Marty and the other hands, enjoying Olivia's delicious meal of steamed potatoes and baked squash, fresh from the garden, and big T-bone steaks which Bob had brought in from the spring house. Marty broke the silence when he said, "I guess some of us must be getting absent-minded. We had four or five good axes around the barn and the workshop and we're now down to two." And Bob added, "That's interesting, because I've recently missed my best heavy hammer. Also that one-man crosscut saw. I remember laying it carefully across a log the last time we went out to cut wood. I'd better ride up there tomorrow and bring it home before it starts to rust." But he still doubted that he had left the saw in the woods.

With supper over, Olivia led the way to the front porch, where they all sat in the bent-willow settees which Bob and Marty had fashioned from limbs gathered along the creekbed. The sun had dipped behind the mountain, leaving only a soft yellow-gold glow that blended into the pale blue sky above. The mares and their foals dotted the dusky meadow, some bedded down in the grass and now only shadows in the soft orchid-gray twilight. All on the porch became drowsy except Marty, who quietly arose, walked down the steps and around the house, to head for the corral, wondering absently why the dogs had not, as usual, been on the porch with them. "They're around somewhere, and they'll show up later," he thought. "That older mare was limping on her near front leg after work today, and I need the ointment out of the barn to treat her."

The foray as planned by Welweyas had gone well, and the timing was perfect, for while everyone at the Cone ranch was eating supper Welweyas and Gopher had carried the bags of corn to the far end of the field, along with the bean and squash and melon seed. "We will pick this up as we leave for the cave," explained Welweyas. They went back through the corn stalks and slipped into the barn, where they were met by the tail-wagging dogs, who caught pieces of jerky in mid-air, chewed vigorously, drooled, and waited for more.

Welweyas and Gopher had been at the far end of the cornfield when Marty entered the barn, got the linament, and walked to the far side of the corral to find the mare with the lame leg. From where Marty tied the mare to the fence, his view of the barn was blocked by a large haystack, so that he could not see Welweyas and Gopher run through the open barn door; nor could they see him. "I'll watch while you search for tools," directed Welweyas, and Gopher disappeared into the barn, planning to enter the connecting shop, where the best tools were kept. The dogs, which seemed to like Gopher, followed behind.

Welweyas was dangerously relaxed, but he did see Marty as he rounded the big haystack and walked toward the barn, the bottle of linament in his hand. Welweyas ran partway through the center aisle of the barn, and gave a low whistle, the warning agreed upon with Gopher. Then he nimbly climbed the steep steps into the haymow, crawled over the hay to the big door on the opposite end of the barn, grasped the rope hanging from the extended ridge-pole above, lowered himself to the ground, and disappeared into the cornfield, remembering Three Ravens' warning: "If danger is near you must take care of yourself, and under no conditions must you disclose the way to this place." Gopher heard the warning whistle and hurried from the shop to follow after Welweyas; but suddenly, seeing Marty enter the barn, he darted into a stall, crawled into a manger, and covered himself with hay.

The happy dogs had followed Gopher, but as he disappeared into the manger they trotted on toward the center of the barn, sniffing about for possible crumbs of jerky, and there they met Marty, who wondered about their strange behavior, and why they were in the barn in the first place, for they seldom went there alone. So he set the linament bottle back on the shelf and turned toward the ranch house. "Come on, boys," he said to the dogs, expecting them to obey, but they had returned to the barn. More alert now, Marty followed them to the stall where one stood with his nose thrust between the poles and his tail wagging vigorously while the second attempted to climb into the manger.

"The dogs have something—or somebody—cornered in a manger out in the barn." Marty announced to the group on the front porch. "Will one of you go with me to see what it is?" And Olivia quickly arose, saying she could use a little walk. She followed Marty, who had removed a rifle from its pegs above the fireplace, and now levered in a cartridge as the two walked through the barn door, where they were met by the two frisky dogs who led them to the manger.

"You take the rifle, Olivia, and keep it cocked and leveled," directed Marty cautiously as he seized a pitchfork and began to remove the top layer of hay. Meanwhile the dogs stood on their hind legs, put their front paws over the top pole, panted and dripped saliva into the manger. Marty pushed them aside and started to lift out a second forkful of hay, but felt something more solid. There was a grunt of pain from within the manger and Marty drew back the fork as the hay began moving. Two hands grasped the top manger pole and a hay-covered head appeared between them. Olivia, only a few feet away, had tensed, and cocked the rifle, and Marty stood with the pitchfork held menacingly.

The head was shaken vigorously, the hay fell off, and Marty heard Olivia's quick gasp and the word, "Gopher!" He turned to see the tears streaming down her face. Then she carefully lowered the hammer on the rifle, handed it to Marty, and stepped forward to embrace Gopher. But the pitchfork, and the rifle, and the fugitive years between, conspired to recall dark memories of white faces, and Gopher stood stiff and unsmiling.

"You must come with us, Gopher," Olivia said softly, and urged Marty to put away the rifle. But he was suspicious, held the rifle at ready, and walked behind Olivia and Gopher to the house. There they met Bob, who knew and had tacitly accepted Gopher, and the cowboys, who had heard only sketchy reports about the Nez Perce kid who got lost and was taken in by Olivia up on the prairie.

Then followed days of quiet terror for Gopher. He was not confined or restrained in any way, and knew that he was free to go. "But the dogs know me, and there is no way that I could conceal my scent from them. They would follow me all the way to the cave, and riders would be behind them. I must not fail Welweyas and Three Ravens and Little Bird, and all the rest up there in Hey-ets Pah."

For Olivia there were long, tense days of wondering, and sleepless nights when the blackness hammered in her ears and at times almost distorted her mind. "He is different," she mused, as she stared across the dim room, seeking the faint light of the window she knew was there. "But he is as dear to me as ever. Marty found two moccasin trails in the cornfield, so there was someone with Gopher who got away." While Marty and the other cowboys and, to some extent, Bob, fumed and threatened and even talked of torturing the truth out of Gopher, they knew better than to defy Olivia, who knew that he would never talk. Days passed, during which Gopher communicated with no one, and during that time Olivia convinced Bob to let him help with the fall work. Bob grudgingly agreed, and though the ranch hands were resentful they soon found that Gopher could ride with the best of them, and realized that he was making no attempts to escape. Olivia had given him a fine Thoroughbred mare, a deep blood bay, to replace the gray Morgan gelding. It was the mare that eased his mind, so that one evening when Olivia said, "Tell me about the gray Morgan," his imprisoned tears erupted, and he told her the story of his long flight with Three Ravens and Red Necklace, and that the gray gelding was with the other people. But he stopped short of describing anything which might mark the way, though he did try to describe the beauty of the valley. Then, in almost a casual way, he expressed his love for his 14-year-old bride-to-be, the daughter of Three Ravens and Red Necklace, adding finally, "Sometime next spring, she will have my baby." Olivia thought she could comprehend the torture and conflict in his young mind, but she would never fully understand the barriers which now separated him from his bride and baby. The next morning, he was gone.

## CHAPTER 45

"Papa Lucas doesn't seem happy," said three-year-old Zola Jones as she watched him walk toward the barn. And her mother Geneva agreed, thinking, "Even the children have noticed it for some time now." For in spite of the constant company of Herb and Geneva and their two children, and at least weekly visits from Kirby or Cornelia and their three, Lucas had become increasingly withdrawn; and those periods became longer, while the happy times became shorter. He still had plenty to do, supervising the ranching operation and counseling with Kirby, but the energetic Herb had caught on quickly and was soon a competent foreman, strongly supported by the steady Geneva for whom Lucas felt an increasing fondness. Morty Martin dropped by occasionally, and once in a while Seth Jones drove over from Mt. Idaho, preferring his buggy seat to a saddle, and sometimes commenting, "I'm not getting any younger, and certainly no lighter. My horse groans when I get on him, and sighs with relief when I get off, so I don't ride much anymore."

But in spite of plenty of attention, love coming from all directions, and the children lavishing their affection, Lucas could not escape his dark moods. He'd often lay awake in the small hours of the morning searching for warm memories of encouragement by his father and the tender affection of his mother. But those memories did not exist, and remained only as hungry longings within his mind.

On a bright spring morning, when the creek rippling through the meadow west of the barn ran full and the scent of sweet grasses and buttercups filled the air, Lucas announced to Herb and Geneva during breakfast that he was going on a trip. It was something he had been planning for some time, and he would be gone for several weeks. "I'm going to visit that country south of the Salmon River where I lived more than 25 years ago." Herb and Geneva, sensing Lucas' anticipation, were delighted for him. By noon he was ready to go, and left right after lunch, saying almost eagerly, "I can make it to Whitebird Creek by evening." Now Lucas rode at a leisurely pace up the Little Salmon river, the old iron-gray gelding, Monty, moving steadily along the rocky trail. Lucas had vacillated when he prepared to leave the ranch. He had first saddled Ollie, the tall sorrel given him by Olivia, thinking that this trip might last for several weeks and wondering if the aging Monty still had the necessary endurance. "But it's a trip for old times' sake," Lucas said, almost aloud, "and Monty is more a part of my past."

So he changed the saddle from the sorrel to Monty. And Monty had traveled well, appearing to enjoy the company of Lucas' pack mule when they stopped at Slate Creek. The next morning, well fed and rested, he had once again loaded the packhorse, saddled Monty, and that night camped where the Little Salmon tumbled into the main Salmon River.

Three more days took Lucas up the Little Salmon, past the Circle C Ranch where the first of the Campbells' Herefords dotted the meadows; over the hill and down to Payette Lake, then eastward to the divide, where small streams again ran into the Salmon River. Then he thought of Warrens, only a few days ahead, wondering why that should excite him. "Warrens can't be anything but a ghost town by now, and will probably be entirely deserted." But the good feelings remained and, without questioning, he welcomed the change. Monty had struggled a little climbing up the slope from Payette Lake, but now seemed to sense Lucas' rising spirits and moved more easily. The pack mule hurried to keep up. Lucas too felt refreshed, and actually looked forward to seeing the old mining camp again. But there was no friendly welcome, for he rode along a rocky street still muddy from winter snows and spring rains, a discouraging, rutted trail between a handful of vacant, untended buildings with missing clapboards and gaping holes in the shake roofs. Two aged Chinese men sat on a rickety bench in front of the only building that showed any signs of occupancy, and both of them immediately arose and disappeared.

Lucas identified the old General Store and Assay Office, knocked on the door and rubbed holes in the grimy windowpanes to peer into the interior, wondering why these windows were not broken like most of the others. But no one answered. He finally found three old men living in a battered shack not far from where his own cabin had been. They looked like they had been there forever, but none of them remembered him. One thing the town had plenty of was dogs, and they all looked alike—narrow heads, close-set eyes, floppy ears, wobbly legs, scraggly tails. A look of despondency and listlessness hung over all of them. One was larger than the rest, and reminded Lucas of the big, friendly dog at the ferry when Bess and Gus lived there. Then it occurred to him that not long after the first dogs were brought to Warrens the only mates available to them were their mothers, sisters, brothers, fathers, cousins, and their own offspring; all were on the downward trail of inbreeding and declining mentality. It was a discouraging thought, and increased Lucas' depression as he rode on to find his old cabin, where in dismay he looked at a pile of rotting boards and a broken column of rock crumbling over the fireplace hearth. Then he walked toward the spring, wondering if he might still get a drink there, and on the way encountered the only thing that was still whole—a little half sphere of hard, baked clay, the kiln in which Mei Ling had fired her pottery.

Lucas felt despondency stealing over him again, and rode back westward a few miles to camp for the night. The bright memory of the hot springs was his first thought upon awakening, and within two hours he was relaxing in the hot spring. Watching the stars at night helped to erase the dismal memories of Warrens, but it took several days. But one morning Lucas realized that he had been gone from home over three weeks, and that he had no way of informing anyone there of his plans. He must be moving toward home.

Clouds had moved in during the night, and as Lucas rode away from The Springs he heard the low rumble of thunder. "Way over there on the divide, by the headwaters of the South Fork of the Salmon," he thought to himself. "Too far away to be any problem here." And he started down the mountain toward the ferry. From a half-mile above the river he could see Gus's old cabin, but there was no ferryboat to be seen. The cabin looked lonely and unkempt, as Lucas had expected. The trail looped back and forth across the creek twice before Lucas could again see the cabin, and he was surprised to see a thin column of smoke rising from the chimney. "Some tired old prospector taking life easy," he mused.

The foot of the trail was behind the cabin and some distance away, and there Lucas tied Monty and the mule and walked toward the cabin, thinking it best to go around to the front porch. As he circled the east side of the old house he glanced to his left and was suddenly transfixed by vivid splashes of color in sharp, brilliant contrast against the coarse grain of the rusty-gray pine planking. For long seconds Lucas' mind groped for connections, struggling to perceive, not yet accepting the beauty of form, the glowing loveliness of turquoise, flaming crimson, clear pale blue, deep metallic green, shell-like pinks, and whites with the delicate shading of apple blossoms. The forms were exquisite, and varied from tiny two-inch vases to tall, graceful urns of eighteen inches. All sat on a rough plank shelf, each casting its shadow to complement the rich grain of the weathered pine wall. Lucas' mind came slowly into focus, as the colors were accepted and belonged here, and as he saw that somewhere on each lovely creation, often as part of a delicately painted leaf or flower, was inscribed Mei Ling's signature character. The sudden shock almost overcame him, and he struggled to erase the bitter, remorseful image of moonlight on her white dress as she plunged into the Sacramento River. How could she be here now?

She had made no sound, but he sensed her presence and turned to find her there, her face calm and serene, the faintest of smiles tugging at her lips and wrinkling the corners of her almond eyes. She was still slim and erect, and the half-smiling eyes sparkled with vitality. "Yes, there are wrinkles, but they are smile wrinkles, at the corners of the mouth and eyes, but there are no frown wrinkles," he thought.

Her hair, so often the calendar of time, was no longer black, but shades of soft gray, still full and luxuriant, and braided into a neat que. Her hands, now folded serenely across her waist, were thin, and showed wrinkles and worn skin from working the clay, shaping the vases and urns, firing the kiln. Lucas could see little but her eyes: the same clear, soft brown, the same sparkle, always calm, often on the edge of a smile, expressive, understanding, patient, accepting.

There was for Lucas no eager surge of excitement or urgency to speak, no immediacy, just a quiet contentment to be there looking at her, seeing that she was well, and much the same as he remembered her. The years between seemed unimportant. He wanted to touch her, perhaps to embrace her, and he reached out to her. But her eyes said "No."

"Polly," a strong voice boomed out, "There's a horse and a mule tied over by the creek. Have you seen anyone?" Then a burly looking man sauntered around the corner of the cabin, and stopped as he saw Lucas. His bearded face was quizzical but not unfriendly, and he smiled as Mei Ling moved to his side. "This is Lucas," she said to the big man, then turned to Lucas: "This is my husband Bemis. He knows about you. Calls me Polly."

The night Lucas thought, "More than twenty-five years, and I'm back here, sleeping in the same little shack, only this time Mei Ling provided the pillow for me instead of Bess. She'd said, 'This is my husband Bemis. He knows about you. Calls me Polly.' Of course he knows about me! Everyone in Warrens knew everything about everybody. We were never married. I had no real claim on her. What kind of life has she had, here in this far-off, lonely place? He seems steady enough, and she seems content. But what choice did she have?"

He frowned and thought about their conversation during supper. "All they said was that she met Bemis in Warrens. Were there more poker games? And was she again part of the pot? Well, they're married, and she looks happy enough. But has she ever really forgotten? At times, I thought I saw sadness in her eyes. Was it really there, or something I want to believe?"

Lucas said good-by to Polly and her husband Bemis the next morning, saying that he planned to ford the river just below the white sand beach, where there was a broad, shallow riffle. Monty groaned a little as Lucas mounted. The steep trail down the mountain the day before had stiffened his hind legs, and as he carefully picked his way along the rocky bank toward the beach, Lucas was glad that they were homeward bound. A few big clouds drifted above the mountain to the south, and he remembered hearing thunder the day before, but the storm had bypassed the Salmon River, or at least this part of it. "Tonight we'll camp up there in the high country around Florence, perhaps close to where I buried Gus and Bess by their little boy."

The beach was broad, the sand clean, white, and deep, and as Monty trudged through it slowly Lucas was concerned that only two miles of shoreline had tired him. So he dismounted, and they rested. Lucas sat in the soft sand, soothed by the river's lisping murmur, for here it ran quietly and deep.

Lucas never knew when the loneliness would return, for it had seldom been far away, ruthlessly pursuing him from Vermont, across the ranges and plains to California, and back into Idaho's mountains and canyons. Even on the prairie during the good years with Jenny and Phoebe and Kirby, it sometimes lurked in the shadows around him. Now it stealthily returned, and he failed to recognize it, for he was aware only of his longings. Then, remembering last night's poor bed and restless half-sleep, he lay back on the sand, surrounded by the whisper of the river, and the rustle of the breeze against the rough cliffs.

He didn't hear her arrive, but suddenly there was the familiar, intangible fragrance of perfume mingled with the earthy scent of her body; the thrill of her soft, inviting mouth; the welcome of her encircling arms; the warmth and tenderness which fulfilled him; the closeness which freed him.

Slowly he realized that she was no longer in his arms, and he reached out to her as she lay beside him. But she was not there, and he turned to the other side, smiling at his own confusion. Nothing! Quickly then, becoming alarmed, he arose and scanned the beach, seeing only a strange horse and a mule nearby. But the bay mare? We always ride here on the bay mare! And where is Mei Ling? Then he ran clumsily up the beach, to peer behind piled driftwood where they sometimes sought shade on the hottest days. Only shadows. And the rocky shore beyond was too rough to show tracks. Frantically he stumbled back, searching for the spot where they had been together, looking for small footprints; but his ramblings had obliterated all but his own big ones. A horse nickered softly, and Lucas turned, to slowly recognize Monty and the mule, standing in a narrow strip of shade below the cliff.

Still not accepting, he hurried back to search the beach again. No one! His numbed mind had cleared a little now. "There is no bay mare here," he said, half-aloud. "But certainly she was." Then as he walked toward Monty his foot encountered a hard object in the sand; and he stooped to pick up a small, brilliantly colored ceramic vial, to which still clung her familiar fragrance.

Some 30 miles upstream from the beach where Lucas had been resting the South Fork contributes to the Salmon River from many streams and springs along its course; it has its beginnings on the high divide above the headwaters of the Payette River to the south. There, among yawning canyons and immense peaks, massive thunderstorms are spawned. One such storm had occurred some 12 hours earlier, the one which Lucas thought had missed the Salmon River.

As the bloated mass of clouds, churning and pregnant with water waiting to be delivered, swept across the lower ranges to the west, it was forced to rise, and it dropped millions of gallons into the South Fork and its tributaries. It would not have been called a dangerous flood by people familiar with those streams, and of course it had a long way to travel, perhaps a hundred miles, before it joined the larger, main Salmon River.

Below the beach where Lucas now stood the river broadened, to run smoothly over a wide gravel bar, a shallow ford where Lucas planned to cross. "Looks easy and safe," he thought. "I can ride all the way; may have to lift up my feet part of the time to keep them dry." And he wondered about the mule. "Has he ever crossed a river before? Probably will need a little help." So he lengthened the lead rope, and tied it to Monty's saddlehorn. The water was limpid and clear, and the high sun cast flickering shadows among multi-colored stones on the river bottom. Lucas relished the hot mid-day sun on his back while welcoming the coolness of the water now lapping at his ankles. Monty plodded firmly over the rocks. The mule on shorter legs was belly-deep but moved calmly in the imperturbable manner of his kind, the current forcing him gently downstream at the end of the lead rope.

Lucas, his eyes half-closed against the reflected sunlight, almost dozed, but was alert to Monty's course—slightly downstream, aimed for a point on the far shore well above the river's rapid swing to the left. All was going as planned, and as Lucas felt the increasing warmth of the sun he caught the faint fragrance of the vial in his shirt pocket. "Was she really there on the beach with me, just an hour ago? It was all so real, and she was so young, and so was I."

The rise in the water was not a sudden surge, and at first was barely noticeable, for here where the river was over 200 yards wide the increased depth was only one foot. But it was enough that the mule could no longer reach the bottom. Monty's feet were slipping as he struggled for a foothold in the rocks, and Lucas suddenly saw that they were drifting downstream, in water too deep to wade and too shallow for effective swimming. At first he was not alarmed, for though the water deepened as the river narrowed, both Monty and the mule began to swim, and were moving toward the rocky shoreline. But suddenly, the shores converged rapidly, and the scant one foot of floodwater over the riffle was now four added feet in the narrow channel, and its multiplied force was overpowering.

Lucas quickly saw that the animals had no chance to climb out on the shore. He must save himself! He stood up on the saddle and leaped toward a rock shelf. But he fell just short, his fingers clutching desperately, holding briefly on the rough surface before his bruised hands were torn loose and the irresistible current swept him into a narrow gorge between vertical bluffs. Monty and the mule, now dumbly accepting, no longer struggling, entered the gorge together, the lead rope stretched taunt between them. Monty's great thigh muscles, essential for swimming and once so powerful, depleted now by age, the hard trip down the mountain, and his frantic efforts against the power of the river, no longer responded, and he began to sink. The mule sank with him under the weight of the water-logged pack, and as the two doomed animals drifted deep in the water they were suddenly stopped, as the rope caught around a rock between them; and there they swayed in the dark torrent, the lead rope holding them in place, their last desperate inhalations filling their lungs with water.

Lucas knew that his efforts to swim might, at best, keep him afloat until he was through the gorge. But what lay below? More rapids? Another gravel bar with shallow water? A quiet place by another beach? Surprisingly, his mind was placid, free of the terror he had felt as a boy in Vermont when he had fallen through thin ice on a deep pond. He'd been rescued by his father and craved his comforting. But he received only stern criticism for bad judgment, with his mother standing by in thin-lipped silence. The relentless power of the river was a simple, abstract force in conflict with his need to survive but against which he could not contend, and he no longer tried.

The change in the river was only a visual thing, for suddenly there was a wide arch of sky overhead, the dark, constricting bluffs were behind, and Lucas was carried on the crest of plunging rapids between fields of massive boulders, the current still frighteningly swift. But his mind did not rebel, seeming only to accept the continuing reality of his impotence, his inability to move himself toward either shore. Then came a lull in the deafening roar of the rapids, and he drifted through a flat, almost serene, stretch of water. The primal demand for self-preservation said, "Stroke! Pull for the shore!" But he lacked the will, and the moment was gone. A blur of rocks and willows was rushing past, and the roar returned to fill his ears and his mind, and he knew that the river had won. Acceptance pushed away the last faint need to struggle, and a nepenthean calm, the ancient forgetfulness of sorrow, swept over him as he was spun with cyclonic force and drawn into the depths of a swirling eddy.

---

"He left here about two weeks ago," said Bemis, trying to recall the day and date which had been little different from all others along this isolated stretch of the Salmon River. "He looked good, and was cheerful enough, but I did notice that his horse seemed tired. Let me ask Polly if she remembers anything," added Bemis, opening the cabin door and calling her name. Olivia and Bob were more than mildly surprised when a trim, half-smiling Chinese woman came through the door and Bemis asked her about Lucas. "No big talk," she replied. "Glad to be going home. Said he would take trail through Florence to Grangeville." Without knowing why, Olivia suddenly asked, "Did you know Lucas in Warrens?" To which Bemis said, "No," but Polly nodded, "Yes."

Olivia and Bob had left Slate Creek three days before, after talking with Kirby and Herb Jones, who had ridden down from the prairie, concerned because Lucas was more than three weeks overdue on his expected return to his ranch. As they rode out of the corral Bob called back to Kirby, "When you cut the southbound trail this side of Florence, look for tracks of Monty and that pack mule. The mule shoe tracks should be easy to spot. If you find no tracks, go south to the river, and we'll meet you there by the ford."

Then Olivia and Bob ascended the Salmon River and the Little Salmon, following Lucas' intended route around Payette Lake and over the divide to Burgdorf Hot Springs. They rode hard, and their worries increased when Fred Burgdorf told them Lucas had started home over three weeks before. They looked at each other with quiet fear: three weeks! "He knew this country so well! He's not lost!"

That same day they rode down to the river. Now as they heard more disquieting news Olivia asked Polly for a drink of water, and followed her around the cabin. There she suddenly saw the brilliant colors of the exquisite vases and urns in vivid contrast against the old weathered boards. She caught her breath, and was about to ask Polly about these lovely things, but Polly walked quickly into the kitchen.

There were no clues here, and both Bob and Olivia were indecisive, a rare mood for either of them. He was about to suggest they ford the river and ride up the steep north side, commenting that Kirby should have been here by now. As they prepared to leave, Kirby and Herb Jones appeared—but they were not alone. Following closely behind them trotted a wizened little Chinese man, with a decrepit burlap bag over his shoulder. "He says his name is Hong Liu," said Kirby after greetings and introductions. And Bemis quickly added, "He's a prospector, and I have a feeling he knows something about Lucas, but he speaks no English." There was a quick conversation between Polly and Hong Liu, whereupon he untied the cord around the burlap bag and dumped out on the ground several pieces of tarnished silver with stamped floral designs. Then he dug through the pile, and all watching gasped as he held up a medallion, for etched on its half-black, oxidized surface were the initials LP. Polly asked Hong Liu a quick question, and then reported, "He found dead horse in mud and rock, cut off the saddle and got this silver."

"Ask him to take us to the horse," Kirby directed. Hong Liu agreed, and led Kirby and Herb, followed by the Cones, on a grueling trip down the river. Stumbling over rock-covered beaches too rough for horses, the four saddened friends followed behind the seemingly tireless Hong, wading around the face of a bluff, climbing a high, steep point below which the river ran black and threatening, then sliding down a rocky, treacherous hillside to the edge of a deep eddy where they found Monty. A frayed lead rope was still knotted tightly around the horn of the saddle which Hong had left nearby.

They combed the riverbank for a mile, then Kirby and Herb swam to the other side and came back upstream; and all finally accepted the harsh reality that their search was hopeless. All returned to the Bemis cabin, where Polly silently fed them hot food and shared their sorrow. But there was a puzzling depth of empathy in Bemis' eyes as he looked at the visitors and then back to Polly as she moved quietly about the cabin serving the food. "He's sharing something with Polly," Olivia suddenly realized. "He's comforting her! But why?"

It was near noon when the mournful group reached Florence. They had ridden the steep, winding route above the ford in silence, the horses eagerly following the homeward trail. Olivia, deeply depressed, had searched her mind through a sleepless night, groping for an illusive, missing piece of the puzzle which she knew somehow involved Lucas and Polly. "Bemis knows something too," she mused. But the pieces did not yet fit, and the answer still evaded her on this final leg of the trip to the Phelps ranch, where Herb Jones' wife Geneva listened in shocked silence, then prepared and served a hot meal as her own glistening tears fell, for Lucas had been like a father to her. With supper over, Olivia and Bob tried to relax in the stillness of the bedroom once shared by Lucas and Jenny. As Olivia reached up to extinguish the lamp she idly noticed a brilliant cobalt-blue vase sitting on the same shelf, her exhausted mind telling her only that she had noticed it there before.

---

"He blessed our lives here on this prairie for well over twenty years," said Seth Jones, his broad shadow falling over the spot which Kirby had chosen to place a memorial for Lucas. But there was no ominous, gaping hole, no pile of rocks and soil and sod, for Lucas' body was not there. Here there was only a softly gleaming, newly-hewn stone column of modest size sitting next to the graves where markers said JENNY and PHOEBE.

"All those years," Seth continued, "we knew and loved him, and he shared his life unstintingly, always available when a neighbor was short-handed at branding time. He taught us all about compassion and endurance during the Indian uprising. Most of us here today have houses or barns which we all helped to build under his direction as we shared the joy of being neighbors and being with him. Yes, we will always wonder, how far did the river carry him, and where did it leave him? I like to think of his great, loving spirit being here close to us, and I'll always feel that way when I look at this stone."

Then Rev. Henley, who had at first felt left out at not being asked to preach a sermon, said a short prayer, and all prepared to leave, except Kirby and Cornelia and Olivia. They stood together, no one speaking, as Kirby unwrapped a burlap bundle he had been carrying under his arm. "That Chinese woman down on the river gave me this just before we started home," Kirby explained. "All she said was, 'people who lived in Warrens remember your father.'" And Kirby held firmly in both hands an exquisite ceramic urn some twelve inches tall, graceful in its contour, and glowing with the colors of the river: its deeps and its shallows, and the sun through the crest of waves, the soft olive-brown lights reflected from moss-covered rocks and the sky when there is nothing to be seen but sky as daylight fades. The colors were so entrancing that no one except Olivia saw any detail, and for her the puzzle was now complete: for etched in black and contrasting against a splash of soft blue was a single Chinese character, the signature character, the same one which Olivia had seen on the vase in Lucas' bedroom the night before.

"I saw it in her eyes," thought Olivia, "and Bemis knows about Lucas and Polly also. I saw the way he was comforting her silently when they both learned about Lucas' death. Now a lot of things are clear, including his lack of passion for me. Jenny never said much, but she knew in spite of his devotion to her that he didn't have as much love to give her as he wanted to."

Kirby and Cornelia had walked toward the carriage where Bob stood waiting, and Olivia's love for the three of them now seemed deeper than ever. "Thank Heaven there is no ghost between me and Bob," she thought. "But there is the memory of that Indian girl between Kirby and Cornelia, and both of them know it. And of course there's that little half-breed girl, lost somewhere in the wilds of the Salmon River; like Lucas, of whom we now have only memories. What a strange world! Father and son, each left with the ghost of a tragic, star-crossed first love."

That night in the big bedroom of her own ranch Olivia lay awake listening to Bob's even, contented breathing, feeling grateful for him but comfortably alone with her own thoughts, with Lucas and Kirby still on her mind. "Star-crossed loves," she again thought. "First loves, so different and yet so alike. But were they really tragic? I saw Kirby's Indian girl and Lucas' Chinese love. Strange as it seems, Lucas would at one time have called them 'Heathen Women,' but I saw in both of them beauty, and strength, and dignity. But there was more, for I sensed their capacity for comfort and tenderness, and deep passion in its finest sense. Many people spend a lifetime searching for such things. How many ever find them? Perhaps Lucas and Kirby were among the fortunate few who did."

# CHAPTER 46

Gopher had wandered for weeks after leaving Slate Creek. Once he was finally sure the dogs had gone home, he returned to Hey-ets Pah. The gardens now covered several acres and produced better crops, for the women had learned to select the best seeds and to plant and harvest at the right times. The grinding stones selected by Red Necklace from beside the stream were now well used, producing corn meal for the winter. And everyone now knew which berries and nuts and roots were safe and most edible. But beavers had become less plentiful near the cave, and the mountain sheep had moved upstream. The men must go farther to hunt, carry their game back home, and risk more danger from the wolves. To make things worse, three horses had died, and there were no young foals because there was no stallion.

The cave was now crowded, for three marriages had already produced five babies, and the parents were stressed and restless. A second cave nearby had been occupied, but it was crowded also, and the separation complicated protection from the wolves. Old Swan Woman, the matriarch, had died while Gopher was away. Three Ravens and Red Necklace, now pushing 60 winters, were losing their vigor, though not their wisdom. Carefully and quietly they were schooling Welweyas and Little Bird to gradually assume leadership of the little band and help them survive.

Those of Joseph's band remembered their comfortable migratory years in Oregon, when each spring they tore the old covers from the winter homes, leaving them to the wind and sun for the summer, and moved to the cool highlands. In a small way they could do the same here by cleaning and abandoning the caves and moving to summer shelters in the shady coves at the base of the tilted south wall. "Everything we need is there," said Welweyas. "Plenty of timber, fresh water, grass and ferns to make mats for coverings. And there we can live from spring until late fall." The plan was approved and, though it took several weeks to build, the communal longhouse was well worth the effort. It was spacious and airy, a delightful place to live, and they were free of the dark cave, at least for a time. Still, the same threat remained, for the women had to travel across the valley to tend their gardens, as the new plots at the summer home would not be fertile until next year. The old wolf, now barely limping, and two vicious young males lounged at times in the mouth of the slot where they could overlook the valley, watching everything that moved for a mile or more; so ever-watchful guards were still necessary.

Welweyas became increasingly concerned about the horses, for two more had died and others were no longer strong, so he talked to Three Ravens. "We could live without horses," the old man said at first, "as our people did for so long. But it would be very hard, for we ride them on the hunt, they carry our game home, drag in our logs and firewood, and sometimes help us to escape if we are attacked by the wolves. Though getting more horses will not be easy; there may be a way, but it will be very dangerous." And summoning Gopher and Eagle and other strong young men he proposed the plan already discussed with Welweyas.

Bob and Olivia Cone had all but finished the transfer of their horses from Slate Creek to Camas Prairie, first moving more than a hundred mares, many already carrying foals by the Clydesdale and Percheron stallions. They left for awhile a few younger mares and geldings too small for the Paloos fields as well as several young stallions which they hoped would be bought by someone on the prairie. The spring grass was good, and these remnants of the herd would do well until there was time to move them. On a May morning, Welweyas, Gopher, and Eagle watched these horses from the timber above the pastures.

"Many good horses," exulted Welweyas. "Now we must know exactly how those men on the ranch spend their time: where they go and what they do all day, when they go to bed and when they get up, and how well they guard the horses." So through that day and night, and the next day, the Nez Perces watched, and clocked in their minds every move of the few men now in routine charge of the horses. "We must have two good stallions," explained Welweyas, "and of different kinds. And as many mares as we can handle. Don't worry if a few geldings are mixed in; they will help to quiet the herd as we travel."

It was Gopher who was chosen to select the stallions—one Morgan and one Thoroughbred—and get them out of the pastures during the night. Welweyas and Eagle would get the other horses. All knew the ranch layout by heart from former trips, and just after midnight Gopher led the stallions out, following a peaceful old bell mare without her bell, and tied them in a thicket a mile up the trail. There were tense moments as Welweyas and Eagle assembled the mares one by one in a small corral farthest from the ranch house, for a dog started barking, and then two dogs trotted toward the corral. But the old trick worked again, as Welweyas threw several pieces of jerky to the dogs, leaving them chewing and drooling while the men drove the horse herd up the trail, each riding a horse he had selected for himself. Eagle led and Welweyas kept order in the middle of the string, while Gopher, riding a nervous three-year-old stallion, kept the stragglers in line.

It was mid-morning when Marty, now the ranch foreman, discovered that at least 20 horses were missing and found their departing trail. "Someone had to open gates and get that bunch together," he said, although the three thieves had carefully avoided leaving footprints. But Marty, though irritated, was not really upset, saying to his cowboys, "We've got a lot of horses like them, and they'll probably be hard to sell."

The ranch crew had barely finished lunch when someone said in disgust, "There comes that old bastard Harry again." And up the lane slouched the occupant of a decrepit shack a few miles down the river. Harry was all anyone ever called him, for no one knew if he had a last name. None of the cowboys were old enough to know his history, though Bob Cone would have. He was an Indian- hater who had badgered the Nez Perce women and children along the river in the years before the war, and was one of those sought by Sarpsis Ilppilp while on the vengeance trip that started the killings on the Salmon River. Now the old man stood by the back door of the ranch house, his scraggly, unkempt beard stained with the drippings of tobacco juice, a trail of which trickled over his sagging lower lip. His battered felt hat sat on the greasy hair which hung to his shoulders, and a frayed piece of rope ran diagonally from right to left across his filthy shirt to hold up the ragged trousers stretched over his pendulous, half-naked belly. There were also some ugly things about Harry himself, for his bulging eyes were bilious and bloodshot and his slack jaw and half-open mouth revealed ulcerated gums supporting a total of four yellow-black teeth.

At first sight, many people missed the incredible details of this unlovely man, for all they could see was his dog. Harry, a few years back, had adopted a huge Irish Wolfhound bitch abandoned by three former owners. Her surly temper matched Harry's, and she developed a fierce attachment for him, and he for her, so he named her Witch. Witch was thirteen years old, and while still acceptably ferocious by Harry's standards, was going downhill sexually, and soon after becoming attached to Harry she came in season for the last time, and her scent was picked up by a wandering timberwolf, who came boldly to find her. She was too far in heat to be defensive, much less selective, and was promptly mounted by the wolf, an immense creature weighing some 150 pounds. Witch's failing ovaries produced only one egg, but her union with the wolf begat a pup who inherited the size, rough, scraggly appearance, and fierce, aggressive nature of his parents. Witch died birthing this monster, named Bruno. He slept with Harry, and for weeks was fed on demand with milk stolen each night from a neighbor's cow. In this way, Harry replaced Bruno's mother, and the resulting bond was the only joy either would ever know. Now four years old, Bruno was covered with wiry, blue-gray hair, stood a rangy 42 inches at the shoulders, and had massive square jaws with inch-long fangs. He was always growling or on the edge of a snarl, and wore a broad collar with sharp studs on both sides to which was attached a heavy chain, for even Harry could not otherwise control him.

Now as the repulsive Harry stood looking at Marty and his helpers he mumbled through his drooling gums, "Saw the trail of them horses as I come down from a hunt in the hills. Injuns took 'em, I bet." At this Bruno rumbled deep in his chest and bared his teeth, for Injun was a fighting word around Harry's shack. Marty drew away from Bruno, feeling fear and intense dislike, and tried to change the subject. But Harry persisted, and soon was challenging the cowboys to go after the Injuns with him and asking for the best horse they had. "After all, I'm the only guy who really knows these mountains and can get them horses back!" Finally Marty reluctantly gave in. Two of the cowboys, angry and insulted, accepted Harry's challenge, and the three pursued the still-warm trail, with Bruno snarling and foaming ahead.

No rattlesnakes had been found when their skins were needed to cover the horn bows, but there was at least one nearby; for as the last of the mares entered the slot a huge, thick-bodied snake sleeping in the shade beside the cliff was disturbed by the rumble of hooves. Now fully awake, he lay coiled in the trail, tail shaking furiously, ready to strike. In one screaming, twisting explosion, Gopher's already-edgy stallion shied and reared, then leaped back, trampled the recoiled snake, left its bloodied body writhing in the dust, and plunged through the wild cherry thicket after the mares. Gopher was thrown from the horse's bare back to crash against a granite boulder. Then there was only blackness as his limp body slid into the brush at the base of the rock.

---

As the sleek horses filed out of the slot and streamed into the valley Welweyas paused and felt deepening satisfaction at what had been accomplished. The new longhouse stood beneath the trees at the base of the south wall with smoke curling through the slot in its roof. Women worked the gardens, still guarded by several young men with powerful horn bows. Other people were fishing, and some were exploring a third cave which they hoped to occupy in the fall. As Welweyas rode into the valley and watched the vigorous young horses mingle with the old ones he thought with confidence, "The worst is behind us."

Unseen by the busy people, the old wolf and his two fierce followers slunk up the trail and flopped down at the mouth of the slot, watching the enticing new arrivals, their hungry eyes on the young foals which had followed the mares. Welweyas, exhilarated at the success of the foray, had seen Eagle ride past, followed by several excited mares and, finally, a fiery Thoroughbred stallion; and through lonely nights he would wonder why he had failed to notice that Gopher was not close behind.

Anyone who ridiculed the aging Harry—and most people did—would have been forced that morning to grudgingly admire him as he rode close behind the charging Bruno, gripping the saddle firmly with his scrawny legs, pushing his horse unmercifully. And the two cowboys following him were glad to let him lead. Bruno, his nose down, raced up the steep granite slope, all three riders now struggling to keep up. Then they plunged down the other side, leaning back in their saddles, their stiff legs thrust forward in the stirrups as the horses slid on their haunches. At the cherry thicket below the blank wall Bruno clawed and whined while the three riders pulled back the branches concealing the opening and followed him into the slot. Harry was off in hot pursuit of the panting Bruno, leaving the cowboys yards behind and disappearing around a slight bend in the slot.

Gopher didn't know how long he'd laid crumpled in the thorny brush, the harsh granite surface hard against his back, his head throbbing. When the urgency to move, to do something, anything, outweighed his pain, he tried to turn away from the rock, to see beyond the close-grown shrubs. But even that slight movement stabbed him, and he lay back, suppressing a groan. Then came the sharp sounds of steel on stone, and his dulled senses shouted, "Horses!" He turned enough to part the branches and peered cautiously through, to see an immense, scraggly gray dog rush by, followed closely by three riders.

"They've trailed us here," Gopher realized, then rose unsteadily to his feet and stumbled toward the cherry thicket. But as he started, the sound of rifle shots echoed faintly from inside the slot and the big gray dog, battered and bleeding, tore his way through the thicket, knocked Gopher off his feet, and ran toward the mountain trail.

Gopher, now determined to hurry into the valley to join whatever fight was going on, regained his feet and again struggled toward the slot. But something was strangely wrong; his legs failed to support his trembling body; a great roaring surrounded him, assailing his mind; vertigo swept over him and fought for control. The terrible roaring and the uncontrollable trembling increased and the earth rose up to meet him. And he lay, stunned, his head still reeling.

Within seconds after the Slate Creek cowboys lost sight of Harry, the narrow slot became a reverberating chamber of clashing sounds bounced back and forth from wall to wall in ear-splitting volume. There were howls, snarls, shouts, and rifle shots, and around the bend came a blue-gray streak—the yelping, tail-tucked Bruno, with three huge black wolves slathering at his heels. As the four vicious canines raced beneath their bellies the horses screamed in terror, reared, and crushed their riders against the walls, to fall unconscious to the rocky floor.

Harry had been close behind the raging Bruno when the wolves attacked, and his horse threw him as he frantically fired his rifle; then he scrambled to his feet to follow his fleeing dog. But he had made only a few steps when he was transfixed by the grinding and groaning and trembling of everything beneath him, around him, over him, the invasive horror shattering his mind; and the terrified scream which exploded in his throat died a whimper on his lips as the massive granite slabs fused, making his body part of the mountain. Only the desperate Bruno escaped.

When the roaring subsided and the trembling no longer controlled his body, Gopher arose unsteadily, bathed his face and hands in the creek, and again turned toward the slot. But as he came closer a strange, pungent odor burned his nostrils; the cherry thicket was a scorched, twisted tangle. And when he struggled through to the cliff he faced a blank wall; only a faint seam with crumbled edges remained. Groping for answers to explain a welcoming place suddenly turned forbidding and hostile, he dragged his complaining body back through the blackened branches and collapsed beside the creek, to stare upward at the granite face soaring above him; smooth, bare, without ledge or crevice or outcropping, its half-mile high crest looming against the darkening sky.

Those at Slate Creek had felt the earth shake, and waited through the night and into the next day for the men to return. They had given up all hope when Bruno, slashed, bleeding, and barely able to walk, dragged his torn body up to the back porch, where he collapsed. They waited another day while Bruno rested; then his love for Harry helped him to rise on unsteady legs and lead the riders back up the trail. He revived a little, and moved more resolutely as they climbed the granite slope, his nose to the rock surface. Then, not far from the top, they stopped before a towering mass of newly broken stones.

When the tremor closed the slot, enfolding within its fused walls three men, three horses, and three black wolves, its vibrations toppled a tall rock face which slid across the trail just after Bruno limped by. Now the cowboys faced these countless tons of rock; they returned sadly to Slate Creek, where they reported to Marty: "A rockslide covered all of them."

---

When Welweyas followed the vigorous new horses into Hey-ets Pah the people quickly gathered about them on the meadow, everyone secretly choosing a favorite. But their joy turned to terror! For the earth shook, the mountains shuddered and grumbled, and overwhelming noise assaulted their ears as the walls of the slot ground together. Slabs of granite split from the high faces and thundered down the cliffs, and huge boulders bounded across the meadows. The destruction was over in a few seconds, but for long minutes the people huddled together, paralyzed by their fear, while the wild-eyed horses ran about them in near-senseless panic. Then as the frightful echoes subsided, the people looked toward their cave homes, to see only jumbled granite where there had been openings. But their longhouse was intact, and they sought comfort there while Three Ravens and Welweyas picked their way through tumbled rocks, seeking the slot entrance which no longer existed.

The trail to Hey-ets Pah was closed forever!

In the excitement of seeing the new horses, Gopher's bride, Syringa, had not missed him, and the earthquake had brought great confusion. But now, with everyone in the longhouse, she knew he had not returned. And she mourned in the silent, stoic way of those who suffer deep and repeated loss, for all of her own family had perished somewhere on the long trail. Now she must raise Gopher's baby by herself.

Gopher had spent a sleepless night hugging the warm granite at the base of the cliff. By morning the rocks had cooled, but it would be hours before the sun reached the spot where he lay. He shivered, and his aching body complained as he arose on trembling legs and tried to move his bruised arm and stiff joints. The cold morning air pierced his thin buckskins, but he ignored his pains, swung his arms, pumped his legs and stretched to regain use of his muscles. A few small pieces of jerky intended for the dogs at Slate Creek revived him slightly. Then he looked up at the granite dome rising above him. Always before it had meant refuge, shelter, security. The slot, once a welcoming door, was now an ugly, dim scar on the unscalable wall, and the mountain a mute barrier between him and those he loved. But what was there behind him? Warmth in his memory of Olivia and Cornelia and Herb Jones; polite, obvious tolerance by a few others; hostility and hate from the rest. Precious little joy out there. And he started climbing toward the north where a secondary ridge joined the big mountain.

For awhile the way was not hard, and the climbing thawed his bones and raised his spirits. He had no real idea of how he would reach the summit, but knew he must, and through the long day he clawed his way over talus slides and granite slabs, then inched, crablike, up slender chimneys. The rough granite tore at his bloody hands and tortured his feet through holes in his moccasins. The far-off Seven Devils range devoured the sun as he dragged himself out of the last thin chimney, barely able to stand. He was at the top, not the rounded dome he had imagined, but the rough, broken edge of the turned-up slab forming the north wall of Hey-ets Pah. Before him lay a maze of tumbled rocks and sharp gullies. His depleted body cried out for food and water, and he slumped against the still-warm stones as darkness closed around him.

His tortured dreams with tantalizing visions of water springing joyously from the rock beside him were finally relieved by the presence of his Guardian Spirit. He lost all conscious thought, all sense of time or place, but near evening of that second day he stood on the rim above Hey-ets Pah. Across the valley he saw the longhouse, very small in the distance, and on the meadow the grazing horses were like tiny ants. Heady jubilation swept aside his hunger and weariness. He was home! But as he moved closer, reality returned with sickening force, for the beckoning meadows lay far below at the base of the smooth, bare cliff.

It was night again, and Gopher slept in sodden detachment. At daybreak he crawled on blindly, knowing barely enough to avoid the precipice to his right. The rocks radiated heat from the high-noon sun when he stumbled over a bluff and landed heavily, gasping for breath. The earthquake had split from the mountain the great wedge of granite on which he now lay, and it hung precariously over the lip of the precipice. He slid fearfully to the edge and peered over. Empty air! He could see the jumbled rockslide where the mountain sheep sometimes found refuge, and the tips of tall fir trees rising from its top. No hope. As he lay back in despair, his bloodied feet slid on the steep rock, and he fell over the edge, closing his eyes in numb acceptance.

Eagle and Welweyas found the crumpled Gopher as they pursued a mountain sheep across the top of the rockslide. They were sure he was dead, for his battered body was ashen gray, there was clotted blood in his ears and nostrils, and his arms and legs were bent at strange angles. He was smeared with pitch and fir needles; and the men looked upward, to realize that the great tree had caught Gopher near its tip and slowed his fall through its stiff-ened branches. A shred of buckskin still clung to the large branch closest to the ground, and his body was stripped naked. Welweyes and Eagle bent to lift him, and there was a soft sigh, a faint twitching of the lips, nothing more. If there was life they must have help, and Eagle ran to the valley to bring back other strong men. They cradled the body in a beaver skin and bore it gently down the rockslide and home to the longhouse.

Weeks passed before Gopher knew anything but pain. Little Bird helped Red Necklace nourish the tiny spark of remaining life, both missing the wise Swan Woman but thankful for her medicine pouch. The pregnant Syringa waddled about, fetching water, gathering the things needed to make poultices. Three Ravens helped Red Necklace to straighten a broken arm and leg and secure them in padded splints.

And they waited.

Autumn was in the air before anyone thought Gopher would live; and to all except Syringa his needs were now less important than the need of the band to survive the approaching winter. So by the time he could limp about with Syringa and Little Bird on either side, the rest were busily finishing a second longhouse at the meadow's edge, beyond the winter shadow of the overhanging wall where there would be some sunshine. And the new house was stronger, with vertical log walls and a permanent roof. Now they would live year round beside their gardens and near the north wall, for the earth-quake had destroyed their cave homes.

Gopher welcomed his first son in late autumn, and during his tortured convalescence came to appreciate the maturing microcosm of Hey-ets Pah. Three Ravens and Red Necklace continued schooling Welweyes and Little Bird to assume leadership, and they were obviously receptive to the wisdom of the elders. Syringa's baby was the ninth child born to five couples, and all were healthy. Old Swan Woman had had some influence on the parents of the brides in the mating selections, but Red Necklace knew that too-close marriages could soon be a problem, so she instructed Little Bird, adding wryly; "This will be hard, and you must be very persuasive."

Gopher sensed that isolation and deprivation had deepened the deter-mination of the young men to protect their families and to help provide for the band. He watched and listened while Three Ravens and Welweyas took care of the enlarged horse herd.The new stallions had been busy, so in the spring there would be several foals, and a year or two later the herd would be too big. So how to limit the herd to match needs and conserve pasture?

Before the snows came, the new longhouse was secure and warm, the wood supply was piled high along the sheltered side, and the winter's food was stored. Gopher hated the winter, languishing on his bed, yearning to be out with the other men, ashamed that he could not seize a weapon and rush out with them when the wolves howled in the night. But he survived, though he would never walk far again or spring easily onto his horse.

Though the older ones were much aware of the group's total isolation and reliance on its own efforts, they never spoke of it. Gradually, ties to the white world dissolved and the last rifle cartridges were fired; store-bought clothing, blankets, and saddles wore out. Only axes, and a few hammers were still usable. But the earth and their own hands would provide, as they always had, and each new generation would celebrate the joy of independence.

As for the future, there would always be the turning of the seasons; the next hunt; the new foals; the planting and harvesting and storing; the begetting and birthing and nourishing and burying; the mastering of their harsh, unfettered world.

Within a few generations this peaceful continuum would be broken, for a great bird that droned louder than swarming bees would soar above the deep valley, then return to fly low across the meadow and swoop over the longhouse with a roar to shake the walls and an echo to deafen the ears. Then it would fly away, and soon there would be no more peace in Hey-ets Pah.

# CHAPTER 47

We consider the opening of the reservation and the development of the Clearwater country by railroads as matters of very great importance to Idaho County, and toward the accomplishment of those ends we will labor without ceasing.

So wrote Frank Parker, the first editor of the Idaho County Free Press from Grangeville in 1886, echoing the desires of the white population, who for decades had had their eyes on the land. And those who had engineered the impending change soon had the force of law behind them with passage of the Dawes Severalty Act in 1887. "You must all learn basic selfishness in order to become more civilized, know about real estate, and respect private property," was the message impressed upon the Nez Perces. "You will now have your own land, and you will come to realize that you will never make more progress until that happens. No one will get less than 40 acres, even a child will get that much, and some will get 160 or even 320." Joseph rode up from Nespelem and looked across a quarter section—160 acres, a half mile square, hardly wide enough for a fast horse to get started on a good run. "This is certainly not for me," he thought, "even if it is the best land available. Besides, if I settle here, no one will ever allow me to return to the Wallowa." So he refused his allotment.

Only a few of Joseph's band accepted land on the reservation. One of these was his old friend Yellow Bull, who was soon dealing with Miss Alice Fletcher, the determined little spinster-anthropologist, former assistant at the Peabody Museum at Harvard University. She was a veteran at land allotment, having recently completed that process with the Winnebago tribe. Patient, tactful, and persistent, she was skilled at handling the local ranchers who wanted the Indians to settle in the canyons, not on the good prairie land. And not only was the land good, but the reservation lay squarely across the best trails and future roads to the Salmon and Clearwater Rivers, with priceless reserves of timber and minerals. Yellow Bull contended with Miss Fletcher over a rather poor piece of land which contained running water called Red Rock Springs, saying he drank of it as a boy, and dreamed of it when tossing with fever in Eikish Pah. "Give me Red Rock Springs, or I want nothing." And Miss Fletcher, in her honest way, allotted him the springs, along with a good piece of farmland. So through the year 1889 and into the 1890s the planned, systematic fragmentation of the reservation continued. Some 175,000 acres were allotted to the Nez Perces, while 542,000 acres were declared, "Surplus," and sold to white ranchers and speculators for $3 per acre.

---

"This will give me an opportunity to talk to President McKinley," said Joseph to Moses as they prepared to depart for Washington D.C. "Perhaps he can do something about the white miners moving onto your reservation. And I will certainly talk to him about returning my people to their homeland." And they made the long trip to the nation's capital and on to New York City, to be exhibited in a parade.

"Joseph, I want you to travel with me. You will be the star, the main man, in my show. We will see the world together!" The speaker was a flamboyant, athletic showman in fringed buckskins who well over 30 years earlier had fought the Kiowas and Comanches, and shortly thereafter gained fame by helping to exterminate their primary food supply, the buffalo of the great plains. He claimed to have personally killed over 4,000 buffalo. Then, while fighting with Custer, he became even better known through his aggrandized account of killing and scalping the Cheyenne Chief, Yellow Hand. He parlayed that fame onto the stage, and during the time the Nez Perces were struggling in Indian Territory he organized his traveling exhibition. "I call it 'Buffalo Bill's Wild West Show," he now said proudly as he tried to recruit Joseph, thinking, "What an attraction he would be!"

"I had Sitting Bull with me for two years, you know," said Cody, not adding that Sitting Bull had refused to travel to England, saying that it was bad for the Sioux cause for him to parade about, and that he was needed at home to fight the taking of Sioux land—ten million acres of it, at fifty cents per acre. So Sitting Bull went home, and the Sioux, after several years of contest got $1.25 per acre.

Joseph politely declined the choice role in Buffalo Bill's Wild West Show and rode in the buggy with Generals Howard and Miles. The parade ended before an impressive tomb beside New York's Riverside Drive, overlooking the Hudson River. The tomb was dedicated that day to the memory of the former Commander-In-Chief Ulysses S. Grant, a president who knew about Joseph though they never met.

President Mckinley and Generals Howard and Miles were sympathetic as always, but Joseph sensed they would do nothing about his request for repatriation. But the parade accomplished an important purpose: it displayed to the public two valiant Indian chieftains and their victorious conquerors.

---

"Johnny, look at these teeth. They will help me explain how I will fix your teeth." Johnny was not looking at the teeth held up by the dentist. He was clutching his mother's hand and staring at a grinning, half-bleached skull sitting on a shelf to the left of the dental chair, and had seen little else since entering the room. Johnny's mother also had noticed the skull but said nothing, for Baker, Oregon in the 1890s was little more than a village, and the story of the skull in the only dentist's office had long since made the rounds.

Not surprisingly, it was the dentist's wife who first told the grisly tale: "My husband and I were visiting my sister over in the Wallowa Valley," she would start, a touch of the mysterious in her voice, "and one day we went for a picnic. And what do you suppose we found? The grave of Old Joseph—I guess his real name was Tuekakis. It's on land owned by my brother-in-law Mac, and he had been there many times before. So we decided it would be fun—scary maybe, but fun—to dig up the corpse."

At this point she would pause and enjoy the rapt attention of her small audience, who sat wide-eyed while their coffee got cold. "It was a little creepy, especially when we found the skeleton, or what was left of it, almost naked. Somebody had dug it up once before, must have been several years ago, and probably took out some of the stuff that was buried along with him. Anyway, the skull hung sort of loose, and was easy to pull off. So we washed it in the creek—not to look too clean, of course—and brought it home with us. Nobody else around here will ever have a souvenir like that!"

After his last trip to Washington and meeting with President Mckinley Joseph had again traveled to the Wallowa Valley, where he visited his father's grave. In spite of the deplorable condition of the site Joseph probably never knew the grave had been robbed and Tuekakis' body dismembered. Though the government inspector who stood by as Joseph mourned may have been personally sympathetic, he recommended against returning land to the Nez Perces and the matter was closed in the eyes of the government. The white rancher who owned the land surrounding the grave was there that day and assured Joseph that he had taken good care of the site. But he had also been there when his sister-in-law and her dentist husband had removed the skull and washed it in the creek before taking it to Baker.

The failure of his talks with President McKinley and with two other presidents, repeated pleas to Howard, Miles, and a long succession of agents, commissions, and associations had not stilled Joseph's voice. He made other trips to talk to other people, and more investigations took place. But of course by now the rights of the settlers in Oregon were well established by law and guarded by multiple layers of citizens, politicians, and officials with no inclination to do anything but enforce those laws. So the ranchers in the Wallowa Valley were doubly adamant—no land for the Nez Perces under any conditions—not even if they have money to buy it.

---

Yellow Wolf sat in the outer ring surrounding the impressive inner circle of special guests. An elaborately dressed elder droned on in a language Yellow Wolf did not understand well, eulogizing, praising, counting the great feats of the man being honored at this potlach; for Moses, the ostentatious Sinkiuse Chief and for years an influential figure on the Colville Reservation, was dead at age 71. All present would eat heartily and the prominent guests would receive gifts, some very valuable. Yellow Wolf recognized some of the honored guests, whom he had seen when they came to visit Moses; they occupied the most prominent positions around the inner circle and would receive the most lavish gifts. Among these celebrities sat Joseph, invited to validate

Moses' rank and prestige, for all knew Joseph's widespread reputation as a war chief.

Joseph was near the top of Moses' list, and soon one of Moses' sub-chiefs approached him. Yellow Wolf smiled with pride as he recognized the first gift offered to Joseph, for he was the only one watching who had been at the Sioux camp in Canada when Sitting Bull welcomed the Nez Perce refugees and wore this same bonnet. At some gathering of chiefs well in the past Sitting Bull had given the bonnet to Moses—now it was to be Joseph's. The tall loop of eagle feathers, more than six feet in length, was placed on Joseph's head, and the ends fluttered around his feet. Then a second bundle was opened, to disclose a supple buckskin tunic and full-length leggings.

When the potlach was over Joseph carried the buckskins but wore the bonnet, walking slowly to his horse where Yellow Wolf held the feathers off the ground while Joseph mounted. Yellow Wolf saw the hesitation, the extra effort required for Joseph to grasp the saddlehorn, lift his heavy body onto his unsteady left leg, and swing his right leg over the saddle. There was a grunt and a little gasp as he settled in. His back was not straight, his body not erect, and his shoulders sagged beneath the trailing eagle feathers as he rode home.

After tethering his horse on the sparse grass nearby, Joseph held up the ends of the long bonnet and walked to his lodge. One of his wives helped him remove the bonnet, found a place to hang it in the tipi, and safely stored the buckskin suit. She had noticed his listless, shortened stride as he approached and entered the tipi. Now she heard his heavy sigh, almost a groan, as he slumped on his bed.

"My old friend is gone," thought Joseph when the tipi became silent and he felt alone. "The Sinkiuse called him Chukatas; the white man, refusing to struggle with that, as with so many of our names, called him Moses. We didn't always agree, he and I, but he gave my people refuge; and we helped each other."

As daylight failed, Joseph peered through the shadowy darkness to where a dim shaft of light through the tipi's smokehole touched the brown and white feather-patterns of Sitting Bull's warbonnet. "He has been gone for some ten winters," thought Joseph. "He escaped temporarily from his white captors, and refused to surrender again. Our friend General Miles would have had Buffalo Bill try to convince Sitting Bull to give up, for they had become good friends during Sitting Bull's time with the Wild West show. But a jealous agent interfered, and some of Sitting Bull's own people, policemen for the whites, killed him. I never met him, for our tracks always crossed after one had traveled on, but he helped to save many of the Nez Perce people."

Before sleep settled over him, Joseph reflected on the 20 years of struggle to get his people back to their real home. "We were a mere 150 when we arrived at Colville," he remembered, "and only 120 survived the few months until we moved here to Nespelem. Most of those think all white men are against us, and refuse to go to Lapwai, and they are still restless."

Then Joseph arose, stumbling a little as he stepped around or over his sleeping family, and eased himself through the tipi flap. His back and legs had stiffened as he lay on his bed, and he no longer needed to stoop to get through the opening, for he had grown shorter through the years.

The late autumn night was sharply cold, moonless and totally clear. A streak of fire burned a pathway across the luminous dome of the heavens, announcing the death of a star countless eons back in time and space. The Milky Way was a glowing swath of silver dust strewn across the sky as if by a giant hand. Joseph felt himself relaxing, his mind calmed by the stillness and the always-new nighttime display so much a part of his life. But he could not escape the deep-down tiredness, the soul-weariness that had stolen over him with years he could hardly count. Now he pushed those thoughts away, thinking again of his people. "There is a new President in Washington D.C. now. Perhaps he will listen. I will try again."

"You will like President Roosevelt," General Miles said to Joseph as they and General Howard walked toward the White House. "He is a fair man, has spent years in the wilds, and knows something of your life."

Teddy Roosevelt arose from his desk in the Oval Office to greet Howard and Miles as comrades-at-arms, and to meet Joseph, whose reputation was even more widespread than theirs. The contrast between the two men facing each other was striking, almost bizarre. Joseph, his sagging body, his drooping, wrinkled eyelids, his general weariness, the effort required to keep his shoulders erect, showing every day of his 63 years. But, Roosevelt was in his prime at 45—tall, robust and erect, his muscular body proclaiming his devotion to physical fitness, his mind keen. He exuded energy and determination. Roosevelt already knew much about the Nez Perces, for he had asked questions after seeing Joseph at the dedication of Grant's Tomb a few year before, and he had been Vice President when Joseph talked with President McKinley not long before his assassination. Now Roosevelt offered chairs to his three guests and calmly asked Joseph to tell his story.

Joseph began in his usual quiet way, telling of his long fight to regain his people's homeland, and pleading for just a small piece of land; then his voice grew stronger with the increasing fervor of his request, his figure became more erect and his eyes flashed from beneath the thick eyelids. Roosevelt was increasingly impressed by Joseph's intelligence, by his humility, and by the agonizing length and terrible depth of the struggle waged by this elemental man to regain something worthwhile for his people. And Roosevelt knew of other chiefs who had lost the same kind of bitter struggles, for he had seen the dying throes of the Sioux in the Dakotas. Now he thought of his own battle to strengthen his once-puny body and achieve his present vigor. "There is common ground here and I understand this man," he thought. Roosevelt told Joseph that he would think on the matter.

"He asked for so little," Roosevelt reflected, struggling with and irritated by his own indecision. "A few Indians on a few hundred acres in that vast Oregon country would be no real problem to anyone. Joseph will not live long, and I should help him find some peace during his final years." Then Teddy, the politician, remembered vividly the angry protests expressed by elected officials, citizen groups, land developers, and ranchers from Oregon: "They will eat me up," he agonized, and turned his mind to other things.

Miles knew when he left the White House, or even before, that Roosevelt would be sympathetic, make no promises, and in the end do nothing, for he had seen this pattern before with other presidents, lesser politicians, and commissions. "Besides," said Miles to Howard, "he won't fight the crowd. He's already started campaigning for another term as President." And Joseph, on the seemingly endless train ride back to the Columbia River, knew that the long battle was over. And he had lost.

---

The buffalo skin lodge sat at the edge of a broad meadow beside the placid river; and along the soaring crest of the mountain a knife-sharp arete sliced the sky. The lodge was empty on this morning in late September, for there was as yet no one there to occupy it. A rancher riding down the river felt a strange, pleasant glow as he passed within a few feet of the tipi, but he saw nothing, for it was in a dimension different from his own.

Joseph, upon returning to Nespelem from Washington D.C., had said nothing to his wives; but they knew his moods and that he had nothing good to report. Yellow Wolf also understood Joseph's silence, was encouraged by his apparent peacefulness, and was glad. "He has finally accepted reality. Perhaps now he will try to enjoy life here." And through that spring and summer Joseph did appear to be at peace. He spoke softly and with kindness to everyone, never complained, and did not talk about going home to Oregon. Then in the twilight of a September evening, when the fields were bare of their meager crops and a blue-gray haze caressed the land, Joseph sat in Yellow Wolf's tipi and they talked of their years together, the joy of life when they were young and free, the long, bitter trails across desperate miles, the struggles for survival. But there were good memories too, and they chuckled as they recalled happier times and the people who had been part of them.

There was a farness in Joseph's eyes, and a look of calm anticipation as he said, almost inaudibly, "Tac Kulewit," heard Yellow Wolf's "Good Evening," quietly left that tipi and walked to his own. He touched gently the arm of one wife, caressed the shoulder of the other, looked with loving eyes at his sleeping children, and lay down on his bed.

He half-awakened to the murmur of a river and the clear call of a falcon circling overhead. A brilliant slice of sunlight slanted through the half-open tipi flap, and he could see across the grassy valley to the blueness of mountains. That he was no longer in the drab heat of Nespelem was accepted as naturally as breathing the freshness of the cool air.

Fully awake now, Joseph was aware of the presence of his Wyakin, welcomed the warming glow surrounding him, but felt no need to speak.

Then, hearing the familiar, throaty nicker of a horse, he arose quickly in one effortless, fluid motion, his lean body as light as his soft buckskin leggings, his supple muscles responding eagerly to carry him out of the tipi, where he found his horse standing beneath the aspens. He felt no surprise, only quiet joy, for Ebenezer too belonged here; and leaping easily onto his bare back, he traveled across the valleys and ridges of his homeland. He rode awhile, guiding the unbridled horse with his knees, delighted at the easy, flowing gait and boundless vigor of the young Ebenezer. Then he walked for miles, glorying in his own firm stride and tireless, rejuvenated body, returning to his lodge in the evening refreshed and as strong as when he had left it.

There were songs of birds and the ripple of the river as Joseph became aware of the morning. But there were other sounds, and soon he recognized the laughter of children at play; and he hurried to the river's edge where Springtime's little Early Flower and Blackbird, who succumbed to wolf bites at Hey-ets Pah, were running in the stream, giggling and shrieking as the cold water splashed over their glistening bodies. Watching comfortably from her seat on the riverbank was Springtime, lithe and lovely, while nearby Heyoom reclined on a grassy hummock, her graceful young body relaxed, her eyes closed against the morning brightness. The dun mare who, before the rock-slide claimed her, had borne Springtime so safely up the Lolo Trail, stood quietly nearby.

There were no tears, only joy as Joseph and his family were reunited. They communed together, talking little, and all moved into the buffalo-skin lodge.

The idyllic days of autumn drifted by, and on a golden morning when the mountain was etched in pristine brightness against rain-washed blue, riders appeared far down the river. "Ollokot!" shouted Joseph, and he sprang across the meadow to meet his vigorous brother and the youthful Fair Land, and there was great rejoicing.

And finally came Tuekakis and Aseneth, not bent and wrinkled as the others remembered them, but in the beauty and strength of their youth. And they were embraced by all with great respect.

The reunion of the immediate family was now complete, except for a few still bound to the earthly dimension: Running Feet, Gopher, Wetatonmi, Welweyas, Little Bird, Joseph's other wives and children. But there were other people waiting to greet Joseph, and one by one or sometimes two by two they came to him, not wearily, as when they fled toward Canada or drifted to Indian Territory, but with dignity and confidence.

There were flashes of red in the fringe of the aspen grove, and all looked to see Sarpsis Ilppilp and Wahlitits walking toward them, wearing the same red coats in which they had died at the Big Hole.

Then came a cheer as Rainbow appeared, and with him was his wife Waddling Duck and their son Small Duck. She never got back to her Crow family, and neither survived the bitter flight to Canada. And close behind them came Five Wounds, Rainbow's dearest friend. He had relied on being protected by sunlight but at the Big Hole the dawn had come too late.

Suddenly there stood next to Joseph a wiry young man, intensely energetic, who had moved noiselessly out of the forest as was his way—Poker Joe, whom the Nez Perces called Lean Elk, and he smiled without rancor at Looking Glass, his one-time opponent. And Tabador, happy enough in this place but inquiring about Yellow Wolf and wondering how soon he would join the throng.

Then other Nez Perce chieftains arrived. White Bird, his hatred cooled and his mind at ease but quick as ever to express his opinions.Toohoolhoolzote, still strong and fiery, but savoring his escape from resentment and rage. Looking Glass, just beginning to accept a humble role and the easing of his harmful pride.

Then suddenly the broad meadow in this Indian Valhalla was encircled by stately chieftains whose coming transcended time and space. In the center of the circle, mounted on Ebenezer, sat Joseph, the trailing ends of his magnificent headdress fluttering around the horse's belly. He rode silently around the circle, nodding solemnly at each of the chieftains, who said nothing, for their presence bespoke their honor.

Chukatas, Joseph's close but contentious friend whom the whites called Moses, a great power on the Colville and helpful to the Nez Perces. He had passed on to Joseph the headdress he had received from Sitting Bull, who was next in the circle.

Sitting Bull, the great Sioux chief of the Hunkpapa band, sat next to Crazy Horse of the Oglalas. The two were unparalleled among Sioux warrior chiefs, and their presence here was a supreme honor.

Next sat Quanah, fearless fighting hero and the envy of every Comanche warrior, who had led a fierce but futile attack against white hunters while they rapidly destroyed the buffalo herds on the great plains.

Little Mountain, wise and sagacious chief of the Kiowas, who tried for years to make peace with the white man, then fought them fiercely, again struggled for a just peace, and died on a reservation, confused by an agreement that was unjust.

The Shoshone chiefs were two: Washakie, steadfast man of steel and friend to the white man; and Cameahwait, brother of Sacajawea, who had greatly assisted Lewis and Clark. And then the haughty Wolf Chief, austere head of the Mandans, whom he had ruled with an iron hand.

And of course there was Cochise, Chief of the Chiricahua Apaches, shrewd and fearless, who finally submitted after a long talk with General Howard. But Geronimo, the Apache chief fully equal to Cochise, was not there, for after surrendering to General Miles and spending years in exile he was now the last of the human exhibits in parades and fairs, still awaiting release from that vale of tears.

Next, the genius Sequoyah, the superb leader who devised the

Cherokee alphabet; and Tecumseh of the Shawnees, who died trying to unite widespread tribes against the onslaughts of the white man.

There were others who had fought and died leading the many tribes across the land and now shared the peace of this dimension. Joseph was awed at this solemn assembly, this gathering of eagles, and humbled by the honor they accorded him. All had sat in respectful silence, and now they made a gap in the big circle for Joseph to ride through. As he entered his tipi alone he said to his guardian spirit, "How long will it take them to get to their homes?" And his Wyakin answered, "They are already there." And Joseph looked out across the broad meadow, now completely deserted.

---

It was roundup time in the Wallowa country, and riders criss-crossed the valley and combed the ravines, gathering their cattle. Often they rode among the Nez Perces, and once two men watered their horses within a few feet of Joseph's tipi, unaware of Heyoom and Springtime, or the children playing in the river. This confused Joseph, and he asked his guardian spirit, "Do they not see us?"

"Sometimes they sense your presence, but only after they have put aside resentment and distrust."

"But today a beautiful young woman rode close to me, and it seemed she looked into my eyes, and I felt sure she knew I was there. Will these people ever be able to see us?"

"A few who have cleansed their hearts will feel your nearness. The rest will never see you, or enjoy the presence of your people living in their own dimension, until they overcome their need to feel better about themselves by scorning others. That will happen slowly, perhaps one by one, and you must be patient."

"But surely, sometime, they must hear us."

"Some will, if only when you spread your laughter upon the wind."

Then his guardian spirit was gone, and Joseph returned to his family.

"Well, the old rascal is dead, and I'm not sorry. I never cared much for him anyway," said the white agent when Joseph's body was found in his tipi at Nespelem. A more compassionate person who had known Joseph said simply, "He died of a broken heart."

---

There were only a few cattle to be seen on the Phelps-Martin pastures, but they were not lonely, for hundreds of horses wandered across the meadows and up the timbered slopes to the south: shaggy-footed, blaze-faced Clydesdales; staunch, blocky Percherons; sleek Thoroughbreds and Morgans. And each year a hundred or more of their offspring, just the right size for pulling the big grain harvesters, were trailed to the Palouse wheat fields north of the Snake River.

Kirby and Cornelia Phelps conducted the drive now, and their children helped, as well as Herb Jones and his son. Olivia and Bob Cone sometimes went along for the ride, but it seemed farther every year, and more often they stayed home; a short evening ride was more appealing than the long one to the Palouse country. So on this autumn afternoon they rode to the lake, along with Kirby's granddaughter Madeline, Olivia's first great-grandchild and now four years old.

"Papa Bob, why is this called Tolo Lake?" asked Madeline.

"Its named after an Indian woman; actually, her name was Toolah. Some white man changed it to Tolo."

"Was she a special Indian?"

"Some people think so. She was a great poker player, and often won the big games at my old ranch down at Slate Creek. But that's not why the lake is named for her. She liked the white people, and when the Nez Perces attacked us in 1877 she was at Slate Creek, and rode to Florence for help, which may have saved my life. Some say her people hated her for helping us; she cussed them out when they came back trying to make trouble again."

"Was she one of Joseph's people?"

"I'm not sure. Probably White Bird's."

"Was Joseph a bad Indian? My friend Josie Randall says he was."

"Most of the people around here would agree, I'm sure. And some of the Nez Perces—not Joseph personally—killed your great-grandmother Jenny and your great-aunt Phoebe, and your great-grandfather Jethro."

Madeline was silent as they rode toward the ranch. Then, looking across the prairie, she saw a fast-moving whirlwind stirring up a cloud of dust, and she said, "There goes Joseph!"

Soon after Olivia and Bob returned from their ride to the lake Kirby and Cornelia arrived for a visit, and all sat under the outer limbs of the walnut tree where they could see the barn. Almost 30 years of wind, rain, and sun had weathered the pine siding to a soft gray-brown patina, but the post and beam framework was still strong and straight, supporting the long Tamarack ridge-pole so that it did not sag. The cedar shakes were now a warm gray but showed no cracks, and on the shady north side of the roof were covered with velvety bumps of green moss.

Sitting on a table beside the family was the graceful urn which Mei Ling had sent to Lucas many years before. Kirby and Olivia both admired its glowing beauty but could never agree on who should keep it; so they traded it back and forth, and it was now Olivia's turn.

"I"ve often wondered about that Chinese woman down on the Salmon," Kirby mused, not speaking to anyone in particular. "All she said when she handed me that urn was, 'People in Warrens remember your father.' I suppose he would have called her a heathen."

No one responded, and all sat quietly, lost in their own thoughts. Cornelia looked at Kirby, who was now dozing. She squeezed his rough, calloused hand and he awakened with a start and the crinkly half-grin she had come to love. There was a calm serenity in their life now, for over the last few years they had welcomed the ghost of Little Bird, and now talked openly and wondered about the daughter whom they had seen only once. They would never know that her name was Camas Blossom.

Olivia's thoughts were of Gopher, whom she had last seen at Slate Creek before he disappeared. And after months of agonized nights she finally found some comfort in remembering that, after all, he was a survivor. And she smiled to herself as she looked up at the bronze weathervane swinging gently on the crest of the barn, the running horse still facing into the wind.

## Then What Happened?
## **An Epilogue**

Many of the Nez Perces who found refuge with Sitting Bull in Canada returned to Lapwai within a year or two. Wottolen, the historian, and his son Black Eagle later returned to Canada. Joseph's daughter Running Feet, and his older wife Heyoom Yokikt (whose described death at the Big Hole was fictitious), stayed on the reservation and Running Feet married there; historical accounts read by the author are silent as to whether Joseph ever saw either of them after their return from Canada. Yikyik Wasumwah, Yellow Wolf's mother, also returned to live at Lapwai. Two Moons drifted from the Sioux in Canada to the Flatheads in Montana, to the Lemhis in Idaho, and finally to the Spokans in Washington. Then he met other exiles at Lapwai and was sent to Nespelem to be with Joseph.

Ollokot's widow, Wetatonmi, after two years with the Sioux, spent a year with the Spokans before returning to Lapwai where she remarried. Whitebird was killed in Canada as described.

After Joseph's death in 1904 Yellow Wolf remained at Nespelem, where he married and fathered sons and daughters. In 1908 he met a most remarkable white man, Lucullus Virgil McWhorter, and the two became close friends. Yellow Wolf, over a period of 24 years, told McWhorter his story of the Nez Perce tragedy, as together they retraced the entire flight to Canada, with Yellow Wolf describing each battle in detail. These accounts and more are vividly recorded in McWhorter's superb book, "Yellow Wolf, His Own Story." (See also McWhorter's "Hear Me, My Chiefs.")

Yellow Wolf died in 1935 and is buried beneath one of the rough, unmarked rocks in an unkempt cemetery at Nespelem, not far from the well-marked grave of his Uncle Joseph.

Mt. Idaho declined rapidly after Grangeville became county seat of Idaho County in 1902. For awhile it was almost a ghost town but now attracts a growing number of those who like solitude. Florence and Warrens have been true ghost towns for many decades. Grangeville has prospered, and is now a delightful and growing prairie town. My corpulent great-uncle, Seth Jones, died when I was eight years old, and for no apparent reason my mother inherited a pair of his immense, tent-like trousers. In fact, with the fly buttoned and the sixty-four inch waistband slipped over two chairs set back to back, they made a dandy tent; the stubby legs, pointing up, served as ventilators.

After Charles Bemis' death, Polly, known as Mei Ling in this story, stayed on their Salmon River ranch, alone but not lonely. She was carefully watched over in her old age by two prospectors who lived directly across the river and called her twice daily on a telephone line strung over the water. Polly was the darling of people living along the Salmon River and in the surrounding mountains.

In 1933 she sickened, and friends carried her out of the canyon and over the still-rocky roads to the Grangeville Hospital, where she died at age 83. Polly Bemis' cabin is now a National Historical Site on the Salmon River, across from the mouth of Crooked Creek. You can't drive there, but you can reach it by way of a spine-tingling, two-hour jetboat ride upstream from Riggins, Idaho. Or you can float in a rubber raft down the Salmon River from Shoup, just below the Idaho-Montana border. It takes most of four days, but you'll never forget it!

Native Americans have made a variety of valuable contributions to mankind; but if the thousands of Appaloosa horse lovers were asked, "What did the Nez Perces contribute to the world?" they would surely answer, "Spotted Horses!" The U.S.Army slaughtered many of the Nez Perce horses after the Bear's Paw battle. The Appaloosas nearly died out, but the breed was rescued and greatly improved beginning in the 1930s. Very influential in that process was George B. Hatley of Moscow, Idaho, who spent his life at it and has been called "the architect of a breed." Under his guidance the Appaloosa Horse Club was firmly established, and its registry is now the third largest in the world.

And speaking of horses, the described method of breeding draft horses for wheat farming in the Palouse hills of North Idaho and Eastern Washington was actually used there, starting in the 1880s. Soon the development of right-sized breeding stock simplified the process and shortened it from three generations to one. Finally, by the late 1920s, tractors replaced horses and an era became history.

Long after the Nez Perces were gone from Whitebird Canyon, and civilization as we perceive it had replaced them, a road was built through the battleground, allowing travel by car past a simple stone column marking the site and over some fifteen miles of serpentine switchbacks to Camas Prairie. Now a modern highway sweeps across a high bridge overlooking the little hamlet of Whitebird, and, after seven or eight miles and a few gentle curves, crosses the mountain by way of an obscene, 400-foot-deep cut blasted out of its top. It is easier, safer, and quicker—and serves to diminish the beauty of the canyon. Beside that highway a few miles above Whitebird is a visitor's center, where a memorial marker reads:

**NEZ PERCE WAR**

*Near the base of this hill over 100 Cavalrymen and volunteers met disaster in the opening battle of the Nez Perce War. Rushing from Grangeville on the evening of June 16, 1877, Captain David Perry planned to stop the Indians from crossing Salmon River to safety from pursuit. At daylight the next morning, he headed down the ravine below you. Some sixty to eighty Indians wiped out a third of his force and the survivors retired in disorder. No Indians were killed.*

The stone column beside the original road bears the message, "Before you to the Westward lies the historic Whitebird Battleground of the Nez Perce Indian War, in which 34 men gave their lives in service for their country, June 17, 1877. Beneath this shaft lies one of those men, who rests where he fell." It seems pertinent to ask: in so dying, what did these 34 men do for their country?

The Nez Perce tribe today claims a membership of about 4,000. Most of them live within the boundaries of the reservation. A few hundred descendants of Joseph and the Dreamers who were sent to Colville in 1885 still live there. But the "Reservation" as delineated on the Idaho State map is not entirely reserved for the Nez Perces, for when it was "opened" in 1893 most of it was homesteaded or purchased by white men. Of some 220,000 acres still under tribal control the majority is leased to white farmers. But, of course, the Nez Perce never claimed to be farmers, and the sale and continuing lease of land has been of substantial economic benefit.

The clusters of Nez Perces along Lapwai Creek and on the Clearwater River at Kamiah, Kooskia, and Stites live in orderly homes and seem to lead contented lives. But it was not always so. For years after 1877, animosity and ridicule regarding the non-treaty people marked the attitudes of the "civilized" Nez Perces on the reservation. Many Christian Indians, influenced by authoritarian missionaries and agents who diminished the powers of chiefs, began to lose touch with their own history and culture. It might be said that they lost their pride as a tribe because they saw no real heroes.

One of the ironies of history is that so many words are written and so much remembered about wars and the people who won or lost them; and that lacking or not remembering more important heroes, people embrace those who arise out of conflict. And so it was with the Nez Perces. As time passed, the non-treaty chiefs, once derided, became the tribal heroes. Many of today's Nez Perces proudly claim direct lineage to Joseph, Whitebird, Looking Glass, and other "patriot" chiefs.

To many people these days, most everything about the Indians stirs chords of sympathy, curiosity, guilt, even genuine concern and appreciation; and more ways are sought to look into their lives—or to exploit them. Indian legends, art, craft work, pow-wows, religious ceremonials—all become increasingly popular. Such deepening interest is sorely needed, but will help bring greater understanding and result in better lives for the Indian people only if it leads to real change in attitudes and in the way we relate to them.

"I know my race must change. We cannot hold our own with the white men as we are." So spoke Joseph at Lincoln Center in 1879. But neither he nor any other Indian leader at that time could envision the magnitude of the changes they faced; nor could few, if any, white men. Just what changes Joseph had in mind is hard to say, but his words "hold our own" seem to indicate that he anticipated ongoing struggles; and, of course, he was right. But the road toward change has been long, hard, and agonizingly slow, and it will continue to be so for most Indians, for which there are many reasons.

Indians, when the white man arrived, did not have to look further ahead than the next hunt, the next run of salmon, the gathering of food and storing it for the winter. It sounds idyllic, especially to a man, for, it is said, the women did all the work. Actually it was a demanding life, full of struggle, uncertainty, and discomfort; and there were lean periods, some ending in starvation. But it required work and self-sufficiency and it gave back a sense of pride and accomplishment. Our government replaced those positive elements with reservations, where handouts were required to sustain life; idleness and the humiliation of dependency followed. Some Indians still live in that dependent state.

Change and lasting progress depend not only on the wisdom of the federal government but also on the attitudes and strength of Indian leaders; as well as white.

Regarding attitude, the San Francisco Chronicle on July 22 1996 reprinted a New York Times article by Timothy Egan:

**COUNTY IN OREGON HOPES INDIANS WILL AID ECONOMY**

Headed at Joseph, Oregon, the article tells of people in the Wallowa Valley who hope to boost their sagging economy by bringing some Nez Perces back to stage cultural events and become a "tourist magnet." At the annual rodeo there, now called Chief Joseph Days, Nez Perce pow-wows attract more people than bucking horses, bull dogging, and calf-roping.

"I was approached by this economic development guy, from the city of Wallowa," said Earl "Taz" Conner, a direct descendent of Old Joseph (Tuekakis). "He said he thought the Indians could save the county. I had to laugh at that. It really is ironic asking the Indians to return after booting us out of there in 1877."

Equally ironic is the comment of Soy Red Thunder, a descendent of Joseph, who said, "The tribe will have to be careful, given that anti-Indian sentiment still lingers in the valley." He was speaking of a current white population yet unborn when the Nez Perces roamed the Wallowa more than 120 years ago and were never involved in violence against white settlers there. Perhaps the greatest irony is that Red Thunder apparently had reasons for his remark.

My own observations on several Indian reservations lead me to conclude that the attitudes of surrounding white populations are usually negative. In some towns bordering reservations (as well as among people who never see an Indian except by chance, and would not recognize one) the

Indians are resented, sometimes deeply: for government assistance which the critics do not try to understand; for controlling resources on the land where the government placed them by treaty; for fishing and hunting rights guaranteed by treaty; for education grants which are aimed at improving their lives; for preference in hiring and promotion in industries located on or near their reservations, often on Indian land set aside for such purposes. And in such settings some white citizens meet Indians on the streets and simply do not see them.

How and when will real and widespread progress be made toward Indian self-sufficiency? Thousands of dedicated people have striven mightily to answer that question, with limited success. I believe such progress will begin when determined, selfless leaders, both Indian and white, are willing to neutralize their own attitudes and literally dedicate their entire lives to the process. They must work cooperatively as a permanent non-partisan group jointly supported by a coalition of tribes and the U.S. Government but independent of both. In this way atavism might be replaced by realism so that more of the Indian people can accept the present and truly work toward the future.

Relating my own life-long experiences to the recent newspaper report from Oregon's Wallowa Valley reinforces questions about our attitudes toward the Indians: How soon will we really see them? And will we listen to their voices when, once in awhile, they spread their laughter on the wind?